Everlasting

by

Carol Johnson

Also by
Carol Johnson

Autism: From Tragedy to Triumph

DEDICATION

To Sally, Rilla, and the Monday night fiction group, for reading and listening to endless versions of Vada's story; to Michelle, for poring over the final draft; and to Jim, for his steadfast love.

1947-52

Chapter 1

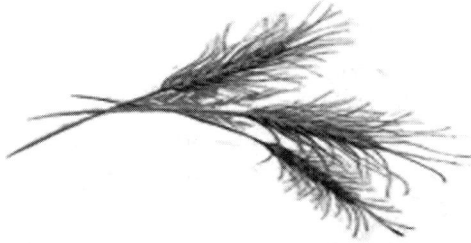

"Lavada June Ross!" Shrill with menace, Mama's voice soared across the heads of Vada and Addy where they crouched on the edge of the field separating them from the house. "You come here to me!" The silence following her words felt heavy, like it would fall to earth and break into sharp, stabbing shards, but it didn't last long enough for that. "Adelaide! If I got to come find you two, I swear, I'll wear you out!"

The girls looked at each other, and Vada put one finger to her lips. Addy lowered herself to sit on the ground, milkweed and wildflowers surrounding her like a cocoon. Vada did likewise, and simultaneously, as if on cue, they scooted closer together. Knees under her chin, arms wrapped around her thin legs, Vada twisted and released the hem of the faded dress that covered her legs, watching Addy pluck first one and then another of the colorful wild blooms and grasses that surrounded them, depositing the flowers in the skirt of her dress.

"Help me," Addy whispered. Vada hesitated, then grinned, and they both began picking like someone was paying them to do it. When they'd gathered enough to fill Addy's lap, Addy began to tie them end-to-end by their stalks— jimmy weed to holy clover to daisy fleabane to sweet william. "Why's Mama always so mean?" she asked, eyes on her nimble fingers connecting the flowers.

"Nobody else's mama acts like her." When Vada didn't reply, Addy continued. "When I stayed the night with Mary Ella Shanks, her mama didn't hit her once. Didn't even *holler*, even when Mary Ella dropped a whole pitcher of tea." Vada still didn't reply. Addy, straight dark brows curved over eyes whose color shifted with her mood and place, dark to light to dark, stared at her older sister, the intensity of her gaze a demand for some kind of satisfactory answer.

"Quit staring," Vada said. "Giving me the fish-eye won't make me no smarter." Lips pursed, she scooped flowers from Addy's lap, then let them drop back.

"Giving me the fish-eye won't make me no smarter," Addy mimicked, and Vada made a mock lunge for her little sister. Addy ducked and Vada fell to the side, landing hard on her bony elbow.

"Ow!" Pulling herself upright, she re-crossed her legs Indian-style and rubbed her arm.

"That's what you get," Addy told her. "You won more prizes the end of school than anybody, then you sit there and act like a dummy."

Vada shrugged, still rubbing. "Toting up numbers or memorizing some stupid poem is nothing anywhere but school. I could do them things all day long and still not know what makes Mama act like she does." She hesitated, her eyes on the hazy sky above the tallgrass that surrounded them. "I reckon she just don't like us." But even as the words slipped from her, Vada knew the answer was not good enough. This meanness of her mother's was a mystery to her, too, a mystery whose answer seemed as remote as the horizon. Over most of her fourteen years, Vada had taken up first this theory, then that, and then another, but each fell apart in time. Only the plainest and most unassuming one held up: "She just don't like us," she repeated, and pulled a strand of dark hair in front of her face, inspecting it.

Addy made the snorting sound that had earned her many a backhanded slap from Mama. "She *has* to like us. She's our *mama*." She negotiated a final connection between a buttercup and a sprig of something that looked like thistle, only more delicate, then reached forward and slipped her creation over Vada's head. Hands clasped, Addy tilted her brown curly head to one side. "There!" she announced. "You look like Miss America nineteen and forty-seven."

Vada removed the floral necklace as quickly and decisively as Addy had placed it on her. "Stop. I'm too ugly to be Miss America any year." She held it in her lap, stroking a golden head of jimmy weed.

"Vada! You are *so*—" Both girls jumped at the sudden shuffling behind them. Vada started to scramble to her feet, then saw who it was and sank back.

"Papa!" they said in unison.

Papa squatted between the two, taking one girl's neck in the crook of each arm, pulling the heads toward each other amid muffled squeals of protest. "I ought to crack your noggins together," he grunted. "Your mama's up there roaring around, fit to be tied."

"I wish *somebody'd* tie her up," Addy said, and Vada giggled into Papa's shirt front.

"The rope's not been made that'd hold her," he said. Arms still around his daughters' necks, he tugged one of Addy's chestnut curls, then one of Vada's straight-as-string locks. "I swear. Will you look at this mess you all call hair? Addy's got the bedsprings and you got the slats." he said. He laughed and tried to release the two girls, but Vada clung to him, inhaling the scent that was Papa. The mixture of sweat, lye soap, and hair oil made her feel safe and secure as nothing else could. The one thing Mama's ill temper brought Vada was this closeness with Papa, this us-against-the-world feeling, and sometimes she almost felt like any amount of unpleasantness was worth it. Almost.

Papa seemed to read her mind. "Why you always got to be deviling her? You know how she gets."

"But we didn't do nothing." She looked up into his sunburned, freckle-splotched face, and her eyes locked on his. *He knows we don't do nothing to her. He knows.* She leaned more heavily on him, suddenly drowsy with relief. "Why is she so mean, Papa? We do everything she says, even when we know it's stupid."

He tilted her chin so her eyes met his, shaded by the sweat-stained fedora. "I wouldn't say 'stupid' when you're talking about your mama. She's not stupid by a long shot." He rested his chin on the top of her head and sighed. "And I don't know why she does you like she does, but I know you got to not run off. She won't do nothing but yell."

Sometimes Vada thought Papa must be blind. He had to be not to know that Mama did a lot more than yell. She switched Vada's legs and back with a limber hickory switch, smacked her in the face at the least provocation—there was no telling what she'd do. But if Mama told Papa Vada's welts and bruises were from roughhousing with Addy, then that's what Papa believed. *Shoot! If Mama told him a cowpatty was good to eat he'd tell her to fry him some.* A slight intake of breath from Addy drew Vada's attention, and her heart sank. She could tell by the look on the other girl's face that Addy was going to tell. She was going to tell, sure as the world. Vada jerked her head *No!*, two short, quick shakes of warning. Addy barely hesitated before plunging on.

"Mama's gone past yelling. She hit Vada with—"

Vada scrambled across the ground in front of Papa and knocked Addy flat on her back, flowers scattering. "Don't you dare!" she cried. "You *promised.*" She did her best to clamp a hand over Addy's mouth, but although small, Addy was a wildcat. With one shove she sent Vada sprawling backward into Papa. Vada winced as her already sore back connected with his knees.

"Here, you two." He caught Vada and held her upright with one hand, then grabbed Addy with the other. "The way you carry on!"

Addy shook loose from him. "She hit her with a board, Papa! Mama done hit her with a board, and Vada didn't do nothing to deserve it." She glared at Vada. "Show him what she done." Her face almost glowed, mottled red and white, and her breath came in furious gusts.

"Your mama wouldn't do no such—" His voice trailed off as Vada and Addy exchanged a glance. "Let me see, Sister." Papa's voice was gentle as the breeze that lifted the hair from the nape of Vada's sweaty neck, and she stood, slump-shouldered. Papa's hands shook as he undid the half dozen buttons holding the dress across her bony back. As he parted the material, the contrast of the air against her skin raised goosebumps and she stared straight ahead, ignoring the tears that rolled unchecked down her face and dripped onto the bodice of her dress. Papa's whistle was so low it was almost overwhelmed by the breeze rustling through the field. In a moment, he refastened the garment and turned her toward him, then drew her to his chest.

"Jesus God, Sister. I didn't have no idea she'd—why in tarnation didn't you tell me?"

Face against his hard chest, she listened to his heart's steady beat and let the tears roll down her face to wet the front of his work shirt. She could never say the words aloud, but they rang clearly in her head. *Why do I have to tell you? Why can't you open your eyes and see?*

* * * * *

Sometime in the middle of the night, Vada awoke and sat bolt upright. She heard Mama screeching like a trapped badger, using words Vada had never heard. She knew instinctively they were bad words, *very* bad words, and ones that Mama would deny with her last breath. Come Sunday, she'd be first one up to lead Testimony Service, and she'd do it with a clear heart. Vada *knew* her Mama.

"I work my fingers to the *bone* around this place, Kenneth Ross, and when I tell her to collect the goddamned eggs, I want them collected, then I want them brought in here in one piece, not broke all over the ground." Vada couldn't hear Papa's response, but Mama's next words were distinct: "That girl is lying. I never seen no snake out there, and if there was, it'd take one look at that face of hers and take off."

Vada felt Addy's hand creep into hers. She lay back down, clinging to her sister like it was Addy who ought to take care of her. Soon, five-year-old Johnsie crawled into the bed with them, dragging two-year-old Roxanne behind him like an oversized pull-toy. The four of them lay huddled almost on top of one another, listening to the battle rage around even scarier periods of silence.

The following morning, Mama's unconcealed anger terrified Johnsie and Roxanne, and Vada and Addy avoided her all day, tensing when they heard her voice. She called Papa "Mr. Ross" now instead of Kenneth, and that made Vada giggle even though she could tell it was supposed to be some kind of punishment. Papa ignored Mama, though, and went about his business. In following days, the only real difference, not counting the tight-lipped glares Mama sent Vada's way, was that now Papa often took Vada and Addy with him to the fields.

Oklahoma was working up to a blistering summer, already so hot at the first of June that Vada found it hard to sleep at night. In the fields, she didn't care about the heat, though Papa often sent her and Addy to the shade of the nearest hackberry tree as they tagged after him. Vada loved shadowing him as he followed along behind their horse, Jack, and the plow. She never strayed far except when Papa sent her under the tree, but Addy roamed the lush land roundabout, bringing back wildflowers and weeds to challenge Papa's knowledge.

"What's *this* one, Papa?" she always yelled, like this time he'd never guess.

"You'll *never* mess up Papa when it comes to them flowers," Vada said. "He knows them all." She was so proud of him that it was almost as if she was bragging on herself. He knew their names not only in English, but in another language too—Latin, he called it—and he knew which ones were everlastings and which ones weren't. That was what most impressed her. She loved the notion that some of them would return year after year, forever and ever, even when she did not.

Chapter 2

Vada's eyes swam with tears as she stood in the front yard, staring hard at the field where she and Addy had hidden earlier that summer. She wanted to hate the Queen Anne's lace, the jimmy weed, the bright, saucy sunflowers, still so bountiful, but she couldn't. She could only hate the thing being done to her now, and love the beginning-to-fade flowers Papa called everlastings. They were not dying, he had reminded her again the other night, but doing what they must to return next year. That idea had pleased her earlier in the summer, but now she felt sad. Still, it was comforting. "Everlastings," she told herself. "They'll be gone a spell, then they'll be back."

Mama's voice was everlasting, but it never went away. As hard as Vada tried to shut it out, the voice was an angry, insistent buzz that would not be stilled. Vada might as well try to turn herself into Veronica Lake, or maybe Miss America, like Addy was always saying.

"Vada." There it was again. *Bzz-bzzz.* "Say hello to Mr. Priddy. Now." Mama's stony tone softened only when she turned to the tall man beside her. "My Vada's a mite shy with strangers."

My Vada? My foot! Vada choked back a nervous giggle, struggling to keep her face rigid. Where her mother was concerned, a twitch was as good as a smile and either one could send the woman into a fury.

Mama simpered up at the man. "My lands, when her daddy came home from the army, it was a good six months before she took up with him, and him her natural born daddy."

Vada stared at her own feet, planted like roots in the poor soil of the yard.

In silence she concentrated on keeping all emotion from her face until a sharp pain in her behind startled her.

"Ow!" Vada rubbed her backside and blinked back the tears. Mama's pinches were vicious grab-and-twists hard enough to keep pain eddying long afterward and leave bruises. Mama hadn't done anything to leave a mark on Vada for weeks, ever since Papa had had it out with her. Oh, there was the occasional whack on the head with a wooden spoon, or, once, the heel of a shoe, but those didn't leave marks, just lumps, and Mama knew Vada wouldn't tell. Addy might, though, so it never happened when Addy was around. But now. Vada gritted her teeth against a queasy feeling. *Oh, Lord, save me from whatever she's up to.*

Mama's voice jerked her back to the right-now and right-here. "Girl, I told you to say hello to Mr. Priddy." Stone had crept back into her voice, giving her words edges sharp enough to cut, and Vada slowly raised a trembling chin, brought her eyes up to the man's face—or almost, anyway.

"Hel—hello," she managed. She tried to look through him or around him— she couldn't look over him, because he was *tall*, real tall, even taller than Papa or Brother Pappan from over at the Cottonwood Freewill Baptist Church, who was supposed to be the tallest man in Creek County.

He leaned toward her, holding out a hand as big as a skillet. "How do, Miss Vada. I'm right pleased." His voice was deep and rich, carrying an unfamiliar rhythm—slow, twangy, yet somehow lilting. He talked like he was from the hills, not at all the kind of person Mama liked to associate with. He held the hand out for a good long time before she realized he meant for her to shake it. By the time she understood, he had stuck it back in the bib of his overalls where the other one rested. He rocked forward and back on his heels, forward and back, eyes still on her.

Even from his great height, those eyes drew her. They were black as lumps of coal, yet illuminated, like thunderheads covering a full moon. She almost winced, expecting to be blinded any time by the lightning. He seemed to read her thoughts and grinned at her, baring small, tobacco-stained teeth. To make up for failing to shake his hand, and for staring, she forced a smile back.

"Now, then," Mama said. "That's better." She took Mr. Priddy's arm and led him across the yard to the sagging porch, their feet kicking up puffs of Oklahoma dust like so many sighs. "Let's sit a spell, Harmon." She gave him the place of honor, a rickety rocking chair with a cornshuck pillow in the seat, then arranged herself on the porch railing, smoothing the bodice of her Sunday dress over a shelf-like bosom. Mama flashed a smile at Vada, who still stood in the yard. "Go fetch Mr. Priddy a cold jar of that lemonade you fixed, Vada."

He stopped the motion of the rocker. "Now, Esther, I don't want to trouble you." Mama extracted a handkerchief from the depths of her bosom and laughed, a high tinkling laugh more frightening to Vada than the earlier grimace. "Land *sakes*, Harmon, you are *company*. It's no trouble *at all*. I can tell you that right now." Her head swiveled toward Vada, the look in her eyes so full of naked menace that Vada didn't wait to be told twice. She crossed the yard to the porch, then darted to the sagging screen door, and gave Mama a wide berth. It usually paid, but when Mama looked like *that*, it *always* paid.

When the screen door banged shut behind her, kids seemed to pour out of the very walls. Johnsie's froggy voice was the first to sound off. "Who's that old man, Vada? Are you going to live at his house like Mama says?"

Vada clenched her jaws for a moment, then shook her head at Johnsie. "No. Papa won't let that happen." Johnsie scratched at his bottom through ragged overalls, and she rapped him gently on the head. "Stop digging." She pulled a quart Mason jar from the doorless shelves above the pump.

"I itch," he said, scratching more vigorously.

She sighed. He probably had worms again. All the children had them occasionally, and the thought almost gagged her. Roxanne barreled across the floor and collided with Vada's leg, then tried to simultaneously wind herself around and climb up the leg.

At three, she sported a flurry of golden curls and dimples deep as the holes on a Chinese checker board. "Pi' me up," Roxanne demanded, dimpling up at Vada. Even at her age Roxie thought she could wrap anybody around her tiny finger. But not Vada, not today anyway.

"I can't now. I'm busy." She tried to walk to the icebox, but Roxanne hung on. Vada jiggled from hip to ankle, attempting to loosen the child, but it was like trying to shake loose a tick. "Addy, get her. I got to take that man some lemonade or Mama's going to be on me like I don't know what."

Addy peeled Roxanne off Vada limb by limb, and it took some doing. Finally free, Vada scrambled to the icebox and chipped ice into the jar. At least having company meant they had a block of ice besides the one that cooled the icebox. She could almost feel the silken chill of it on her lips, but she knew better than to take without asking, and knew even better not to ask.

"If Papa doesn't get here pretty fast, that old man is going to haul you off," Addy said.

Vada's scalp prickled at the thought, and she shook her head. Turning from the icebox, she saw Johnsie still digging at the seat of his pants. She thumped him a little more sharply this time. "Stop digging, I said."

Behind her, she heard Roxanne whining, "Vad-a, Vad-a, ho' me," as if her heart was broken. Lord knew Vada loved her brother and sisters—had practically raised Roxanne—but she was so tired of children, their wants, their needs, the way she was required to fill them. *Diapering and making sugar-tits gets old. Real old. Like Mr. Priddy.* The sudden thought almost brought a giggle to her lips, but she pushed it way down and walked carefully out to the porch, holding the sweating glass of lemonade with both hands. Wouldn't do to spill it. Wouldn't do at *all*. She reached Mr. Priddy and placed the jar in his enormous hands.

"Much obliged, Miss Vada." He bared those little teeth at her again.

She blushed, the heat rushing from the neck of her thin calico dress to the roots of her hair in sweltering waves. She turned and took a step toward the house, but made it only a step or two before Mama's voice stopped her dead in her dusty tracks. *Bzzz-bzzz.* Vada faced her mother, hunching her shoulders against the voice, but couldn't shut it out.

"Come sit a spell and visit with Mr. Priddy here. He's come all the way from Kellyville to see you and you haven't said two words to him." Mama was using the voice she used when the preacher came, and she dabbed at her freckled chest with a flowered, lace-edged handkerchief. Vada's stomach rolled at the sweet smell of *Evening in Paris.*

"My children's all been raised Christian, Harmon, but I guess you know enough about me to know that's how it'd have to be." She dimpled at him. "And Vada, she's been taught to play the piano—she can't do much yet, but she will. She ought to fit right well with you and your fiddle."

Vada stared at her mother. "I can't play nothing but 'Amazing Grace.'"

Mr. Priddy shrugged. "We ain't got no piano at our place anyway."

Mama stopped a moment, frowning. "But I thought Sarah—God rest her—played."

Vada watched Mr. Priddy from beneath her lashes, saw his Adam's apple bob as he took a long drink of lemonade. He nodded. "She did. I had to sell her piano to bury her. Already sold most ever'thing else to pay for her doctoring." His accent, wherever it was from, was so thick Vada had a hard time understanding some of the words, but when she did, she wondered why he didn't sell his fiddle, then decided that since a piano was bigger, he probably got more money for it.

The man watched Mama as she went on and on about how she—Mama—taught in the Sunday School and collected money to send missionaries to minister to the Unsaved over there in Africa. Mama was big on doing for the Unsaved. Vada had learned at school that many people who fell into her mother's Unsaved category had their own gods, yet when she'd mentioned that fact, Mama had washed her mouth out with lye soap. Mama said there wasn't but one god, the one who spelled his name with a big "G," and that if those heathens didn't worship God with a big "G," they were Unsaved. Period. Now Vada didn't ask questions about God, not the one with a big "G" nor any other. She could still taste that lye soap. She watched Harmon Priddy and wondered if he went to church, and if he did, did he hold with big "G" or little "G"? Occasionally, he glanced at Vada, but his look revealed nothing. It was not unpleasant, just curious. Still, she felt a frantic desire for the safety of the house, a desire much like a drowning man might have for air. Finally, she edged toward the screen door.

"I—I got to go see what them kids are into."

Mama laughed again, a tinkling laugh, bizarre coming from her, like a chicken mooing, or a cow clucking. "Land sakes, Vada, you can't be looking after those kids every *minute*." Mama came toward her and clamped a hand like a vise grip on Vada's shoulder, then pulled the girl to the porch, and leaned her against the railing like a rake or a broom. "I'll swan to goodness, Harmon, my Vada can't get enough of those young'uns—been that way all her life. Worries over them, chases after them—why, sometimes I wonder whose young'uns they *are*."

Vada stared at Mama, mouth agape and powerless to look away. Mama met her eyes defiantly, daring Vada to dispute her word.

"Mr. Priddy here has three motherless babies, Vada." She said it like they were kittens left on the doorstep. "Their mama passed away and left them all alone in this old world." Mama clapped her hand to her bosom and looked skyward. "God rest her soul."

Vada dropped her gaze, moving it to the bib of Mr. Harmon Priddy's overalls. She peeped up through her dark lashes and saw him looking her over, not a casual glance, but one of intent, speculation. She felt like asking him did he want to see her teeth.

"She ain't no bigger'n a minute." He studied her some more. "A mite puny for seventeen, ain't she?" His voice was reflective, and the words had barely died away before Addy's outraged shout and then Addy herself burst through the screen door, letting it bang back against the house, then against the doorjamb, the sound like gunshots in the silence that followed her shriek.

"You told him she's seventeen! She's not but fourt—"

"Back in the house, Adelaide," Mama said, but it didn't sound like that. "Backinthehouseadelaide" was one long word, as two-edged and dangerous as a sword. "Nobody asked for your two-cents' worth." For just that long, the real Mama escaped in the snarling words. Addy stood her ground briefly, but even she, the bravest of them all, wilted when confronted with the heaving bosom and mottled face that was Mama. She went to the porch and slipped silently behind the screen door, hanging there, a shadowy guardian of truth. Vada sneaked a peek at Mr. Harmon Priddy.

He was looking at Mama like he smelled something bad and was too polite to say so, but when Mama turned to face him it was as if a window shade had dropped down over his eyes. He turned his attention to Vada.

"Fourteen," he said. Harmon Priddy didn't appear surprised—she looked fourteen, and barely—or mortified at his almost-mistake, but more like Papa trying to decide whether to pull a watermelon from the patch or give it another day.

Vada lowered her eyes, felt the heat creeping up her neck and face again.

"Tell Mr. Priddy about your garden," Mama said, voice bright. "Why, we put up green beans for three days. You never seen the like. I was saying to Miz Calvert at the dairy the other day—"

The sudden clip-clop of hooves sounded from the other side of the sagging barn, and Vada's heart jumped up into her throat. *Papa Papa Papa Papa.* The litany accompanied her as she leapt from the porch and sprinted toward the back of the barn, feet seeming to skim the ground. Papa stood there, a V of sweat darkening the back of his rough cotton work shirt, and when Vada hurdled to the other side of the plow he was unhitching, she saw a matching V on the front.

"Oh, Papa, Lordy me, am I glad to see you. Mama's got company. Mr. Harmon Priddy, and Addy heard Mama—he's got three motherless babies and me and Addy are—and she wants—and I don't aim—" She paused, gulping the heavy late-August air. "I'm so glad you're home."

"Now, Sister. Simmer down." Plow unhitched, he swatted at old Jack, and the horse ambled into the barn. Papa faced her. "All right. Now what?" He didn't sound curious, just resigned, and Vada was suddenly, frighteningly, speechless. This "what" of her Mama's was the worst in a long line of "whats," and maybe Papa couldn't stop it. The premonition that he couldn't—worse, wouldn't—stop Mama sent a tremor of fear up her spine, and no amount of effort brought words to her lips. Papa put his arm around her anyway, and she leaned into him, briefly comforted. A silent prayer began to take shape inside her as she clung to Papa. *Lord, make him tell her this time. Make him tell her good.* But even as it moved silently in her, she knew that her prayer was as useless as a hammer without a handle.

As they approached the porch, Mama stood, smoothing the front of her dress down with an almost-nervous hand. "Kenneth, this is Mr. Harmon Priddy. I told you about him."

Vada's head swiveled in Papa's direction. *He already knew?* This was the most scarifying thought of all, and the force of it took her breath.

Papa looked at the taller man, a long, penetrating look. After a silence made even more uncomfortable by the measurement each man took of the other, Papa held out his hand. "Mr. Priddy. Proud to know you." They shook, and Papa moved to the only empty chair on the porch, ladder-backed and rickety, and lowered himself. Removing his hat, he wiped his face with his forearm, glanced at Vada and then away, like Johnsie when he'd been into something he shouldn't have been. Her bowels weakened, and she was afraid for a minute that she would have to run to the outhouse and miss Papa telling Mama what was what. Because he would. Surely he would. *Please, Papa. Oh, please please please, don't let her do this.*

"Vada!" Mama was talking to her. "Get your papa a glass of that lemonade. And pour yourself one, too."

Vada stared at her. Pour *herself* one? She waited for the punch line. The last time Mama had been this nice to her was when they'd got word Papa was coming back from the Army, all in one piece. Now Mama always said him being in the Army was nothing since there wasn't even a war going on, but then she'd been happy. Vada was only four when he returned, and couldn't even remember who her Papa was then, but she remembered Mama swooping her up and dancing her around the kitchen, laughing and crying at the same time.

"Go on, Vada, land sakes. Don't stand there with that ugly mouth of your'n hanging open." Mama flushed geranium red, blue eyes pinning Vada to the porch, never mind her instructions to get going.

Vada glanced at Papa, saw he was looking straight ahead. He seemed to sense her gaze upon him, but he didn't look at her. "Go on, Sister," he said. "Do like your Mama said." His voice, soft, undeceived but firm, sent fear skittering up her spine.

"Papa. Please. I don't—"

Now he faced her. His eyes were barely familiar, like when he first woke mornings—Papa's eyes, but not Papa's eyes, as if he'd gone off and only part of him had returned. "Go on."

The gentleness of his voice held both apology and regret, and for the first time in her memory, was void of hiding places. A prayer sprang to her lips but went unspoken, unacknowledged. Why should God help her when her own father refused? When she moved at last, her body was no longer light with the hope of redemption, but heavy with the knowledge of her father's betrayal.

Chapter 3

Vada fingered the limp pink ribbon tied around the stems of her wedding bouquet. The smell of the wildflowers suddenly nauseated her, and she laid them on the porch railing. Staring down at her cheap, hastily-purchased shoes, she twisted the thin gold band on her left ring finger, and finally raised her gaze to rest on her sister's flushed face.

"It's not right. It's not!" Addy's ragged whisper was loud as thunder and soft as dew. "I'll come for you, Vada, soon as I can. We'll go to Tulsa, even Oklahoma City, and they won't never find us." Addy had been in an almost uncontrollable state since the Sunday morning church service three days before when Mama had stood and announced before God and the whole congregation Vada's impending marriage to Mr. Harmon Priddy of Kellyville. Some church folk had looked at Vada with pity and at Mama with something akin to disgust, but even Vada had to admit the ones who seemed so disapproving were the ones Mama called Nosy Parkers and Busybodies. Papa had sat still, like he wasn't there in the church at all, his gaze off on something Vada couldn't see.

In the intervening days, Johnsie and Roxanne had been skittish and whiny like they were when Mama and Papa fought, and Roxanne clung to Vada with uncommon desperation, refusing to allow anyone else to feed or comfort her.

Only Vada was resigned. Frightened, unable to sleep, but resigned. She knew Johnsie and even Roxanne would do all right as long as they had Addy to look out for them, and Addy would make it, too. *What about me?* Vada wanted to cry out, for as welcome as a world without Mama might be, she would also be beyond Papa's protection and Addy's love, and those seemed like the only useful things in the world.

No sense fighting after you done lost. That was how she looked at it, but now here was Addy, clutching Vada's arm, promising things that would never come to pass. "Don't talk crazy." She was amazed at how her hands could push Addy away when all she really wanted to do was hold onto her and everything that was familiar, even Mama. The familiar was bound to hurt sometimes, but was still better than the unknown. *But it won't kill me. It sure won't.* She drew a shaky breath and went to Harmon Priddy where he stood by his 1930 Chrysler.

"I guess I'm ready," she said. Her carpetbag had been loaded earlier and sat in the back seat at the feet of Mr. Priddy's three starey-eyed children. Mr. Priddy—Harmon—had named them off to her earlier—Nelda, Cordell, and Dempsey—but they could've been Winken, Blinken, and Nod for all she cared.

She glanced at them, taking in the pasty-faced girl's eyes, so hard and dark they could be mistaken for a couple of Johnsie's playing marbles; the middle boy, ignoring her as determinedly as his sister stared at her; and the littlest one, who would have been cute with his taffy colored hair and light hazel eyes if he hadn't been picking his nose and wiping the result on his ragged overalls. Vada turned away, revolted. *That's worse than having worms.*

Mama's mouth stretched into a smile. "We're shore honored to have you in the family, Harmon. Shore enough." She preened and squirmed in her Sunday dress as if she and not Vada had stood in front of the preacher and gave away her future to a man she hardly knew, a man twenty years her senior with backlit eyes and hands big as skillets.

But it wasn't Mama, it was Vada, and the act had numbed her. She let Harmon guide her to the car's passenger side, his big hand rough on her elbow, but as he pulled open the car door, she turned back for one more look at those she was leaving behind. Somehow she knew that years later, the picture would remain clear in her mind: Johnsie swinging from the porch railing; Addy, face tear-stained, holding Roxanne on her hip; Roxanne sobbing, still reaching for the sister whose leaving she was too young to understand and too old to accept easily; Mama's back as she disappeared through the crooked screen door; and last, but more achingly vivid, more lost to her than any of the others, Papa. As he raised a hand in farewell, he knocked from railing to dirt yard Vada's fading wedding bouquet. He descended the wooden steps, retrieved the flowers, and offered them to her as she met his gaze through a mist of tears. Steeling herself, she turned her back and allowed Harmon Priddy to guide her into the waiting car.

Carol Johnson

Vada slipped silently into the front seat, feeling like she didn't even need the door open, because she was air and could have passed right through it. Once in the car, she twisted again to look at Addy, beautiful, chestnut-haired Addy, face perfect even when blotched from crying. Vada stared hard at her sister as the vehicle moved slowly away. When it was almost too late, she waved with all her might like she was never going to see any of them again. Facing the front once more, she felt a fat tear trace her cheek and drop onto the front of her pink and white flowered dress, the only new dress she remembered having. She wiped her eyes with the heels of her hands, but more tears welled and spilled down her face, more tears than she'd thought were in the world. At the feeling of a light touch on her shoulder, she looked over to see Mr. Priddy—*Harmon. Harmon, my husband*—offer her a big handkerchief. She took it, clutched it tightly. At least it was something, some little something, to keep between her and the unknown.

Chapter 4

The ride from west of Bristow to east of Kellyville went on and on. And hot, Lordy, Vada couldn't remember heat like this. Was she really only thirty miles from home? The silence of the car was broken only by Harmon's occasional comment on a passing landmark or by a brief squabble from the backseat. "Buy my seed there." He tilted his head at the Farmer's Co-Op near Kellyville. "Yonder there is where we bring the cotton after it's ginned." She looked at the long white building, the tin roof winking in the high, hot sunlight.

She hugged her side of the car, letting the hot wind lift the hair from her sweaty neck, picturing how Mama had looked simpering up at Harmon. *I could scratch her eyes right out, I had me a chance.* No. More than that. *I could kill her, kill her dead.* Vada no longer felt the mixture of love and fear that had marked the relationship. Now it was hatred, pure and simple: a hatred for what her mother was and wasn't, a hatred that felt everlasting and complete. *I'm never going to forgive her, not as long as I live, and I'm never going to be like her, neither.*

Her rage became a seething simmer as she counted the ways she would not take after her mother. Resting her arm along the groove that held the lowered window, she lay her cheek on her forearm and closed her eyes. *I won't disrespect my man, or tell him he's not fit for nothing.* She glanced sideways at Harmon. He was her man, now. She felt dizzy, as if she couldn't absorb that knowledge all at once, and she closed her eyes again, tight this time. *And if I ever have me any young'uns, I won't beat on them, nor tell them they're ugly.* She stopped, considered. *Unless they are, and I reckon they'll already know it then.* Grinning against the moist, warm crook of her arm, she thought of the time when Addy had told Ethelene Baumgardner, the school librarian, that she had a face like the north end of a southbound cow. Vada nearly giggled aloud, but a sudden shift in the direction of the car brought her upright.

Harmon had turned down a dirt road between two endless fields of cotton. Dust flew up and surrounded them, provoking a chorus of complaints and coughing from the back seat, where, for most of the trip, the children had remained blessedly silent.

"Pa, can't you roll up them windows?" came a nasal voice. "We're going to choke to death back here."

Vada turned her head only enough so she could see the face of the girl who spoke—Nelda, that was her name. The child stared at her with undisguised hostility, and in spite of herself, Vada shivered. *What did I ever do to her?* She jerked her face quickly back to the front and stared straight ahead, shivering again even in the heat.

"Pa? You hear me?" Nelda hacked like an old woman who'd swallowed her snuff. "I'm choking to death back here."

Harmon rolled his window up. "Satisfied?"

"Can't she roll *hers* up?"

Vada crossed her arms over her chest and made no move to do so, but the girl yammered on about choking to death until finally Harmon sighed and touched Vada's folded arm. "Raise that window why don't you? She ain't going to shut up until you do."

Vada stared straight ahead. "I don't reckon I care to do that. Little dust never hurt nobody, and I'm about sick from the heat anyway."

Harmon sighed again, and the girl in the back seat moaned about hay fever and choking to death and how sorry they would be when she lay dead from the dust. Suddenly, Harmon slammed the car to a stop, jerked on the emergency brake, and turned in his seat.

Vada shrank against the door. *Do Lord! Surely he won't beat her right here.*

He squeezed Nelda's knee in one big hand. "I don't want to hear another word from you, girl. That dust won't kill you, but I might if you don't shut your yap. Understand me?" Color tinged his high cheekbones.

The girl mumbled something, and Harmon slapped her knee. "Don't try me, Nelda Faye." Finally, he rearranged his long body to face the front, put the car in gear, and released the hand brake.

Vada turned her head to look out her open window, then extended one arm through it, letting the hot air flow through her fingers and raise the fine hairs on her arm. For the first time that day, she smiled, just a tiny curve of her lips, but a smile nonetheless.

After what seemed a very long time, Harmon pulled to a stop in front of the sorriest looking place Vada had ever laid eyes on. "This is where you live?" she asked.

Harmon hauled her bag from the back seat as the children slipped from the car. "This'd be it."

Dempsey, the littlest of the two boys, maybe four years old, barreled across the dusty yard and threw himself upon a red hound that lay beneath the edge of the porch.

"Aw, Dempsey," Nelda said. "Pa, make him get up offa Red. It's too hot to be wallering him."

Harmon ignored her, coming instead to Vada, who still stared up at the house that wasn't a house at all. A box on stilts was what it was. Both the pointed roof and the porch sagged as they ran the width of the house, and each was missing a board here and there. The second step leading up to the porch was mostly rotted away, and there wasn't even any glass in the windows, or a screen between the hot dusty world and the splintered door. The poorest people Vada knew had screens on the doors and glass in the windows. It was—civilized. Topping off this whole sorry mess, the building sat three or four feet off the ground. The dog that lay under it, minus Dempsey who was now running full tilt around the yard in frenzied pursuit of half a dozen scrawny chickens, thumped his tail in greeting, but made no other movement. Vada didn't blame him—without the benefit of trees, this place seemed thirty degrees hotter than back home. *Than my Papa's place*, she corrected herself. This was home now.

"I know it ain't what you're used to," Harmon said, leading her up the steps. "But it's what we got, and it ain't fell down around us yet."

Vada wanted to say something smart, like "It's a thousand wonders," but she didn't. She nodded even though he couldn't see her, but when they crossed the porch and entered the house, her heart sank even further. Two rooms. Pallet in one corner of the one where they now stood; against the wall closest to the door, a broken down couch, one end propped on a chunk of wood. Iron cookstove against the back wall. Ice box. A bowlegged table. Two chairs in even worse disrepair. She closed her eyes briefly. *Lordy, Lordy. Couldn't Mama give me to a rich man as easy as a poor one?*

Harmon led her through a curtain to another room and put her bag down on the bed in the corner. It was covered with a quilt that, although worn nearly through in places, was so beautiful it almost took her breath. The double wedding ring pattern was shot through with the colors of not just any sunset, but a desert sunset, melting one into another. All vivid pinks and purples and blues, this was no rag quilt, but made of store-bought material put together with exceptional skill. Worn or not, it outshone anything she had ever seen, and certainly surpassed anything else in this poor mess of a house.

Harmon cleared his throat. "My wife done that. My first wife." Vada heard him swallow. "When she was a girl." After a few moments of silence, he added, "She come from a good family, over in Arkansas," as if that explained something.

"It's beautiful," Vada said. Before she could say anything else, or examine the room more closely, he pulled her back to the other room.

"'Bout time you was making supper. I got to go check on some things out yonder, and I'll take them boys out from under your feet. Nelda can stay and help." He said "hep" instead of help, and for a moment it didn't register. When it did, it didn't matter, because he was gone, through the door, boots clattering, not even changing from what must have been his best overalls, unpatched as they were.

As Vada looked around her, a spasm of homesickness nearly doubled her over. Although her eyes burned, she refused to allow a single tear. What was the use of crying? There was nobody to care, no Addy to hold her, no Roxanne to cry in sympathy. Nobody.

As if to confirm those thoughts, Nelda appeared in the doorway, silently regarding her. "You going to cook something or just stand there?" The child was maybe nine, smaller even than Vada, with a sprinkling of freckles dusting her pale cheeks.

Vada looked at her, a flat, unwavering gaze perfected by the many hours of staring contests between her, Addy, and anybody at school who dared challenge them. Nelda held her own briefly, but finally succumbed.

"Hope you don't cook like you look," she muttered, and flounced out to the front porch, slamming the door behind her.

* * * * *

"Vada?" Harmon's voice startled her and she felt the hesitant weight of his hand, hot on her shoulder. She stiffened, waited until she felt the cool rush of air as he withdrew. "Four o'clock comes early," he said.

She stood in the black silence, broken only by the squeak of an oil well pump in the distance. The smell of honeysuckle was everywhere, but she had yet to see any. "What happens then?"

He laughed from deep in his chest. "Then we go chop some of that."

Vada's eyes followed his pointing finger to row upon row of cotton, only then becoming visible by the light of the sudden, fat, yellow moon. She let her gaze drift over the cotton, realizing that she had not even noticed it before. Searching the sky desperately for a bright star to wish upon, she saw that the moon's brightness had dimmed them all. She looked back to the endless, eerily lit fields. "You want me to chop cotton?" So numbed was she by the day that it was barely a question. Of course he did. Why else would he bring her to a ramshackle house set down in the middle of acres and acres of it? It didn't matter anyway, what she did. *Chop cotton. Die. Live my life at the bottom of a well. I don't care.*

He patted her shoulder. "Just till picking time." She heard the smile in his voice. "It's like the Good Book says. A man wants to eat, he's got to work."

Her thoughts returned to the disastrous meal she had prepared earlier, with Nelda first sulking on the porch, then hovering near the cookstove, watching with disdain and commenting on Vada's efforts to cook.

"Ain't you never made gravy before?" the girl would ask. Or, "You call them sorry things biscuits? Even Red wouldn't eat those." Vada had finally had to threaten the child with the business end of a saucepan to get rid of her.

"Supper wasn't much, was it?" she asked Harmon now.

He laughed a little. "Oh, that Cordell. He's liable to go to vomiting over near-about anything. Don't take it too serious." He remained silent for a moment, then cleared his throat. "I did have in mind your mama might have taught you to cook."

"My mama might have told you near anything to get you to haul me off." Her words sounded more bitter than she meant them to, but not as bitter as she felt.

He cleared his throat again. "Cooking ain't nothing you can't learn. Nelda done a good bit of it after her mama passed on. She can prob'ly help you there, you get on her good side."

Vada almost choked on the words she wanted to utter. *That little she-devil hasn't got a good side, and she don't want to 'hep' me do nothing but get on down the road.* She held back, though, just let him lead her into the house, through the front room, darkened but alive with the sounds of sighs and turnings and the dreams of children. By the moonlight spilling through the glassless windows, she saw Nelda, sprawled, her arms flung to either side over the bodies of the boys, wide open and trusting. Vada envied her.

Harmon prodded her through the curtained doorway and into the bedroom. He stepped to the bureau and quickly lit the kerosene lantern. Vada went to it also and removed her nightgown from the top drawer. When she raised her eyes to the top of the bureau, she saw sitting there, next to the lantern, a Mason jar filled with a cluster of wildflowers, clumsy looking, as if the bouquet had come together accidentally. She touched the petals of a sunflower with one finger.

"I picked 'em." Harmon's voice was quiet, almost shy.

Vada looked up at him, then returned her gaze to the flowers. Biting her lower lip, she fingered a primrose, a Sweet William, some Queen Anne's lace, and a tiny orange flower she didn't recognize. "I never had nobody pick me flowers." She paused. "'Cept Addy," she whispered, almost to herself. When he made no reply, she turned and let her gaze move around the dim room, to the iron bed with its uncommonly beautiful quilt, to the one window, to the silent fiddle on the battered three-legged table in the corner, to Harmon. He stood, hands inside the bib of his overalls, then behind his back, then arms crossed and hands stuck up in his armpits, like he didn't know what to do with them. "You going to turn around?" she asked.

He frowned briefly, and when she indicated the nightgown in her hand, he smiled, revealing the small teeth. "Oh. I'll go one better." He stepped to the bureau. She heard a sound like a sigh, then the lamp went out, and the room fell into a dark nothingness that gradually took on shadow and contour.

Wishing he had just turned his back and left the lamp on so he could not sneak up on her, Vada slid down the top of her dress so it hung around her waist and hastily dropped the gown over her head. With it around her shoulders, she removed her brassiere, then slipped her arms through the gown's armholes and let her dress fall to the floor. Stepping out of it and her shoes, she picked up the garment, placing it and her bra on the bureau top.

Harmon moved beside her, and he took her hand and led her to the bed in the corner. The smell of wildflowers clung to her, fresh and strong, filling her with sorrow and some other emotion, overwhelming but unidentifiable. When they reached the bed she stood beside it as if rooted to the floor. Arms crossed over her chest in an X of fear, left hand grasping right shoulder and right grasping left, she resisted his efforts to move her onto the high iron bed.

"I don't aim to sleep here." Her eyes had adjusted to the dimness, and her gaze was riveted to the beautiful quilt, brilliant even in shadow, searching it as if for an answer to the fearful situation in which she found herself.

He nudged her with his body. "Why, shore you are. It's the only bed we got, and you going to be in it in about two shakes of a dog's hind leg." When she still didn't move, he leaned around her to peer into her face. "I ain't going to do nothing you don't want me to."

She stared back at him, again biting her lower lip. He sounded as if he meant it. Of what "nothing" consisted, she had a fair idea—not many details, just an idea—and she couldn't imagine what made him think she would ever want him to do it to her. She and Addy had discussed the little they knew about it endlessly. *The man puts his thing in the woman's belly button and fills it up with something, and they get a baby.* Jimmy Sue Anthamatten had told them so, and she'd be the one to know, what with fourteen in the family besides herself. But Vada didn't want a baby, thank you very much, and anyway, her belly button didn't hold much—she couldn't even get her littlest finger in it. She was pretty sure there wasn't room to deposit enough—whatever—to make a proper baby.

Cool air replaced Harmon behind her, and she heard the clink and rattle of his overalls as he removed them. When he nudged her this time, fear and anger combined to bring tears to her eyes, yet she felt hysterical giggles bubbling up within her. *It's not fair. I don't want this—this…*words failed her, and anger suddenly outweighed both fear and nervous laughter. Angrier than she ever remembered being, she fought to control her breathing. No one could help her, no one could save her from what was about to happen, and she tried desperately to keep the anger inside. It seemed more important to protect that core of anger than her virtue, for after all, being good had never gotten her anywhere. Again, as she had the day she met Harmon, she tried to form a prayer, but the words, the shape of it, eluded her.

He suddenly pushed her down onto the bed, his rough, callused hands raising her gown up around her neck till she felt like she might as well have not put the thing on. Still, she hung on to the material, refusing to let him pull garment over her head. If he had wanted her naked, why did he make a production of darkening the room for her to put on her nightclothes? Not that she would sleep naked. No sir. She would win this battle, if no other. Harmon must have read her mind, for he quit trying to pull the gown off. His harsh breath smelled of tobacco, and she struggled to turn her face from him. His big hands squeezed her breasts, those breasts that only in the last year had begun to develop. The hard little bumps were painful and barely in need of the brassiere she had shed, but he pawed and pinched them as if they were the size of cantaloupes while she whimpered beneath him.

Don't. Don't. Don't. The words stayed in her head even as he moved her higher on the bed, tugging at her cotton panties until he had them off. She felt his fingers spreading her apart down there, felt a ragged nail tear the delicate skin, then felt something bigger, harder, hotter forcing its way inside her, and even when his breathing became tortured and the fiery outer pain moved inside, she kept her words and her tears to herself. They were all she had, and she would not give them to the man pumping away on top of her, oblivious to the moans and whimpers of pain she couldn't stifle. But she would tell Addy. She sure would. She would tell her that the curse Mama complained about was not the monthly bleeding but this hammering assault, and Vada would certainly tell her to not, under any circumstances, let it happen to her.

When it was finally, mercifully over, Harmon rolled off her onto his back and patted her leg. "You'll be all right," he panted, while she pulled her gown down, her panties up, and lay balefully silent. Within minutes, his breathing slowed and snores filled the room.

Vada curled on her side as far away from him as she could get, her hands clamped together between her legs. *Lordy me, what I wouldn't give to sit in a bucket of ice cold water.* The throbbing down below did not abate with the night, and between bouts of seething anger that almost lifted her from the bed she planned all that she would tell Addy, all she would warn her against. *And if I ever see that lying Jimmy Sue Anthamatten, I'm going to slap her stupid.*

Chapter 5

She finally slept, and when she awoke, lay still, disoriented. A soft buzz seemed to come from all around her, then stop, then come again, just often enough to aggravate her. As she squeezed her eyes shut against it, the collection of her thoughts seemed to be a process almost too overwhelming to attempt. Was this a school day? She reached for Addy, intending to shake the sister who had slept next to her every night for almost as long as she could remember. Instead of soft girl-flesh and the worn-to-a-wisp cotton of a nightgown, her fingers brushed wool on skin, and the memory of the night before slammed into her. She moved her fingers away, but the feel of the long johns remained, and somehow the fact that this man wore long underwear in the dead of summer made what had happened to her all the more horrible. Face hot, she slowly pulled the quilt over her head and turned onto her side, curling into the tiniest ball possible.

The buzz she'd heard before had died away, but as it picked up again, she realized it was whispering. A probing began, like little cat feet kneading her through her covering, but more persistent. *Poke. Poke. Prod.* She flipped the quilt with her fingers.

"Get away from me." *Poke. Prod.* She jerked the cover from her head, surprised at first by the bare light of the lantern next to her, then by the three faces, one level with hers, the other two stair-stepping up. "What do you want?" she whispered. "Get away. I'm trying to sleep."

The little one, Dempsey, jabbed her under the eye with a chubby, sticky finger. "'Ungry," he said. The lantern light glinted in his hazel eyes. The other two stood silent, both faces a little puffy with sleep. Nelda looked at her with a bit of a smile curving one corner of her mouth.

Vada closed her eyes against that smile. *She knows. She knows what he done to me.* Harmon's grunting and hoarse breathing, her own whimpers, probably carried loudly enough that they woke Nelda, and the girl knew. Shame flooded Vada all over again.

"'Ungry," Dempsey said again.

"That's none of my concern," she said. "And putting my eye out won't get you fed." He started to poke her again and she grabbed his hand. "Jab me again and I'll break your dang finger," she whispered. "See if I don't."

He grinned, wrinkling his nose and revealing tiny, perfectly shaped, but discolored teeth. "Poke your goddamned eye out," he said, and before Vada could react, Nelda smacked him on the back of his head, hard. His forehead slammed into Vada's nose, and both began to howl at almost the same moment, he lustily and she through blood and mucous and tears involuntarily brought on by the blow.

"What in Sam Hill is going on?" Harmon's voice, quiet and tight, stopped Dempsey's wails immediately, but Vada's continued a little longer.

"S'e hit me," Dempsey said. "S'e hit me wif her face."

Vada tipped her head back to slow the blood pouring from her nose. "Did not. Laying here minding my own business," she said, the words accompanied by gurgling. "Why don't you teach these young'uns some manners?" Still holding her head back, she canted her eyes at Harmon where he lay sleepy-eyed in the lantern light.

"They been taught manners." He yawned. "Their mama was real big on manners. They ain't using 'em, is all." He stretched, his long body becoming even more elongated and almost comically thin. "What time's it getting to be, Nelda?"

Vada watched as the girl padded away with the lantern, casting the room into momentary darkness. She returned and announced, "Quarter to five." Giving Vada a narrow-eyed stare, but speaking to her father, she said, "She's going to get blood all over that quilt, Pa."

Vada leveled on the girl a look that was known to send school-yard rivals scurrying in all directions, but Nelda didn't flinch, just glared back and said, "My mama give me that quilt. Said I was to have it when she passed."

The bed shook as Harmon reached across and grasped Nelda's shoulder, pulling her partway across Vada, whose face lay inches from the lantern.

"You all are fixing to burn me to death," Vada said, and grabbed the lantern.

Caught as she was, all she could do was hang on to it, arm outstretched off the bed.

Harmon's voice was quiet, but in a dangerous way, like when the wind stops in the midst of a storm. "Girl, you want to get out of here while the getting's good." Nelda's body tensed as if she were going to speak, but Harmon pulled her even farther onto the bed and halfway across Vada. "On your own two feet or asshole over elbows, Nelda Faye. I won't tell you twice." He shook her once and released her. Sliding off the bed, she jerked the lantern from Vada, turned, and stomped away.

Vada stifled a groan. *I not only got to lay in this bed with a pile of sticks in long johns, but I got to take guff off that little brat.* As the sound of the girl's pounding footsteps became irregular thuds—and Dempsey shouted from the other room, "Nelda kicking the wall wif her feet, Pa,"—Vada consoled herself with the thought that at least she'd be taking guff from a girl with stumps instead of feet.

Beside her, Harmon stretched and groaned. "Gawdamighty," he said, arms and legs still extended. "I'd stretch a mile if I didn't have to walk back." Relaxing, he poked Vada. "Better get out of bed. Shoulda been up a hour ago."

It didn't even feel like she'd been asleep an hour ago, but she swung her thin legs over the edge of the mattress, fingered her nose, sticky with partially dried blood, and winced at the soreness that had already set in. She thought of Dempsey. *Stinking little brat.* The pounding in the other room had stopped, and now the three kids stood in the doorway, staring at her. She wanted to scream, "What're you looking at, you buncha monkeys?" but she didn't. As she slid off the bed, the thought struck her that she didn't have to worry about it anyway, because she wasn't going to be here that long. The idea both surprised and pleased her. Being married was like being grown up. She could go anywhere, do anything, and couldn't nobody say "Scat" to her. She glared at the children, conscious of the stickiness between her legs. As if on cue, the children turned and headed for the other room, taking the lamp.

"I'm going to need that light," she called. "I can't get dressed if I can't see." Dempsey looked back and grinned at her, wrinkling his nose. "I can't get dressed in the dark," she said again.

Harmon appeared beside her, barely visible in the gloom, his long body bent double as he rustled around for his own clothing. "Guess you'll have to," he said. "Ain't got but the one lantern, and it went thataway." Above the sound of him pulling on his clothes , she heard him clear his throat. "You fixing to cook breakfast?"

"Do I have a choice?" She slid from the bed and felt her way across the floor to the bureau. Poking about in a drawer, she pulled out something that felt like a dress. *Probably wrinkled as Grandma's butt.* She pulled it over her head anyway, and, pushing the heavy hair from her eyes, looked into the dimness to where Harmon sat on the edge of his bed pulling on his boots and grunting. Finally, he clumped from the room, the wood floor squeaking with his weight. Running fingers through her hair, she sighed, rubbed her eyes, and sat on the bed, moaning slightly at the pressure on the area between her legs. She was so sore. And tired. *Lordy me.* She sat a moment before she heard Harmon calling. Sighing again, she rose and trudged toward the kitchen. Now the lantern sat on the rickety table, illuminating Harmon in one of the chairs and Dempsey on his knee. Dempsey crinkled his eyes at her, but she glared at him until his smile wavered then faded, finally disappeared entirely, and was replaced by what was probably the meanest look he could muster.

"S'e ain't going to hit me wif her face, is s'e, Pa?"

Harmon laughed. "I got a suspicion it weren't her done the hitting." He finished rolling a cigarette one-handed, put it between his thin lips and flicked the head of a match with a thumbnail. When he had the cigarette glowing, he looked at her. "What happened in yonder? Your nose looks like a mule kicked you."

Nelda had drifted into the kitchen area, Cordell shadowing her, and she glared at Vada as if daring her to tell. The girl's pale hair and skin were accentuated by her eyes, as black as Harmon's, but with a defiance written in them that Vada both hated and envied. *Won't nobody never walk on her.*

"Nothing happened," Vada said, shifting her gaze from the girl to Harmon. "You want me to fix some breakfast, I need some flour." For a moment the room remained silent, then Harmon burst into laughter.

"Godamighty. I got four of you ag'in me now. Just what I been needing." He stood, dumping Dempsey in an unceremonious heap on the floor, where the boy set up a howl that could probably be heard in Kellyville. Moving up behind where Vada stood looking at the nearly bare shelves of the cabinet, Harmon reached over her head and retrieved a half-empty flour sack. He set it on the counter and moved even closer, chuckling as he squeezed her butt. She jumped, and he patted her shoulder. "We'll get on fine, girl. We shore will."

Vada jerked a bowl from a shelf beneath the sink closer to her, and dumped flour, salt, water, lard, baking powder, and whatever else was handy into it. Taking up a heavy wooden spoon as she might have an ice pick, she began violently gouging the mess. She stabbed it over and over, losing herself in her rage. When she finally looked up, exhausted and sweaty, breathing rapidly, Harmon still stood there, his gaze resting heavily upon her for a few moments before he moved away. The *clump clump* of his boots faded as he moved outside and off the porch, but Nelda stayed put, like an appointed watchdog, measuring every movement Vada made.

Almost an hour later when Vada had both biscuits and gravy done, she put it on the table and looked at Nelda. "Go tell them it's on if they want to eat."

Nelda didn't move, just opened her mouth and brayed, "Breakfast is ready," never removing her gaze from her new stepmother.

Vada glared at the girl and made a disgusted noise, a cross between a sigh and a snort, then looked away from her toward the table. This meal didn't appear to be any more a success than last night's. The biscuits, flat, misshapen and nearly burned, resembled small cowpatties. The gravy would've been all right had it not been hidden under a layer of grease floating on top. Here she had done the best she could and it still fell far short of edible. Not only was she stuck in this house with these hyenas and their nasty old daddy, but it looked as if she would never again eat a decent meal unless somebody else came in and cooked it. Her hopes that Harmon and the children would eat the sorry mess and leave her be were destroyed when they trooped in and stopped, almost as one, in front of the table.

Cordell looked a little sick, and Dempsey jerked on Harmon's overall leg. "Pa, s'e ain't done it right."

Harmon looked at the table, then at Vada and took a deep breath. "She done a fine job. We're going to eat it." Nelda started to speak, but he silenced her with a look. "And like it."

Vada stared at the floor, so embarrassed and angry at everything that had happened to her in the last twenty-four hours that she could not look at any of them. When they began to eat, she took two of the sorry biscuits and went to the front porch to gnaw on them in private.

* * * * *

By mid-morning, sweat drenched every article of clothing Vada wore, and her skin felt as if it had been dipped in water, stretched across her bones, and left to dry in the sun. Perspiration dripped from her face to the dusty ground as she bent over the cotton plants, and her sunbonnet felt glued to her head by the wet hair beneath. *I've died and gone to hell.* She straightened and sucked on a finger, then a place on her palm rubbed raw by the hoe. Sore, red and blistered already. She didn't see how she would make it today, then tomorrow, then the day after and the day after that.

"S'e stopped again, Pa," Dempsey said, and Vada glared at him. Stinking brat.

"Mind your own business and let her mind hers, Dempsey," Nelda said, and lugged a gallon jar of water to where Vada stood.

"Drink some more water," the girl told her, holding out the dipper. "You're liable to get heat stroke you don't drink enough."

The voice wasn't as snotty as it had been, but Vada eyed her with suspicion. "Heat stroke'd be a blessing." She drank deeply and wiped her mouth with the back of her hand.

Nelda shrugged. "You get used to it. I been doing it since I was a young'un."

Vada almost laughed in her face, but one look into those coal-smudged eyes and she swallowed instead. "Don't feel to me like I'll get used to it." She looked down to see Dempsey glaring up at her.

Without moving his eyes from her face, he shouted, "Pa, they bof am stopped n—ow!" The smack of Nelda's open palm on the side of his face even made Vada jump, and she almost grabbed the girl's wrist to prevent the second blow. Then she caught herself. *I'm not having that brat look to me to fight his battles.*

"You shut up and mind your own business, you stupid little tattletale," Nelda said over the sound of his wails. Shouting sob-filled recriminations at his sister, Dempsey bent to pick up the ridiculously wide-brimmed straw hat her slap had knocked from his head.

A few rows over, Harmon straightened and removed his own sweat soaked hat. "I'm fixing to come over there and wallop the both of you." Wiping his face with a forearm, he put his hat back on and stood watching Nelda, Dempsey, and Vada.

"I had to give her some water, didn't I?" Nelda stood, hands on hips, giving Vada the full force of her evil eye. "Look at her. Got a face like a tomato. She won't last a day." Whatever acceptance had been in her a few minutes before had flown, and only disgust remained in her attitude and on her face. "Won't last a day," she repeated, and shoved the dipper of water at Vada again.

Vada pushed the dipper back. "Stop saying that. I worked in worse than this," she said, but she knew it wasn't true. She turned her back on the girl and bent over a cotton plant, her arms screaming at the repetitive movements, her back on fire from her bent position. When she next looked up, Dempsey stood before her, shiny tear tracks smudging his dirty cheeks.

"You my mama now?"

She stopped, hoe half through a weed. Where had that come from? "Your what?" she asked, pretending she hadn't heard him.

"My mama," the little boy repeated, louder this time like she was hard of hearing. He resumed chopping the weeds around the cotton stalks as if born to it and moved on to another, sliding his gaze her way.

"Why would I be your mama?" She felt itchy in her clothes, but didn't know if it was the sun or his question. Couldn't he see she wasn't old enough to be anybody's mama? And if she was, she wouldn't want it to be this tattling little monster who seemed so bent on making trouble for her.

"Cordell say whoever Pa marry be my mama." He said it like Cordell's word was the gospel truth.

Vada glared at Cordell, bent over his sack a few rows beyond her, then looked back to Dempsey. "I ain't—I'm not." *Lordy me. I'm starting to talk like them.* "You can forget about such as that." Even as she said it, a heavy sadness crept over her, for both herself and the boy. If only she could walk off this place right now, not chop another weed or answer another stupid question from another stinking brat till she died. And if only he had somebody who would love him without him having to ask. She chopped faster to get away, but he easily kept up while she left behind more weeds than cotton stalks. *Outworked by a four-year-old. If that's not something.*

"You can be my mama if you want to." From beneath the huge hat, he wrinkled his nose and smiled, and for a brief moment she felt a stirring. He reminded her a little bit of Johnsie. If he'd dig at the back of his drawers, there'd be an outright resemblance.

A stab of homesickness pierced her, and she could barely breathe. Struggling for air, she kept her eyes on the weeds, determined to avoid looking at the child again.

"Can't you be my mama if you want to?"

"It don't matter, 'cause I don't want to."

"You marry my Pa," he said, as if that explained everything.

"That's no fault of mine," she snapped, eyes on the red dirt around the cotton plant.

"Don't you like me?" The tremor in his voice drew her gaze back to his face. The tan-going-to-green eyes shimmered with tears, and she tried telling herself the tears were because he was stuck in the hot sun, chopping cotton when he was barely old enough to pick his nose. But they weren't, and it suddenly seemed like the most important thing in the world to keep those tears from falling.

"You're all right," she conceded.

"Then you can be my mama!" he said, and flashed a discolored but still brilliant smile through the tears glistening on his cheeks.

She gave him the look she had always used to stop Johnsie dead in his tracks, but whatever the resemblance, this boy was not Johnsie. He rushed straight into her knees, wrapped his arms around her legs, and nearly knocked her over.

* * * * *

When the day finally ended, the ends of her fingers were on fire and her back felt as if her mother had been at her with a board again. Making supper, Vada tried to handle everything with the palms of her hands, dropping most of what she picked up. By the time she had cooked the the poke greens with the bacon and made gravy, she was ready to scream from pain and frustration. To make matters worse, the pale, lumpy things she removed from the oven looked even less like biscuits than those she had previously cooked.

She took it all to the table, grimacing at the pressure on her fingertips, and set it down. Harmon and the kids were already there, he in one chair and Nelda in the other. Vada stood for a moment, waiting for Nelda to vacate the seat for her, but the girl didn't move. Instead, Nelda poked at the biscuits with one finger, then used her fork to stir the sad looking greens and bacon.

"I can't eat this mess," she said finally.

Vada glared at her. "Fine. Cook it yourself next time."

Nelda curled her lip slightly and wagged her head at Vada. "Cook it yourself next time," she mimicked.

Vada clenched her fists, saw the room and the girl through a swirling red film. "Don't you mock me! I don't have to put—"

"Don't you mock me! I don't—"

Both Harmon's fists came down on the table at once, sending a tin drinking glass over on its side and off the edge of the table. "Stop it!" he said, and the anger in his face made her stomach contract momentarily, made her feel like the outhouse wasn't nearly close enough. Vada felt a trembling begin in her, and even in the heat, her teeth chattered with growing intensity.

Harmon rose from his chair, face growing darker, jaw muscle jumping. "Nelda Faye, you get your young ass to bed. You can't eat this mess, you can do without." The girl started to say something, but when her father drew his hand back as if to slap her, she burst into tears and ran to the other side of the room, throwing herself onto the pallet.

Cordell shifted from foot to foot, brown eyes wide on his father, while

Dempsey sidled up to Vada, caught a fistful of her dress and hung on. Harmon pointed at Vada. "Plant your butt in that chair." When she had done so, knees trembling, he seated himself. "It's bad enough listening to the bunch of you sniping at each other out there—" he jerked his head in the direction of the fields—"but I ain't breaking up fights in here all night."

He pulled biscuits from the pan, forked bacon and greens from the chipped bowl, dipped gravy onto the biscuits and slapped plates in front of both boys, then Vada, then himself. He took a bite. Vada sat frozen in place, stomach churning. When he next spoke, his voice had softened. "I know you ain't full-grown yourself, but somebody has got to act like an adult, and it looks like you'd be it."

She stared down at her hands, twisted together in her lap, and fought the urge to cry from fear of him and outrage over Nelda's insults. *I won't bawl in front of him. No sir. And I'm not about to show her I care.* But neither could she eat, and she spent the remainder of the meal pushing soggy biscuits and watery gravy around on her plate. When it was over, Harmon went to the porch, followed by Cordell, and while she collected the dishes and heated the water for washing them she could hear the mumble of their conversation, smell the smoke of Harmon's roll-your-own.

Dempsey followed her from table to sink to stove, not saying a word, but picking up a spoon when she dropped it, finding a clean rag to replace the smelly one used for the morning and noon dishes. Vada let him follow her as long as he was quiet, and while she washed the dishes, he sat at the table in the chair she had been ordered into earlier. He sang quietly, something about rabbits dancing jigs and tree frogs playing banjoes, and Vada resisted an inclination to smile. *Won't catch me making up to no stinking brat.*

A couple of biscuits and a little gravy remained from the meal. She stood still, pondering the merits of throwing the food away. A voice, not Dempsey's, came from behind her. "I might eat that."

She turned to see Nelda, eyes swollen to slits. Vada glanced from Nelda to the food, sarcastic words a breath away.

Dempsey stopped his song. "They good, Nelda. Them biscuits. They—" He frowned, as if searching for the most appropriate term. His face brightened. "They *chewy*."

He spoke with such seriousness, such sincerity, that Vada had to smile. She was probably the sorriest cook in Oklahoma, but this little boy was willing to lie for the sake of peace, or maybe just for her sake. She dumped biscuits and gravy into a bowl and handed it, with a spoon, to Nelda.

"Better eat it 'fore your pa comes in," Vada said, and returned to the final few dishes awaiting her.

When she had finished, she stood at the sink, arms hanging at her sides. She felt suddenly numb, her mind fogged, as if fatigue had only then rushed in to claim her. Without a word to Dempsey or Nelda, both still at the table, she stumbled into the other room and fell onto the bed. Groaning, she seemed to feel an ache in every single muscle in her body as she sank into the lumpy mattress. Her dress, smelly and stiff with the salt of her sweat, bound and irritated her sunburned neck and arms, but she hadn't the energy to rise and strip. She tried to relax, reached to rub a leg cramp, then lay still.

Sighing, falling into an almost doze, she thought of Addy. What would she be doing now? Sitting on the porch with Papa, probably, him smoking and the little kids deviling him for a story about the Army he'd served in, or the Land Run he'd heard his own papa tell about. She could almost hear Addy's words: "I'll come for you, Vada, and we'll go where they won't never find us." Even in recollection the words were filled with hope, determination, Addy's voice fierce as she had declared them. How Vada wished it could be so! But lying here in the house of a man she barely knew, she didn't see how she would ever get away, be able to leave this place and survive it. *I've never been nowhere, done nothing. Put me somewhere on my own and I'd be like a turtle without a shell.* The thought of her own helplessness depressed her and she sighed heavily.

A small movement shook the bed, interrupting her thoughts. She turned to see the middle boy, Cordell, leaning over her.

"Want to see what I got?" He grinned, revealing gapped teeth and a small scar near the corner of his eye, invisible except when he smiled. One hand was hidden behind his back.

"What?" She eyed him and scooted a little further away.

"You can't ask what. You got to say yes or no."

"No."

He bumped the bed with his skinny hip, and the movement seemed to jar every sore muscle. "You can't say no. It ain't polite."

"It's not polite to wake people up when they're sleeping, either," she snapped back.

"Ain't supposed to sleep in the daytime nohow. You want to see what I got or don't you?" His hand was still behind his back and he fairly jiggled with anticipation.

"I said no! Leave me be." She turned toward the wall, but felt the bed move. She rolled over and glared at him. "All right. Show it to me and get out of here."

Anything to get rid of him. But when he threw the garter snake onto the bed, she shrieked as if she'd had a hot poker put to her and leapt off the bed after him. Out of the room and through the front door Cordell ran, Vada hard on his heels.

"Pa! Pa!" he shrieked as he sailed off the porch, over the steps, and hit the ground in a small cloud of dust. "Make her quit! She's going to—"

"I'm going to kill him is what," she screamed, and jumped off the porch after him. Catching him in the middle of the yard, she captured his head in the crook of her arm. "Dang little brat," she said, punctuating each word with a smack on his skinny behind. "Don't you never do nothing like that to me again!" With one more *whomp* on the butt for good measure, she thrust him from her. Both stood in the dirt, glaring, breath coming in gasps, Cordell's eyes streaming tears and his nose running.

"I hate you!" He shook with obvious rage, kicked dirt at her, and ran up the steps to Harmon's side, where the boy stood glaring.

Harmon had not moved, still sat smoking, hands clasped behind his head, chair tilted to rest on the back two legs. He let it thump onto all fours. "What the Sam Hill is goin' on with you two?"

"I asked her did she want to see it, Pa. She said she did and I showed it to her."

"What? That garter snake you been carryin' around?"

Vada mounted the steps, hands clenched into fits. "I only said I'd look at it so's he'd leave me alone. And he didn't tell me it was no snake." She looked from Harmon to the boy and back to Harmon, who tilted his chair back on its hind legs and grinned.

"Aw, quit looking so sour. He didn't mean to scare you. Just being a boy's all." He took a pouch from his overall bib pocket and began to roll another cigarette.

"He put a snake in the bed with me. I've never had no boy do that."

"Garter snakes won't hurt you." Harmon stuck one end of the cigarette in his mouth and lit up.

Vada stood an arm's length away from him, torn between turning around and walking all the way to her daddy's house and shoving Harmon off the porch. She watched him until he'd smoked the cigarette nearly down to his thin lips. Even if she made it to her daddy's house, he had shown he was no refuge. Not anymore. And Mama would make him load her up and bring her back to this hellhole, no doubt about that. Life seemed to hold no choices anymore, and Vada felt like an ant under the boot of the world. She released her pent-up breath slowly.

"You going to get that snake out of the house?" she asked Harmon.

He laughed. "That snake ain't going to hurt you. Ain't hardly bigger than a worm, and anyway, he's more scared of you than you are of him."

Her head swam and she sweat trickled down her back. She was so tired, and if Harmon would do this one thing—just this one. She felt as if she could collapse onto the porch and fall into a dead sleep, but somebody would come along and throw a snake at her or want her to fix supper or poke her in the eye. The sight of Harmon tilted back in the chair, smoking his cigarette, hands behind his head, made her want to slap him stupid. *The king of the world. Got him somebody to take care of his heathen kids and fill his bed at night, and he's happy as a pig in mud.* But some instinct told her she had one more card to play.

"I'll tell you one thing. You want me in that bed in yonder, you better be for finding that dang snake and getting it out of the house." For the first time, the small grin left Harmon's face. She motioned with her head toward the old Chrysler. "Reckon I can sleep in that back seat about as easy as I can in a house with snakes in it." The front chair legs slammed to the porch floor, and the look on his face was fearsome. She stared back, determined and exhausted, with one strengthening the other. Half of her hoped he'd tell her to go on, go sleep in the car if that's the way she felt. But no.

Eyes still on her, Harmon glared at Cordell. "You get your young ass in there and find that snake, boy."

"I can't—" Cordell started, but Harmon cut him off.

"Don't 'I can't' me. Get in there and find it, and don't you ever let me catch you pulling a stunt like that again, you hear me?"

Vada turned and lowered herself to sit on the porch's top step, ignoring Cordell as he stomped into the house.

* * * * *

That night went much like the one before, with Harmon on her like white on rice, her with her eyes squeezed shut and fists clenched. Lying beneath him, she suppressed the grunts his weight tried to force from her, and got through the act by doing what she'd done all her life—looking for the bright side. If she rated things on a scale of zero to five, and being in the fields with Papa and Addy was a five, then this was a zero. But if having whooping cough or the back door trots was a zero, then this was at least a two. *Then there's that time Roxanne upchucked all over me, and Mama whipped me for getting my clothes dirty. That was a definite zero, so maybe this is a four next to that. Well, a three, anyway.*

Finally, Harmon gave a mighty groan and collapsed, squeezing the breath out of her. She nudged him with one hand, and he rolled onto his back.

Breathing hard, he patted her thigh. "Wasn't so bad this time, was it?" She was pretty sure he didn't want to know the truth, so she remained silent, and he patted her again. "You're going to be all right here, girl. See if you ain't." The words were hardly out of his mouth when she heard the first snore.

She turned on her side, curled into a ball, and lay uncomfortably with the sticky mess seeping from her. *Shoo. This is worse than when Addy used to pee the bed.* On whispering feet, she went to the chest of drawers and the trunk beside it where Harmon always left his overalls. With a grim smile, she clutched what was probably a pant leg and wiped herself clean, then climbed back into bed. Although she knew that the fragile cocoon of satisfaction that surrounded her was as temporary as a summer shower, she fell almost immediately into sleep.

Chapter 6

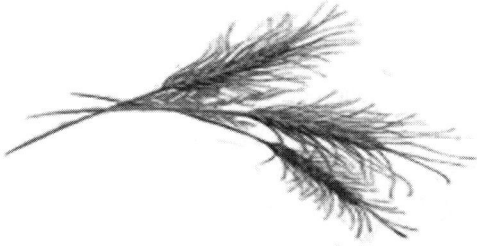

The unending heat and toil of the days worked on Vada, making her short-tempered and teary. *Stinking Oklahoma sun.* Why couldn't she live somewhere normal, where September and October meant fall, colored leaves and cool nights? She knew there were such places because she had seen pictures. Why did she have to live somewhere it was so almighty hot for so long? *And the cotton, Lordy me, the cotton.* How could there *be* so much cotton in the world? And why did *she* have to be the one to chop it, to live in this hot, dusty, sweaty, place and pick cotton?

She comforted herself with memories of Addy and the fields full of wildflowers, and allowed herself to dream a little about how her sister might yet come for her, and how they would go away, far, far away, and take care of each other. Surely together they would be all right. Surely they would. And oh, how she wanted to be away from Dempsey's continual picking at her to "be my mama," and from Nelda—Nelda and her badgering, her spitefulness, her spying—her eternal spying. Vada could turn from almost any chore or even come back from the outhouse and find Nelda somewhere nearby, pretending not to watch her. *What's she think I'm going to do, grow horns?* And then there was Cordell. Cordell was a hard one to figure. Ever since the incident with the garter snake, he had steered clear of Vada, canting his light brown eyes at her, as if afraid she'd hex him or something worse. Once or twice he had muttered something in passing, something she didn't quite get and he refused to repeat.

But most of all, she wanted to go away from Harmon and his nightly invasion of her most private places, his bemused glances whenever she complained, his constant pushing her to do more than she felt able to do. When he took the car and went to town for supplies, always leaving her and the children behind, she had often thought of striking out on her own without waiting for Addy. But she never did. Every time the idea came to mind, she pictured herself alone somewhere with too many strangers, too much noise, too many opportunities for disaster. Maybe she didn't leave just because she was so blamed tired. In the last few weeks the exhaustion had grown, glomming onto her and holding her captive. She barely got supper over in the evenings before she found herself looking longingly toward the bedroom. As weeks passed and the nights became cooler, she had to almost be dragged from bed in the mornings, a job Dempsey took on with great relish.

"'Mon, Mama. Get up. 'Mon. I helping," he would say, and tug on her arm. When she finally sat up, he'd grin at her, say, "Get up, Mama. Fi' breakfast." Too drained even to tell him to quit calling her "Mama," Vada usually got up because it was unavoidable.

But as the days wore on, and the heat abated, Vada began to realize that she didn't need anybody to rescue her. If she had a mind to go, she would. Biding time, that's what she was doing.

Now wasn't a good time, though. Lordy, she was so tired, and a bit queasy all the time. When November had come, Harmon had covered the windows with clear plastic that popped and snapped with the late autumn winds, and the place seemed airless. In spite of cracks in the walls where daylight and even an occasional field mouse crept in, smells lingered of greasy food and too many people who bathed too seldom.

Hands still in the soapy water, Vada looked toward the bedroom that held the lumpy bed with its beautiful faded quilt. To lie down, bury her face in that quilt, sleep till she awoke on her own. The thought was seductive, almost irresistible—that is, until she thought about the nights she spent there, and Harmon and his demands. Then, she wanted no part of it.

She yawned and dropped her forehead onto the cast iron sink. Even though winter approached—or at least the unpredictable extremes passing for winter in Oklahoma—the temperature must have been near seventy degrees, and the coolness of the sink sent a thrill through her. One tiny thing for which she could be thankful.

Harmon's voice broke into her reverie. "Aw, I seen you eyeing that bed in there. Getting to like it a little, ain't you girl?"

Dang him! Always sneaking up on me. I'm going to start shutting that front door even if it's a hundred and ten out there.

He squeezed her butt as he reached over her head for a Mason jar. He gave her another squeeze and leaned around to peer into her face. "I knowed you had it in you to be a hot one. You wasn't fooling me none." He filled the jar with water from the pump, drank long and noisily before he set the empty jar back on the shelf. He grinned at her. "Yessir, a hot one."

A hot one? That was a hot one. The only time she was hot was when she was in the blazing sun chopping cotton. Even when frost came, she was still in the sun; she'd thought at least now she could pick the cotton without the sun turning her skin red and tight, but she'd been wrong there too. *Dang Oklahoma weather. It's no weather at all, that's what.* Stifling a snort, she waited for Harmon to leave. *Like to give him something hot. Burning stick up his—*He grabbed her behind once more, this time with both hands, and she slapped her palms into the dishwater, sending sudsy water all over the warped wooden floor and herself.

"I wish you'd quit that!" She turned on him. "Quit it."

His head drew back like a goose preparing to hiss. "What in the Sam Hill is wrong with you?"

She removed a plate from the dishwater. "Nothing wrong with me. I'm tired of you grabbing my backside every time I turn it, that's all."

He acted as if she hadn't spoken. "It's your time of the month, ain't it? That's it. Sarah always got crabby—"

Suddenly paralyzed, hands in the water, she frantically tried to remember when her last monthly was. She'd been menstruating less than a year when she'd come here, and often as not its occurrence came as a surprise to her. She barely breathed as he droned on in the background and she mentally toted up the numbers. No matter how she calculated, her last period had been the week before she'd married Harmon. *Three and a half months ago!*

Motionless in front of the dishpan, trying and failing to form prayers to spare her this final blow, she was vaguely aware of the rumble of an engine, then a familiar voice from the front yard.

"Vada? You in there? Where's your manners, girl? You got comp'ny on the doorstep."

Harmon raised his eyebrows at her. "Why, that sounds like your Mama," he said, and went to through the open door to the porch.

The voice startled her and all other thoughts scattered like so many birds. Mama? Homesick as she'd been for Addy and the little kids, and yes, Papa, in spite of what he'd allowed to happen, she'd had no desire to see Mama. She couldn't remember a single act of tenderness on her her mother's part, even when she tried. She thought only of a red-faced, blue-eyed screaming woman who hated her and lived to make her life miserable. Vada's heart pounded in her throat until Mama's voice no longer penetrated the roaring in her ears. Quickly drying her hands, she smoothed the front of her dress and moved quickly to the door.

She stopped just over the threshold. "Papa!" He looked up from where he leaned against the porch post watching her mother in animated conversation with a motionless Harmon.

"We had us a chance to borrow this old car from Kenneth's brother," she was saying. "He's bad to drink, you know, drunk more often'n not, to tell you the truth, but he does keep his vehicle running fair—and we up and decided to drive over and see how you all was making out." She spied Vada hovering in the doorway. "Lord, girl, if you're not a sight. You look like you been wallowing in flour. You always was the sloppiest—"

"You care to set a spell?" Harmon broke in. "Because if you do, I'd be right happy to fetch a chair."

"Why, yes, I believe I would. And I sure could use me a glass of ice tea." Mama cooled herself with a funeral home fan as if to emphasize the need, and Vada looked back to Papa. He barely met her eyes before he looked away, and in the brief moment when their gazes did connect, she saw both anger and shame there.

"We don't have no tea, nor no ice neither," Vada said, her eyes still on her daddy. "We got water, though, if you want that." She hesitated, looking at her father and wishing with all her might for him to throw his arms open to her and say, "Come here, Sister," like he used to. But he didn't, probably never would. Still, her anger at him seeped away with each breath she drew, and she felt only longing and love.

"Can I fetch you a glass too, Papa?" She would do anything to take that look from his face, that hardening of the jaw, the twitch at his temple. She wondered at first what she had done to bring it on, but then she saw that his jaw became even more rigid, and the shadows in his eyes deepened even more, when he looked at Mama. He finally moved his gaze to Vada and nodded, said he guessed he'd take a glass if it wasn't too much trouble.

When she returned to the porch with two jars of water, Harmon had brought out another chair and Mama sat in it like queen of the world, shawl around her shoulders, fanning and talking, laughing to hear herself laugh. Vada hovered near, glancing from time to time at Papa, longing to feel his rough hand on her hair. Dempsey circled her legs, making buzzing noises, till she felt like she'd scream. She finally bent so her face was even with his. "Can't you go out yonder with Nelda and Cordell?" she asked, grasping his upper arm.

"Nope. Stay wif you." He grinned, crinkling his freckled nose.

She sighed, wishing she could throw him off the porch like a tow sack of rotten potatoes. But she knew full well that if provoked, he'd start screaming, and then where would she be? "You better keep shut. I'm going to talk to my daddy while he's here, and I don't want you butting in."

"Okay, Mama!"

She pulled his face toward her and squeezed it till his lips looked like those of a fish gasping for air. "And I'm not your mama!"

"Okay, Mama!" Dempsey said, eyes gleaming.

She edged toward Papa, finally came close enough to catch the familiar smell of Tiger Rose hair oil and lye soap, and a new one—maybe after-shave of some kind—and her heart caught in her throat. He'd wanted to smell nice to come and see her. The fact, simple as it was, almost brought tears to her eyes. When she could trust herself to speak, she did. "How you doing, Papa?" she asked. "You been working hard?"

He grinned his slow, tobacco stained grin and spat a stream of juice off the edge of the porch, then looked back to her. "Toler'ble hard. Leastways, it seems hard without you and Addy following me around."

She inched closer, brushing at his arm with her fingers as if there was something on it, but she wanted to touch him, reclaim the Papa she'd always known, the one who gave her piggyback rides and helped her make her ABC's, and took her to Sunday school even when Mama was in a snit and wouldn't go. "How come Addy don't go around with you no more?" He spit again, swallowed hard, and looked out over the near-bare cotton fields. "Aw, she's got school, and all. And you know your mama. Always got something for her to do in the house, what with the young'uns and all."

Vada followed his gaze to bare fields where cotton had grown a few short weeks ago, wondered what he saw there that was so much easier to look at than her. Red dirt, an oil derrick in the distance, the sun setting on the horizon—to her they didn't seem like much of a substitute for a daughter he hadn't seen in almost four months.

He nodded toward her mother. "Better go visit with her. We're going to have to go pretty soon." He looked at her for a moment, and his eyes were dark with—something. Something hurtful and mad and sad at the same time, something that made her want to hug him and tell him *she* was sorry. Instead, she moved across the porch, sidled up near her mother and waited for a break in the one-sided conversation. Nelda and Cordell had filed past and into the house to wash up for bed, dragging Dempsey with them, by the time Mama took a breath. Vada knew her mother had seen her approach, but the woman still jumped.

"Land sakes, girl! What you got to sneak up on me like that for?" Even though the late afternoon had turned cool, Mama's fanning went into high gear and her face reddened, visible even in the growing dusk. "You know I can't take that sneakiness of yours." She looked back to Harmon. "She always was the sneakiest child! Why, she'd creep around and come up behind me and pert near give me a heart attack. I'll tell you, Harmon, I don't know how you—"

"I's over by Matt Hensley's place the other day," Harmon cut in, looking at Papa. "He's sure enough got a stand of peach trees, ain't he?"

Papa and Vada both looked at Mama, who was puffing up like a toad. Then Papa moved toward Harmon, squatting between Vada and her husband. "Yeah, I reckon he'll start him a fruit stand come next summer—he's got that apple orchard back of his place too, and a good many plum trees."

"I never did like plums," Mama broke in. "The red ones give me the hives, and I'm not aiming to try no others. The young'uns all love plum butter, though, so I reckon they're all right, if you can tolerate 'em." She motioned with her head toward Vada. "Vada here's the only picky eater I ever raised. All my othern's are good as gold, but with this'n, if it wasn't one thing, it was another. Just the smell of turnips made her vomit, and never mind trying to get her to eat a good piece of pork. Why, I don't know how in the world you stand her, the way she's so *delicate* and all." She fanned herself, dabbing at her freckled chest and red face with her hanky as though oblivious to the near-dark and rapidly cooling air. "Do you believe this weather? I'll swan, seems like May instead of pert near December." She eyed Vada, who tried to shrink away from the building tension and into the shadows on the porch. "Will you stand up straight? I'll swan, you act like you're an old—"

"Can I fetch you some more water?" Harmon broke in, the front legs of his chair crashing to the porch. The sudden noise caused Vada to bite the inside of her cheek, but she held back a cry of pain, wanting only to sink into the porch before the dirt came down. "If another jar'd cool you off some I'd be mighty pleased to get it for you. But if you're bent on hammering my wife into this here porch with your tongue, you can get back in that car there and get on down the road."

Vada blinked at him and looked at her mother. Mama looked like she'd swallowed a June bug as she gaped first at Harmon, then at Papa. *Nobody* had ever talked to her that way. Vada would wager ten years of her own life on that one. She looked again at Papa, but he was studying the cracked and splintering wood of the porch like he'd never seen such. It was nearly too dark to tell, but she thought one corner of his thin mouth was twitching.

"Why, I—Kenneth—I—" her mother said, as near to sputtering as Vada had ever heard her.

Papa's voice was quiet, and he didn't look at Mama. "You want that jar of water? Reckon you might ought to answer him 'fore he changes his mind."

Mama stared at him, then at Harmon, then, finally, at Vada. In Mama's face was every nasty thing she had ever said to Vada, every slap she'd ever delivered, and Vada shrank from it. At last, her mother heaved herself from the chair, gathered her pocketbook and handkerchief, and moved off the porch with all the dangerous majesty of a funnel cloud advancing across the plain. She nearly jerked the car door off its hinges, and after seating herself in it, slammed it so hard Vada fancied the ground shook. Papa stayed in his squatting position on the porch, talking quietly to Harmon, for a good long time after Mama had gone to the car. Mama, for her part, sat and screamed out the window every so often for Papa to come on, she was ready to go, ready to go *now*. Papa ignored her for a good bit, then she blew the horn. When he still didn't move she blew it again, alternating blowing the horn with screaming shrill demands. Finally, he unfolded himself and went down the steps to the car, back straight, fists clenching and unclenching.

Opening the car door, he said something in a low voice, something Vada could not hear, and both the horn and her mother fell silent. Papa returned to the now-dark porch, squatted again, and talked to Harmon for another fifteen minutes. Vada leaned against a post, weak with fear and wonder, and shivering with the growing chill in the air. Dempsey had wandered back out, and rather than argue, she picked him up and set him on her hip. When her father rose to go, he came to where she stood, Dempsey asleep in her nearly numb arms.

"You be good, Sister," he said, kissing her on the forehead. "Don't pay no attention to your mama. You know how she is." He hugged her the best he could with Dempsey between them, then released her. "It don't seem like it now, maybe, but this is the best place for you. He's a good man." He patted her shoulder and turned to descend the steps.

"Papa?"

He stopped, looked back over his shoulder.

"Will you bring Addy to see me sometime?"

He nodded. "Do what I can." With that, he was gone.

* * * * *

For once Harmon let her alone, and if he never did another thing for her, she had that to thank him for. It was a hard thing, knowing her mama hated her and her daddy was unable to stand up for her. *But he did, in his way. He stayed there on the porch with Harmon, stayed there and talked for the longest time, even with Mama sitting in the car screaming at him to come on, come on NOW, and blowing that horn.* She wished he could've grown a backbone sooner, maybe back in the summer, when Harmon started coming around. Vada turned over and over, her gown twisting around her in a sweaty shroud. Finally, she rose, went to the front porch and gingerly sat on the top step, body and mind feeling bruised.

Elbows on her knees, chin in her hands, she listened to the sound of the distant pump jack, its lonely squeak company for the sorrow within her. A slight breeze came up and she tilted her face toward it, eyes closed, as it caressed her skin, lifted her hair, let it drop to her shoulders, soft as a sigh. When next she looked, Harmon squatted behind her in his long johns, a cigarette between his lips.

"You orta come on to bed. You'll catch a chill out here."

As if he had prophesied it, she shivered and hugged herself, but did not yet move to rise. Looking up at the sky speckled with stars, she pulled her gown tighter over her knees, down to her feet. Harmon smoked in silence, then pitched the butt into the darkness and stood, knees cracking.

"You come in 'fore long, you hear?"

She nodded, and a while later, she followed him into the house. When she lay back down in the bed, curled on her side, he placed a hand on her hip, and she stiffened. But he only patted her twice, gave her a little squeeze, and snores filled the room, at first softly, then loudly, and for once, she felt comforted by the warmth and sound of him.

Chapter 7

After the visit from Mama and Papa, Vada didn't think so often about leaving. It wasn't only her pregnancy, although another missed monthly and the violent nausea pursuing her any time she was upright confirmed her fears, but also Harmon's defense of her in the face of her mother's badgering and insults. How bad could a man be who would face the wrath of Mama, and it not even his battle to fight? Her father had certainly rarely done so, and for Harmon's willingness Vada was grateful.

But sick. Lord God, she was sick. *Sick enough to die.* The words circled in her mind, vultures waiting to light, as she heaved, heaved, and heaved again. "Oh, Lordy me, I can't stand this no more." Still unable to straighten, she kept her eyes closed against the sight of the outhouse hole and tried to breathe through her mouth. Solemn vows made with her head over this very hole bound her to forsake food for all time if she could stop vomiting. *Have to stop pretty soon. Nothing left but teeth and toenails.* She wobbled out of the leaning, unpainted building and retreated to a tree a dozen feet upwind, hoping to control the her stomach muscles' contractions by removing herself from the stench. Harmon always said the smell was mostly in her head, but she had her own opinion about people who thought their outhouses didn't stink. Removing herself from the immediate vicinity worked finally and she headed for the porch on rubbery legs. Too weak to pull herself up the four steps, she collapsed onto the second one. She buried her face in her lap, trying to shut out the other offensive smells that had kept her in the outhouse the last few weeks—food, dog manure, cut hay, air.

A warmth and slight breeze alerted her to another presence, but she could not even summon the energy to look up or speak. She had a good idea who it was though—her shadow, he-who-couldn't-be-avoided, the living, breathing one who stuck to her like a locust to tree bark.

"'Frow up again, Mama? Wan' me get you washrag?" Dempsey asked.

She raised her head a little, looked at him through eyes made watery from gagging. "No," she whispered, then buried her face in her lap again, breathing shallowly.

"I 'fro up once, inna bed." A brief silence followed, then he continued. "It was stinky. I ain't never eating succotash aga—"

"Oh, Lordy, me," Vada said, and broke for the side of the house, where she heaved until her sides hurt even more than they had. When she could finally stand, she turned to find Dempsey hovering behind her with a wet cloth. Grateful in spite of daily resolutions not to slide any further into affection for the child, she took the ragged cloth and wiped her face and mouth.

He held a small, brown object out to her. "Pa say pe'rmint make you feel better, but I only got this one. It root beer."

Vada hesitated. The piece of hard candy, shaped like a tiny barrel, was covered with lint and grains of things she refused to consider, but she would have hesitated had it been wrapped in pristine cellophane. She knew that candy was his favorite thing in the world, and that in his world there were few things he both loved and possessed. The look in his eyes, though, was so wide open, so trusting, that she took it. He watched her so long that she finally had no choice but to touch one end of it to her tongue, try to lick a little place that had nothing stuck to it.

Dempsey beamed. "There. That better now, ain't it? You look pinker."

She nodded, swallowing bile. "Sure enough. If I can lay me down a bit, I'll be right as rain." She tried to move up the steps, stumbled, and found the boy instantly at her side, so close she could scream. To be alone in her misery would be heaven, but it seemed a luxury she would never again have. She let him help her up the steps because it took less strength than shaking him off would have.

Harmon stood in the door. "We got to get breakfast on, girl. Time's awasting."

"Har, I can't. I'm sick enough to die. Can't you see that?"

"Oh, hell, girl, you ain't nothing but pregnant. My mama had—"

She clenched her teeth against the words she wanted to shout at him. If she'd heard once, she'd heard a thousand times how his mama had a half dozen children and never missed a day in the fields. She didn't believe that for a minute, but arguing was fruitless. *I can think of one his mama had that shoulda run down his daddy's leg.* Saying it out loud would have probably made her feel a hundred million times better, but right then she was afraid to open her mouth. She went to the kitchen and took down flour, lard, salt, and baking powder, and began to prepare the eternal biscuits that had to accompany every meal. By the time they were mixed, she was so weak she had one arm laid out on the cabinet, head resting on it, and was using the other arm to roll them out, all the while wishing she was dead.

When the biscuits—sorrier even than usual—were in the oven, and the gravy was bubbling, she lurched toward the bedroom, Dempsey on her heels. She hit the bed half on her stomach and half on her side, one arm beneath her, incapable of movement. "Oh, Lord," she moaned into the mattress. "I'm sick enough to die. I wish I'd go ahead and do it." She buried her face in the quilt to momentarily block the smell of food cooking, then raised her head and looked at Dempsey, standing beside the bed with a stricken look on his face.

"You ain't going to die, are you, Mama?" His eyes brimmed with tears and his lower lip jerked and twitched. "I don't want you to die."

"Oh, Lord." Even thinking nauseated her. "Go ask Nelda to watch breakfast."

"'Kay. Nel-l-l-da!" He screamed the name before he even turned to trot from the room, and Vada winced. She heard Dempsey, self-importance in his voice, delivering her message to his sister, and presently, two sets of footsteps approached the bed. She opened the eye that wasn't pressed into the mattress to see Nelda and Dempsey standing near.

"I thought Pa brought you home so you could cook and take care of us. You been sick four months now." When Vada didn't answer, but only closed the one eye again, Nelda continued. "Pa says you ain't nothing but pregnant. He says Granny had six young'uns—"

Vada opened the eye again and regarded Nelda, then grabbed the front of the girl's dress and pulled her down until their noses almost touched. "How many babies your mama have before it killed her?" she whispered.

Nelda went even whiter than usual, jerked away from Vada and stomped from the room. Vada hoped with all her heart that the girl was cursed with "nothing but pregnant" ninety-nine times at the very least. Dempsey watched his sister go, then crawled onto the bed. "I lay here case you need the bucket." The bucket was his special job—hiding it from Harmon, getting it for Vada when she needed it, emptying it afterward. Harmon had flatly declared the outhouse the place for all bodily functions—not beside it, not behind it, nowhere but in it.

"That's what a outhouse is for. I ain't cleaning up no messes that ought to have been done in there to begin with." *Like you ever clean up anything anyhow.* Her frustration with his insistence that she was not really sick, "nothing but pregnant," was almost worse than the pregnancy itself, but she knew he wasn't about to change his mind. Stubborn old goat. He had no pity, insisting that she cook three meals a day, no matter how the children complained about her cooking, do the washing, what ironing there was, and be ready to receive him at a moment's notice on any given night. *That's sure going to stop when I get over this. I'm not having no part of that nasty old thing of his, and I'm not having no more young'uns.* With that assurance, she drifted into a sleep made sweaty and fitful by her nausea.

* * * * *

She awoke to a crash and a small voice. "Uh-oh. S'e going to get me." Lying on the bed, she listened to the shuffling and mumbling coming from the kitchen, where Dempsey seemed to be holding another of his many one-sided conversations with himself. Soon she heard the whispery sound of a broom across the floor, and sighed. No telling what he was into. Pulling herself erect and swinging her legs over the edge of the bed, she waited for the dizziness to pass, then rose and went to the door.

"Lord God," she said, and stopped. Flour covered the kitchen floor, and in some places had been turned to paste by spilled liquid of some kind. Feathery places, like misshapen snow angels, marked the areas where Dempsey had attempted to sweep. Vada resisted the urge to scream, fearing if she started she would never stop. "What are you doing? Haven't I got enough to put up with without you making messes I got to clean up?" Weak as she was, she covered the distance between them in three steps and did something she never had before—cuffed him soundly on one side of the head, then the other. "What's wrong with you? Are you stupid, or what?" He stared at her in disbelief, mouth open, and this further angered her. "I asked you a question. Are you stupid?" She slapped him again, and it was like she was watching someone else do it. It couldn't be her. Never in her life had she done more than thump a child on the head, but here she was delivering an open-handed slap, and she felt both the terrible power that comes to the tyrant and a sense of relief that came from doing something concrete to rectify her own situation.

Dempsey's eyes glistened with tears and his lower lip trembled, but he didn't cry. He took the slaps, the cuffs, the outright punches one after another, backing up a step with each one until he was against the cookstove, hands and arms covering his head and face.

"Don't hit me no more, Mama. Don't hit me. I won't help you no more, I promise."

It wasn't his plea that stopped her, but only her inability to continue, and as she stood looking at him, her breath coming in gasps, a familiar nausea slammed into her. This time, though, it was not pregnancy, but rather the knowledge that she had imitated her mother to the fullest extent possible under the circumstances. Visions of herself at Mama's hands flashed before her and she stumbled to the chair and fell into it, covering her face with her hands to try to shut out the ugliness of her actions. Rocking back and forth, she moaned softly, and whispered, "Oh, God, I'm sorry, I'm so sorry. Oh, God, God, oh please." She wished she could cry, and felt like slapping herself in the head, the face, anywhere that might sting enough to bring tears to cleanse her. She squeezed her eyes shut, trying to produce tears where there were none. Sorrow washed over her like a wave, then small, sturdy arms encircled her. Removing her hands from her face, she looked down into Dempsey's dark eyes, and saw not fear, but a desire to comfort, to be comforted. She grabbed the child like he was the only log in a raging river.

"I'm so sorry, Dempsey, so sorry," she whispered. "Please don't hate me. Please. I'll be your mama, I will. Just don't hate me." He started crying then, still clinging to her, and his sobs soon brought tears to her eyes as well. The harder he cried, the harder she cried. Soon the front of her dress was wet with his tears, and her own dripped onto his thick, bright hair. After a few minutes the sounds of sobbing died down, and they seemed to simultaneously run out of tears with much sniffling and rubbing of eyes. She dried Dempsey's face with the hem of her dress and held it to his nose. "Blow," she told him.

He looked up at her. "On you' dress?" He backed up a step. "Huh-uh. You hit me again."

She pulled him toward her. "I won't neither. I got to change it anyway—feels like I took a bath in it." She held it to his nose once more. "Now blow. You got snot running all over your face."

Reluctantly, he blew, and, holding the skirt away from her, Vada hugged him. "I really am sorry, Dempsey, and I swear it won't never happen again."

He beamed up at her, face radiant. "'Kay."

Just that. 'Kay. How long had it been since she had been able to trust the word of someone else that something would or would not take place? She had had the illusion that she could trust Papa, but that had been shattered when he'd allowed her to be handed over to Harmon. And Mama. She could not even imagine trusting her. Vada sighed, tiredness and nausea fighting for equal time.

"I can't clean this mess up right now, but you leave it alone. I'll do it after while when I feel better." She turned to go back to the bed, then a thought struck her and she turned back to Dempsey. "What were you doing, anyway?"

He looked at the floor, then away, as if the mess embarrassed him. Eyes on the wall to one side of Vada, he mumbled something.

"What?"

"Bi'cuits," he said. "I going to make good bi'cuits. Pa say you make the worst ones he ever et, and I thought that what make you sick alla time."

"He said that?" She laughed aloud. "Good thing he didn't marry me for my cooking." Dempsey looked at her, eyes wary, as if afraid she'd lost what little mind she had left. She turned from him, shaking her head, and went to the bedroom. Changing from the damp, snotty dress, she laughed again, and when she lay back on the bed, she grinned even through the queasiness that plagued her.

As she was about to doze off, she felt the bed move, heard Dempsey reminding himself "Don't jar the bed," her words to him every time he came to lie with her when his daddy wasn't around. He snuggled up to her back and patted her shoulder softly. The last thing she heard as she slipped into sleep was, "You my mama now."

Chapter 8

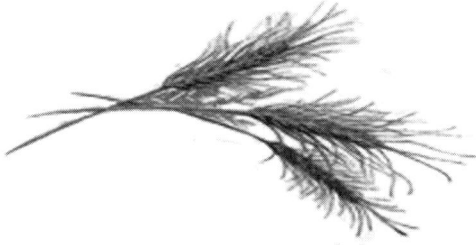

She remained so nauseated that it was almost spring before she even developed a belly. When she did, it was with a vengeance, and every time she walked by Harmon, he seemed compelled to comment.

"Looks like you swallowed a watermelon, girl," he'd say. Or, "What you got under there, a basketball?"

No matter what he said, his words made her mad. Her anger wasn't because she cared about no longer having a figure; as far as she could tell, she hadn't had one to begin with. Slim hips, small breasts, and "no ass a'tall," as Harmon liked to say, usually when he had a handful of it. What made her mad was the fact that she would be responsible for another life. She had pretty much given up any thoughts of leaving the Priddys behind, but every so often, a small inner voice reminded her that she *could*, if she wanted, and no one would be hurt by her going. Well, perhaps Dempsey, but he would surely get over it. A baby, though. It wasn't done, not among the people she had known all her life. A woman didn't take off on her husband, even if he beat her and made her life miserable, and only the worst kind of person left her child. Vada had a sneaking suspicion that she was miserable mostly of her own account, that in many ways she must be the kind of person her mother had always accused her of being—lazy, spoiled, contrary. What, after all, was Harmon's great sin against her? He was old? He wanted her to cook and clean and work in the fields and do all the other things a wife was expected to do?

If she really was the bad person Mama had always accused her of being, who was to say that she would treat her own child better than Mama had treated her? Look at what she had done to Dempsey. She could try to be a good mother, but who ever had children with the idea that they would abuse them? Not even Mama could be guilty of that, Vada was sure. Well, almost sure. But how likely would Vada be to treat her children well if she were saddled with two or three or four more?

Something else troubled her, too. She'd been changing diapers since before she'd started school, and could remember even at the age of nine or ten feeling like Beulah, Papa's old coon dog, who'd had a record litter of sixteen pups. Papa sold the first nine right off, but for months—*months*—poor old Beulah walked around with five, six, or sometimes all seven pups hanging from her teats like big, fat, greedy ticks, sucking the life right out of her. The dog had finally lain down and died, and Vada didn't blame her a bit. Child though she was, Vada had felt like giving up the ghost at times, after getting so tired of chasing after kids and wiping noses and changing diapers.

But at least I knew someday I'd be rid of them, that they'd be somebody else's problem. Not so with the one she carried. She'd be responsible for it till the end of time. Some people wouldn't be, but she wasn't built that way.

"Shoot," she said. "I don't want a young'un anyway."

"What's that?" Harmon asked, leaning against the porch where she sat on the top step, knees under her chin and dress pulled down to her ankles. He placed a roll-your-own between his thin lips and struck a kitchen match against the porch post.

"Nothing. And don't sneak up on me like that." Lately, just the sight of him made her mad.

He took on an injured look. "I wasn't sneaking. All's I did was walk up here like anybody else."

"Like anybody else," she repeated. "You got that right. Every last one of you is always sneaking up on me and spying, trying to see what I'm doing and thinking. I haven't got a minute to myself around here." She stared straight ahead at the horizon, where hazy sky met blurry ground, but his eyes were so hard on her that she felt pressed down, squeezed into a flat little mass of mad. She glared at him. "What are you looking at, I want to know. You're always looking at me like I'm some kind of bug or something."

"You women." He shook his head and drew deeply on his cigarette. "You get you a man and ever'thing that goes with it, and you still ain't happy."

She felt her jaw drop, then snapped it shut, breathing shallowly to ease the tightness in her chest that had begun at his words. "You think I waited fourteen years on a man to haul me off and marry me, stick me in two rooms with three kids and get me in the family way, you got you another think coming, mister." She jerked her dress more tightly, tucked the ends under her toes. "My idea of life never was to be chasing after a bunch of snot-nosed kids that don't even like me."

He smoked the cigarette down to nothing before he spoke. "Dempsey'd be right unhappy to hear that. That little feller worships the ground you stand on."

"Huh!" she said, unable to dispute Harmon. Still, she refused to give up. "Well, them other two. You try running after that pair of two-legged hyenas all day every day and see how you feel." Her chest felt like it was going to explode, and she knew she was getting ready to say something *real* bad, but she couldn't seem to stop. "You try having something squirming in your belly keeping you awake and running to the outhouse all night and giving you a backache all day. Try having some kind of—of—*thing*, like worms or something, inside you, and knowing it's going to come out whether you want it to or not and you're going to have to take care of it till you *die!*" She almost choked on the words, almost but not quite, and managed to spit out the ones that she knew would probably break the camel's back: "Till you *die*, Harmon Priddy. And I'd rather. I don't blame Sarah, not one bit. If I's her, I'da laid down and died, too."

Dead silence greeted the words, and for a brief moment, she wished she could take them back. Then innate stubbornness took over and she didn't care. Let him get mad. Let him send her to Mama. Mama would send her straight back. There were worse things. She waited for him to say anything to break the silence, but he didn't, and when she finally turned to look, he was gone, as silently as he had come.

"I guess I told him." But the words offered precious little comfort, far less than she had thought they would the many times she had imagined them. Uneasiness stole over her, along with a nagging guilt; she sat where she was, though, unwilling to apologize. When the chill became too much, she went into the house. Harmon sat with Dempsey on his lap in an overstuffed chair he had dragged home from somewhere. Cordell was on the arm and the three talked quietly, all squinting through the haze of Harmon's cigarette smoke. Nelda hunched over the kitchen table, fat pencil clenched in her fist as she labored over the evening's homework.

Harmon glanced up, and Vada expected his look to cut her, but it was mild, and she gave him a tentative smile. "Going to bed," she said. "You coming pretty soon?"

"Pretty soon," he agreed, and returned her smile with his own, old-ivory teeth glinting in his dark face. "You go on. I'll get the young'uns down."

Heat rose in her face. Some slave-life she led, sitting on the porch sulking, with never a thought of getting the children washed and in bed. She lowered her eyes, ashamed and cold, but evidently, forgiven. She crawled dress and all into the bed, pulled the quilt to her chin, and fell asleep without even a final visit to the outhouse.

Chapter 9

The day didn't start out right. Vada had spent a restless night, her sleep punctuated with sweaty awakenings and mumbled reprimands from Harmon, and no matter which way she turned, there was some part of the baby inside her wedged some place it shouldn't be. Finally, feeling like a turtle on its back, she tried several times before bringing herself upright, then made for the porch where she lowered herself to the top step, huffing and puffing.

She couldn't get enough air nowadays, and the bigger she got the more suffocated she felt. She wondered if she could survive another month. Her knees wouldn't even meet anymore when she sat on the porch as she now did. "It sure don't seem like I'm going to make it," she said, and regarded the faint glimmering of morning as a personal affront. If it would stay dark and everybody in the house would stay asleep, she'd be fine. Her moods wouldn't go up and down like an out-of-control pump handle, and nobody would get on her nerves or ask her stupid questions or make her wish she'd never heard of Harmon Priddy and his band of brats. Just yesterday Cordell had thrown a daddy longlegs at her where she'd sat on this very porch step. Vada had reared like a runaway horse, batting at the spider in such a frantic way that she had fallen backwards onto the porch and lain there, legs waving like some big bug while the children and Harmon doubled over in laughter. When she had threatened Cordell with a spanking, he had run behind his daddy.

"You ain't my mama nohow," he'd said.

"I wouldn't be your mama if you was the last young'un on earth, you miserable brat!" she'd retorted, and darned if he didn't look hurt. Harmon had promised both of them the back of his hand if they didn't shut up, and Cordell slunk off to wherever he went when he was peeved.

Vada still smarted from Harmon not taking her side against the boy. *Buncha heathens. All of 'em.*

Her back had hurt ever since, and she thought she might have pulled something out of place. Last night, her belly began to hurt, not a stomachache exactly, but an *ache* just the same. She kept feeling as if she needed to go to the bathroom, but when she reached the outhouse, the ache had subsided and she no longer felt the urge.

Resting her chin on her knees, she thought about the ways she'd make Cordell's life miserable if he weren't his daddy's favorite. But he was, and in Vada's mind there was no way the child inside her was ever going to mean to Harmon what Cordell did. Not that it ought to matter to her, since she didn't want a baby herself. But, somehow, it did, and if she was stuck with having it, the baby should at least have a fighting chance of being the favorite. She felt a twinge of jealousy that Harmon could love someone else's child more than the one they made. The more she thought about it, the madder she got. Why did he marry her anyway? *He don't like my biscuits, he don't like my belly, and he don't like my baby. I oughta haul off and go to my daddy's, that's what.* As soon as the thought came, it left her, along with the anger, and her chin sank down onto the cloth held taut by her spread knees. *I act as stupid as Cordell. What do I care what that old man thinks?* Foolishness cloaked her in an itchy blanket, but she still took some comfort from the fact that Harmon never said he loved Cordell more than his other kids, and he was happy as a kid himself about the coming baby. *I done sat here and got myself all worked up out of my own mind, and peed myself to boot.*

This last came to her at the same instant the wetness streamed from between her legs, as if her brain knew it before her body did. "Lordy me," she said, and was in the process of lifting herself from the step when the water became a gusher rather than a stream, and a pain shot from her back around the front of her belly, gripping her and holding her motionless for a span of time just short of her limit. "Harmon!" she screamed. "Harmon Priddy, you get out here right now, you hear me?"

She heard pounding feet while she clung to the top step, turning herself toward the house to see him standing in long johns, hair in black spikes, face panicked. "What? What is it?"

"I peed on myself, and it's not my fault, you hear me?" Her face was wet with sudden sweat, and she held her soaked gown away from her as she tried to mount the final two steps to the porch, trying to avoid the one with the missing board without falling on her face. A searing pain stopped her and she bent, panting, till it was over.

"Let me get my pants and my boots, girl," he said. "This is a mite too early. We taking you to Sapulpa."

"No," she screamed. "I'm all wet, can't you hear? I can't be going nowhere all wet like this." She made her way into the house to see the kids huddled together on the pallet, Nelda's face puffy with sleep and Dempsey in silent tears, while Cordell blinked at her from a prone position.

"What's wrong?" Nelda asked, hanging on to Dempsey as he tried to scramble toward Vada.

Vada took a deep breath and tried to calm herself. "I—I'm not sure. I—it—"

Harmon rushed from the bedroom with flapping overall straps and unlaced boots, clutching the quilt pulled from the bed. Throwing it to Vada, he said, "Cover yourself. I'll get the car started."

"I'm wet! Will you listen to me?" she panted, seized by another pain. Gritting her teeth, she kept talking through it, knowing if she stopped he'd be gone. "I need some dry step-ins and a dress," she grunted. "And shoes, and a hair brush."

Dempsey started crying in earnest now. "Don' whi' her, Papa, p'ease. S'e can't help it."

Nelda slapped the back of his head. "Shut up! What're you talking about? He ain't going to whip her."

The boy cried harder and Harmon looked from him to Vada and rubbed his face, hard, with both hands. "Will you people shut up? A man can't think around here for the caterwauling. Vada, get that blanket around you. We going to the hospital. Nelda, take care of your brothers till I get back."

"But Harmon, I'm wet," Vada wailed, and Dempsey finally escaped Nelda's grip and ran to her.

"Don' cry, don' cry, Mama. Pa won' hit you. It not you fault." He wrapped himself around her legs, seeming oblivious to her soaked gown. As another pain captured Vada's attention, Harmon seized the moment to grab the quilt, throw it around her, and haul her out the door, leaving behind a squalling Dempsey, and Nelda on the porch screaming about a geography test she was going to miss.

"Get back in there and take him with you," Harmon shouted at her.

The old Chrysler coughed and sputtered its way down the bumpy road, forcing a groan from Vada. "Please. I can't go nowhere looking like this." She glared at him, ignoring the muscle jumping in his jaw. She hadn't done anything wrong. Why was he mad at her? "Harmon, listen to me! I'm all wet and in my nightclothes. What'll folks think?"

He glared at her, eyes fierce. "If you say 'wet' one more time, I'll take you to Livermore's pond and drown you." Breathing hard and fast, he turned his eyes back to the road. "I'm wet, I'm wet. That's all I been hearing outta you, and you sitting here miles from the doctor, fixing to have a baby it ain't time for." He reached into his overall pocket, seemed to realize he had no tobacco and glared at her like that was her fault, too. "I'm wet," he repeated. "Your waters broke. Don't you know nothin?"

Another pain grabbed doubled her over. When it passed, Harmon's words echoed in her head. *Waters? What waters? I'm having a baby, not a fish.*

Harmon's terse words made her feel stupid now and she held her tongue, enduring with equal stoicism the bumpy dirt roads and the intermittent pains until they arrived outside a low, one story building. Harmon leapt from the car with an energy Vada could hardly believe he possessed. A phrase of her daddy's came to mind—*Acts like his tail's on fire and his butt's a'catching*—and she would have giggled had not another pain, worse than any before, come upon her. She bent double again, gasping, and the door was suddenly jerked open.

Through a halo of pain, she saw a man with dark Cupid's bow lips, wide, womanly hips, and a behind with a mind of its own maneuvering a wheelchair into position. When she turned around, she saw through his white shirt breasts bigger than hers—which granted, even with her pregnancy, wasn't saying much, but still—and a name tag that said "Oliver." He lifted her into the chair like she didn't weigh a pound and whisked her through the double doors. That's where Harmon stood, looking for all the world like it was him that was in pain, face pinched and white, cheekbones jutting out.

Being hauled into a public place in a gown, soaked in her own fluids, turned out to be the least of her embarrassment. As Oliver pushed her at top speed down a short hallway and toward a dingy room, she heard a gravelly voice grow louder.

"Whoo! Goddamn," the voice bellowed. "Jesus Godallmighty cockSUCKER!" Oliver pushed Vada up next to a high, iron bed, then crossed the room in four or five mincing steps and jerked back a curtain to reveal a gaunt woman with an enormous belly, wet red hair plastered to an oversized skull, and a sharply etched face shiny with sweat.

"Shut that stuff up, Donna Mae. I don't want to hear any more foul language out of your mouth." He planted small, dimpled hands on his wide hips, and his butt twitched as if it, too, wanted to give the redhead what-for.

The woman grimaced. "Why don't you lay your fat ass down here for seventeen straight hours and try to push a baby out—see if you don't cuss, you—you *man!*" The words were no sooner out than the redhead paled and sucked in her breath, then let loose a string of curses the likes of which Vada had never heard.

The orderly snapped the curtain back into place and helped Vada situate herself on the bed. "White trash," he whispered. His voice held the cadence of some place much further south than Oklahoma, and each word, no matter how short, was drawn out into more syllables than it had begun with. "She's in here once a year, sure as God made little green apples, so I'd say she likes men well enough when they suit her." He looked from side to side as if someone might be listening, then lowered his voice a bit more. "Nobody knows who all those babies belong to. Not even her, I'll wager."

"Son of a bitch!" came the voice from the other side of the curtain. "God damn Jesus H. Christ on a fucking broom crutch. Whoo. Whoo. Whooooeeee!"

Now Vada could not attend to what Oliver was saying, nor even to the words Donna Mae was screaming. She felt her own stomach tighten as pain began to build, and she clutched at Oliver's sleeve. "Seventeen *hours?*"

Oliver giggled. "Aw, now, don't you worry about that. You'll not go no seventeen hours, I can tell that right now." He moved to the side and looked at the small, bird-like woman who bustled up to the side of the bed with a red bag like the one that had hung on the back of Mama's bedroom door. "Isn't that right, Beryl?"

"Isn't what right?" the nurse asked, simultaneously rolling Vada onto her side and whipping the wet nightgown above her belly to expose her underpants and distended belly. Beryl tugged on the wet panties.

"No!" Vada grunted, and tried to pull the gown down. "Don't. Please, I don't want—"

"Now, let's don't be that way, sugar." The little nurse was far stronger than she appeared, and Vada felt the nozzle connect with its intended target. Beryl easily held her with one arm and administered the enema with the other hand. "Oliver, get her a dry gown," she said. "No wonder she's fighting me—she's soaked plumb through."

"Why are you doing this to me?" Vada asked, but she couldn't be sure she really said it. Maybe it was only inside her head, because no one answered her. She lay on her side, fear, anger, and pain all tangled together, her insides being pumped full of water by the ferocious little nurse on one side and her clothes being stripped by Oliver on the other. When they finally replaced her gown with a dry one, she felt air on her back and bottom and realized they hadn't even given her a real gown, just some piece of material with armholes and an opening in the back that exposed her butt to the world. She squeezed her eyes shut against the humiliation, tears sliding down her cheeks. *I hate you, hate you both. And Mama and Daddy and Harmon, every last one of you. Hate you hate you hate you.*

* * * * *

She fought waking with her whole being, and fought, too, the sound of the voices that surrounded her. She could make them out—Mama and Harmon and Papa—and they were all as unwelcome as a cold wind. Somehow, too, they were associated with the pain between her legs, and she didn't want to look at any of them, afraid that if she did, they would see the hate in her eyes. All she wanted was quiet, and more sleep. The twilight world in which she floated was wonderful, like nothing she had ever experienced. She almost felt as if it were touchable, and as she stretched forth her hand to feel the softness of it, she felt someone latch onto her hand, and none too gently.

"Vada, Darlin', you awake?" a voice cooed. "Mama's here, going to take care of you and this young'un, you hear?"

She squinched her eyes even more tightly against the voice. That could *not* be her mother, for if it were, the words "darling" and "Vada" would not have been uttered within days of each other. And if it were not her mother, Vada didn't want to see the woman desperate enough to pretend to be. Another voice, this one more dear, more welcome, drove the first away.

"Vada? It's me, Addy."

"Addy?" She opened one eye, still wary. It really was Addy, looking not simply a year older, but practically grown up, dark lashes sweeping almost to the arched brow, changeable blue-gray eyes flecked with a knowledge that hadn't been there when Vada last saw her.

Addy stroked her sister's cheek with two fingers and smiled, all sunshine and white teeth. "I can't believe you got you a baby! Not a big 'un, but it's a baby all right."

Vada pulled Addy's head closer to her own, put her lips near Addy's ear. "That belly button thing—what Jimmie Sue Anthamatten told us—that's not right."

"Aw, shoot, I knew that." Addy giggled. "Everybody knows that." She gazed at Vada, smoothed her sister's hair back from her forehead. "What're you going to name that baby?"

"Adelaide," Vada said. "Adelaide."

Addy's laughter made Vada's head spin with joy, even though she didn't know the reason for it. They had always laughed together, and to have her sister with her again filled her with a gladness and well being she had not felt in months and months. It was short-lived though, for Addy was abruptly and roughly replaced by their mother.

"Don't be your usual stupid self, girl. You can't name no boy child 'Adelaide.' Where's your brain?"

A chill traveled down Vada's back and surrounded her; she pulled weakly at the crisp sheet covering her and tried to move away from Esther Louise's red-faced reprimand. "I didn't know," she whispered. The further she tried to retreat the more her body hurt and the sharper the words became. Finally she closed her eyes, sank into the welcome darkness, realizing at last that sometimes the only way to get along was to go away.

Chapter 10

Gerald looked up at her, his blue-brown eyes nearly crossed as he tugged at her breast. Stroking his tiny nose and dark eyebrows, she wished she never had to let him go. He was the cutest thing, a little doll. As she rocked him in the brand new rocking chair her father had brought her, she marveled all over again at how good it felt to nurse a baby. It had been humiliating the first few times, with nurses grasping her breasts, pinching the nipple, and guiding it into the mouth of the bellowing, constantly squirming infant, but it quickly became second nature, and Vada figured she looked forward to feeding almost as much as Gerald did.

Almost as wonderful as the baby in her arms was the presence of her sister. Addy sat crosslegged in the middle of the bed, elbows on knees, chin propped on fists.

"I still can't believe you're here," Vada said, her voice soft to avoid startling Gerald. Sometimes she felt guilty at the pleasure she derived from Addy's presence, almost willing to have half a dozen more babies if it would keep her sister there.

Addy giggled. "I can believe it. I knew I'd be the one taking care of you soon as Mama found out there was work to be done." She eyed the baby and sighed. "I can't wait to get me a baby."

"Aw, no, Addy. Don't let her do it to you, too."

Addy smiled, dreams reflected in her eyes like high clouds in a pond. "It's not the same thing."

"It *is* the same, only worse." Vada pulled the now-sleeping child away from her breast and covered herself, then placed him in the cradle that had served all Harmon's other children. She went slowly to the bed, knees weak even after three weeks of almost constant bed rest. Addy made room for her, and she climbed onto the bed and lay there, breathing hard. She couldn't remember a day when she wasn't worn out.

Addy covered her with the quilt, then lay on her side facing Vada, twirling a piece of long dark hair. "Me and Alex—we're not the same as you and Harmon. He's not old like Harmon, and he's got a house in town, and no bratty young'uns, and no cotton to pick—"

Vada pulled the quilt to her chin, chilled in spite of the sunlight spilling through the narrow window. But Vada knew it wasn't about Alex Bookout. "You're twelve years old. At least I was fourteen."

Addy scooted closer to lay her head on Vada's shoulder, one arm across her sister's middle. "Don't think about what all's going to happen to me. You got your own young'un to worry about now. Don't have to take care of Mama's no more." She chuckled softly. "That Roxanne don't mind nobody since you left." She was still, then took up their earlier conversation as if they had just left off. "And anyway, I'm going to be thirteen in two months, and we won't even get married till next year, so I'll be fourteen. Almost, anyway." She paused, then shrugged. "That's how old you were."

That's what makes it so wrong, Vada wanted to say, but instead, she looked away from her sister and stared at the dust motes that floated in the stream of sunshine. "You ever think you'd like to do something besides get married?"

Addy raised her head and looked at her, wide-eyed. "Like what? Live at home with Mama till one of us dies?"

"There's other things," Vada said.

Addy let her head drop back onto Vada's shoulder. "I don't know how to do other things."

Vada knew she sounded desperate, but she was desperate. Marrying Harmon wasn't the worst thing that ever happened to her, but wouldn't it have been nice to have a choice? "You could be a...a teacher!"

Addy giggled. "Oh, sure!" She pitched her voice high and did a more than passable imitation of Mrs. Bierman, the woman who taught fifth through eighth grades at their small school. "All right, students. Whoever put the cowpatty in the heating stove needs to own up and take what's coming to them. Remember, confession is good for the soul." She collapsed in laughter next to Vada, then immediately sat up. "I didn't hurt you did I?"

Vada shook her head, searching desperately for the words that would make

Addy see that if she let herself be married off now it would be the end of something that, although Vada could not name it, was precious as gold and never regained once lost. When she found her voice, the words still eluded her and she could only look at Addy, at the child she knew would be made into a woman far before her time, at the sister she loved more, yes, more, than the baby in the cradle, or herself, or anything on earth. Finally, she whispered, "Please don't get married, Addy. Please. Come here. Live with us. Harmon won't care. I know he won't." She felt her chin tremble and steeled herself, resolving not to cry, no matter what.

"I know he probably wouldn't care, but Mama would. She don't like what's not for sure, and she wants me gone for sure. I don't take her guff like you did, like Papa does." Grinning, she added, "She says I'm a thorn in her side, and I take that as a compliment." She lay down beside Vada and put her arm over her again. "You rest, and don't worry about me. When I get married, I'm having a whole passel of young'uns." She giggled. "And I'm going to teach every last one of them to run far and fast when they see their Granny Ross coming to the door."

Vada lay still, inhaling the smell of Addy's hair as it tickled her nose. Sunshine and wildflowers. That's what Addy smelled like, always. "You had a hissy fit when Harmon come to call. How could things change so fast?"

Addy raised her head and looked up at her. "Vada, I was a *kid* then."

Vada started to laugh, realized Addy was serious, and stifled it. "But still. You act like you *want* to get married."

Her sister was still for so long Vada thought she'd fallen asleep, but finally, Addy exhaled and spoke. "For one thing, not the main thing, just one, Harmon was old already when he come to the house, old as Papa." Her voice thickened and lowered to almost a whisper. "But I reckon he's all right anyhow. What's not—" Addy cleared her throat and her voice cracked a little. "What's not all right is trying to live with Mama without you. I didn't have no idea how much you took from her till you was gone." A single tear stood shimmering on her lower eyelid, then trickled slowly down her cheek. She wiped it away with an almost angry motion. "Maybe I don't take it, but it's like she's wearing me down, day by day. She's not just mean, Vada. She's plumb crazy."

"But you don't have to get married. Please, come here, stay with us." When Addy didn't answer, Vada knew talking was useless, but she had to try. "Listen, we'll send you to some kind of school! Just think! You could be one of them career women, live all by yourself, have your own car—you could be a bachelorette!"

Addy lay mute for a few moments, then sighed, a sound as full of despair as any Vada had ever heard. "I thank you for the offer, Vada, but it—" She shrugged. "It's not the kind of thing folks like us do." Vada shivered. A girl not yet thirteen, and Addy had no more hope than somebody who'd been told they'd be dead in a year. Addy pulled the quilt around her sister's shoulders and tucked it in. "You best get some rest now. That young'un's going to be awake and hollering to eat 'fore long, and feeding him's something else I can't do."

Vada raised herself on one elbow, her other hand clutching the quilt so tightly the knuckles were white. "But listen. You don't know what—what happens when you get married." She swallowed hard, surprised to find herself embarrassed to speak of the subject with Addy. Her voice fell till it was barely above a whisper. "Harmon—men—they—their—you know, their thing—it gets real hard, and they ram it in you even though it don't nowhere near fit." Vada felt as if she were dying of embarrassment, but Addy's eyes sparkled and her lips were pursed as if she had a secret. "What?" Vada asked. "Why are you looking at me like that?"

It was Addy's turn to whisper. "Sometimes it fits." Vada looked at her, not comprehending until Addy whispered, "Alex. *You* know." She colored, then jumped onto her knees and got as close to Vada as she could. "*We* done it." They both squealed, Addy wiggling all over like a happy puppy.

In the cradle, Gerald stirred and whimpered, and Vada put a finger to her lips. "Shh. Don't wake him up." When he became still again, she grabbed Addy's arm. "When? You and Alex?"

For the next hour Addy regaled her with tales of sex in haylofts and corn fields, beneath bleachers and behind barns. Vada laughed until she thought she would cry at times, but underneath it all, she feared for her little sister.

"What if you get caught?

"Then Mama can't change her mind about letting me marry Alex."

Addy's look was defiant, and in it Vada saw a little of what she wished she had—fearlessness, determination, and a wild, almost crazy energy. She gazed back at Addy, as if seeing her for the first time, and fear seized her.

"Addy, please, don't—" She stopped as an involuntary shudder wracked her body, and Addy suddenly became Addy again.

"Look at you. You're shivering!" Pushing Vada back on the bed, Addy covered her to her chin.

Vada looked up at her through eyes that suddenly felt gritty and swollen. "She won't ever stop, Addy. She won't stop until she's got rid of us all."

Carol Johnson

"Sh-h. Quit worrying about everybody else. Mama's not going to do nobody no permanent damage, least no more than she's done already." She grinned. "You think I'm feisty, you ought to see Roxanne. She'll stand up and tell Mama to go to the devil, and her not but three years old." She tucked the quilt around Vada on both sides. "If Mama could understand what that girl says, she'd probably beat the pants off her." Leaning over, she kissed Vada's forehead. "You rest. I'll be right here if you need anything."

Vada turned to the wall, huddling under the quilt. She closed her eyes, sure she wouldn't sleep, but she needed the silence in order to conjure a solution. In her heart, though, she knew the only solution was to let nature—or Mama, whichever struck first—continue on the course at hand. Very soon, almost against her will, she began to drift off, a cocoon of sorrow and rising fear wrapping her in its web-like embrace.

Chapter 11

Addy stayed almost a month, but to Vada it was not nearly long enough. Papa came for her on a bright, spring-like afternoon, mild for June in Oklahoma, taking her and her belongings away amid much protesting from both girls. Once they'd gone, Vada sat alone on the front porch, dejected and out of sorts. Hunched over on the top step, she picked at her big toe, its cuticle dry and ragged. She wasn't thinking about that, though, but about Addy and how much she would miss her. Why couldn't she have stayed? Why couldn't she just live here with her and Harmon and the children? *If Papa showed a little backbone, stood up to Mama, Addy could be here all the time.* Vada sighed. Backbone wasn't Papa's strong suit, at least not when it came to standing up to Mama. The whisper of bare feet on wood sounded behind her, and she wiped her eyes quickly. Looking up, she saw Dempsey, lower lip stuck out in a pout. He'd been a regular little pill ever since she'd brought Gerald home from the hospital, tattling on the infant for spitting up or dirtying his diaper, pinching him when he thought nobody was watching. *What now?*

"What's wrong with you?" she asked.

Dempsey shrugged and ducked his head, then plopped beside her on the porch step. "Cordell being mean to me. He say I got to stay outside." He stared morosely out at the dirt yard.

"Cordell can't keep you out of the house. If you want to go in, go in."

The child moved to a lower step and stood, his face level with hers. Putting a sticky hand on each side of her mouth, he squeezed her lips together, then pursed his own. As he spoke, he manipulated each side of her face so that her lips moved as his did. "Cordell say stay out," he said loudly, as if she were deaf. "He say he gonna stomp a mudhole in my ass."

She slapped his hands away from her cheeks. "Now look what you done," she said, wiping at her face where his fingers had been. "Got me all sticky. You been into the honey again, haven't you?"

"I on'y ate a little," he assured her, and began to lick his fingers, one at a time.

"Stop it. You're not no dog. Go get a rag and wash yourself, and don't give me no baloney about it."

He started to protest, but she grabbed his arm and shook him. "Mind me, or I'll wear you out." Vada had not spanked him since the day he'd tried to make biscuits for her, and Dempsey surely knew her threat was empty, but he seldom refused to obey. He did not this time, either.

"You don't even like me no more, now you got that stupid baby," he said, shooting her a dark look as he stomped into the house.

She heard Cordell's voice, then Dempsey's, then a howl, and Dempsey shot back out the door. Vada stood abruptly and grabbed him, jerking his small body around and marching him back into the house. "Cordell, I won't have this," she said. It took a moment for her eyes to adjust and find Cordell sitting at the kitchen table with a block of wood, a hammer whose head was barely connected to its handle, some nails, and half a dozen wooden spools. He ignored her and placed a spool on the narrow side of a block of wood, then began to hammer a nail through the hole in the spool.

"Did you hear me?" she asked Cordell, at the same time pushing Dempsey in the direction of the sink. "Anybody can come in this house any time they got a mind to, and you got no say about it."

He didn't look at her. "You're in, ain't you?"

She squeezed her eyes shut, then opened them. "Just don't be telling your brother he can't come in here. And don't be cussing."

Cordell selected another spool and placed it a few inches from the first. "I ain't been cussing."

Lord, the boy made her head hurt. "You told Dempsey you was gonna stomp a mudhole in his ass."

The older boy looked at her as if she were a complete idiot. "Ass is in the Bible. If it's in the Bible it ain't cussing, and if Dempsey would leave my stuff alone I wouldn't have to stomp no mudhole in his ass."

"That tears it, little man." Vada strode to the table and jerked the hammer from his hand, then pulled him from the chair by his upper arm. Holding on to him, she swatted his rear end, then swatted it again as he danced around in front of her, trying in vain to elude her hand. "Now get outside, and don't come back in here till I call you."

"Don't you tell me what to do!" he screamed. "You ain't my mama!" Red-faced with anger, he looked wildly around the room, and then returned to the block of wood. Before Vada had time to grab him again, he picked up the wood and threw it at her.

The point of it caught her right above the eye on the brow bone, and she sucked in a sharp breath. Blood spurted from the cut, immediately blurring her vision with its wet, red haze. The silence in the room was absolute, as if even the world around them had stopped to witness this.

Dempsey's shrieks filled the air, his speech almost incoherent. "She bleeding. Cordell you—you bastard! I telling Pa," the little boy shouted, and the sound of his rapidly pounding footsteps echoed the throbbing that had begun in her head.

In the wake of his leaving, it seemed a very long time that Vada stood with her hand to her eye and forehead, stunned. Finally, Cordell broke the silence. "I didn't mean—it was a accident, honest—"

"Cordell Priddy, you stinking little brat." She put forth one hand and searched blindly for the sink and something with which to staunch the blood. She heard the whisper of feet moving away from her, then loudly on the porch and steps, and she shouted after Cordell. "You better run, boy. You just jumped from the frying pan into the fire." Finally laying hands on the dishrag, she wet it and put it to her eyebrow. "Stinking Cordell," she mumbled, pulling the rag away from her forehead. It was covered with blood, and she fingered the cut. It didn't seem too bad, but blood had run down in her eye again, so she re-wet the rag from the pump and put it to her brow-bone again. Making her way into the bedroom, she peeked at where Gerald lay peacefully sleeping in his cradle. "I'd kill you now if I thought you's gonna turn out like that rotten Cordell," she said aloud, and dropped into the rocking chair between the cradle and the wall.

She was still there when an outraged Dempsey led his father into the room. "See? Show him, Mama. Cordell frowed 'at wood at her and broke her face."

Vada had to grin. "He didn't break my face. It's just a cut." But it hurt like the dickens, and a little attention was always a welcome thing. She tilted her face up to Harmon, who grunted and lifted the rag.

"Huh. Got you a pretty good goose egg coming up, too." Shaking his head, he re-folded the rag and handed it back to her. "Where's he at?"

"Where's a goose egg?" Dempsey asked, and tried to climb onto Vada's lap.

Harmon pulled him back by the collar of his over-sized shirt. "Get on out of here. Go outside and play."

"I want to see 'at goose egg," Dempsey insisted, trying again to get to Vada's lap.

His father jerked him from her once more, shook him briefly, and gave him a light shove toward the bedroom door. "Do like I tell you. I'll stomp a mudhole in your ass, you fool with me."

The boy staggered a bit, then righted himself. "Ever'body always yelling at me. How come don't nobody yell at that stupid baby?" he asked, and kicked the cradle, startling Gerald into wakefulness.

As the baby emitted a strangled cry, Harmon acted as if he would step toward Dempsey, but the little boy ran out the door and through the front room. Vada heard him shout something from the porch, then all was silent but for the hiccupping of the baby that Harmon now held.

She glared at Harmon through one eye. "No wonder Cordell cusses like he does. He gets it straight from you."

He ignored her remark, patted Gerald's back, then jiggled him until the baby quieted again. Placing the infant back in the cradle, he straightened and began to roll a cigarette. "Where's he at?" he asked, tapping a bit of Prince Albert into the paper.

She shook her head. "I don't know. He went tearing out of here like he was on fire." Removing the rag from her eye, she let her head fall against the high back of the chair. "I thought he'd get over this, but he just gets worse. If I hear 'You ain't my mama' once a day, I hear it a hundred." She pushed the chair hard and set it to rocking. "And Dempsey. I don't know what's come over him. He's so jealous he stinks. Won't let me out of his sight. Dadburned little—"

"Where's Nelda?" Harmon cut in.

Vada glared at him. "Gone to a picnic with the Pauley's."

Harmon sighed, exhaling a plume of smoke. "I'll talk to Cordell when he comes back. He's probably gone down to the pond to pout." After bending over the cradle to run a finger down the sleeping Gerald's cheek, he left to return to the chicken coop he was building out back.

Vada felt like a failure. Nelda wasn't as hostile to her as she had been, and Vada had treated her the same way she'd treated Cordell. And she hadn't done anything to him she hadn't done to Dempsey, and the younger boy flat adored her. *Maybe too much.* But she couldn't help it. It didn't do to love a young'un halfway, or some of the time. Anybody could see that.

As if summoned by Vada's thoughts, Nelda appeared in the doorway. Her skin, normally pale after the winter and before cotton picking time, had taken on a barely perceptible glow from long days with the Pauley's, fishing and picnicking, and she looked relaxed, more like a little girl than she had when Vada married Harmon. "What happened to your head?"

"Oh, Cordell."

Nelda's black eyes widened. "He *hit* you? With what?"

"Threw a piece of that wood he's been fooling with," Vada said.

Nelda moved closer and put a hesitant finger on the cut. "It's swelling up, too."

Vada winced and ducked away from Nelda's probing finger. "Don't." When Nelda had retracted her hand Vada looked at her. "You seen him?"

The girl shook her head. "But I bet he's down at the pond. That's where he always goes, never mind he'll get snake-bit one of these days." Leaning closer to Vada, she whispered, "Does Pa know?"

Vada nodded. "Dempsey run and got him."

"Little tattle-tale. He'd tell on Jesus hisself."

"Well." Vada hadn't expected sympathy from Nelda, and was somewhat relieved that she hadn't gotten it, but still. "He did hit me." A cry came from the cradle and she rose, hurrying to Gerald before he got up a good head of steam.

"The *wood* hit you."

Removing the wet diaper, Vada cleaned the baby, re-diapered him, and picked him up. "Cordell threw it." Gerald nuzzled at the front of her dress and she quickly unbuttoned it, covering both baby and breast with a threadbare towel she kept for that purpose. "I don't know why that boy hates me like he does."

Nelda lifted one shoulder in a shrug and moved closer to Vada's chair. She stroked one of Gerald's arms, then slipped her forefinger into his fist. "'Cause you hate him, I reckon."

Vada stared at the girl, open-mouthed. "I never. I don't. Why in the world you say something like that?"

Nelda backed up a step as if shocked at the force of her stepmother's denial. "You're always telling him you wouldn't be his mama if he was the last brat on earth."

She couldn't believe what she was hearing. "Only because he's always telling me I'm not his mama." How had Cordell hitting her turned out to be her fault?

Nelda rolled her eyes. "He's a *young'un*. What he says don't amount to a hill of beans." She fell backwards onto the bed, arms and legs splayed, and yawned, but still speaking through it. "He says you ain't his mama 'cause he wants you to say you are."

"That's stupid. How am I supposed to know that?" Gerald began to fuss and Vada switched him to her other breast, patting him on the bottom and jiggling him a bit to calm him. "Dempsey never acts like that, and he wants the same thing."

The girl nibbled on a cuticle. "Dempsey won't never act like that." Nelda spoke around her cuticle, then removed the finger from her mouth and inspected it. "He's too scared you won't love him."

"That's stupid. Even if I said I don't, he'd know I do. And anyway, Dempsey don't always say I'm not his mama. Am I supposed to read Cordell's mind?"

Nelda sat up on the bed and gave Vada a look that would have withered an oak tree. "You're the mama. Mamas know stuff." Shaking her head in apparent disgust at Vada's thickness, she went out of the room, leaving an almost palpable trail of disapproval behind.

Vada stared at the doorway. *I'm the mama?* When had *that* happened? Oh, sure, Dempsey had long insisted she was *his* mama, but that was a game they played. Well, not a game, exactly, because he was a likeable little boy, even in his fits of jealousy, and being his mama wasn't an unpleasant task. But Cordell…she let her thoughts travel back over the year and more that she had been here. The snake he'd thrown at her. The taunts. Bugs in her bed, down the back of her dress. Spitting in her drinking water. How was she supposed to know that meant he wanted her to mother him?

Nelda's words echoed in her head. *You're the mama. Mamas know stuff.* She expelled an irritated sigh. All right then. Fighting back had not worked. She would try it Nelda's way.

* * * * *

Vada picked her way through the half-mile of tall grass between the house and the pond, steeling herself against all thoughts of snakes and other critters that might live in the growth. The wind blew gently, rustling the grass and lifting the hair off her neck and shoulders. Bright blue sky reflected the unusually low humidity, and she wished she could just go back and sit on the porch, watch the day turn to evening, and keep herself to herself. There wouldn't be many more days like this, with the end of June already here, and she hated to spend it down here in this snake haven.

Cordell's back was to her, its narrow brown form giving off a loneliness that produced an unexpected ache in her heart. He sat on the edge of the pond and chunked dirt clods, his dark head resting upon his drawn-up knees. A dragonfly occasionally lit on his shoulder, and he barely twitched shaking it off.

"Cordell?"

He didn't jump as she had expected he might, but turned a tear-streaked face slowly toward her. His eyes widened slightly when he caught sight of her forehead. "Did I do *that?*" He sounded somewhat impressed, and when she just shrugged he let the question drop, replacing it with another. "What you doing down here? Ain't you scared of snakes and such?"

She nodded, moved up to stand awkwardly next to him as she stared at the murky green water. "I just wanted to see if you was all right."

The boy turned back to the water and chunked another clod of dirt into it. "What do you care?"

She shrugged, even though he couldn't see her. "I just—" Nelda's words again came to her. *You're the mama.* She looked at the hard little back, rigid in its distrust, and ignored every instinct that rose up in her. "Because I'm the mama. And mamas care."

The wind in the tall grass, the ripples in the pond, the buzzing of insects— all seemed to stop as if on command, and she waited for Cordell to turn on her, to scream his customary "You ain't my mama!" and run to the next hiding place. None of the expected happened. Instead, he spoke without looking at her. "Want to see what I got?" They were the same words he'd used when he'd thrown the garter snake at her as she lay on the bed.

Again going against her instincts, she shrugged, then said, "Okay."

Rising, he went around the pond as she followed. He stopped beneath a cottonwood tree. A small crate sat there, topped with a piece of cardboard weighted with a rock. He removed the rock and started to pull the cardboard off, then stopped and looked at her. "You won't scream?"

Oh, Lord, what did he have in there? Fighting against the sound already forming in the back of her throat, she shook her head.

The boy lifted the cardboard, and the biggest frog Vada had ever seen stared balefully up at them for a split second before leaping for the top of the box. She closed her eyes and clenched her teeth and lips against the shriek trying to escape. When she had it under control, she opened her eyes again and saw Cordell offer the enormous creature up to her.

"You want to hold him?"

She nearly swooned at the thought of touching the frog. Her father had often brought home frogs for her mother to clean and fry the legs, but Vada had never been able to touch even the cooked legs. She tried not to show her feelings. Cordell's eyes were fixed on her, but not in the way they usually were—belligerent, looking for a way to torment her. Now they were wary, but frank and without guile.

"Won't I—won't I get warts?" she asked in a voice that sounded unfamiliar.

"Only if he pees on you." As if on command, the frog released a stream of urine, and Cordell looked down at it, then back up to her, grinning slightly. "Don't look like he'll do that."

She wanted to run screaming back to the house, but in some strange way she felt that this was a test of her mettle as a mother, and she planted her feet more firmly, stiffened her spine, and held out both hands. "Let me have him."

Chapter 12

When the heat finally did come on, in the middle of July, it did so with a vengeance. Vada found herself too exhausted to worry about much of anything but what Harmon called "picking them up and putting them down."

"You say the dumbest things," she told him the first time she heard the phrase. "What's that supposed to mean?" It didn't matter what he said, not really, because she stayed cranky from the heat and the way the cotton bolls tore at her hands, then clung to the roughness they had created.

"You asked me how you was supposed to get through this hot weather with a young'un in the field and all, and I was just telling you. Ain't no way to get through it but to pick 'em up and put 'em down." When she didn't answer him, he added, "Your feet, girl, your feet! Don't you know nothing?"

Straightening, she placed one hand on her lower back, and with the other wiped the sweat from her face. She hated the way her hands had been so darkened by the sun where they stuck out from one of Harmon's tattered shirts. When she took it off of an evening, she looked like she was wearing dark gloves. *Guess if it wasn't for this stupid looking hat I'd look like I was wearing a mask, too.* Nevertheless, she removed it and let the breeze—what there was of it—move over her hair, as it lay plastered to her scalp.

"Oh, I know something, all right," she said, but let it go at that. She had thought that surely, with a baby to be tended, she would be relieved of this job, but here she was, in the field again, this time with Gerald gurgling in an old, three-wheeled baby carriage Harmon had hauled home from somewhere.

Dempsey positioned himself beneath the carriage and served as an automatic alarm, sounding off at every change in Gerald's position, mood, or diaper state.

"'At baby's fixing to cry," he'd say, or "'At baby done wet hisself again," his own face twisted in absolute and total outrage that Vada should allow such a thing. Dempsey often—too often for her taste—told Vada his Pa would wear him out if he was to cry every time anybody said "Boo," and the child couldn't even find words for what would happen to him if he was to dirty his pants. Cordell, Nelda, and Harmon all ridiculed Dempsey for his jealousy, infuriating him by calling him "titty-baby." Everyone but Dempsey loved Gerald, oohing and ahhing over everything the baby did, right down to burping, or grunting during a bowel movement.

Whole family's baby crazy, Vada often thought, but secretly, she was pleased. With her own body she had produced this perfect little human being who now recognized and desired her presence, something she could scarcely remember ever happening, and it made her happy. Still, she did not intend to go through the struggle of pregnancy and birth again. *No, sir. Be a cold day in h-e-double-l.* Harmon, however, was unremitting. The more she refused, the more inflamed he became, and on a few occasions he had simply forced her legs apart and took her anyway, with her lying rigid, staring murderously up at him.

She lived in fear of pregnancy, but deep within knew it was inevitable. Each time Harmon took off for town, she instructed him to bring back some of those rubber things like the doctor had given them before, but somehow, he always seemed to "forget." If she ever made it to Sapulpa, she knew she would not "forget," but chances of her getting there before the worst had happened were slim.

Vada sighed, replaced her hat on her head and bent over in the blazing sun, back burning even through her dress and shirt. Worn out was how she felt, what with middle-of-the-night feedings and the day-in, day-out fieldwork. From daylight to dark she labored at one thing or another, and the work still seemed to stretch on forever.

"'At baby stinks," came Dempsey's voice behind her. "He been shitting hisself again."

She straightened slowly, hand again cradling the base of her spine. "Dempsey," she warned.

Brow furrowed, he put his fists on his hips. "He did. Been shitting hisself." His insistence was typical. He would not be ignored on any count, even when he knew he was pushing it.

"You don't have to use them kind of words, no matter what he did." She walked toward the carriage, massaging the tenderness in her lower back.

Dempsey trotted beside her. "What'm I 'posed to say, then?"

Vada thought about it as she cleaned and diapered Gerald, Dempsey looking on with great interest. "Dookey, I reckon." Deftly unbuttoning the bodice of her dress, she picked Gerald up and put him to her breast, covering his head and her bared nipple with a threadbare diaper. He sucked a moment, then fussed, kicking arms and legs so vigorously she had to adjust her hold or lose him to the red dirt below. He didn't seem to eat right any more, always fussing, like he wasn't getting enough milk. More often than not, she ended up making him a formula from canned milk and Karo syrup.

"Dookey!" Dempsey scoffed. "'At's not even a real word, I bet." He watched her a moment while she fed Gerald. "Mama?"

"Hm?"

"You ain't having no more babies, are you?" His brow furrowed as if it hurt him to ask the question.

"Lord, I hope not. Why?"

"'Cause I don't want no more. I don't like 'em."

"Well, I don't want another one either, but a body don't always get what it wants."

Dempsey eyed her for a long silent moment, then crawled back under the buggy, settling in the shade with a few sticks, rocks, and blocks of wood, and began to construct one of those things rocks and wood were meant for in the hands of little boys. He had pretty much given up doing any work when Gerald began coming to the field, and no one objected but Nelda, who objected to everything.

His voice came from under the buggy. "It ain't a real word, is it, Mama?"

"What?"

"Dookey. It ain't a real word, is it?"

"'Course it's a real word. You heard it come out of my mouth, didn't you?" Vada murmured, eyes on the horizon. Cotton grew as far as the eye could see, interrupted only by the occasional brilliant purple of thistle or a clump of golden ragweed. She knew there were fences too, and although she couldn't see them, was glad they existed. Without fences, she might have to pick or chop into eternity. At least with only these few acres, the end was always in sight. Barely, and seldom actually reached, but still in sight. "Praise the Lord and pass the biscuits," she said. Her voice, though soft, seemed to startle Gerald and he flailed about, batting at her breast with tiny furious fists. When she switched him to the other, he seemed no better. She sighed. "Guess it's the bottle for you." Turning, she spotted Harmon far down the row, overalls so faded the sun seemed to glint from them.

"Har?"

He glanced over his shoulder at her, then straightened, shading his eyes. "You going to the house?" he asked.

She nodded, glad to have Gerald as an excuse to go, but too worn out to shout back.

"I can't hear your head rattle, girl." His voice was irritated like it always seemed to be lately, and she realized that because of the sun, he couldn't see her well enough to know she was nodding.

"Yes," she managed, then, a little louder, "Yes."

He waved her on, and she turned to Dempsey. "Bring the buggy." He was already at it, pushing, shoving and pulling. She struck out across the field, too tired to take the long way down the rows. She heard Dempsey shouting behind her.

"Wait on me," he called, panting. "Mama, wait on me. I coming too."

She stopped and turned, struggling to hold onto the squirming Gerald. Placing him upright with his head on her shoulder, she shaded her eyes with the other hand and looked toward Dempsey. "If I was going any slower I'd be stopped. You just come on." But she didn't move toward the house again until he decreased half the space between them. When she turned to continue her trek, she heard him muttering behind her.

"I got to do ever'thing. Don't nobody wait on me. That baby ain't got to do nothing."

She grinned as she mounted the steps. Dempsey griped more than any four-year-old on the face of the earth. *Spitting image of his daddy.* This last thought gave her a sick feeling in the pit of her stomach. Harmon's irritation of late had a reason, and she knew what it was—her attempts to stop his nightly groping, poking, and grunting attacks had become more and more adamant, more staunch until, finally, he stopped. Just like that. Quit pestering her, quit trying to force her, even stopped asking for it or making lewd comments about it. Turned over in the bed one night after she had clamped her legs together and begun her litany of "No, Harmon. Don't, Harmon. I don't want to, Harmon," and that was the end of that.

It was, however, the beginning of something else. His good-natured tolerance of her poor cooking, half-hearted cleaning, and bickering with the kids turned into barely concealed hostility, and he picked at her continually over things that he had ignored before. To return him to his former easy-going state required nothing more than her giving in to his desires, but the thought of another pregnancy so terrified her that she couldn't. Not just wouldn't. *Couldn't.* Gerald was almost ten weeks old now, and between working in the fields and in the house, holding Harmon off, and caring for the baby, she felt like she'd been holding up the world single-handedly. With some of her tasks—picking cotton and housecleaning, even caring for Gerald—there was at least a projected end. Not so with Harmon and his demands. If the sex didn't kill her, pregnancy and childbirth would, and if they didn't—well, there was something about the idea of being at the beck and call of *two* squalling bundles of want 24 hours a day that almost made her *wish* she were dead.

She fixed Gerald's bottle, and laid him on the bed surrounded by pillows and rolled up blankets to keep him from falling off. Propping the bottle on one of Harmon's wadded up shirts, she lay beside him, raised on her elbow, and traced the lines of his perfect face and silky head. He sucked greedily, his eyes almost crossed as he tried to focus on her, one fat little hand stretched toward her face.

"You're just Mama's boy when Papa's not here, isn't that right?" she said, and grabbed his hand, alternately kissing and blowing into the palm. He squealed loudly and waved his arms and legs at her, losing the nipple of the bottle in the process. "You silly." She kissed his forehead and stuck the bottle back in his mouth. "You stay here, now. Mama's got to go see what that Dempsey's up to."

Dempsey awaited her in the kitchen, sitting beneath the table, knees drawn up to his chest, arms wrapped around the bent legs. "You didn't wait on me," he said, lower lip protruding.

"Oh, hush. You're here, aren't you? Want to help me cook dinner?" The thought of the freshly killed chicken Harmon had brought from the Fleetwood's down the road made her a little nauseous, but she removed it from the icebox, keeping her hands off the pimply skin for as long as possible. She got the butcher knife and looked at the chicken, pale and bumpy, plump with lots of extra fat around the body cavity.

"You gonna cut it up or not?" Dempsey had pulled a kitchen chair beside her and now stood on it, poking one dirty finger at the bird's breast. "'At musta been a fat old chicken, right, Mama?" He wrinkled his nose at her and grinned, but the grin slowly died as he looked at her. "What wrong wif you? You look funny."

Afraid to open her mouth, Vada walked quickly, almost running, from the house to the outhouse, still clutching the butcher knife. She barely made it into the rickety wooden structure before she lost everything from her toenails up. When the spasms subsided at last, she leaned against the wall, looking through the crookedly rectangular, glassless window to the cotton field.

Harmon, Cordell and Nelda formed a silent trio as they worked their way down their respective rows, dragging burlap bags behind them. She focused her gaze on Harmon, his bony figure bent in a U, the smoke from a roll-your-own drifting above his head into the now windless air. She looked down at the whitened knuckles of her own hand, the one that clutched the butcher knife, then back out at Harmon, and felt rage gathering in her like storm clouds.

He had won. No matter how she looked at it, that man out there, both stranger and husband, had won. All the strength she had expended refusing him, all the complaining she had had to listen to about her cooking, her cleaning, her general incompetence, all had been for nothing. The few times he had entered her body had prevailed over the many times she had managed to hold out, and, once again, he had won. Pressing her free hand to her stomach, she swallowed against the slow-rolling nausea, and, carefully, deliberately, used one hand to pry the rigid fingers of the other from the knife, then released the heavy, wooden-handled tool into the deep, stinking safety of the outhouse hole.

Chapter 13

Vada was going to lose her mind. She was sure of it. Gerald toddled around the house, continually under her feet, clutching her leg or her thin nightgown whenever he got close enough. Baby Margaret alternated between crawling and tottering after Vada, whining because she was in the middle of cutting a pair of jaw teeth, while Jacob had pulled himself up by the railing on the baby bed and stood, wet diaper drooping nearly off of him, screaming to be fed, changed or both. In the midst of the uproar, Vada rushed desperately around the slap-dash kitchen, trying to get some breakfast on the table.

Cordell planted himself in front of Vada. "I can't find Dempsey. If Pa comes in here and I ain't got Dempsey right by the hand, he'll whomp me, and I don't aim to be whomped because he's a mama's boy."

"I can't help you none. Go look under the house. That's where you found him last time." She stepped around Cordell and set a pan of oatmeal on the table. "And he's not a mama's boy," she added. "He's just not used to going to school yet."

Just then Harmon stomped into the house, pulled a chair out from the table and sat. As he seated himself, Vada placed a cup of coffee and bowl of oatmeal before him, distracting him while Cordell slipped out the door.

"I know you don't like oatmeal, but it's all we got till you go to town next. You reckon we could have cheese when you do? Cheese sandwiches would be awful good in this weather." Just when she thought she'd succeeded in keeping his attention, Harmon snapped his attention to the door just closing.

"Cordell, get your young ass in here."

Cordell slowly moved back into the room, stopping several feet shy of Harmon. Cordell and Vada exchanged looks, and she let her breath out slowly, hardly aware she'd been holding it. Poor Cordell. He was in for it now.

"You find your brother?" Harmon did not look at his oldest son, but kept his eyes on the oatmeal as he stirred it.

"No, sir." The boy studied the floor like he was going to be tested on its covering, contours, and degree of slant.

Harmon tore off a piece of toast and dipped it in the oatmeal, then put it into his mouth. "Get your ass out there and don't come back without him."

"But Pa—" Cordell started.

Harmon half-turned in his chair. "Don't 'but' me. Find him." He stared hard at Cordell until the youngster left through the front door. Then he looked at Vada, eyes accusing. "I don't know what you done to that Dempsey. Didn't neither one of the other ones act this way when they started to school. Here he is in second grade and you got to just about give him a sugar-tit to get him to go."

Vada restrained the urge to shake her head at him like he was the most pitiful sight she'd ever seen. Instead, she picked Gerald up and put him on his daddy's lap, then went to the bedroom to take care of the now-shrieking Jacob. She didn't need to hear what Harmon had to say. She could almost predict his words. *They's glad to go to school, 'specially Cordell. He didn't want to stay home and do women's work like that Dempsey.* But she didn't say anything, because he didn't deserve an answer. All she'd done to Dempsey Priddy was be a mama to him, and any fool could see he was scared to death he'd go to school and come home and find her missing. He was a joyful boy, as a rule, but sensitive, easy to cry. His jealousy of the younger children had abated to a large extent, but that didn't mean he wanted to lose the only mama he'd ever known. He'd been sick with terror when Vada had gone off to have Margaret and had to stay an extra three days in the hospital because of an infection, and when Jacob had come along the boy had become so hysterical that Harmon had relented and taken Dempsey to the hospital to see that Vada still lived.

She looked down at Jacob as she deftly changed his diaper. Like Margaret and Gerald before him, he had remained on the breast only a short time before Vada became pregnant again and lost her milk. He was only seven months old, and already she was five months gone. This was it, though. Forever and ever. If Harmon couldn't find a way to prevent it, she'd find a way herself. She sure would. A shuffling of footsteps at the door drew her attention, and she looked up, expecting Harmon, or maybe Cordell. But it was Papa, his face red and swollen, and Harmon behind him, hovering in an uncharacteristic way, clutching Gerald around the middle like a sack of potatoes.

Confused and embarrassed by the thinness of her gown, she tried to cover herself first with the baby, then the burp rag she always seemed to have flung over her shoulder. Her frantic motions came to an abrupt stop as she realized in horror that her father had been crying. *Papa! Crying.*

"What is it? Is it Mama?" she asked, forgetting for the moment her resolution to call her mother by her given name. She half rose from the chair, but his next word knocked her back into it.

"Addy," he said, voice cracking. At first, only for a split second, she imagined he had gotten her confused with her sister, because imagining that was easier than knowing what he was really about, why his face twisted when he said the name "Addy." She felt her bowels loosen, a sudden tingling began, and she rose almost involuntarily. Harmon came and took the baby from her, stood holding and jiggling a child in each arm while Margaret whined at his feet.

"No," Vada said. "Not Addy." She shook her head at her father, as she would have at Dempsey or Cordell when they got into something they shouldn't have. Backing toward the bed as if distance would change the nature of what she knew had happened, she said again, "Not Addy."

"It wasn't nobody's fault, the doctor says. She miscarried…but Addy…she didn't know. She waited too long to go to the hospital…I aimed to come for you soon's it happened, day before yesterday, but I…your mama…" Her father moved toward her, eyes beseeching. "You got to come to the house. Your mama needs you." He looked down at his hands as if they had betrayed him, then up at her, tears rolling down his face onto the cotton shirt he wore. "I can't do nothing for her no more."

"No!" The word was a screech, and she flew at him, fists flailing. The attack was so sudden that he was forced against the wall, and she landed a couple of solid punches before Harmon could drop one child—Gerald, as it happened—and get to her.

"Here now, that ain't no way to act." He grabbed her by the upper arm and pulled her away from her father, who had made no move to block the blows or even restrain her.

Now he seemed to realize she had hit him, and he massaged his chest, a stricken look on his face. "For the love of God, girl. What ails you? Don't I have enough on my plate with Addy dead and your mama took to her bed and nobody to take care of the young'uns?" When Vada didn't answer, but simply stood before him, body rigid, he took her by the upper arms and shook her, once, hard. "What ails—"

She jerked away from him, backed up and nearly knocked Harmon over, her gaze never leaving her father. "You killed her." She rubbed her arms, trying to stop the chills she felt moving up and down her body. "You might as well held a gun to her head, you and Mama."

"Aw, now, Vada," Harmon said from behind her, voice nervous. "You ain't got no call—"

"You shut up!" The words were like a slap, but she didn't care. She didn't have it in her to care about anything but getting to Addy, seeing for herself what had been done to her little sister. "Just get the car and take me to my sister. I want to see what they've done." She glared at her father, both pained and vindicated to see the whiteness of his face.

"Vada, sugar—" Papa began.

"Don't you 'sugar' me. Don't you *ever* sugar me." She spat the words at him, but at the same time saw that mixed with his sorrow was a large measure of guilt, and she knew as well as if he'd spoken them aloud that it was there because he had never stopped Mama from doing the things she had done. Vada slumped, grabbed the bedstead to keep from falling, and looked at Harmon. "Get the car. I want to see my sister." Her eyes moved around the room and stopped to rest on the children motionless in the doorway. Even Dempsey was there, his face a study in fear.

Harmon started to speak to Vada but seemed to think better of it, and looked at Nelda instead. "I reckon you better stay home today. Take care of the young'uns."

Nelda only nodded, but Dempsey spoke up. "Me too, Pa. I want to stay home too." His voice quivered, and when the door shut a few moments later, only Cordell went through it to catch the school bus.

Harmon handed Jacob off to Nelda, who already had Gerald clinging to her, and went to fetch the car. After a last, longing look at Vada, Dempsey turned along with Nelda and went to the other room.

Papa looked at Vada, started to say something, but like Harmon, seemed to think better of it. His shoulders slumped, and he looked years older than his age. Without another word, he turned and left the room. Vada stared after him, but all she saw was Addy as she had looked all those months ago, scared and proud at the same time, as she stood beside Alex, the man who had planted the seed that took her life.

Chapter 14

It had been an uncommonly warm winter, and the trend had continued into March. The day of Addy's wedding, she and Vada had stood in the small room off the fellowship hall of Beaver Creek Free Will Baptist Church, taking turns letting the fan blow up their dresses. The giggled as they had in the old days, when they had eluded Mama by hiding in the fields around the house. Even though she was her sister's matron of honor, Vada had still spent the week before wedding alternately pleading and demanding, searching for the words that would convince Addy to come live with her and Harmon. But Addy wouldn't hear it. When she put her mind to something, nothing could change it. Vada was glad Addy was having a real wedding, with store-bought flowers and a cake and all, but still, the marriage wasn't right. It just wasn't.

"Don't let Mama do this, Addy. Please. You got so much life ahead of you, and me and Harmon wouldn't like nothing better than for you to stay with us a while." Addy faced the mirror now, and tilted her head to set the circlet of flowers atop the mass of curling chestnut hair that spilled down her slender back. Her changeable eyes gleamed like moonlight on a wet blacktop road, and the small scar on her chin, reminder of a rock Vada had tossed at her when they were small, dimpled as she eyed herself in the mirror.

"I'm not *letting* her do nothing." Satisfied with the angle of the flowers, she turned to Vada and hugged her tightly. "I love you for caring, Vada, but I *want* to marry Alex." Holding her sister at arm's length, Addy grinned. "Maybe you're just a little bit jealous." She arched her dark eyebrows, a caricature of the vamps she and Vada had gazed upon in movie magazines. "He's mighty good looking."

Vada felt the heat rise in her face and she slapped at Addy. "Stop it. I couldn't never be jealous of you." But she was, just the tiniest bit. It wasn't because Alex Bookout was handsome—which he was—or because his family had money—which they did—but because Addy loved him so much and was so happy. Vada did not know what that felt like, to be in love. She had not even really gotten around to thinking about it before Harmon had come along and married her. It made her head ache, though, thinking about things like that, things that couldn't be helped and that would never come to her, even if she lived to be a hundred.

"Vada?" Addy's face was solemn now, and expectant, as if Vada had said something that had made her sad and owed her an explanation. Addy brushed something wet from Vada's face. "Why you crying?"

"I'm not," Vada whispered as another tear, and another, slid down her face and dripped onto the bodice of her cotton dress.

"Well, then, your cheeks are leaking." Addy hugged her. "You just don't worry one minute about me. Mama might think she's doing something to me, but she's not. She's just pushing me where I want to go a little bit sooner than I meant to go, that's all." After a long, searching look into Vada's eyes, she grabbed her sister's hands and squeezed, then released them. "Looky here. Don't act like this is a funeral. Let's be happy." She pirouetted away from Vada. "You never said how you like my dress. Isn't it swell?"

The pale pink dotted Swiss made Addy look like a fairy princess, with its little cap sleeves and scooped neck, and the grosgrain ribbon tied in the back. Alex's mama had said the pastel material wasn't proper for winter, but as far as Addy was concerned, the dotted Swiss was the only bolt of cloth in the world. And besides, wasn't it almost spring?

Around Addy's neck was a wide band of black velvet with a cameo, a gift from Alex's grandmother, suspended from it. Nylon stockings and white pumps—again, according to Alex's mama, not right for March—completed the outfit, and when Vada could separate the outfit from its purpose, she thought she'd never seen anything so grand.

"You look beautiful," she said. "Prettier than a whole field of sweet williams."

Addy's eyes were drawn back to the mirror, like she couldn't help herself, and she grinned. "I do, don't I?" She put a hand to her hair, then dropped it and turned to her sister. "Vada, I—" Interrupted by the opening of the door, both turned toward it.

"Hey, Mama," Addy said. "Me and Vada—"

"Addy, Addy, Addy, didn't I tell you—oh, Vada. Didn't know you were in here." Mama stopped just inside the door and dabbed at her flushed face with a lace hanky, then tried to push tendrils of hair back into the bun she'd taken to wearing. Sighing, she placed her pocketbook on the nearest chair. "I guess it's just as well you're here. It'll take both of us to get that mess of hair up. She produced a brush and a handful of hairpins, along with a can of hair lacquer, from a paper sack she'd brought in. As she advanced on Addy, the girl responded by backing away.

"Huh-uh, Mama. No, sir." Against the wall, she put her hands and arms clear over her head. "I told you, I ain't having my hair stuck up on my head like some kind of old woman."

"Don't you 'ain't' me. Sound like white trash."

Addy responded by turning away from her mother. "Vada, help me."

Mama's face became redder and more blotched by the second, and she pointed her hairbrush at Addy. "A lady wears her hair up. I won't having you shame me in front of all my friends." She tried to pull one of Addy's hands from her head, and Addy swatted at her.

"No! Leave me be. Vada, tell her."

Even though she'd been gone from home three years come next July, Vada still harbored a fear of her mother when the woman was riled, and this was bound to rile her. But it was Addy's wedding after all. "Let her be," she said, and took hold of the soft flesh above her mother's elbow. "Come on, Mama."

Her mother shook loose. "Leave off me, Vada. This is none of your concern. This is my child and I know what ought to be done."

"Come on, now. Let her be. It's her wedding day. If she wants her hair down, let her wear it down." Vada tugged on her mother's arm again, and this time Mama turned on her, arm drawn back, hairbrush clenched in her fist.

"Don't you tell me what to do, missy," she said, face twisted into a knot of ugliness. "You and your high and mighty ways—don't think I haven't seen what you been doing, trying to turn your daddy and Harmon and Addy all against me." With every word, she came closer to Vada, and Vada, stunned at the attack, backed up accordingly, until she was against the flowered pink and green wallpaper.

"What are you talking about? I've not seen Papa in months, or Addy either, not since Margaret was born." She placed a protecting hand upon the belly that strained against her dress. "Why, Papa didn't even know I was in the family way again till this week."

"Mama, stop it," Addy said, and tried to pull the furious woman away from Vada, but was shaken off like a cow swatting at a fly.

"That's just what I mean," Mama said, said, ignoring Addy. "You haven't been to the house once since you left it. Not *once*, Vada." Mama whacked the hairbrush against her ample thigh, and Vada knew by the look on her mother's face that she wished it was her, Vada, she was hitting, and not on the thigh.

"You've not been to mine either, but once."

"It's not my place. And besides, when I did go, your man disrespected me. Lucky your daddy didn't take a horsewhip to him."

Vada bit her tongue, determined not to ruin Addy's day, but her mother wouldn't have it. The older woman placed her fists on her hips, the hairbrush still clenched in one hand. "Not one time in all these years have you been to my house. How do you think that makes me look?" Before Vada could answer, her mother continued. "I'll tell you how it makes me look. It makes me look like a—like a rotten mama. That's how."

Vada kept a tight rein on her words, her expression, everything that Mama could use against her. It galled her, but she said, "All right, Mama. I'm sorry if I hurt your feelings." She swallowed. "We just got so much to do—so many young'uns and all...and I can't drive..." Her voice trailed off.

"Got so much to do," Mama mimicked. Beads of sweat dotted her red, twisted face, and she looked set to explode. "You don't have so much to do when you want something though, do you? I know you and your sly ways, sneaking around behind my back, trying to make out like I mistreated my children."

"I never," Vada protested. "Please, don't do this. We can talk about it later, can't we?"

"Yeah, Mama, leave her be," Addy said. "Come on, I'll let you put my hair up."

Mama shook Addy off again, and her breath burst out in shallow gasps. "You've always hated me, Vada, always snuck around behind my back, tattling and carrying tales. Folks round here treat me like I'm some kind of—of leper or something, all on account of the way you carry on." With every word, her face grew redder and she seemed wound tighter.

Remaining silent, Vada knew there was nothing that her mother would believe, or even want to hear. The best thing to do would be to leave, at least the room, and hope that Esther Louise would not follow. Just as she started to turn away, her mother smacked her on the side of the face.

Vada put one hand to her stinging cheek and grabbed her mother's arm with the other. Words tumbled out of her in a rush, rolling and bumping against each other as they pelted the other woman. "Don't you ever lay a hand on me again," she said, her face close to her mother's. "And don't go blaming me for the way people treat you, 'cause it's not me that makes you look bad. You look bad 'cause you *are* bad, hateful, and spiteful, and ugly, not just to me, but to other people, too." Vada could not believe she'd said it. *Do Lord! Tell me I didn't say that out loud.* However, the look on Mama's face told her that she had not only said it, it had hit home.

"You little heifer," her mother screeched. "You skinny-legged, stringy-headed, snot-nosed little heifer." She came at Vada with the hairbrush and Vada went to her knees, crouched with her hands and arms over her head, unable to cry out, but overcome with mortification. "I'll beat you till you piss your drawers then beat you for pissing them," her mother cried, and Vada felt five years old again, terrified and straining to hold back both tears and urine lest either one get her killed. She vaguely heard Addy screaming, then the door slamming open, Harmon's voice and Papa's, and after a short spell of pitch darkness, the room was bright and Mama was gone. Addy squatted beside her with a wet washcloth and dabbed at her arms and forehead with it.

"My stars and garters, Vada, I didn't mean for you to get yourself killed. I would have let her put my hair up before I'd have had this happen." Addy smiled and shook her head, her hands tender on Vada's face. Finally, she motioned to Harmon, who hovered just behind Vada. He moved forward and pulled Vada to her feet.

"Don't you know better than to get your mama going?" He brushed her hair back from her face, peeled it away from the wet blotches left by tears.

Vada rubbed her arms. "I didn't do anything," she muttered.

"You must've done something." He looked at her for a long moment, and she saw his Adam's apple bob. "All right, all right. I forgot who we're talking about here. You ain't got to do much." He helped her straighten her dress, then bent and retrieved the hairbrush from the floor and handed it to her. "Fix yourself. Your hair's all undone and you got pins hanging everywhere."

Looking into the mirror, she examined first her tear-stained face, then Addy's high-colored, smiling one. She couldn't help but note that Addy's hair was even more glorious in its current disarray, curlier and with more shine, as if to spite Mama. Vada laid the hairbrush on the vanity table and, with trembling fingers, picked the remaining hairpins from her own almost black hair and let it fall. It was straight, not curly as Addy's was, but it hung heavy and shining past her shoulders to the middle of her back. As she drew the brush through it, over and over, she inhaled one shaky breath after another until she had calmed herself. At the first strains of organ music, she laid the brush aside and motioned toward the door.

"You better go on, Har. It's time." Vada picked up the bouquet of baby's breath, lilies of the valley, and forget-me-nots and handed them to Addy. Harmon wavered uncertainly, his black eyes regarding her with careful scrutiny, but finally, he turned and left the room. She looked at the hairpins in her hand, then at the silky dark hair on her shoulders. As the organ segued from "Oh, Promise Me" to the wedding march, she dropped the hairpins into the wastebasket, picked up her own, smaller bouquet and preceded her sister out the door in precise, measured footsteps, hair lying warm and heavy on her back.

Chapter 15

And that had been that. Addy had married Alex, and Mama had refused to speak to Vada the rest of the day. Hadn't spoken to her since, in fact, and now Papa wanted her to go help with the little ones. *Not on your life.* Vada sat like a stone on the seat beside Harmon as they drove to Sapulpa, to Harrison's Funeral Home where Papa said Addy had been laid out.

When they reached the place, Vada slipped from the car almost before it had stopped moving.

"Wait on me," Harmon called. "I'll park the car." His voice faded into the background as she stared at the ground in front of her and kept walking. Picking them up and putting them down, like Harmon always said. She knew now as she never had before that to put one foot in front of the other was the only way she would make it, the only way she could walk into that building and see Addy dead. And that sometimes it was easier said than done. Picking them up and putting them down. She was counting on that now.

Inside the door of the funeral home, it looked like somebody's living room, but the smell of flowers was overwhelming, sickening, and Vada stood unmoving in the center of the beige carpet until a short plump woman whose taffy-colored hair sported dark roots, and whose face resembled a Pekinese, bustled toward her, her silk encased bosom preceding her by a foot as she met Vada.

"You must be some of Miz Bookout's folks," the woman whispered.

"I—I must be," Vada whispered back, stricken to realize that in her distress she had forgotten Addy's married name. "That is, Addy—Adelaide—"

"Yes, yes," the woman said. "Adelaide. Of course." She guided Vada into an even dimmer room, more deeply carpeted, all light shut out by maroon and cream striped drapes. A brocade sofa and two overstuffed wing chairs flanked a coffee table at one end of the room, and the casket occupied the other. There were a few sprays of flowers in front and a blanket of yellow roses covering the lower half of the casket, but nowhere near enough to explain the cloying sweetness in the air.

"She looks real fine, if I do say so," the woman whispered, and pulled Vada toward the dark coffin.

Vada dug her heels in as they reached the last wing chair. *Too soon! Too soon to see my baby sister dead.* "I-I think I'd just like to set a spell, if that'd be all right," she said, and dropped into the chair before the woman could stop her.

"Why, surely." She patted Vada's hand, smiling. "You just take all the time you want, dear. I'll be yonder in the other room if you need me."

She gave Vada a final pat and was halfway to the door when Vada stopped her. "Ma'am?" The woman turned back, eyes questioning, pug nose twitching. Vada hesitated, then plunged on. "There's a man come with me—tall, thin fella—he's gonna be coming in any second now. Could you—could you just tell him one at a time?"

The woman looked at her for a long time, eyes bright and curious, then nodded. "Sure thing, dear. I'll tell him just that." Easing out the door, she closed it softly behind her, leaving the sisters alone together.

Vada tried to think about anything but the fact that Addy was lying up there in a box, dead. Who would pay for the fine casket, the luxurious carpeting and drapes? She guessed it would be Alex's people. They surely had it to spare. But if that was the case, why weren't there more flowers? These few arrangements were barely respectable. And why wasn't Alex here? How could he leave Addy here all alone? Vada sat in the chair staring at the coffin, trying to dwell on the things that didn't matter so she wouldn't have to think about the things that did. She bit her lip, tried to induce a pain more fierce than the one in her heart that held her breathless. Finally, she rose, moved forward on legs like iron weights.

First, she saw Addy's nose, then her cheeks and forehead, her entire face, and, finally, her torso. She stopped at the casket, sucked in what little air she could. *She looks so alive.* And Addy did. Her dark lashes swept cheeks tinged with peachy-pink, her lips were pursed just a bit, like they always were when she was thinking about something. But something was missing. Vada searched her sister's face, tried to see below the cosmetic perfection. After a few moments of scrutiny, she realized that the tiny scar on Addy's chin, the one she herself had put there with a rock so long ago, was gone, covered over by the makeup. For some reason, that scar, so artfully hidden, undid Vada, and the tears she had been holding back all morning overwhelmed her.

"Oh, Addy. I tried to tell you." Her shoulders heaved with the effort of speaking through sobs. "I tried. Oh, God, my God, my God." Her knees gave way and she sank down beside the coffin, hanging onto the side, crying so hard she couldn't catch her breath. She was aware of nothing but the deep pit of her grief until firm hands lifted her to her feet. Not even caring who it was, she cried out, "I should've stopped her. I should've done it no matter what." The odor of Prince Albert surrounded her, and Harmon's voice was more of a comfort than she ever thought possible, so welcome she couldn't even be angry at the taffy-haired woman who hovered in the background, twisting a handkerchief in both hands.

"You couldn't do nothing, girl. And you can't do nothing now but get it all out. It's all right. You just go ahead and bawl." He held her against him and patted her back, and although she felt comforted by his presence, she could not cry in front of him. Her tears did not so much cease as retreat, making her chest ache as if they still flowed somewhere deep inside her. She gradually dried her face, wiping her eyes and blowing her nose on the handkerchief he offered. As if of one mind, they moved to the sofa and sank down on its edge. He held her hand awkwardly, as if she were an unwieldy object he was forced to keep safe.

"How can she be dead?" she asked, voice a dull monotone. "How can my baby sister be dead, and her not even fifteen years old?" She looked at Harmon for a moment, through burning eyes, as the ache in her chest moved back up in her throat. Tears blurred her vision, and she turned toward the casket, toward the shimmering peach satin and the dark cherry wood. *I wish I could just crawl in there with you, Addy, go where you go, feel what you feel, even if it's nothing. Especially if it's nothing.*

Harmon cleared his throat. "We need to go to your folks'." The words were soft but firm, and Vada looked at him, then slowly shook her head.

"No. I got nothing to say to either one of them." She set her mouth and drew away from him, rose and went to the coffin.

Harmon followed, showering her with an annoying and unwanted barrage of words. "I know you ain't, but you got to understand, they're hurting same as you. You have to know that. A body just don't lose a young'un and go on like nothing happened. They'll be needing you, and you got to go." He moved up beside her, hesitated, then said, "It's the decent thing to do."

"Decent? Were they worried about the decent thing when they killed her?" She twisted one hand in the other, staring at Addy.

"You got to leave off that kind of talk. Your mama's mean, and her way's the only way, but she wouldn't've had this happen for the world." He put a hand under her chin and turned her face toward him. "She wouldn't, and neither would your pa."

Vada glared at him in silence and tried to turn her face from him, but he wouldn't allow it. She glared at him. "You don't know her like I do," she said, enunciating each word clearly. "You. Don't. Know. Her." Swallowing convulsively, she looked at the carpeting under her feet. "Mama done this, and she'll do it to Roxanne too, when the time comes."

His voice continued, soft, insistent. "I might not know her, but I know people. She might be mean, and she might be spiteful, and she might be a piss-poor excuse for a mama. Hell, she might even be crazy, but she ain't no monster." He swallowed hard. "For whatever reason, maybe just because people are going to think what you do, she wouldn't have had this happen." His black eyes seemed to swallow what little light there was in the room, and his narrow face was all she could see. "She hit you and she screamed at you and she married you off when you wasn't nothing but a young'un, and it don't make no sense to you. But it don't matter." He was breathing hard, and he shook her gently. "She's your kin. That's the long and the short of it. She's your kin, and you just got to go through this with her and your pa." His eyes locked on her face as if judging her reaction to the words. "And I'll tell you one more thing. You don't watch out, you'll turn out as mean as she is, holding all this bitterness in you."

"Maybe I will. But I won't stand by no more to watch her do her work. I should have made Addy come live with us—and now she's dead, and Roxie—Roxie—" Her back, rigid and upright, suddenly loosened and she slumped, twisting away so he couldn't see her face. Sitting silently, breath coming only with great effort, she stared at the floor until her eyes burned, then stood unsteadily and made her way back to the coffin. She didn't even realize she was crying until spots appeared on the peach satin around her sister's sleekly upswept hair. Wiping her eyes harshly with the heels of her hands, she gently kissed Addy's cold cheek and straightened, trying to control her trembling chin. Harmon took her elbow and she started to let him lead her from the room, then pulled away and went back to the casket.

Taking a tissue from her skirt pocket, she hesitated, then scrubbed gently at Addy's chin until the small scar was once again visible, shining up at her. Harmon tried to pull her away, and she almost let him, then removed herself from his grip again. With careful fingers, she pulled the pins from the lustrous dark hair, lifted her sister's head and let the vibrant mass fall, fanning out on the pillow. With Addy once more resting on the peach satin, Vada arranged the locks around the shoulders and small face. When she was finally satisfied, she dropped the pins into her pocket and left the room.

Chapter 16

At Mama's the kids were huddled on the porch, so grown up Vada scarcely recognized them. She hadn't seen them since Addy's wedding, and they looked like they'd each grown a foot since then. Roxanne, at almost six was beginning to lose her baby fat, and Johnsey's face was full of freckles he'd never had before. Vada felt a rush of sympathy. With Addy dead and her so far away, they had nobody who cared for them. *Nobody but Mama and Papa, and I've seen how well they take care of a young'un.* As she stepped out of the car, Roxanne bashfully came forward, head down and bright, curly hair blocking her face from Vada's view.

Vada squatted in front the girl. "How you doing, honey?" she asked, voice barely above a whisper.

The little girl glanced up and back down, quickly. "Mama bees crying," she said. "'Cause Addy am dead." She stared at the dusty ground in front of her feet and held onto the hem of her dress, slowly raising her hands until the dress was over her head, revealing clean, but worn and oversized underwear.

"Put that down, Roxie," Johnsey said, and came to where she stood. He jerked the garment hem down to cover her panties.

"Don't!" she shrilled, turning on her brother and throwing herself at him in a fury. "You dang bastard, Johnsie. You dang—"

"Hey, hey, hey!" Harmon pulled the little girl off Johnsey and picked her up, holding her straight out from his body, his hands under her arms, while she kicked and screamed and tried to slap him. "Settle down, there, big 'un. What d'you think you're about? Where'd you hear them kind of words?"

"He better not be messing with me," the little girl muttered, lower lip jutting out and brows knit tightly.

"What's going on out here?" Papa's voice through the screen door was rough, like he had a cold, and when he stepped out onto the porch his eyes were almost hidden behind puffy redness. Seeing him like that nearly ripped Vada's heart out, and she could no longer deny that his suffering ran as deep and true as any river. He stuck both hands inside the bib of his overalls. "You come after all, did you?"

She nodded. He sounded like he wanted her to say something he could take issue with, but she was too tired. It wasn't Papa she blamed anyway. It was Mama who was like a freight train when she got a notion, and if she decided Addy was going to get married, couldn't nobody stop her, not even Papa. *Maybe especially not Papa.* She didn't know where the thought came from, but it seemed true. She mounted the steps and hugged him.

"I'm sorry, Papa." She wasn't sure what to be sorry for, wasn't sure if she was guilty of many things or nothing, but it seemed like the right thing to say. His body was straight and unmoving as a porch post at first, but she didn't let go, and it wasn't long till his shoulders began to shake. He held tight to her and cried with such anguish that she was embarrassed for him. It wasn't seemly, a man crying, but she patted his back anyhow, just like she would anybody else.

"There, Papa, don't—please don't take on so." Although she felt sorry for her father, a faint resentment at being once more cast in the role of caretaker bubbled up within her. When was it her turn to grieve, to let go and be comforted? Maybe she couldn't. She thought about Harmon at the funeral home. He'd tried to ease her suffering, but she'd stuffed it deep inside her rather than let him see her take on like Papa was doing. Maybe too many years of playing mother, and then becoming one, had robbed her of the ability to be comforted in her own sorrow. Well, there was nothing to be done but play it like she was born to it, and she led him into the house, stiffening her back and her resolve in preparation for seeing her mother.

* * * * *

The bedroom was dim, lit only by the light that crept in around the edges of the heavy curtains. Vada closed the door softly behind her, inhaling deeply. When she let the air out, she tried to release all the mean feelings she had toward the woman who lay on the bed.

"Mama?" At first her mother didn't move. She lay motionless, a washcloth covering her forehead and eyes, the smell of vinegar wafting up from it. "Mama?" Vada tried again. "Can I get you anything?" Mama raised one hand slowly and pulled the cloth away as if it took every bit of strength she had. She lay there, unspeakable tragedy writ large upon her face, mixed with something Vada had not often seen there—fear.

"Mama?" Her mother looked right at her, gaze flat and staring, for the longest time. Then, slowly, her eyes closed and her breaths began to come evenly, deeply.

Torn between leaving and staying, fearing her mother's wrath no matter what, Vada stood beside the bed until the ache in her back demanded relief. Lowering herself onto the rag rug, she grunted as her swollen belly rested heavily on her thighs. She folded her arms on the bed next to Mama, and rested her tired head upon them.

Vada was almost asleep when she felt a slight pressure on her fingers. Without moving her head, she peeked from beneath lowered lashes to see her mother's hand on top of hers, squeezing lightly. Keeping her eyes slitted, Vada peered at the other woman's face. The telltale twitching of eyelashes and unevenness of the chest rising and falling told her Mama was not truly asleep. If Mama did not sleep, neither would Vada. Instead, she closed her own eyes again and turned all her attention to the unfamiliar feeling of a mother's gentle touch.

Chapter 17

It seemed an eternity, but really it had been only three, almost four, months since they had buried Addy in the little cemetery at Mounds. Vada had walked about in a blanket of grief, barely eating, barely answering when spoken to. In her mind, she saw not the turning of the trees in response to the season's first frost, or the faces of her children, but only the heap of fresh dirt covered with the meager floral tributes under which Addy lay. Her loss consumed Vada, eroding not only feeling but hope. She sat long hours on the porch step, staring out at the summer-scorched fields and hazy sky, trying hard to think about nothing. She pictured a big blackboard like in school, and on it was written the word "nothing."

Sometimes, she was successful. Then, nothing was everything, all she knew. But the nothing board was really only superimposed over the heap of dirt, and by and by, little by little, the remembrance of Addy, of her voice, her way of being, penetrated the nothingness Vada cultivated.

"Scat," she sometimes whispered to the memory, as if it were a barn cat who'd suddenly decided to enter the house. And like a cat, it receded into the shadows to wait until she had ceased to pay attention, then sprang full-force upon her, bringing with it the sound of Addy's voice and a revival of the pain. And Vada cried. She cried a lot. She cried when Papa came to visit, bringing her a jar of honey, or jelly, or a fistful of wildflowers. She cried when he drove over with Roxanne standing on the seat beside him, cried harder when Roxanne squealed at the sight of Vada, reminding Vada that Roxanne was her only sister now. And she cried when she looked at Roxanne, seeing only the girl she would grow into, the girl Mama would shove into the arms of the first man who showed an interest. Vada had never cried as much in her life as she had since marrying Harmon, and she was sick of it. *Sick. But this is the worst. The worst that can happen.*

That day in the bedroom, when both she and her mother had been bound together in their grief, they had somehow each given a measure of comfort to the other and forged a fragile bond. Although they had not seen each other since Addy's funeral, Mama must have felt that it still existed. On one of Papa's trips to see her, he had brought a nice piece of material from Mama.

"She said you ort to make yourself a dress."

Vada looked down at the fabric, gray, with pink primroses dancing across it, soft as old flannel. "I don't sew much anymore."

Papa cleared his throat and spit to one side, then looked at her. "Harmon says you don't do much of anything anymore." She didn't reply, but only stared past him until he finally went away.

Another time, he brought a jar of jelly—albeit one Vada had made when she was at home. She had looked at it until he set it on the table beside her and, once again, went away.

Some weeks after that—she didn't know how many, because she had ceased to keep track of time—she sat on the porch step, knees drawn up under her chin, and gazed across the field at the pump jack's rhythmic motion. She tried to pay close attention to it, wondering why it was called a pump jack, how the rocking motion made oil come out of the ground, or did it? The questions mesmerized her, helped to keep at bay the things she wanted to forget, at least for a while. Trouble was, those things always came back, sent waves of sorrow washing over her. But she didn't cry. *Nothing will ever make me cry again.* When it seemed as if tears were inevitable, she bit the inside of her mouth, hard enough to hurt and make her forget all about crying. Until the next time.

Suddenly, she became aware of a noise in the house behind her, and tried to think what day it was. A weekday, surely, because the older children were at school, and Harmon had gone off somewhere in the truck that morning. The last cotton crop had been dismal, and he'd been doing odd jobs most of the winter.

As the sound came again, she turned and peered inside. The babies were asleep. What if some tramp had happened along and come in the back door, maybe waited in there right now for her? The thrill of fear was electrifying, and the first thing she had felt, other than sadness, in many weeks. She heaved herself to her feet, wincing at a sharp pain in her belly and the popping in her knees, and approached the open door with caution. As she peered in, the man at the table let out a groan and dropped his head to the table.

"Harmon Priddy! How'd you get in here? What're you doing, sneaking in the back way so you don't have to talk to me?" She couldn't imagine him doing it, but how else could she explain his presence? Hadn't she been out there on the porch step all this time?

He looked up at her, his elbows on the table and hands clutching tufts of his thinning hair on each side of his head as if he wanted to tear it out. "What're you yammering about?" His forehead wrinkled both above and below the tan line that marked where his hat usually perched. "I walked right past you." She shook her head uncertainly, and he went on. "Truck's sitting yonder in the yard. You mean to tell me you didn't even see that?"

Vada went to the door and looked out. Sure enough, there was the rickety truck that had replaced the worn out Chrysler. He *must* have walked past her, practically stepping on her, probably even spoke to her. It scared her, thinking she could have missed something like that. She moved slowly back to the table, bare feet quiet on the wood flooring. Perching on the edge of the chair across from Harmon, she craned her neck to see the piece of paper he'd been scratching on with the pencil he clutched in his right hand.

"What're you doing?"

"What's it look like I'm doing?"

She studied him for a long moment, then shrugged. "Trying to squeeze the lead out of that pencil, I reckon."

He grunted. "Trying to squeeze one more drop of blood out of a turnip's more like it." He flung the pencil down and watched it roll northward on the sloping floor. With a grunt, he kicked at it but missed.

Vada followed the pencil's movement until it rolled to a stop, then pulled her gaze back to Harmon. His dark face looked pinched, showing white around the sides of his nose and mouth. He pulled a bag of Prince Albert out of his bib-overall pocket and emptied the last of it into rolling paper, not speaking until he had it lit.

"There's no use putting it off." He inhaled deeply, then fell into a fit of coughing. When he recovered, he stared out the front door. "We ain't going to be able to stay here no more after the first of the month."

She followed his gaze out the door, a sudden shiver running down her back. "Where would we go?" The house might be barely a shack, but life anywhere but there was unthinkable. This rut she'd made for herself brought comfort, and she didn't want to upset that.

Harmon shook his head. "I ain't for sure. I reckon I could get a job over to the glass plant, get us a place in town."

"Town?" Her belly flip-flopped and her knees weakened. "Town?" She hated the squeak in her voice. "What town?"

He looked at her as if she'd lost her mind. "What town you think?" He blew smoke through his nose and sighed. "Sapulpa, like as not."

"Sapulpa?" Her voice squeaked again. "I don't know anything about town, about living there." Panic rose at the thought of being anywhere that she'd have to meet new people, make an effort to speak when they spoke, smile when they smiled. *And what if they don't speak, don't smile?* "I don't think I ought to go to town."

Harmon laughed a humorless laugh that didn't reach his eyes, and barely brought a curve to his lips. "Ought to ain't got nothing to do with it. *Got to* is what rules the roost around here." He stubbed out the cigarette in a dirty tin ashtray and immediately started patting himself down, looking for more tobacco. When he didn't find any, he looked at Vada, and she rose, went to the bedroom and got the big round tin he used to refill his bag.

While he tended to that chore, he talked, not really to her, it seemed, but just thinking out loud. "Old man Cozort is taking more for rent than I'm making, and he ain't about to take less just because the crops are down. It's been getting worse every year, and I don't aim to stay here till we can't move off." He gave the cigarette a final lick and a pinch and put it between his lips. "I'm going to Sapulpa first thing in the morning, and I ain't coming back till I got a job and a place." He let go a plume of smoke. "You just as well set to packing."

She stared at him, at his long, narrow face, the flat black eyes. Married five years, and she still didn't know him. What if she said, "I don't want to. I don't want to move to town"? The words beat an insistent tattoo inside her head and it matched the throbbing beginning behind her eyes. She pictured herself jumping on top of the table, big belly and all, and screaming at Harmon over and over: *I don't want to move. Don't want to move. Don't want to.*

But she didn't. She looked down at her hands, where the fingers on one twisted the gold band on the ring finger of the other. The band had been Sarah's, until this life had killed her. Now it was hers. Her wedding band. Her husband. Her life. She forced her gaze back up, met his dark, impenetrable eyes. "No more picking cotton?"

He shook his head. "No more picking cotton." He said it as if he were losing his best friend.

"I reckon you better find me some boxes," she said.

Chapter 18

The Priddys didn't have much, but packing seemed to take forever. Vada might have been faster if not for the insistent ache in her back, the weekends which meant the older children were home all day, and the ever squalling babies. *At least it's not hot.*

"Dempsey, get out of there," she said, for what seemed like the one-hundredth time.

"Ain't no Dempsey in here," came a voice from the depths of a large cardboard box with *Delsey Toilet Tissue* printed on the side.

She dropped the stack of ragged towels she held and slapped the cardboard, then reached in and grabbed his arm. "I said get out, and I mean it. Don't make me tell you again." The box was too big to use anyway, but it didn't matter. She meant for him to mind. Pulling him from his cardboard fortress, she shook him. "I tell you to do something, you do it, you hear me? I'm—ah!" The pain sliced through her and knocked the air from her lungs.

She bent double, a grunt forcing itself from between her clenched teeth. Dempsey emitted a small sound, his own note of pain, and Vada saw she still held his arm. When she released it, the imprint of fingers lay red and angry on his pale skin. Straightening slowly, she breathed in shallow gasps, clutching her swollen belly with one hand and a ladder-back chair with the other. *Lord, what now? It's not time.* Sweat stood on her forehead, and she felt it trickle down the sides of her face.

Dempsey's eyes were wide as dinner plates as he jerked quick looks from her to the door and back again. "I better get Pa." Tears thickened his voice and

Vada tried to smile.

"It's all right. I've had worse." She told the lie in a desperate attempt, not just to wipe the fear from Dempsey's face, but to avoid having to deal with anything but the all-consuming pain. Before the first one ended, she felt another begin in her back, creep around her taut, swollen belly and squeeze her like a too-small corset. None of her other children's births had begun like this. Painful, yes, but a pain that built, not one that arced through her like a shaft of hot steel that threatened to burn her up with the heat of it.

She groaned while spots danced before her eyes like dirt devils, spinning and bouncing, until the pain finally released her. Dempsey's sturdy little body suddenly replaced the empty air between them, and she leaned on him. His eyes moistened as he struggled to support her weight.

"We need Pa, Mama. He'll know what—"

"No. He'll be back directly. Help me to the window." All she could think of was air, more air. With Dempsey's help, she struggled toward the window, trying to beat back the specter of the coming birth, of lying exposed before a doctor and having another child pulled from inside her, leaving behind only fear, resentment, and the aftershocks of lightning sharp pain. The boy shoved a rickety chair under her, and she collapsed, so breathless she could not stop him as he blasted out the front door. She lay her head on the rough wood windowsill and groaned again.

* * * * *

Vada remembered all those months ago, way before Addy had died, when she was sick enough to die, and upchucking her toes morning, noon, and night. She hadn't dreamed that she was pregnant again, because Jacob was still a week shy of three months old, and besides, God just wouldn't do that to her. He said He'd never put more on a person than could be borne, and He *knew* Vada couldn't do with another baby. Instead she blamed her prolonged nausea on the greasy diet they lived on, and her constant state of exhaustion. She'd avoided Harmon as much as possible, had begged him to leave her be, or at least to use one of those rubber things the doctor had given them after Jacob was born. It was like talking to a wall. Nevertheless, she had done what she could on her own: used that awful dia-whatsit from the doctor, slick with jelly and as likely to hop-toad across the floor as to slide in her, gone to the old Indian woman she heard about, gotten herbs, and been faithful to use them. Not a new moon passed but what she buried outback a bit of foxglove tied up in burlap, and every time Harmon finished his business, she'd gotten up and brewed a cup of bitter root tea as the old lady had directed. *I can't be that way again*. The sickness persisted and so did her denials. If she didn't say it, maybe it wouldn't be true.

One evening in April, she had come back from the outhouse for the third time in an hour, weak and empty, to crawl onto the bed and lie as still as possible with a wet cloth on her forehead. Addy and Alex had visited that day—the last time she'd seen her sister before the girl's death, and all Vada could do was lie on the bed with that wet rag on her head, answering Addy's chatter with groans and nods. Addy glowed with health, her own stomach barely pooching proudly out in front of her. All Vada could think was *Better her than me. Better her than me.* It was like a hymn she sang over and over.

After seeing the couple off, Harmon's footsteps had come into the room and stopped at the bedside, and she felt the bed sag as he eased himself down beside her.

"You feeling any better?" he asked.

"No. And I don't know how much longer I can stand this." She breathed shallowly so as to shut out the normal smells that made her so abnormally ill.

"I figure six-seven months," he said.

"What are you talking about?" *Don't say it. Don't say it.*

He chuckled. "I'm just saying it looks to me like you been to the gittin' place, girl."

Stubbornly resistant, she refused to understand him. "I haven't been anywhere but to the outhouse, and all I'm 'gittin' is mighty tired of having my head in a hole."

He laughed. "Aw, you know what I'm saying. Acting like you don't ain't going to make you un-pregnant."

Vada had lain still, hating him for saying what she would not, for making it true by putting it into words. After a few minutes of silence, Harmon lifted the rag and looked at her. She stared back, breathing shallowly, trying not to smell the homemade cigarette hanging from his mouth. He dropped the rag back into place right quick, but even after he did, Vada saw his glittering black eyes before her. Soon, he left the room, and she heard him talking to the children, cooing at Jacob, carrying on with the others. In her mind, she thrust ice picks through those black eyes and imagined their light flickering and fading away. Fury ran through her, but it was not all toward Harmon. He had only said what she already knew, and it sickened her that she could so easily convince herself of whatever she wanted to believe. That was just like Mama. *Just like her!*

Soon, she had heard Harmon's fiddle, and she lay flat on her back the rest of the night. Her self-hatred grew as disproportionately as her anger at Harmon had, and she lay seething until the sickness and the intensity of her feelings wore her out, and she slept. When morning came, she rose early and ran out back, sick enough to die, mad enough to chew barbed wire. She squatted against the side of the outhouse, bare feet in the cool dust below. Hugging herself and staring out over the cotton fields in the pinkening dawn, she saw in her mind's eye the full roundness of the bolls to come, cotton that would have to be picked, baby or no baby. Tears ran down her face and dripped from her chin, plopping into the dust or onto her feet.

She could have had that operation Hattie Elkins had, the one that fixed a woman so babies stopped coming, but Harmon wouldn't hear of it. It didn't cost, not if you were poor enough, and Lord knew they were, but his face had frozen in those granite lines she knew so well, and he had lectured her on the evils of do-gooders and charity and taking a man's God-given dignity away.

"Where is it wrote down?" she whispered. "Where is it wrote down that God sets more store by a man's dignity than a woman's?" She squatted, watching her tears turn the dirt into bits of mud until she heard Jacob bawling, then struggled to her feet.

* * * * *

Finally, Vada heard the chugging of the old truck. Harmon's long shadow preceded him through the doorway and he stopped. For a minute, Vada was afraid he would refuse to take her to the hospital. She knew he blamed her because she'd had to have all three of their children while confined to one. He often said that after three babies, Vada ought to be able to deliver them standing on her head in the cotton field. After all, Sarah never had a doctor, but just pushed out those babies and went on being perfect in every way. At least that's how Vada heard it.

But the doctor had told him months ago that if Harmon didn't want to bury two wives in six years he'd better see that Vada had this one in the hospital, too. Harmon had accepted the news with tight-lipped silence and a sideways look at Vada that said, "See what you done now?" Vada felt some satisfaction right then to see that he looked scared.

Dempsey fit his small body to Vada's and helped her from the chair to Harmon, who took her arm with surprising gentleness. In spite of herself, she leaned on him. As he led her to the truck, she was barely aware of Margaret toddling about on the porch, and Nelda struggling to hold onto not only to Jacob, but also to a frantic Gerald.

"Mama. Mama!" Gerald twisted and turned like an angry badger, arms stretching out to Vada, but Nelda held on with grim determination.

"I'll take good care of the young'uns," Nelda said.

Vada nodded. "I know you will." But she didn't care now, and it didn't seem like she ever would. Harmon settled her into the pickup and ambled to the driver's side. She gritted her teeth, partly against the pain and partly against her urge to slap him. He never moved at more than a snail's pace, even when she was sitting there *dying*, for pity's sake. She groaned and looked out the side window at Dempsey, standing alone in the dirt yard, face pinched and white. As Harmon pulled away, Vada tried to smile at the boy, but he showed no sign that he had seen.

The ride to the hospital went on for an eternity. "Are you hitting every bump in the road because you like it, or because you think you'll bounce this baby out and won't have to pay a hospital bill?"

He looked at her, reproach and long-suffering battling for an equal place on his face. "You act like I got the others paid off."

"Well, maybe you will when you find out what causes this," she retorted.

Another look, as if she were being completely unreasonable, then he focused again on the road. She glared at him between pains, but he ignored her, just drove like he had all the time in the world.

"Can't you drive any faster?" she asked in a few minutes, teeth clenched against the contraction now ebbing. "You hoping I have this baby right here?"

"That's the second time you said that in the last two minutes. You're having this young'un in the hospital. I'm going to get you there before you have it, and don't no more need to be said about it." He still didn't look at her, and the words were mild, but a muscle in his jaw jumped like somebody was sticking a cattle prod to it.

She watched the muscle as another pain pulled her into its grip, and wished she'd never been born. Before the pain had subsided, she changed her mind, and wished *he'd* never been born, the idjit.

Chapter 19

She awakened slowly, squinting against the whiteness of the room, and groaned, half in pleasure at the crisp sheets under her and half because sleep felt so good, like a drug she never wanted to quit. As she was drifting off again, the door whooshed open and Dr. Smith ambled in.

"Morning," he said. He took the clipboard from the end of the bed, looked it over, and put it back. Then he pulled back the sheet, raised her gown and commenced to poking and prodding and making noises as if it were his tender belly he was poking and prodding. He parted her legs and she turned her head away, humiliated even after all this time. Staring at the soft shapes that floated on the other side of the frosted glass window at her bedside, she let her breath out slowly. That was how her head felt then, hazy and full of barely shaped figures. She liked it.

"You're doing fine, Vada." He flipped the gown down and the sheet up and seated himself on the edge of her bed, bringing a barely suppressed groan to her lips. He took her small cold hand in his warm ones. "Don't blame yourself, you hear? It's better this way—no telling how long or how tight that cord was wrapped around her neck."

She stared dry-eyed at the shapes through the frosted windows. "It don't matter."

He acted like she hadn't spoken, like he already had the way she ought to act all worked up in his head, and it didn't matter what she really said or did. "Now, don't you fret. You'll have more babies." Her face snapped toward him, and his own face creased into a smile so fake she thought he must have practiced it before a mirror.

"I don't *want* no more babies."

The doctor moved his torso back as if she had spit at him. "That's something you and the mister will have to work out."

"My 'mister' don't want to work it out. And I'm not depending on him for it, neither." She stared at the frosted glass and wondered what shape misery would take if it could choose. She felt a weight lift from the bed, and a subtle warmth moving away.

"I think what you need is rest, Vada. Ladies sometimes get a little emotional at times like this." His voice turned hardy. "I'll speak to Harmon, how about that?"

Don't do me no favors. She stared at the window, straining to see a recognizable shape. After a few moments when the only sound was the dinging of some other patient's call bell, she heard the squeak of rubber soles on the floor, then the door whispered open and shut.

* * * * *

Harmon did not appear until Vada's release a week later. When he arrived, she was in the lobby with her bag packed. "You 'bout ready to come home?" he asked, holding out a clump of mistletoe and late feverfew with a little holly thrown in, his eyes soft and hungry and full of roads that all led somewhere she didn't want to go. As if ashamed of his own thoughts, he dropped his gaze to a spot near his feet.

"Have you talked to the doctor?" she asked.

He looked up. "What about?"

"He wants to talk to you." She clasped her pocketbook and fixed her own eyes beyond him. Soon, she heard his slow heavy footsteps cross the lobby.

When he returned within a few minutes, still carrying the flowers, he said nothing, only shoved them at her, picked up the suitcase and helped her rise from the vinyl settee. She stood but refused to move.

Harmon looked at her, mouth grim, that muscle in his jaw jumping. He nudged her forward, but she held her ground.

"What did you say to the doctor?" she asked. Her palms were sweating and she felt the flowers disintegrating, falling in bits and pieces from her hands to the floor.

"Same thing I told you. Priddy's ain't never took charity and ain't starting now."

"What's the difference if we take it to keep from having more young'uns or if we take it because we can't afford to feed 'em all?" Her voice grew shrill but she couldn't seem to prevent it. "For the love of God, Harmon, are you trying to kill me? Didn't losing Sarah teach you anything?"

He turned white for a moment and Vada trembled but didn't drop her gaze. He jerked his head toward the parking lot. "Let's go," he said, and went to the door, then stopped and turned to look at her. His face reddened. "I said, let's go. I ain't airing our dirty laundry in public."

She stared at him through a prism, a color for every feeling in the flood threatening to drown her. She searched for the words that would pierce him, that would reach behind the dark eyes and touch the tender places inside him, the ones he never let her into, where no one but Sarah had ever been. "I'm eighteen years old. I've had four young'uns since I was fourteen. Four, Harmon. Some people don't have that many in a lifetime, let alone in more than four years, and me sick as a dog with every one of them." She took a deep breath. "If I'm anything to you but a brood mare, you'll understand me when I say I'm not having another."

The grim set of his mouth warred with the tender confusion in his eyes. "I hear you talking."

"Hear me good. No more."

"It happens." His voice hardened, but uncertainty lingered in his gaze.

"Not to me it don't." Weak-kneed and dizzy, she stepped forward, slipped briefly on the slickness of Harmon's crushed flowers that lay beneath her foot, then righted herself. Marching out the hospital's double doors and to the truck, she heard his slow step behind her. As she climbed into the truck, she dropped the remainder of the disintegrating bouquet and wiped her hand, hard, on the skirt of her dress.

Chapter 20

Two weeks after Vada left the hospital, Harmon drove her, the children, and everything they owned to Sapulpa in a single trip. When they passed the library and turned off Route 66 onto Main Street, Vada sank into the seat, wishing she could stop time so she wouldn't have to face the coming changes. The truck chugged up the steep hill, north on Main, and she wondered if the vehicle would survive the climb. The hill was that steep. Or the truck was that old. They turned left on Okmulgee Street and passed a trio of dilapidated homes, all in nearly as bad a shape as the place in the cotton fields. As they passed the worst one, she released a breath she hadn't known she was holding. *Lordy me, at least it's not that falling down pile of...* The brakes of the pickup squealed and the gears ground harshly as Harmon slowed and shifted into reverse, backing it into the rutted driveway of the one they had just passed. A feeling midway between pleasure and dismay seized her. Holding Jacob on her lap, she looked at the white paint that peeled from roof to foundation, the wooden porch listing slightly southward, and the screen door that hung crookedly on its hinges. She remained in the truck, eyes on the house, while children swarmed the yard of the sorry looking place.

Suddenly, a whoop split the air as Cordell barreled through the screen door of the house, only to careen almost immediately back out. "Pa, it's got a inside privy!" he bellowed from the porch, then spun to charge back inside.

Harmon, with a roll-your-own hanging from his thin lips, looked at her and raised one eyebrow. "Now the neighbors know what we ain't been used to."

She grinned, shook her head. "I reckon." Pushing on the door of the truck, she opened it with a tremendous *pop!* of its hinges and slid from the seat to the ground with a grimace. Dr. Smith said the last baby hadn't been any bigger than the others, but that had sounded like something men tell themselves to feel better about what they do to women. She walked carefully across the yard, balancing Jacob on her hip, and surveyed the houses surrounding theirs. A square gray stucco squatting to the north was just as run-down, but was bordered neatly with flowers and carefully trimmed hedges. A statue of a black jockey in a short red jacket and white pants, red hat perched on his head, sat squarely in the middle of the tidy square of grass.

"Have to get us a lawn mower," Harmon said from behind.

She looked for the first time at her feet. A surprisingly thick layer of grass grew in and around random patches of weeds, and Vada felt interest stirring. She'd never lived anywhere where there was actually grass. Papa's place was too shaded by hackberry and mulberry trees, and the sharecropper's place was nothing but a shack set down in the middle of a field of dirt. Jacob twisted in her arms and let out a cry. She handed him off to Harmon, then slipped off one shoe, wiggled her foot, and grasped the thick grass with her toes. Finally, she bent over and pulled a few blades. It needed watering and cutting, but seemed healthy. She smiled and kicked off her other shoe. Maybe living here wouldn't be so bad.

Harmon bounced the baby a bit and patted him on the back, laughing. "It's called grass, girl. Ain't you never seen it before?"

Vada cut her eyes at him. "Course I have," she sniffed. Head high, she stalked off to the house, shoes in one hand, and dropped the few blades of grass into the pocket of her faded housedress. As she banged through the crooked screen door, she stopped dead. Her view was unobstructed, clear to the end of the house and out the back door. She stopped in a welter of confusion and delight. Who would ever have thought of such a thing? It reminded her of something, maybe a train, one of those with sleeping rooms like she'd seen in a magazine. Or maybe...a trailer house! She gaped at it, enchanted.

"Harmon! It's like a tr—"

Harmon passed her with a still fussing baby. "It's like a house we can afford," he said. Turning, he motioned behind her with his head. "Front room up here, kitchen back there, four bedrooms and a bathroom off the sides." He sounded a little mad and a little proud all at the same time.

That stopped her ruminations. "Four! Lordy me! Whoever heard of such a thing?"

"Well, there ain't no inner doors yet, but we'll manage."

Vada stood absolutely still, feeling rich beyond measure as she looked at the dark walls, lumpy wooden floor, and dirty windows. It looked like the trailer house her third-grade teacher had lived in a few blocks from the school. Harmon didn't need to know that, though. She didn't want to make him feel bad that it *wasn't* a trailer house. It was a fine house even so, much better than she'd thought possible given the outside of it. A sound like a buffalo herd pounded across the porch and banged through the screen door, and a swarm of children surrounded her. She looked at them, Nelda with Margaret, finally walking, tagging after her, thumb locked firmly in her mouth, Dempsey trailing his fingers along the wall, a dreamy look on his freckled face, Cordell with Gerald on his back.

"Hey!" All eyes turned to Margaret, who had thus far only managed to say "Mama," "Daddy," and "poopie." "Me yike it!" Everyone fell silent, then the laughter of the whole family bounced off the hallway walls, spinning away into the late autumn sunshine.

* * * * *

Vada worked furiously on the place for nearly a month, even pounding nails into boards pulled loose from the outside of the house. Although Harmon was never home, or no help if he was, because the shift work, heat, and odd hours at the glass plant kept him worn out, she was happier than she ever remembered. Cordell, Dempsey, and Nelda attended school all week, and she usually sent the younger children into the back yard to play each day. Although it was now December, daytime temperatures rarely fell below 40, and sometimes soared to near 70. When she was alone inside, she sometimes whirled through the house on tiptoes, a ballerina astonished at the room to pirouette, to leap and jump and celebrate, enthralled by the dust motes dancing in the weak sunshine and the smell of soap and water and her own sweat.

The house swallowed up their few possessions, but they began to slowly acquire needed items. A co-worker gave Harmon an old wooden table and half a dozen rickety chairs, and they found an icebox at a rummage sale for ten dollars. They created extra beds from blankets purchased at the second-hand store and washed over and over again, their cleanliness making up for both lack of newness and the fact that all the children still slept on pallets on the floor.

Finally, near the middle of February, Vada stood in the center of the living room and surveyed her home, and the sparkle she had produced in it. She took in the gleam of the windows, the pale stream of early winter sunshine spilling through the glass, and felt a warmth growing inside her. Although the floor sagged in places, the linoleum was ripped in the kitchen, and the bathtub and commode held rust stains that defied Bab-O and bleach, too, the house had become hers in a way nothing else had ever been. She neither knew nor cared who the previous tenants had been. What mattered was that it wasn't Sarah, who, through no fault of her own, had become a symbol of everything Vada was not and could never be, if only because she was not Sarah, but Vada. For the first time in her life, Vada was happy to be exactly where and who she was.

Padding down the hallway barefoot, she stopped a yard from the kitchen window, stood in the puddle of sunlight collected there, and hugged herself, smiling, eyes closed. The space for her body was delight enough, but the space for her soul, the almost daily nine-hour stretch of just her and her children felt like a balm, soothing all the places chafed by the friction of Harmon and his demands. At that moment, she could not have asked for another thing.

1955

Chapter 21

V ada squinted up at the sun, pushing her recently bobbed black hair
back from her damp forehead. It must be close to three o'clock.
School would be out soon. She looked around her, taking in the four o'clocks,
the zinnias, the marigolds. The rose moss was slowly but steadily taking, filling
the small bed by the porch, and the morning glories on the fence were surely
going to take over the world. A slight resentment filled her at the thought of
going in to start dinner and the endless round of chores it took to care for six
kids.

"Vada, how are you doing?"

She shaded her eyes, watched the postman cross the green velvet square of
grass, saw the footprints he left in its perfect cut, the result of hours spent each
week pushing the rusted old mower back and forth across it.

"I'm all right, Mr. Newman." It irritated her a bit that he always acted
surprised to see her. He knew she lived here, he came on purpose to deliver
mail, and if the weather was fine she was most likely working in the yard.
What was there to be surprised about? Sighing, she pushed herself to her feet
and tried to wipe her grimy hands on her washed-thin dress.

He pushed his cap back on his head. "I'll tell you, it may not be very big,
but you've got the finest looking yard in the whole town." His admiring glance
swept through it, stopping first here then yonder, and he shook his head. "It's
hard to believe you do all the work yourself."

"Sure can't afford a gardener." She looked down at her dirty hands, feeling the heat creep up her face.

"A professional gardener couldn't do a bit better than you have." Mr. Newman handed her some circulars and the light bill. "You've got a green thumb, I'll tell you that. If you entered the Garden Club contest this summer, those women would be handing you that $25 prize come August." When she didn't answer, he said, "I see a lot of yards, and not many look as good as this one." After another admiring glance and a shake of his head, he touched his hat brim and crossed the yard in a different direction, leaving more foot-shaped areas of crushed grass behind him.

The Garden Club! As if she would *dare*…as if she was even *interested!* Vada shook her head, and glancing around, duck-walked along where the postman had trod, fluffing the grass with sideways swipes of her hands. Halfway through the first set of footprints, she laughed aloud. "People see you now, they'll sure enough say you lost your mind." She returned to the flowerbed where she had been working and laid the mail beside it. Caring this much about a piece of land was probably wrong, but she couldn't help it. This yard was the only thing she had ever had in her life that was hers to make beautiful, and every seed she planted, every weed she pulled, and every five gallon bucket of water she carried to nourish the plants was done with love. In her yard, she was not somebody's daughter, wife, mother or stepmother. She was just Vada.

Maybe I ought to give them ladies a run for their money. Get me that $25. I could buy me a rake with all the tines, and a real edger. She laughed softly and shook her head as if someone stood next to her, suggesting these things. "I reckon not. If I don't know anything else, I know my place." And it wasn't in any garden club.

Vada turned over a few more shovels full of earth, broke up the clumps, then looked at the sun again. It seemed as though the days were even shorter now that all the children were in school. As soon as she had them out of the house, she rushed through housework and laundry, spending afternoons perfecting this little piece of the world. Reluctantly, she put the small spade, the broken-handled shovel and the leaf rake with the missing tines in the kids' old slat-sided wagon and hauled them to the shed out back. She stowed the stuff away and kicked off the mud-caked boots that once belonged to Cordell. The wadded paper she used to make them fit irritated the toes of one foot, but she wore them only to work in the yard.

She shut the shed's plank door and walked barefoot across the yard to the house. Slipping inside, she stopped, letting the wood-framed screen door hit her gently on the behind before easing it to. She grabbed the frayed tea towel hanging beside the big wood stove and wet it under the faucet. Wiping her neck, face, and arms with it, she sighed. *It's not much, but it'll have to do.*

By the time she had meat loaf in the oven and potatoes on to boil, the kids were home. Gerald clamored for store-bought cookies and pushed Margaret out of his way, throwing her into Cordell, who then stepped back and nearly knocked Jacob down.

Nelda rummaged in the cabinet. "Don't we have any peanut butter?"

"No," Vada replied shortly.

"We never have anything *I* want."

"You're the one with the job at the grocery store. You can get it as easy as I can." Vada felt almost claustrophobic as she fixed the swarm of children slices of bread with butter and sugar and sent them outdoors. All but Nelda went.

"You want this or not?" Vada asked her, holding out a thick slice of homemade bread spread heavy with butter.

Nelda shied away from it as if it would bite. "I'm not eating that. That's trashy stuff."

Vada slapped it onto the counter top and wrapped up the bread, covered the butter, put up the sugar bowl. "Fine. Go to work hungry."

"I don't work today," Nelda mumbled peevishly as she slouched down the hallway.

Vada heard the door slam and sighed. "That girl is so rotten salt won't cure her." She went about straightening the kitchen and almost had it done when she heard the sound of a vehicle outside. "Jesus in a tree house! Can't be Harmon already." He wasn't even due off work till 4:30. And why would he be coming in the front door? But he was, and she heard his voice as he shouted at one of the kids, then a noisy clattering of boots from the front part of the house, coming closer until Harmon stood in the doorway, Jacob wrapped around one leg and hanging on to him as if afraid he might disappear. Behind him, Cordell sidled in, wraith-like, and Dempsey shadowed his big brother. Nelda appeared, hovering on the edges of the room as if she could hide in the yellowed wallpaper, but Margaret skipped into the kitchen and hopped around the table on first one foot and then the other.

Vada sighed. *Fifteen minutes to myself, and now look. Harmon and every last child on the place under my feet.*

Harmon took off his dirty cap, held it by the bill and flicked Vada with it. "Look at you, woman. Near on to four o'clock, and you ain't hit a lick on my supper yet. What will my Mama think of you?" He flicked her with his cap and placed it on a hook by the back door, avoiding her eyes. When he turned to her once more, he ducked his head and busied himself with Jacob, letting the boy stand on top of his work boots and walking him around the kitchen with stiff-legged steps.

His mama? "It'll be ready when it's usually ready," Vada said. She watched as Margaret bounced around the kitchen, spinning in front of Harmon, the sash from her dress hanging from a loop and trailing her.

"Looky, Mama," she cried, one cheek full of something that looked to take a great deal of chewing. "Look at Pa! Isn't he like on the picture show? Like Frankenspine, right, Mama?"

Her eyes were deep, dark and round, like the centers on Vada's daisies, and the narrow face was pure Harmon, as was the rest of her: even though she was small, her arms and legs seemed too long for her torso, her lips the pale, thin Priddy line.

"Go outdoors, you kids. I want to talk to your daddy."

"But Mama, he's like Frankenspine—"

Gerald, jaw also filled, pushed his sister. "It's not Frankenspine, stoo-oopid," he said, darting away from her. "And anyway, you never been to a picture show, so how would you—"

Harmon stretched forth one long arm, snatched the back of Gerald's shirt, and held the boy a few inches off the floor. "What I tell you 'bout calling people stupid, boy?"

Like magic, Jacob slid away from his daddy, knowing even at five years old that when Harmon's voice became a razor, it was best to leave the scene or be shaved.

Harmon gave Gerald a not-too-gentle shake. "What I tell you?"

Gerald's eyebrows knitted together, and Vada almost laughed. He was the spitting image of his daddy, from his spiky black hair to his firmly planted feet and stubborn disposition. She clapped her hands together, a movement that seem to break the tension in the room. "I want you young'uns outta my kitchen, you hear? I bet not a one of you's got your chores done."

After one more shake, Harmon released the boy, and Gerald and Cordell made for the back door where Dempsey hovered anxiously at the bottom of the steps. Margaret stayed put, watching her daddy go to the ice box, and stand with the door open, drinking ice water from the jar with great gulps.

"Pa, you said if he called me stupid again you's gonna tan him." She glared at his back as if looking for justice in the faded plaid of his shirt.

Vada slapped at Margaret with a tea towel. "Get on outta here. Now."

"But Mama —"

Vada pointed a finger at her. "Don't make me tell you again."

Margaret looked from Vada to Harmon. "Do what your mama told you." Rolling her eyes, Margaret sighed and trudged toward the front of the house. "And don't step on that thing," Harmon called after her. Without looking back, she grabbed her sash and held it up off the floor. "Not that thing." Harmon winked at Vada.

Margaret stopped at the doorway and turned back, looking first at the sash in her hand then at her daddy. "What?"

Harmon sat on a ladder-back chair and began unlacing one of his boots. "Your lower lip. You'll step on it if you ain't careful."

"Oh, Pa!" She stomped out of the kitchen, and in a few seconds Vada heard the creak of the plywood door Harmon had built for Margaret's room. She turned to him.

"What do you think you're doing?"

"Oh, I know. I ought not to devil her like that—"

"That's not what I mean and you know it. What is it you're up to?" She pushed her heavy dark hair out of the way and narrowed her eyes as if she could use her gaze to squeeze the truth from him. When he said nothing, she turned, and with broad, angry movements began to roll out the first batch of biscuits from the dough she had prepared earlier in the day. "You brought your Mama here, that's what you did. After all we talked about, the room, the work, how hard it'd be on her." *Not to mention me. Not to never mention me.*

"I know it. But—" She heard him grunt, heard the thunks as first one boot, then the other hit the floor. Then she felt him behind her, felt his hands move around her waist. "I knew you wouldn't listen to reason."

She turned to him. "Reason? Why is it always reason when it's something you want, and—and bullshit when it's something I want?"

His head snapped back as if she'd slapped him, and his hands fell away from her waist. "Now ain't that a hell of a note? There ain't no call for you to talk nasty."

"There's no call for a lot you do. And don't change the subject."

His features set into the look she'd seen often when things didn't go his way, absolutely rigid but for one muscle in his jaw, twitching, like it was trying to jumpstart the rest of his face. "I ain't going to dignify that nasty remark with a answer. My mama is here, and if you want her out, you get your little behind in there and tell her so."

Vada looked at him, debating whether she ought to hit him in the head with a hot cast iron skillet. Finally, she sighed. No sense cracking a perfectly good skillet. "All right, Harmon. Fine. Matter of fact, you did me a favor. Now that I got nobody at home during the day, I was afraid I might have five minutes to myself." She turned back to her biscuit dough. "Thank you for saving me from that."

Incredibly, she felt him move up behind her again, put his big hands around her waist. With deliberate motions, she placed the rolling pin on the counter, turned, took hold of his wrists and thrust his hands off her. "Keep your hands to yourself, Harmon, and I mean it."

"You ain't never got a minute for me..."

"I can't believe you. What did we just talk about? We got six kids, Harmon. I must've had time for you at some point." She stopped, turned back to her dough. "Don't look like I'm going to have time to breathe, you bring your mama here."

A chair scraped on the linoleum and she heard the snick of a match head, smelled Harmon's Prince Albert. "I reckon you'll have more time than you think. My mama'll be a help to you around here."

"Still," she said. She quickly cut out a dozen biscuits with the open end of a floured drinking glass, put them into the pan, pan into the oven, and let the door slam. Finally, she turned to Harmon.

"How long is she staying?"

Relief swept across his narrow dark face, but he did not move. "Just till she gets adjusted to Pa being—gone."

Vada let a small sigh slip through her irritation. "Your daddy's not gone, Harmon. He's dead. A woman don't marry a man and live with him her whole life and then get used to him being dead." She tried to control her anger. *It could be worse—could be my mama.* Vada slapped plates onto the table one at a time, and their solid thuds echoed in her head. *Never no peace. Never.*

* * * * *

Miz Priddy barely touched her supper but lingered in the kitchen afterward to help Vada with the dishes. The old woman seemed to have shrunk since Vada had seen her at Mr. Priddy's funeral. Everything she ever had—big shoulders, solid arms and legs—was still there, but had collapsed on itself, a building that had imploded but forgotten to fall, sagging parts supported by only one another. With a heavy sigh, Miz Priddy took a tea towel and began to dry the dishes.

"You don't have to dry them, Miz Priddy. I usually let them air dry, then put them up when I fix breakfast."

Miz Priddy placed a chipped plate in the cabinet on top of a dozen others in as many chipped patterns. "I don't mind. I like to be up and doing." She smiled wanly, and Vada was shocked at how ill-fitting the old woman's cheap dentures had become, giving her a skeletal look. "I can't sit down and wait to die."

"No, ma'am, I guess not." That Harmon brought his mother here without regard for Vada's feelings still irked her, but she couldn't help feeling sorry for the old lady. *Poor old soul. Nobody left in the world but Harmon and me and a bunch of half-wild grandkids she hardly knows. Well. And a couple of daughters that hadn't ought to be allowed to walk around in the world with all us that's got sense. But still.* She went to the back door and threw the rinse water out into the yard. Turning back to the kitchen, she stopped short, almost running into Miz Priddy.

"Mercy! You like to scared the life out of me."

The old lady peered over Vada's shoulder. "I always mop my floor with the rinse water so's not to waste it."

Vada looked down at the empty enamel pan, then back up to her mother-in-law's high-cheek-boned face. "I expect we do a lot of things different from one another." Miz Priddy's gaze met hers dead on, and Vada felt a tremor of alarm. *Not a good way to start.* But something wouldn't let her be the first to look away. Finally, Miz Priddy nodded.

"I expect you're right. No reason we can't mop the floor with the dishwater." She turned, retrieved the mop from a corner of the kitchen, wet it in the pan of water still sitting in the sink, and began to scrub the worn linoleum.

Vada stood still for a moment, holding on to the rinse pan like it was full of gold, a covey of thoughts taking flight in her head—*The floor don't need mopped. The dishwater's liable to be greasy. It's my floor. Go back to Henryetta*—but she allowed none to escape the confines of her mind. She stepped around Miz Priddy and placed the rinse pan on the cabinet, then escaped the kitchen.

* * * * *

Vada rose at five to cook Harmon's breakfast. Voices drifted toward her as she padded barefoot down the long hallway to the kitchen, where she found Harmon and his mama at the table. Miz Priddy's eyes were red-rimmed, and Vada glanced at Harmon, eyebrows lifted in question. Harmon looked at his mama, fidgeted, and mumbled something about a cigarette as he almost ran from the room. Moving to the cabinet, Vada measured flour, baking powder, salt, thinking, *I'll probably die right here making biscuits someday.*

"You doing all right, Miz Priddy?" Vada kept her voice neutral, focusing on the biscuit dough she was rolling.

"Tolerable well, I reckon." Miz Priddy's voice quavered, like she had a chill. The kitchen was silent except for the sizzle of bacon, and Vada could almost feel Miz Priddy's eyes on her back. She slid the biscuits into the oven, then collected potatoes, paring knife, and a newspaper and placed them next to Miz Priddy.

"You mind peeling these for me? Harmon likes fried potatoes for breakfast."

Tears filled the old lady's eyes and her voice seemed to be caught somewhere in her chest. Alarmed, Vada snatched the potatoes, knife, and newspaper back.

Miz Priddy lifted a hand. "No," she choked, but said no more. Instead, she made motions with her hands for Vada to give back the potatoes. When the old lady finally spoke, she looked up at Vada and tried in vain to blink back tears. "It's just—well, his daddy loved fried potatoes better than almost anything in this world, and I don't—and here I am, nothing but a burden to the two of you—"

Vada dropped everything onto the table and squatted beside the older woman, taking the veined, soft hands into her own small, hard ones. "You're not a burden." Her own eyes burned, but Vada willed away the tears. This was not her grief, and she didn't want the pain of it. Still, Miz Priddy's thin voice had moved her. "Miz Priddy, we don't want you to feel that way. You make yourself at home, because far as we're concerned, this is your place as much as it's ours." The words surprised her, but if they could take the sting from the old woman's pain, then she meant every one of them.

Miz Priddy pulled a hand free and wiped her face and eyes. "I know you mean well, but you don't know how it is. I been living in the same place with the same man for 53 years. Now—now it's like them years never happened. Or like they're *all* that happened." Fresh tears streamed down her face.

Vada rose and fetched a tea towel, handing it to the old woman. Miz Priddy wiped her eyes and face. "It ain't that I didn't want to come. It ain't that. It's—at least back in Henryetta I had my church family, and my things, all my things everywhere in the house. Everywhere I went it was like Walter was right there with me, and now I—I—" She cast a look of helpless misery at Vada. "It's like I left my insides back there, and I ain't got nothing but a empty husk."

The words—a version of what Vada had earlier thought—startled her, but she said nothing, just hugged Miz Priddy's shoulders, and thought about how she had felt when Harmon brought her from her daddy's house to the shack by the cotton fields. She'd been scared and empty too, feeling as if she'd left some part of her behind, but she'd gotten over it—well, mostly—and so would Miz Priddy.

"You'll find a church here, and make some friends. It won't be the same life you had, but it'll be a good life, in time. We'll keep each other company till the new wears off, all right?"

Miz Priddy drew in a hitching breath and nodded. "I reckon. I reckon we will."

* * * * *

By eleven o'clock the next morning, all the floors had been dust-mopped and the previous day's laundry put through the wringer washer and hung to dry. Vada perched on the edge of a kitchen chair, eyes straying from the mending in her lap to the back door through which she saw her kids, and what looked like half those from the neighborhood, chasing each other through the buttery yellow sunlight. She sighed and returned her attention to the neat patch she was stitching over Gerald's pants' knee, determined to sit until the heap of mending in her lap and in the basket beside her had diminished to what she thought a respectable pile. A few minutes later, she stuffed everything into the basket.

Can't stand this house another minute. She started for the back door, then stopped. There was Miz Priddy to think of now. She retraced her steps, going to the living room. Miz Priddy sat in Harmon's rocking chair, handkerchief clutched in one hand, face a study in misery. The radio she had brought with her, and which Harmon had hooked up for her, was on, but emitted only static with an occasional burst of country music. Vada hesitated, embarrassed for the old woman, but finally cleared her throat.

Miz Priddy jerked as if she'd been shot, then wiped her face with the sodden hanky. "I was—I'll swan, Vada…" Her voice trailed off and she twisted the handkerchief a bit before dropping it into her lap and clasping her hands on top of it.

"I'm fixing to go out and dig in the dirt a while. You want to go?"

Miz Priddy's face brightened. "Work in the yard? Why, I wouldn't mind." She hesitated. "That's if I won't be a nuisance to you."

Vada forced a smile. "I'm glad of the company." It was a lie, but to leave the old lady alone with her misery would be meanness, and that was something Vada wasn't capable of. "Come on out here a spell. The air'll do you good."

Outside, Vada pulled Miz Priddy from bed to bed, explaining each flower, each plant, future plans and past failures. When they reached the grape hyacinths under the redbud tree, Miz Priddy squatted, her cotton dress pulled tight across her ample hips.

"Why, them looks pert near like my bluebonnets. Walter brung them back when he went to Texas with them WPA folks." With great effort, she straightened. "I been growing them every year since. Some come back on their own—they're some kind of wildflower, you know, and then I save the seeds from one spring to the next." She gazed at the hyacinths. "Didn't get any planted last year on account of him being so sick."

Vada smiled politely. "I bet they're real nice." Her hands itched to be in the dirt, but she waited, hoping Miz Priddy would soon be ready to sit a while.

Apparently, they were not anywhere near that moment. Instead of professing tiredness and allowing herself to be led to the porch swing, the old woman clapped her hands. "Oh! I believe I still got some of them seeds. Seems to me I stuck a few in my sewing basket when Harmon come for me." Her pale cheeks colored, and her black eyes showed the first spark Vada had seen there. "Would you mind, Vada? They don't even have to be planted in a bed, just scattered in a shady place where the grass don't come up too early in the springtime."

"Well—" Vada began. "It might be too late—"

"You wait here. I'll be right back."

And off the old woman went, moving faster than Vada thought possible. Her heart sank a little, but really, how bad could it be? Just one more flower, and it'd make the old woman happy. *But still.* By the time Miz Priddy returned, Vada had gathered her gardening tools and put her boots on, but she still couldn't work her mind around to saying yes, to letting Miz Priddy invade her haven. The old woman tagged after her like a homeless puppy.

Finally, she spoke. "Vada, I believe this spot here would be pert near perfect, don't you?" Miz Priddy dug the toe of one laced-up black oxford into the perfect grass, and Vada winced

"Well." Vada's stomach cramped into a nervous knot like it did when the tenth or twelfth or fifteenth came and her monthly didn't. "The grass is already up," she said, but the old woman wasn't listening. Vada sighed. *Got as much chance of convincing her she don't want these flowers planted as I do convincing a good Baptist dancing's not a sin.* "All right," she said, thrusting into the rich, black dirt. "I'll dig. You plant."

* * * * *

Arms folded over her midriff, Vada gazed through the door at the front yard. The grass lay in a lush green carpet except where it was interrupted by clumps of weeds sporting delicate, hyacinth-like blooms in their midst. The bluebonnets had defied all expectations and pushed their way through the dirt in mere weeks. Now weeds and bluebonnets were so closely intertwined that to pull one would be to kill the other, and clumps of grass further entangled the separate messes that dotted the lawn. Miz Priddy sat in the porch swing with a pile of mending in her lap. From time to time, she glanced at the unsightly clusters, and her lips curved in a smile that seemed much too tender to be directed at anything as pitiful as what was growing there.

Vada felt a presence at her side and smelled cigarette smoke. Harmon. "Them things is about sickly looking," he whispered. He had given up trying to convince her the clumps weren't noticeable when old Gilmartin next door had offered to share his weed killer with them.

Vada nodded, her eyes going from the precisely kept bed of rose moss to the brilliant four o'clocks to the knots of weedy bluebells and back to Miz Priddy, who had now dropped her mending onto the swing beside her, and sat gazing into the distance.

"Want me to talk to her? I know you set a store by your yard work, and that mess don't add nothing to the looks of it."

Vada shook her head, eyes on her mother-in-law. "I've give up a sight more than a few patches of grass in my lifetime. I reckon I'll give up a sight more before it's all over." With her hands in her apron pockets, she padded back into the kitchen, wondering if she ought to make cornbread instead of biscuits tonight, just for a change.

Chapter 22

Regardless of Vada's compassion for her mother-in-law, getting used to her being there seemed, at times, impossible. Miz Priddy crept about the house like a ghost, almost fading into the walls, and yet she created a definite presence. She hadn't so much as gone to the grocery store in the months since she'd arrived. Vada tried to be patient, but the effort sorely tried her, especially in the evenings. Before Harmon's mother had come to live with them, Vada had put the children down when Harmon went to bed, even making Nelda and Cordell go to their rooms. She'd sit in the quiet of the front room mending or reading, or sometimes just sitting. Now, however, Miz Priddy was there, too, and though she rarely spoke, she made peculiar little cooing sounds like a dove as she, too, mended or read. Vada knew it was a nervous, even unconscious habit, but sometimes she wanted to choke the life out of the old woman to stop the sound.

Even now, as Miz Priddy sat reading her Bible in front of the heating stove, Vada heard the quiet cooing, and she fought the desire to say something. Instead, she plunged her needle into the knee of the pants leg she was patching, and bit the inside of her jaw. Just keep shut, she reminded herself over and over. She'll get used to the place and us and she'll settle down.

"Where do you all go to church, Vada?" Miz Priddy asked, eyes large and wavering behind her thick glasses.

Vada shrugged. "We don't go. Never have got around to it."

Miz Priddy seemed to struggle valiantly with the idea of someone not "getting around" to going to church. "Well, I always did say the Lord's in your heart, not some building." She hesitated briefly, then said, "I will tell you I raised my young'uns in church, though. 'Train up a child in the way he should go, and when he is old he will not depart from it,' the Bible says, and I believe it."

"I was raised in church." Vada said, reluctant to broach the subject. Mama had visited twice since the Priddys had moved to town, and each time she had harangued Vada about her "spiritual duty" to her children.

"Law, Vada, I don't know how you live with yourself, you and that husband of yours," her mother had said last time. "How can you worry so much about what you put in your young'uns' bellies and so little about where they'll spend eternity?"

Vada had rolled her eyes and refused to answer, but a virtual whirlwind of thoughts had run through her head: *Because I can do something about filling their bellies, but there's nothing I can say or do that will change where they hang their hats in the next world. Because I don't want to go sit and have somebody make me feel guiltier than you've already made me feel.* But giving up wasn't Mama's way, and she didn't. When guilt didn't work she wheedled, and when that didn't work she whined, but Vada remained silent. When Harmon came home, he had given Vada and her mother a sharp look, then, instead of going out to the backyard to smoke and watch the kids play, he planted himself at the kitchen table where Vada stood folding the last of the towels she'd brought in from the line. He grabbed Roxanne when she came through the room, tickling her until she screamed for mercy, and teased Johnsie about his big feet, but never said a word to Mama. Vada's mother had gone home in a huff, leaving strewn behind her dire predictions about the souls of the Priddys.

"Vada?"

Vada jerked her attention back to Miz Priddy, who sat looking at her expectantly. "I'm sorry," she told the older woman. "I guess I drifted off."

"Oh, don't apologize to me, girl. I wonder you don't lose your mind around here with all you do."

"Well," Vada said, and shifted on the divan, feeling the heat rise up her face. "Since you've been here I got a little more time to get it done in."

Miz Priddy leaned forward. "And that's why I was asking if you'd mind going with me to church somewhere. I'd kind of like to get started back again, and I could help you get all the young'uns ready." Her eyes shone.

Miz Priddy meant well, so Vada didn't feel right shutting her out or refusing to answer. She sighed. "Miz Priddy, I don't think that's something I want to start right now. Whyn't you ask Harmon. Or Nelda." *Anybody but me.* It wasn't *her* mama. And if it was, there was even less chance that she'd go. Why, it'd be like visiting the hen house in the company of a fox. *Lord!* "Ask Harmon," she said again, aware of the desperation in her voice.

"I don't know as I could get Harmon to go." Miz Priddy leaned back in the dark wooden rocker and made the little cooing sounds that drove Vada wild. Her gnarled hands cupped the lion heads gracing the front of the chair's curved arms. "He wasn't never one for church going after he was about twelve or fourteen." *Coo. Coo.*

Vada wanted to scream, but she managed to measure her words. "You did say if you raised them up the way they was supposed to go they wouldn't depart from it." She concentrated all her attention on her sewing so she would not have to look at Miz Priddy. "It can't hurt to ask." And it couldn't, but she doubted seriously that Harmon would go, and, somehow, half hoped that he wouldn't.

* * * * *

At supper the next night, to Vada's everlasting surprise, Harmon not only agreed to attend church but made a suggestion about one they should try.

"It's over at Kellyville," he said, spooning chow-chow into his bowl of navy beans. Vada figured she'd canned 500 jars of the spicy relish since they'd been married, and Harmon had eaten nearly every bit of it. "I been hearing good things about it from a fella at work." He looked at his mother. "Only thing is, it ain't exactly Baptist."

Vada stared at him, hardly believing her ears. She knew he'd been searching for something to cling to after his father died, but she had thought he was slowly coming to terms with the fact that people die, that death was a part of life.

Miz Priddy waved a hand dismissively. "Who cares about that? I'll warrant there's as many good folk in a Methodist church as there is in a Baptist one."

"Well," Harmon began. "It ain't exactly a Metho—"

His mother's dark skin glowed as she interrupted him. "You'ns know what?" she asked, looking around at her grandchildren. "I'll bet they've got a Sunday School class for every one of you."

Dempsey looked at Vada in alarm, eyebrows raised nearly to his widow's peak. "I don't have to go, do I, Mama? I already got to go to school every day." Although they'd lived in town going on four years now, Dempsey had retained his distaste for school, or anything else that took him away from home and Vada. "I don't like church. I know I don't."

"Me, neither," Gerald mumbled, mouth full.

Harmon reached halfway around the table and slapped the back of Gerald's head. Cornbread sprayed from the child's mouth into his beans and onto the yellow and white checked oilcloth on the table. "How many times I got to tell you, boy? Don't talk with your mouth full."

Gerald glared at his father, and Vada felt her stomach tighten as it always did when Harmon reprimanded him—something that seemed to happen a dozen times a day. "Now, you boys don't know if you like church or not. You've never been." Turning to Harmon, she asked, "What about this church? It's in Kellyville, you say?" She gave him her full attention while covertly waving Gerald away from the table.

Harmon watched Gerald leave the room before he answered her. "Yeah. Kellyville. Fella says people are real friendly." He pushed himself back from the table with half a bowl of beans still left, and deftly rolled a cigarette. Flicking a match with his thumbnail, he lighted the cigarette, then dropped the match into his beans.

Vada ignored it, though he knew she hated it when he smoked at the table and even more when he put matches, ashes, or butts in the supper dishes. Rising, she began clearing as first Dempsey, looking crestfallen, then Nelda, Cordell, and Margaret left the table. She could hear the latter three as they went down the hallway, squabbling over who ate the last of Miz Priddy's pear bread.

Jacob struggled down from his chair. "I'm done, too. I don't want no more."

"Come on and let Meemaw wash your hands and face," Miz Priddy said, clucking at him as she led him from the table. "You've got more cornbread on you than in you."

The two left the room as Vada carried a stack of plates and bowls to the sink. She ran water into the dishpan, swirling the water to make more suds from the cheap soap.

"I was right about her being a help, wasn't I?" Harmon asked.

"I guess so," Vada said grudgingly, and turned in time to see Harmon stub a cigarette out in his beans. She grimaced and reached for the bowl with the butt sticking out of it, but Harmon grabbed her wrist and pulled her to him.

"What do you say, gal? How about tonight? You going to give your old man some loving?" He wrapped her in one arm and moved his hand down her hip, around to her buttocks.

The idea appealed to her about as much as the sight of that butt he'd put in the beans. "Harmon, let me be. I got to get these dishes done and—Harmon!"

Slapping at his hands, she laughed uneasily and slipped away from him. "Stop it. Your mama's right there in the other room. Don't you have any shame?"

"No, I don't," he said. He stood, stretching his long arms over his head, and winked at her.

She watched him go, releasing the breath she hadn't known she was holding. The years they'd been together—eight now—and her cooking had finally put a little weight on him. His dark, straight hair was threaded through with silver. She couldn't believe how old he'd seemed to her when she'd first seen him. He might not be called handsome, but she liked the way he looked. Now there were times when she felt like she was the older of the two, mothering and fussing around him.

But she didn't like *that*, sex, and she never spoke of it. Maybe if she'd been older when they'd met—but Addy had been even younger than Vada when she and her husband-to-be had begun to engage in—*that*—and Addy had certainly been excited about it.

"Must be something wrong with me," Vada muttered. "Sure can't blame it on a lack of enthusiasm on Harmon's part." She dawdled over the dishes, then over getting the kids to bed, and decided to do a little ironing. As she was setting up the board, Miz Priddy came into the kitchen.

"Good Lord, Vada, you ain't going to iron this time of night are you? Leave it and I'll do it in the morning." She came toward Vada, shooed her out of the kitchen. "Go on, go on. You go on and spend some time with Harmon. His daddy always did like to sit a spell with me before we went to bed of a night."

"But Miz Priddy," Vada protested, coming back to the kitchen door.

The old lady clapped her hands. "Go on now. I mean it."

Sullenly, Vada trudged down the hallway, scooted past the living room door without Harmon seeing her. Rapidly removing her clothing, she slipped a gown over her head. If she could get in the bed, maybe she could pretend to be asleep.

"I thought you wouldn't never get finished with your messing around in there," Harmon said from behind her.

For a long moment, she stood beside the bed, hands in an automatic X across her breasts, left hand gripping right shoulder and right gripping left. Staring down at the faded glory of the quilt on the bed, she briefly considered pleading illness. Finally, she released her pent-up breath and turned to face Harmon. "I reckon you better shut that door."

* * * * *

Vada lay on her side looking out the long, narrow window next to the bed.

The black silhouettes of trees stood out against the brighter darkness of the winter sky like so many scarecrows, guarding the house. Between the bare branches the black sky was dotted with pinpoints of light, and she imagined floating up there with the stars, finally, because of the great distance, able to see the big picture of her life, maybe able at last to understand what she could not now fathom—Mama, Addy's death, how she, Vada, came to be at this place, at this time.

Heaving a great sigh, she turned on her back, then rolled her head over to look at Harmon. He slept deeply, lying on his back with hands folded on his chest, almost as if he were dead. A small amount of air pushed his lips out each time he exhaled, making a little "puh" sound. Watching the tiny movement of his lips, Vada realized that he never kissed her. Never. She couldn't remember if he ever had. Gazing at his thin lips as they expelled the tiny pockets of air, she decided that was all right. She had enough to bear at present.

Chapter 23

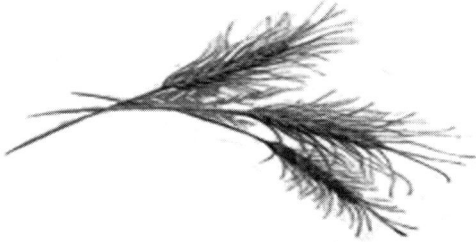

Harmon's mother settled in well enough after she began going to church. To Vada's surprise, the old lady did not nag her to attend with Harmon and the children, but, instead, continued to allow that "the Lord ain't just in the churches." Harmon, on the other hand, slid into the niche of fervent fundamentalist with all the zeal of a man on death row. He was teaching Sunday School within a month and was a deacon within the year, putting to rest his dire predictions of not being fully accepted because Vada did not accompany him.

"Lordy me, has he always been so—whole hog?" she asked Miz Priddy as they snapped beans together on the porch one Sunday afternoon. Harmon hung over the fence, debating with Mr. Gilmartin the likelihood of Indians and coloreds gaining entrance into heaven. Mr. Gilmartin was nearly purple with the force of his denial, Harmon more philosophical in his stance that it wouldn't be the first time God did something totally against the grain of mankind.

Miz Priddy rolled her eyes. "Now and again," she said. "Now and again."

At first, Harmon had at least tried to hold his tongue about the fact that Vada didn't go to church. The few times he'd reproached her about it, it seemed to be more because she hadn't the slightest qualms about staying home while he, Miz Priddy, and the children drove to Kellyville. If she'd felt guilty, maybe he would have left her alone. She didn't think he'd always been driven by guilt himself, not until his father had died. The old man had lingered only four months, and Harmon'd been stuck in Sapulpa most of that time, making the trip to Henryetta on the odd day when he didn't have to work, or sleep in order to go to work. Vada had never seem him cry until the day Mr. Gilmartin had delivered the telephone message from Harmon's sister, that their father had died in the night. Harmon had closed the front door and looked at her, his face crumpling like a brown paper bag while tears trickled down his cheeks.

It seemed to Vada that when he saw the peace his mother's faith afforded her, he wanted the same. To his practical nature, imitating her actions must have seemed the only way to get it. Vada was glad they'd come to terms with their grief, but she wished they'd taken up anything but church. It was true that Miz Priddy did not bother her much about it, but Harmon was beginning to get on her nerves. His burden for her soul was like a sack of dead cats, Vada sometimes thought, and the longer he carried it around, the more it smelled. He wheedled her at odd times: standing behind her when she pulled weeds from the flower beds, when she was hanging clothes out to dry, once even outside the bathroom door while she sat on the commode, overcome with stomach cramps and diarrhea. Wouldn't she like to go once, to see what it was like? He'd bet she'd never been to a church held in the back of a feed store. When she told him she wouldn't and she hadn't and didn't think she'd start now, he sulked. He'd sulk for a while, then it was, "Vada—" followed by a snapping shut of his jaws and "Hmm." That "hmm" irritated her beyond belief.

It wasn't that she disliked church as much as she loved her time alone. Once he'd started wrestling all the children into going, and fearing for the soul of the occasional one—usually Dempsey—who escaped him—it had been just Vada and her flowers, or a book, or blessed peace, on Sunday morning and evening and Wednesday night, too.

On this Sunday morning, she fixed pancakes for the whole family, trying to hide her smiles at Dempsey's resistance to his father's wishes.

"I don't want to go. It stinks in there," the boy declared, hands fisted on his hips.

"That ain't no way to talk about the Lord's house," Harmon said, voice mild.

"Well, it *does* stink. It smells like—like toe jam!" Dempsey insisted. "And nobody never told me the Lord lived in a feed store."

"You better shut that yap, youngun," Harmon said, and drew back his hand as if to slap the boy.

From her perch on the edge of a kitchen chair, Margaret looked up worrying a cuticle and groaned. "It'th not a feed thtore when you're having Thunday Thcool," she lisped through missing front teeth.

Vada had to stifle a laugh. Margaret, with her glossy dark hair and snapping black eyes, dressed in a starched hand-me-down gingham dress, was the image of innocence, but Vada knew the little girl hated traipsing to the back of Dub Shurgesen's feed store for services as much as Dempsey did. Even at six, she was too smart to say so. But she'd come whining to Vada more than once—"*Why can't Papa go to First Baptist like normal people?*" she'd lisp. "*They have ice cream parties there, and church just for kids, puppets and everything*"—only to discover that her mother wasn't interested in helping her avoid church, but only in avoiding it herself.

Vada's attention returned to the scene before her. Dempsey and Harmon face to face was a sight to see. Harmon had more than once lost the peace that passeth understanding in dealing with the eleven-year-old, finally hollering at the boy to get his ass in the truck before he got a lung knocked loose. Today was no exception, and although Dempsey stomped out the door, Vada had an idea that at the last minute he would disappear and Harmon would be forced to leave without him—again.

When she had the last of the children spit-shined and combed, she gave Gerald a little push toward the front of the house. "You look out for Jacob, you hear?" she called after him. Straightening, she looked at the clock on the faded wallpaper of the kitchen. "You best get going, Har."

Instead of following the children, Harmon sank onto the chair Margaret had vacated. "It ain't right, you not coming with us."

She sucked back a sigh, turned to the sink, and began scrubbing the skillet that had been soaking there since breakfast. Not again. "You go on. Don't worry about what I ought to be doing."

"It's my job." She heard the frown in his voice.

Rinsing the skillet, she inspected it over-carefully, hoping against hope he'd disappear, slide away like the soapsuds from the clean pan. *Pretty soon he'll be telling me he's the master around here.*

"Will you look at me when I talk to you?"

Vada slammed the skillet down and turned. "*What?*"

His head drew back while his torso stayed put, like a snake frightened into striking. "What? What? Is that all you can say when I'm sitting here worrying about your soul?"

She dried her hands on the tea towel that hung next to the sink and raked fingers through her hair. "I don't know what to say to you anymore, except 'Leave me alone.' I don't want to hear any more about my soul. I'm sick of hearing about how you're worrying over it, and how I better take care of it now 'fore something horrible happens and it's too late. Get *done* with it, Harmon."

"I'm only telling you the truth. You could drop dead in the next thirty seconds, and your soul would be damned to eternal hellfire. Don't that bother you none?" The aggrieved look he had taken on since he became the guardian of her soul was back, and more irritating than ever.

Placing her palms flat on the table, she leaned over, looking him square in the eyes, her nose almost touching his. "It don't bother me none, Harmon." She held up one hand, thumbnail placed on little finger, measuring the tiniest amount possible. "It don't bother me this much, but you do." She moved away from the table, her back to him. Hearing him take in a preparatory breath to deliver more dire threats, she turned on him. "Don't you say another word to me about it. You're worse than a life insurance salesman, with your predictions and scarifying and trying to bully me into heaven." She knew she was angrier than she should be, but she couldn't help it. "I've had enough of church folk to last me a lifetime, and I'm not having no more. You go eight days a week if you got a mind to, you take the kids, you pray for my soul, but I don't want to hear about it. Not now, not next week, not never."

"But—"

"But *nothing*, Harmon. I'm sorry your daddy died, and I'm glad you found something to make you feel better about it, but I don't need it. When I get ready to trot down the aisle and look to somebody else to take care of my problems, you'll be the second person to know, right after Jesus Christ, all right?"

He started to speak again, but she tilted her chin a little more in his direction, and it was his turn to sigh. He rose, picked up the imitation leather Bible the church had given him when he'd gotten saved and baptized—for the second time, Miz Priddy pointed out, for his church would not accept baptism from other denominations, and apparently any other church was considered another denomination—and trudged slowly from the room.

Vada sank into his vacated chair, the sight of his stooped shoulders and bowed back stamped on her mind, settling there to aggravate her later. She felt almost sorry for him, but not quite. He worked all week, stayed worn out most of the time, and regularly wrestled heathen kids into the truck because he worried about their souls. She didn't even know why she so staunchly refused to go, only that not going felt like the most important thing in the world. Until she'd married Harmon, she'd gone every time the church doors were open, and she could still smell the mustiness that filled the little Free Will Baptist Church on the outskirts of Bristow, still see the sunshine sneaking through the Venetian-blind covered windows in bits and pieces

Churches had always seemed mysterious to her, and she'd often wondered why their windows remained covered. Was God (big "G") a secret only revealed to some? When she was eight or nine, she'd asked Mama, but Mama slapped her mouth and told her smart alecks didn't get into the Kingdom of Heaven. Her mother set quite a store by heaven, and Vada had thought maybe Mama would love her more if she too was assured of entrance there, so, at the age of ten, she'd trekked down the aisle to the strains of *Just As I Am*. It was a *disaster*. She cried at first in relief that someone else could take the burdens from her heart and her shoulders, and then in fear because it was all going so wrong.

Sister Dortha McNamara had come to pray with her, and every few minutes, bawled into Vada's ear, "Do you feel His Holy Presence yet, Vada?" And she didn't. She didn't feel anything but a full bladder, an empty stomach, and sore knees. And, of course, the fear that if she didn't feel what she was supposed to real soon, her mama was going to be powerful mad. Still, she couldn't lie about it, and at the end of two and a half long hours, she'd risen, tear-stained and shame-faced, clutching a handful of wet, balled up tissues, and followed Mama, Daddy, Addy, and Johnsie from the church. Mama, expecting Roxanne then, had waddled from the building, with something in the woman's pigeon-toed stride making Vada wish she had lied. God's wrath couldn't be any worse than Mama's.

Vada had attended every service that ever was—brush arbor revivals, vacation bible school at a half dozen different churches every summer, special Easter and Christmas services—until the day she'd left home, but she'd never again been able to force herself down the aisle. Since then, it seemed that the direr the circumstance, the harder time Vada had talking to God. *Not even when Addy died.* The thought came to her unbidden, and she tried to push it away. It would not have done Addy any good anyway, so why should she have prayed? It wasn't that Vada didn't believe in God. She believed in him all right. Big "G" or little "G," she believed He'd as soon slap her as look at her, and she had long ago made a deal with Him: if He didn't bother her, she wouldn't bother Him. That was how she felt, and it irritated her that people thought He stood around waiting for somebody to lose their glasses so He could help find them, or that He hung out in the Safeway or Warehouse Market parking lot waiting for Harmon to show up and pray for a parking place close to the door.

She changed into a pair of Cordell's old blue jeans and one of Harmon's long underwear shirts and padded barefoot to the back door, slipping out into the late March sunshine. Going to the ramshackle shed, she removed Cordell's old work boots and slipped them on, feeling for the newspaper crumpled in the toe of the boot. She retrieved a spade, shovel, and small bag of fertilizer, hauling everything into the front yard and dumping it next to the plot of ground she had turned over and broken up the day before. With gloved hands, she began to work the fertilizer into the soil, but after a few moments, she stopped and pulled the gloves off.

The cool dirt on her fingers, under her nails, coating her palms, energized her, and she smiled, eyes almost slits, like a cat being stroked. This was where God lived, here in this rich black dirt, if he lived anywhere. This was where she found peace and contentment, yes, even joy. It couldn't be replaced by sitting in a building listening to some preacher spout words from a book written by a lot of dead men. It was only here that she ceased to ponder on the whereabouts of God when little babies were born without legs or with flippers for hands, or when politicians called for wars they didn't want to fight on their own, but instead wanted to send the children or fathers of people they didn't even know. *Or when Mamas send their daughters to marry and die without seeing their fifteenth birthdays.* Her throat tightened, but she pushed the grief back down deep. *Some other time. Some other time.*

She figured that whatever kind of God He was, she was as close to Him there as she would have been in Shurgeson's Feed Store. *And if I'm not, I guess He'll let me know.* And until then, this ground was an altar fine enough for her. If it didn't work for Harmon, she'd face that battle when it arrived.

1961

Chapter 24

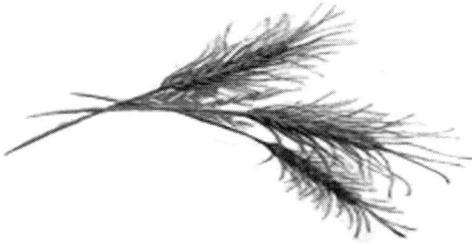

Vada did not know Papa was dying until he was nearly gone. She worried about him unceasingly because he'd grown so thin and pale, but when she asked him if he was all right, he'd always say, "Oh, I got a little touch of gout's all."

Still, she worried, and although nagging Harmon had become a full-time job, she could rarely get him to take her to Bristow. When he did, his grousing was so ferocious it almost made her physically ill.

"Why you got to go over there every time I turn around?" he asked. "What you going to do, sit there and moon over him, badger him about how skinny he is? He told you there ain't nothing wrong."

Crossing her arms over her chest, she rubbed the crop of goose bumps that had risen in spite of the unseasonable May heat. "I want to see him. Something's not right." She picked up her purse. "Will you take me, or do I have to get Dempsey to run me out there in that hot rod of Cordell's?"

"Then I'd be getting the both of you out of jail. You better stop letting that boy tear around town in that jalopy without a driver's license." He slapped the *American Tattletale* he had been reading down on the divan. "Well, don't just stand there. If I got to go, bring me my dadburned boots."

She did, then went to stand impatiently by the door. She'd rather work in the yard, Lord knew she would, but she had to see Papa. *Had* to. Every time she saw him, he had grown grayer and thinner, and sometimes she had seen bits of blood on his handkerchief after he sneezed, coughed, or sometimes, just wiped his mouth. No matter what he said, she knew he was not all right. Glancing sideways at Harmon, she fervently hoped her mother would not let slip that Dempsey had cut his afternoon classes one day last week and driven Vada to Bristow. He did have a license, a learner's permit, anyway, but she knew he was supposed to have a licensed driver with him at all times, which she was not.

Harmon stood, stretching arms over his head, then running a big hand over his face. The years in the cotton fields, under the blazing Oklahoma sun, had taken an early toll on him, turning his skin leathery with darker spots of pigment here and there. He was not quite 45 but looked ten years older. He appeared to be developing a barrel chest, and it contrasted oddly with his long arms and legs and thin neck.

Kind of like a iris bulb, Vada mused, then reconsidered. *Well, only if it was planted upside down.*

"We going, or you going to stand there looking like some kind of idjit?" Harmon asked.

She felt her face and neck flush, and picked up the sack of material scraps she was taking to her mother for quilts. "You don't have to get hateful." When he didn't answer, but simply pushed her out the door ahead of him, she shook his hand off her shoulder, and turned to face him. "If it was your daddy, you'd be crawling if that was the only way you had to go. Why do you have to complain every time I want to go out there?" She hesitated, but in the end, could not resist. "Is that what all your fancy church folk been teaching you? To be selfish and stubborn?"

It was his turn to flush. "All right, don't let that alligator mouth start what your piss-ant butt can't finish." He jerked open her truck door, then went around to the driver's side and got in. He started the motor and looked at her. "You coming or not?"

She stood, unmoving, for a long moment. *I'd like to bite somebody's head off.* Still, it didn't have to be his. He was just there. And it wasn't a little head-biting she wanted to do. No. She wanted to pound on the hood of the truck, scream at the sun, curse God and die, and she had no idea why. It wasn't just her father. It wasn't just Harmon. It was a bone deep aching for something she had never had and could not name, but which Vada knew she was entitled to, and would recognize when she found it. Slowly, she placed the sack on the floor of the truck, her purse on the seat, and heaved herself into the cab.

* * * * *

Vada knew something was badly wrong as soon as they pulled into the yard of the house where she'd grown up. Johnsie and Roxanne hovered around the screen door, peeking in then backing away to stand awkwardly by the porch railing.

Vada stepped from the truck's running board and halted, anxiety and reluctance forming a near-toxic mixture in her stomach.

"You going to stand here all day?" Harmon asked, and poked her in the ribs.

She swatted at his hand. "Stop it! I'm going." But still she stood, staring at the house, called back to days past by voices in her head, until they were drowned out by the thumping of her heart. She had never known the sound of one heart beating could be so loud.

The place hadn't changed much since she'd left with Harmon all those years ago. The weathered wooden porch still sagged, and she knew if she put a marble at the east end, it would roll all the way to the west and off, into the gray dirt below. The screen door still hung crookedly, and the window on the left still sported a crack running from lower right to middle left, remnant of a crabapple tossed by Johnsie and ducked by Addy.

In contrast, Johnsie and Roxanne seemed to have changed drastically every time Vada saw them. Johnsie's hair had gone from ginger to auburn, and at nearly seventeen, he was as tall as Harmon. His biceps and forearms had developed, but he still seemed incapable of holding his arms in any way that did not appear awkward. They almost seemed to be the limbs of someone he didn't know. Roxanne, too, had grown up, or at least looked as if she had. May's blazing sun had already streaked her dishwater blonde hair with deep highlights of ash and silver. They seemed applied by master painter, and even with Papa on her mind, Vada marveled. *Just like a movie star.* The girl's once slim, almost emaciated body was now so shapely as to be a caricature. For some unidentifiable reason, Vada felt suddenly depressed. Roxanne's curvaceousness was unlike any Vada had ever seen outside the women on the covers of girlie magazines she'd found under Cordell's bed. The girl's hips had rounded just enough to accentuate her small waist, and her breasts had assumed a life of their own, moving when she breathed, swaying when she walked.

Vada looked at Harmon and could predict his next words just from the way his eyes flicked toward Roxanne and then away. He cleared his throat, but she cut him off. "I know. She doesn't have to worry about drowning."

"I wasn't going to say that," he muttered, but studiously avoiding looking in Roxanne's direction.

Voluptuous as she was, Roxanne would not be fifteen till September, and she seemed uncomfortable in her own skin as she ran to Vada, burying a tear-stained face in her older sister's chest, which now seemed woefully inadequate to Vada. She pushed Roxanne away more roughly than she meant to and held onto the girl by her upper arms.

"What?" she demanded. "What is it?" Roxanne burst into tears and Vada pulled her little sister close once more. "Shh, Roxie, I'm sorry." She released the girl and cast a look at Harmon, who'd finally come to the porch and stood, one long leg on the top step, holding on to a post. He spit a stream of tobacco juice into the dust below and motioned with his head toward the front door. Vada moved past Johnsie, squeezing his arm as she did. She could tell he was trying to look tough in that way he had lately taken on, but mostly he seemed scared, Adam's apple bobbing as he swallowed repeatedly, his eyes darting from her to Harmon and back again.

"You stay here with Harmon. I'll holler if I need you." She slipped into the house. Her mother's voice, strident and quavering at the same time, came from the cramped bedroom the couple had occupied for as long as Vada could remember. Hurrying down the hall, she came to a stop at the door.

Mama stood at the foot of the bed, still in her nightclothes, hair standing nearly on end except in the back where it lay matted and frizzy. "Kenneth, get up from that bed," she was saying, hands on hips. "You give in to it and you won't make it through."

Vada's heart lurched as she took in his closed eyes and colorless face. In the three weeks since she'd seen him, Papa had gone from too thin to barely forming a lump under the sheets, and one look told Vada he was not going to get up and would not make it through whatever had stricken him. She looked at Mama. "How long has he been like this? Why didn't you send somebody to call me? You got Mr. Gilmartin's number—"

Mama turned the scowl that had been directed at Papa in her daughter's direction. "I don't need to call nobody to get my husband out of bed. I been getting him up many a year now, and he's not going to lay here the whole day long and expect me to take care of this place by myself."

This was her mother's house and that was her mother's voice, but those were not her mother's eyes, glassy and staring and disbelieving. They did not go with the strident voice, the angry words. Vada took her gently by the arm. "It's okay, Mama. Here, you come and sit on the divan." She led her mother into the living room, speaking in soothing tones. "I'll get Papa up, now. You sit yourself here and rest a minute."

Her mother suddenly stopped resisting Vada's pull and looked blankly at her. "I been trying to get that man up out of that bed all day long. He keeps saying 'I can't. I can't.'" She patted her hair and looked around as if for a mirror. "I must be a sight."

"No, Mama," Vada assured her. "You look fine." Patting her mother on the shoulder, Vada sprinted to the door and out onto the porch. "Harmon! Sssst!" He lifted his head and cupped one ear from where he and Johnsie were hunkered down beneath the hackberry tree, each balanced on the balls of his feet as if the position were the most natural in the world. "Come here! Hurry up." She motioned to him, but did not wait on the porch. Meeting him in the yard, she motioned toward the house. "Papa's bad, Har, and Mama's not much better. You got to come in and help me and send Johnsie for the doctor."

Roxanne hovered on the porch, but Johnsie came to Vada's side. "What's Mama doing, Vada? We been shut out of the house all day." For a moment he looked like the scared boy she remembered from childhood. "Papa's bad sick, isn't he? He had another one of them nosebleeds this morning and I thought he was a goner." He swallowed hard. "Mama just stood there, and I reckon if Tandy Bigpond hadn't been here—"

"Another one?" No one had told her he was having nosebleeds. Vada tried to still her racing heart, taking Johnsie by the arm and steering him toward the truck. "He's bad, but you can help. You and Roxanne drive to town and call the doctor. I don't know the number, so you'll have to look it up." She turned to Harmon. "Give him the keys."

"Now, hold on," Harmon began. "That truck ain't used to no—" He looked at her face and changed verbal directions. "I ought to call the preacher and get the prayer chain—"

"Give him the keys, Harmon," she said, enunciating each word. She turned back toward the house, but, failing to hear movement behind her, whirled around. "Harmon, give him the goddamned keys!" He blanched, but handed the keys over, and Roxanne ran across the yard to the pickup, her saddle oxfords kicking up dust.

Vada pulled at Harmon's overall bib. "Come on. I need you in here." She trotted back to the house without waiting to see if he followed. *He by damn better be right behind me.*

She'd been outside only a matter of minutes, but Mama was gone from the divan, and the sound of her voice came from the bedroom. "Kenneth, I won't tell you again!"

"Oh, Lord. If he's not dead already she'll see to it that he is before long,"

Vada said to Harmon, now only a few steps behind her. Bursting into the bedroom, she found her mother grasping one of the sick man's arms, panting and trying to pull him from the bed.

Mama looked up when Vada entered. "Help me, girl. He's got to get out of this bed."

Vada glanced imploringly at Harmon, motioning toward her mother with a dip of her head. Harmon took the hint and crossed the room. "Come on, now, Esther. I can see you're plumb wore out with this. Come and set a spell, tell me about it." When eyes met Vada's over Mama's head, Vada forgave him everything.

When Harmon had led her mother out, Vada went to her father, torn between being glad he was alive and frightened that he would die while she watched. As she tried to straighten him in the bed, he opened his eyes, then closed them again as if in relief.

"Your mama," he croaked. Your—" His gums were bleeding. She didn't know if he was aware of it, but didn't want to frighten him by mentioning it.

"Shush. Don't talk, Papa. I know." Tiny spots of blood dotted his lips, and his eyes shone feverishly bright. "I'll be right back," Vada told him, and ran to the kitchen for a basin of water. As she passed through the living room, her mother called to her.

"Have you got him up yet, girl?"

"Just about," Vada replied, and this seemed to satisfy Mama, for she began telling Harmon about the lack of roughage she believed to be causing Papa's problem.

Back in the bedroom, Vada moistened a washcloth and wiped her father's face carefully, cleaning dried blood from his lips. "Oh, Papa. Why didn't you tell me you was took this bad?"

"Wa'nt nothing to tell," he said, his voice barely above a whisper.

She hadn't meant for him to speak, hadn't really expected an answer, and shook her head. Dipping the washcloth in the cool water, she again wiped his face simply to have something to do. "Johnsie's gone for the doctor. You'll be fine, once he gets here." *And it better be soon.* She held his hand, straining for the sound of a car or a truck, anything that would signal the arrival of help.

Papa's eyes were closed now, and he looked so frail and old that she wanted to cry. How had this happened? He had told her it was nothing, a touch of gout, and even Mama had said it was nothing. If there was a complaint to be made, a ploy for sympathy to be had, Vada knew her mother would have used it. As she gazed down at her father, a sudden thought struck her. Did he even tell Mama? It would be like him not to, but surely, even if he hadn't, anyone with eyes could see that he was dying. *But I didn't. I didn't.*

As if to comfort her, Papa squeezed her hand. After a hitching breath, he pulled her closer and raised his head a bit. "Listen," he whispered.

"Don't talk, Papa," she said. "You got to save your strength."

He shook his head, pulled harder on her hand, until her face was so close to his that she could smell his fetid breath. "I done my best for you."

Vada fought the tears that clogged her throat and chest, finally bit the inside of her cheek once, hard, before she spoke. "I know, Papa," she said, and tried to free her hand so she could soothe him, get him to lie back. "Sh-h, now."

"No!" he rasped, jerking her hand in frustration. "Listen to me." He stopped, seemed to gather strength from somewhere. "I done—my best. It wasn't enough." He paused, licked his lips. "You do your best for Roxanne when I'm gone."

"Oh, Papa, you're not going anywhere," she cried desperately, but he had fallen back on the bed, chest rising and falling with great effort. His eyes were closed, and he looked even grayer, sicker than before.

The crunch of gravel came clearly through the window, and relief flooded her. Finally. She placed his hand on the bed, gently, and as she did, a thin stream of blood began to run from one nostril, becoming more profuse; she grabbed the washcloth, tried to staunch the flow, but it defeated her.

She heard a man's voice and ran out of the room. "Oh, God, Dr. Cavanaugh, hurry! Please!"she shouted. She came to a halt in the front room and looked around, confused. Dr. Cavanaugh wasn't there, just Mama and Harmon on the divan and, standing in the doorway, a short, wiry man with hair black as the cowboy hat he turned around and around in his hands.

Vada could tell Harmon wasn't pleased at the stranger's presence, but her mother clearly was. Her pale face had colored and she put a hand to her chest as if to calm her racing heart.

"Oh, Tandy, he's no better. No better at all," she said.

"Yes, ma'am, I's afraid of that when I seen Roxie and the boy in town just now." He finished the sentence by jutting his chin once, as if to loosen a tight shirt collar, although his own collar was not buttoned. He shook his head woefully. "That little Roxie was crying her eyes out," he said, and with barely a pause turned his light brown eyes on Vada. "You must be Roxie's sister."

"I guess I would be," she said, and moved as if to go back to Papa. Something stopped her though, something she could not quite put her finger on. Turning, she looked him over more closely—late twenties, early thirties, clean-shaven, boots so shiny she could've seen her face in them if she'd been close enough. What was Mama up to now? It was inconceivable that she could be trifling on Papa. Even Mama wouldn't do that.

"And you would be who?" Harmon asked, rising, and Vada'd never been so grateful to anyone in her life.

"Tandy Bigpond," the man said, looking up at Harmon. He offered the taller man his hand, but Harmon stared at it until finally, Bigpond returned it to the hat he still clutched with the other.

Mama touched a handkerchief to her mouth and cleared her throat. "Tandy is—is an old friend." Glancing from Vada to Harmon, she cleared her throat again. "I don't know what in the world I'd have done without him since your daddy took sick."

Vada flicked her eyes from Mama to Tandy and back again, then turned on her heel and went back to Papa's room. She made herself breathe deeply, in, out, in, out, and remembered Papa's words. *"You do your best for Roxanne."* She pushed it out of her mind for the present, because right then she had to do her best for Papa. Roxanne would have to wait her turn.

She sank down on the floor by her father, and took his hand. His chest barely rose and fell. Placing her lips to the hot hand, she shut her eyes to the sight of her big, strong Papa, lying there like he was dead. *Oh, Papa. Papa.* Every other thought gave way to those words and the despair in which they were shrouded.

Chapter 25

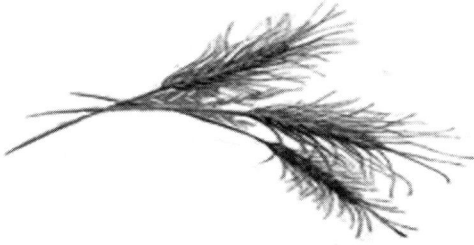

Vada remained at the hospital day and night, hopes temporarily buoyed when medication made the bleeding stop.

Dr. Cavanaugh had come in to her father's hospital room, listened to his chest and grunted. "He got blood in his urine yet?" Vada flushed. It was embarrassing enough to have to assist her father in relieving himself, but to have others know about it was worse.

Dr. Cavanaugh patted her shoulder. "It'll come. Don't you be scared when it does."

When he had gone, she sat by her daddy's bedside, his hand cold in hers, staring at the empty bed on the other side of the room. An elderly man had occupied at first, but he had been taken away, to surgery, Vada had presumed, and never returned. She had not asked Dr. Cavanaugh for particulars, but was grateful that Papa had the room to himself. She concentrated all her energy on him, somehow feeling if she could keep watch, Papa could not die. From time to time, he roused and looked at her, the ravages worked on him by the cancer—leukemia, Dr. Cavanaugh said—making him a stranger. He could no longer speak, and did not need to, for she knew what he wanted: *Mama*. She shook her head, the aching fullness in her chest and throat making speech nearly impossible for her as well.

"She—she's sick, Papa. Dr. Cavanaugh told her to stay in bed." In truth, the doctor had administered a shot to Mama when he had come to the house, and she had slept through the night with Johnsie and Roxanne on either side watching over her. When she awoke the next morning, she asked for Kenneth, and, told by the children that he had been gone by ambulance to Sapulpa, had refused to get up.

"If he can lay up in the bed, so can I," she had said, and that was that. She reigned over her court from the bedroom, demanding that she be brought meals in bed, expressing surprise that she managed to eat as much as she did. "I've never been able to keep anything on my stomach when my nerves is bothering me," she told Roxanne and Johnsie, but, as Johnsie reported to Vada, their mother had eaten "like she was going to the chair."

Nevertheless, both Johnsie and Roxanne came close to tears when they described her sobbing through the night, calling, "Kenneth" over and over.

Vada could not find it in her to feel either sympathy or forgiveness. *That crazy act might be good enough for Dr. Cavanaugh and a couple of young'uns, but it don't fool me.*

Vada refused to look after Mama, refused to leave her father even long enough to make a trip home to bathe. She knew her mother was furious, but she did not care. Her father would not die like he had lived, second fiddle to Mama. This time, it was all about him.

Harmon brought her a change of clothes, and she took a sponge bath, then came back into her father's room and handed Harmon the paper bag with her soiled things inside. He motioned to her father with his head. "He doing all right?"

She felt like rolling her eyes and stomping her feet, but she only poked him in the upper arm, urging him out, into the corridor. Closing the door behind her, she said, "No, he's not all right, Harmon. He's not a bit all right. Folks with cancer in their blood are funny like that."

"You don't have to take my head off. What you want me to say? 'Is he dead yet?'" At the sight of her face, he shut up. "All right. I'm sorry. I know this is hard on you."

"Did you go talk to Mama?" Vada pressed her lips together to keep from snapping at him when he took longer to answer than she liked.

"I did, and that Tandy fellow was there, waiting on her hand and foot."

Vada closed her eyes. *"Damn* her!" When she opened them, Harmon was staring at her as if she'd bitten the head off a live chicken. Taking a deep breath, she swallowed and shook her head briefly. "I don't have time to fool with him right now. Is Mama coming?"

"She ain't having none of it. She swears Kenneth ain't sick, and says if he ain't got to get up, she ain't got to either." He looked toward the ceiling, then back to Vada. "I don't have to tell you your mama is a few bricks shy of a load."

When did he get to be so stupid? "That's what she'd like everybody to believe. She's not crazy, though. She's afraid he'll die and she'll be there to feel it." She'd meant to say "see it," but as soon as the word "feel" came out, she knew it was the right one. Mama pushed down every feeling but anger, and seemed like she'd go any distance to keep a step ahead of her emotions. Vada hugged her midsection, felt the empty gnawing hunger, but knew that even if she could eat, food would not stop it. "If there's any unpleasantness, Mama don't want to be there, that's all."

Harmon sighed. "Well, that's a kind of craziness right there, ain't it? A person that ain't crazy'd be up here with her man, no matter how bad it got."

Vada half opened the door to her father's room, hesitated, then shut it and turned back to Harmon. "I want you to go back out there, take Cordell with you, and bring my mama back. I don't care how you do it, but get her up here."

"Aw, Vada, no." When she didn't reply, he tried again. "You ain't got to do this. It ain't no skin off your nose if she—"

She closed the door again and pushed Harmon a few feet further down the corridor. "You go in there and sit, then. Sit and look in my daddy's eyes every time he opens them, and tell him she's not here." The tears were so thick in her throat that the pressure made her ears hurt. "You go—you—you…" Her voice gave way and she inhaled, eyes shut, and tried to picture that big blackboard with the word "nothing" on it. This was why her mother refused to feel the things that hurt, the things that could not be dealt with by screaming. She opened her eyes. "Get my mama here, Harmon. You make her come." If it made Vada sick to be this weak, so out of control, how must it make Mama feel? She chewed the inside of her cheek and battled against any sympathy for Mama. If she hated it and she had to stand it, so did Mama. In the middle of this internal battle, she felt Harmon's arms around her, felt his hand rubbing circles on her tired, aching back, smoothing her hair, heard his voice, not exasperated, but soft and calm and reassuring, so un-Harmon-like that it was as if another man had taken over his body.

"All right. All right. I'll get her." He tipped her face up toward his. "You better quit chewing on yourself like that." He tapped one of her cheeks gently. "It don't do you no more good than screaming and playing crazy does your mama. You need to let your heart tend to business and give that jaw a rest."

She looked at him, wondering where she might find a heart that could stand such pain.

* * * * *

Papa had drifted in and out of consciousness for hours since Harmon left. Every time a nurse came in, Vada watched her warily, frightened of being given information she did not want. She was tired, so very tired, but she wanted to stay awake, convinced somehow that death could not take Papa as long as she remained alert, watchful. And she tried, she really did, but sometime after dark, with only the light from the hallway spilling through the doorway and the occasional sound of crepe soles whispering down the hall, she dozed in the vinyl chair next to his bed, still holding to his hand. Her mother's voice awakened her, not angry, as Vada had expected, but quavering, thin.

Mama stood in the door with Harmon, Roxanne, and Johnsie, hair disheveled and dress buttoned crookedly. Casting a look at her husband, she moved forward only when Vada held a hand out to her. Mouth working but sending no sound, she allowed Vada to take her hand, then allowed it to be placed in her husband's. Mama seemed rooted to the floor, but she took up his hand and held it in both her own. Vada moved to the other side of the bed, took her father's other hand, and sank into a straight chair. After a bit, her mother lowered herself into the vinyl one Vada had vacated, and Johnsie and Roxanne took up positions beside and behind her.

Vada silently thanked her lucky stars that Tandy whoever-he-was had not accompanied them. She could not have stood it right then. She glanced at Harmon and nodded, and he backed out the door, closing it softly, leaving them to their vigil.

She was in the field outside Bristow again, walking beside Papa as he plowed and told her about the wildflowers that grew there. "Them's everlastings, Sister," he told her when she held up a sweet william. "Them flowers is going to be here long years after we're gone." And in her dream, she stopped, bent in the field for something, maybe to remove a rock from her shoe, and when she looked up again, Papa was far away, across the field, walking faster and faster, and when she cried, "Papa, wait! Wait for me," he turned and waved, waved, waved until tears blinded her.

She jerked awake, heart pounding. Across the bed, Mama made a small sound, and when Vada looked at Papa, she saw the flecks of blood on his lips become pink foam, then a red stream running from his mouth. It was as if she'd been awakened just to witness this and the gurgling which began in his throat and chest, and Mama raising him upright to keep him from choking, because these and the scene that followed would be forever imprinted on her mind.

"Nurse!" Vada shouted. Papa's eyes moved wildly from her to Mama, and when he recognized Mama, he half lunged, half fell toward her. A spasm racked him, and a final torrent of blood rushed forth, covering the bedclothes and splattering everything in its path. He lay partially on his side, eyes on his wife. Slowly, shaking visibly, Mama pulled him toward her, cradling the upper half of his body in her arms, heedless of the blood.

"Kenneth," she said softly, smoothing back his thin, damp hair. "It's all right. I'm right here."

The nurse had arrived by then, but stopped at the foot of the bed, her round face flushed. Mama looked at her and shook her head. "He's fine. I got him." As Johnsie, Roxanne and Vada huddled on the other side of the bed, clinging to whatever part of Papa they could reach, life left his body, leaving his eyes open and empty, his mouth twisted in an almost-smile, while Mama shut her own eyes against the tears that ran down her face. "I got him," she whispered. "I got him."

Chapter 26

Mama took to her bed and would not be comforted, at least not by Vada. Every time Vada went to check on her, she found Tandy Bigpond sitting by Mama's bedside. He was obviously doing her fetching and carrying while Johnsie and Roxanne finished the last two weeks of school, and though he tried to make up to Vada, he disgusted her. Anybody that fond of Mama had to have a screw loose. Finally, Vada left them to it and stayed home herself. She slept little, ate little, and snapped at anyone who came near her. Lord, Lord, what was she going to do about Roxanne? *The last thing I need in this world is another young'un, and Roxanne*—she let the thought die.

"You just as well get over this," Harmon finally told her one night after they'd gone to bed. "Your daddy was out of his head when he said them things to you, about you taking care of your sister."

"He was sick, not crazy." She turned over, staring out the window at the hackberry tree.

"I say he was," Harmon insisted. "He knew your Mama better'n anybody, and he knew she wouldn't never stand for you butting in." He inhaled, then let out a noisy breath. "Besides that, he never come right out and said what he wanted you to do. Maybe he just wanted you to see she had somebody sympathetic around. I mean, he did marry you and Addy off."

"People learn from their mistakes, Harmon," she retorted. "Besides, he knew I was always going to be around." She paused, then continued. "He wanted me to see to it Mama didn't marry her off. It just makes sense." When Harmon did not answer she turned halfway over and elbowed him. "Can't you feature him learning from Addy dying?"

Harmon sighed. "I reckon." They were both silent for a few moments before he said, "You could pray about it."

She made a dismissive noise, then lay quietly for a bit, wondering what in the world she'd do with another teenager. The ones she had were bad enough. Even Dempsey from time to time defied her and Harmon, almost dared them to reprimand him. Vada always let Harmon deal with him, turning a blind eye whenever possible. The boy seemed to take everything she said so *seriously*.

"Well, what are you gonna do with her when you get her?"

Oh! How she hated that! He was always saying what she was thinking, not even giving her a chance to say it. "Leave me alone," she snapped, flopping onto her side. "I'm tired." She felt his eyes boring into her back, but refused to turn over. She wished she could lie there until hell froze over, until the mountains fell into the sea, until...Well, until she could make up her mind about what to do with Roxanne. *I don't need me no more kids. Not even one, and especially not one that looks like Roxanne.* She groaned at the thought of the possible complications.

Still, she could hear Papa's words, hear them as if he were sitting beside her. *"You do your best for Roxanne."* But Lord Jesus in a treehouse, she did not want to take on another child. She was tired of children at fourteen, and raising six had not yet made her any less tired. *Maybe Papa didn't mean for me to take Roxanne to raise. Maybe he meant for me to just keep an eye on her.* She thought about the possibility for several long moments, then rejected it. If that were the case she'd be watching Roxanne trot down the aisle with somebody, anybody Mama could palm her off on. She couldn't let that happen. *Even if Papa hadn't told me to take care of her, I couldn't let it happen.* Frustrated at the box she felt herself in, she turned over and punched her pillow hard a few times before burying her face in it. *Damn!*

* * * * *

Vada was in no better humor the next day when Tandy Bigpond showed up on the front porch. She knew as soon as she saw him exactly what he wanted, and what Mama had been up to. *That battle-axe!* She allowed him only a few steps into the living room, determined to let him have his say and be rid of him once and for all.

Every other sentence, he jutted his chin at her, loosening a collar not buttoned, and twisting the black hat in his hands. "I wanted you to know I'm right sorry about your daddy. I know he set a store by you, was real proud of you. Him and your mama both." Vada let the lie pass, and the man pressed on. "The thing is, me and your mama, we been talking about—about me and

Roxanne, you know, about how I might start to calling on her before too long." He jutted his chin out. "I know what you must be thinking, that I'm some older than Roxanne, but I aim to take real good care of her. I sure do." He licked his lips, a gesture that sent disgust coursing through Vada. He seemed to be waiting for her to say something, and when she did not he stammered ahead. "I don't want no trouble with her kinfolk, and being you're the main one, 'side from Est—your mama, I figured you'd be the first one to talk to. After her, I mean." A bead of sweat began a slow amble from his temple down the side of his face.

Vada watched the slow progress of that sweat bead while inside her a mounting pressure threatened to stop her breath.

"Look, Mr. Bigpond," she began, but he cut her off.

"Tandy," he said, voice pleading. "Call me Tandy. Don't nobody call me Mr. Bigpond." He grinned lopsidedly, revealing a missing upper incisor. "I 'spect to turn around and see my daddy, you say 'Mr. Bigpond'."

"Mr. Bigpond," she repeated. "There's no telling what my mama told you, but Roxanne is only fourteen years old. I don't know how old you are—" She held up her hand as he started to stay something. "Let me finish. I don't know how old you are, and it don't matter. You're right, you're way and gone too old to be sniffing around after my sister."

He looked at her sadly. "Your mama said you wasn't likely to approve, but I like to lay my cards on the table, I sure do. I don't like to go sneaking around behind—"

"Mama," Dempsey's voice floated into the room, and he followed it. "Mama, I can't find my—" He stopped a few steps onto the front room linoleum, his lanky frame, so like his daddy's, filling the doorway. He looked at Vada, then the visitor. "Never mind," he said, and turned back the way he'd come. "Pa!" Vada heard him scream, and she almost wanted to scream herself as his footsteps receded down the hallway, through the kitchen, and out the back.

Vada motioned with her head toward the door. "You better get on out of here. My old man is nobody to fool with when he gets mad."

"Ain't none of this fixing to happen till she finishes ninth grade, come June. I done—"

Vada was suddenly as angry as she could ever remember being, not just at him but at everybody that made this conversation necessary. She heard Harmon's heavy footsteps moving more quickly than usual as she shoved Tandy Bigpond toward the front door. "It's not going to happen at all. Now you get out. Just get out. And don't come around this place or my mama's house no more." She pushed him out onto the porch, and despite the unseasonable heat, closed the door on him. Just as she did, Harmon loomed in the doorway between the front room and hallway.

"Dempsey said there was somebody here—should have knowed it was that damned squirrelly little Indian. I'll tear him a new one," he said, and moved toward Vada, whose back was still against the door.

"He's gone. He's probably running back out to Mama's to tattle on me." The sound of an engine starting penetrated the room, and Vada pulled back the curtain to reveal a turquoise Pontiac with huge tail fins moving slowly away from the curb. She knew what she had to do, but it sure wasn't going to be easy. Removing her apron, she threw it on the couch. "Come on, Harmon. I'm going out there."

Harmon groaned as if her words gave him a physical pain. "Aw, not now. Let's don't do that. Your mama is still grieving over—"

Vada spun from where she stood at the front door. "Harmon Priddy, if you don't get in that truck, her grieving's nothing compared to what you're going to be feeling. My daddy trusted me to look after my sister, and I aim to do it." The look on his face frightened her, even in her state, and she ran back and grabbed his hand, pulling him toward the door as Margaret or Jacob might. "Please, Har. I don't want to do it no more than you do, but I got to." At first he stood rigidly, and she felt hot tears well in her eyes. "I can't lose another sister. Please."

"Aw, Vada. Surely your ma ain't planning nothing right yet."

"But she *is*. She's going to turn Roxie over to that—that weasel." She tugged his hand again. "You've seen how fast the woman can move—like a tornado on roller skates. Please take me to see her."

Finally, he let her pull him out to the truck as he fished in his overall pocket for his keys, grumbling all the way.

* * * * *

They'd driven almost all the way to Mama's before Harmon spoke again. "It wasn't your fault, you know."

She clutched one hand with the other and stared straight ahead, her body slightly forward as if she could get there faster that way. "What?" she asked, never taking her eyes from the road.

He cleared his throat and spat out the window, looking at her from the corner of his eye.

"I saw you," she said. "Least you could do is stop that when you got back on the cigarettes."

"It ain't that easy, and don't change the subject."

She leveled a long look at him. "I'm not the one that spit."

"Spitting ain't changing the subject. Now listen to me." He spat out the window again, almost defiantly, before he resumed. "You couldn't have done anything about it if you'd tried."

"About what?" She stared at her whitened knuckles now as she sought to shut him up by forcing a choice between that and repeating himself, which he loathed.

"Aw, you. You know damn well what I'm talking about. Addy. You couldn't have done a thing about Addy dying."

She looked at him. "I know that." From his look she knew he didn't believe her, but that couldn't be helped. "I'm not gonna let what happened to her happen to Roxanne."

They rode in silence for a few minutes until Harmon cleared his throat again. "Not everybody that gets married dies."

"They might just as damn well," she snapped.

"Well, thank you, Miss Vada," Harmon said, mouth twisting wryly.

"I didn't mean it that way, and you know it. But you can't think getting married is the best thing that can happen to a girl Roxanne's age." When he didn't reply, she turned to face him fully, her back against the door, the handle poking her. "Can you?"

He shifted, glanced at her, then away. "She's older than you was when we got married." He paused, then continued. "A woman don't get married, what'll she do? Your mama got money to send Roxanne to some college, OU or someplace?"

Vada felt a catch in her throat, then an ache as if someone had punched her. There had to be more to a woman's life. She took a deep breath, tried to speak softly though she wanted to scream. "I don't know about college. But she ought to be able to finish high school, don't you think?"

"I guess." He cleared his throat and spat out the window. "Still, you don't know. Maybe your mama ain't even got the money to keep Roxanne till she graduates. Your daddy couldn't have left her much."

"Then I'll keep her," Vada snapped, knowing even as she said the words that no matter how little money Mama might have, she had more to spare than the Priddys did. "What about Nelda?"

He swerved to miss a rut in the road, hit a bigger one, and looked at her. "What about her?"

Vada shrugged. "She'll soon be twenty. You want her to haul off and get married? Or what about Margaret? Here she is almost darn near nine years old and we haven't even got her a hope chest started."

"All right, all right. You don't have to be a smart aleck about it. I get your point. But they're gonna have to do it some day."

"Not if I can help it, at least not till they're old enough to know if they want to or not," Vada retorted, folding her arms over her chest to finish the ride.

* * * * *

A shiny, robin's-egg blue pickup sat at the edge of the yard when Vada and Harmon drove up. An old yellow tomcat perched on the porch railing stopped the furious licking of one paw to glare at them but quickly lost interest and returned to his paw.

Vada slid from the truck, smoothing her dress over her hips and stomach, but Harmon stayed put, leaned both forearms on the steering wheel, and began rolling a cigarette. "I don't reckon I could wait here." He didn't look at her.

She slammed the door. "I don't reckon." Staring through the window at him, she tapped her foot and watched as he ever so methodically finished and lit the roll-your-own.

Finally, he too exited the truck and made a sweeping gesture toward the house. "You first. I ain't gonna get between you and your mama."

Vada wished somebody would, because she knew what she was about to do would infuriate Mama. She stepped up to the screen door and peered in. Nobody. Rapping twice, she pulled it open. "Anybody home? Mama? Roxanne?" Voices came from the kitchen and she went toward the sound, followed by Harmon.

"Well, hey, Vada." Johnsie's voice seemed to have deepened even since the last time Vada had seen him.

Mama and Roxanne sat on the other side of the table, but Roxanne jumped up and ran around to hug Vada. "I didn't know you were coming!" She punched Harmon in the arm. "Don't you ever have to go to work no more?" He grinned at her, but his answer was lost in Mama's sudden bustling about.

"You all want some coffee?" Mama asked from the stove. "Or I got tea." She looked pale, but had apparently eaten a good dinner, for the plate she'd abandoned held the remains of what looked like a meal of brown beans, cornbread, and fried potatoes.

Ignoring Mama's question, Vada asked one of her own. "Whose truck?"

"Truck?" Mama echoed, flushing.

"Isn't it swell?" Johnsie burst out. "Tandy give it—"

"Get out of here, boy," Mama snapped at him. "Nobody asked for your two-cents' worth." She went back to where she'd been sitting and sank down on the wooden ladder-back chair. "You too, Roxanne."

"But Mama," Roxanne began. "I didn't do—"

"Get out!" shrieked Mama, half rising. "Don't make me have to tell you again. You're not too big to whip."

Both children trudged from the room, and Harmon edged after them. "I'll go visit with them a spell."

Coward, she thought, but nodded. When they were alone, she looked at her mother for so long that Mama began to fidget, first with her hair then her dress bodice.

"Mercy sakes, girl, what are you staring at? I grow two heads all of a sudden?"

It took Vada a moment to find her voice, and when she did, she blurted, "What'd you do? Trade Roxanne for that truck out yonder?"

Mama made a motion as if shaking a headful of hair back from her face, even though her own heavy tresses were pinned into an enormous bun atop her head. "I knew you'd go plumb nuts one of these days and you finally done it."

Vada took a deep breath. "Mama, I know what you're up to."

Mama put on an unconvincing act of confusion. "What I'm up to?"

Vada slapped the table with the palm of her hand. "Can we for once talk honestly?"

"Honestly?" Mama's eyes were big and round now.

Vada had to get this over with. "I'm taking Roxanne home with me." She involuntarily cringed away from her mother as if in fear of being hit.

Instead, Mama sucked in her breath and her eyes filled. "I don't understand you. Roxanne and Johnsie are all I got now. Can't you leave me—"

Vada steeled herself, knowing tears were only a prelude to the rage that would eventually come. She stood. "I know what you're up to with Roxanne, and I'm not going to stand for it. I'm taking her out of here today and I don't want that Tandy fellow coming anywhere near her." Vada's insides quivered but she held her mother's gaze.

"You've got no heart, girl, you know that?" Mama rose to her feet, visibly trembling, but didn't move forward. She leaned heavily on the table, breathing hard.

Vada laughed, but there was no humor in it. "This isn't about having a heart. It's about having common sense. You married me off, and Addy, and you're trying to do the same to Roxanne. I'm not having it." Vada backed out of the room before turning and hurrying toward the porch, from which she heard the voices of Harmon and Johnsie.

"Lavada June," Mama shrieked from the kitchen. "Don't make me come after you!"

The words followed Vada and made her feel 14 again, hiding in the fields behind the house, but now she didn't have Addy to help and protect her. Addy had always been the strong one, the one who stood up to Mama no matter how the woman had raged and threatened. *Now it's just me. But I'm leaving here with Roxie if it harelips every dog in Europe.*

"Where's Roxanne?" she asked before Harmon had a chance to say anything.

He motioned over his shoulder. "Out yonder in the tree swing, I reckon. She was a minute ago."

The swing was blocked by the pale blue pickup and a small outbuilding, but Vada could hear the elm branch's familiar *scr-e-e-e* as Roxanne swung herself. She heard Johnsie's voice behind her.

"What's happening? We don't have to give the truck back do we?" Before the words were completely out she heard her mother's angry voice, but she ignored Mama just as she ignored Johnsie and rounded the corner of the small structure. She saw Roxanne in the swing, feet reaching for the sky, eyes closed, head thrown back so that the lowest point of each leisurely arch brought her long, tawny hair almost to the ground.

"Roxie, honey?"

Roxanne opened her eyes slowly and looked at Vada sideways, then closed them again, a slight smile curving her lips. For a moment even Vada could not believe that this was an innocent 14-year-old, but she had only a moment to contemplate the fact before she heard Mama behind her arguing with Harmon, and urgency seized her.

"Stop the swing, honey."

Roxanne opened her eyes again, a slight frown making a crease between her eyes. Dragging her feet, she seemed to just now hear Mama screaming in the background.

"—my daughter, and I do with her as I see fit," she was shouting over Harmon's low rumble.

"What's wrong?" she asked.

Vada ignored the question. "Come on, honey. You're going to come stay with me a while."

"I am? Did Mama say okay?" Mama's voice grew sharply shriller and Roxanne grimaced. "I guess not, huh?"

Vada took her arm. "It doesn't matter. You're coming." She pulled Roxanne toward their truck with one hand and motioned to Harmon with the other.

"Har, let's go."

"But I need my stuff," the girl said. "I need clothes. And my—"

"Vada!" shouted Mama as she followed Harmon to the pickup. "Don't you do it. You think you're so smart, but you're never here. You don't know half of what goes on around here, don't know how I struggle to take care of this place, these young'uns."

Vada shoved Roxanne into the old truck and got in, slamming the door as Mama ran panting up to it. "I don't have to be here to know what goes on."

"You'll rue this day, girl." Mama's full lips twisted into a snarl as she snatched at Vada's arm through the window, grabbing and twisting the skin until Vada screamed and slapped at the pinching fingers.

"Quit it! Get your hands off me, Mama."

Mama hung on. "I'll have the law on you. I will, you mess with me."

Vada grabbed one of her mother's fingers and pushed it back as far as it would go. "You do that, Mama," she said through clenched teeth. "You do that and see what I do to you. You won't be able to hold your head up in this county."

Mama grimaced, finally relinquishing Vada's arm. Angry red marks stood out, and Vada looked from them to her mother. "I'll tell everybody what you're really like, Mama."

"Hey, now," Harmon said. "You're upsetting the girl here."

Vada became aware of Roxanne sniffling beside her. The truck began to move, leaving Mama and Johnsie standing side by side behind the blue pickup. Vada saw her mother's mouth move, but could not hear her over the roar of the engine. She sank back, thankful to be away, and put her arm around Roxanne.

"You okay, sugar?"

Roxanne's hazel eyes, fringed with black lashes wet with tears, were frightened, but she nodded before turning to look out the rear window at her mother, then back to Vada. "She's going to be real mad."

Harmon snorted and struck a match with his thumbnail. "I'd say she's near as mad as she's gonna get." When he had the cigarette going, he canted his eyes at Vada. "I ain't never seen you act quite that way."

"I don't guess I ever did before," she replied, and only then realized how badly she was trembling and how frightened of Mama she had been.

"You acted like you was rescuing me or something," Roxanne said, and laughed a shaky, uncertain laugh.

It was Vada's turn to laugh uncertainly. "I wouldn't call it a rescue," she said, and lapsed into a silence that the three occupied all the way home.

Chapter 27

W hat Vada thought about on the way home was what she was going to do with Roxanne now that she had her. *We don't even have money to take care of our own young'uns, let alone another.* In her blind anger and determination to thwart Mama, she had not considered anything past removing Roxanne from Bristow. Now she and the girl stood in the middle of the front room, accompanied by Dempsey, Jacob, Cordell, Gerald, Margaret and Nelda. Miz Priddy had come in just long enough to *tsk* over the story of the rescue breathlessly reported by Roxanne.

"Where's she gonna sleep?" Nelda asked. "We don't even have room for all of us."

"Maybe we can get some bunk beds like Mena has," said Margaret. "Then Nelda can have her own bed, and I can have the top bunk, and Roxanne can—"

"We're not getting any bunk beds," Vada snapped, unnerved by the growing feeling that she had made a poor decision in bringing Roxanne home. She not only felt unable to cope with another teenager, she didn't even have a place to put another child. "We'll just have to manage," she said. "You three girls can share a room. It'll be fun."

Margaret and Nelda exchanged looks that said it would be anything but, then questioned Roxanne. "You don't wet the bed, do you?" asked Margaret.

Roxanne, who had been perched on the edge of the divan twirling a piece of hair around her forefinger, looked at Vada. "Is she joking?"

Margaret didn't give Vada time to answer. "Well, Gerald does, and you're not very much older than—"

"You creep!" Gerald squealed, lunging at his younger sister. "Mama said you's to quit telling everybody that!"

"He hit me!" cried Margaret, running at him and with a hand already drawn back to hit him.

"Stop it, now." Vada grabbed Margaret's hand, but Margaret jerked away from her and went for Gerald.

He ducked away from her then whirled, slapping her again. Now the fight was on, and in the midst of the melee, Vada heard pounding on the front door.

Jesus in a treehouse! Mama's got the police after me! But when she opened the door, she saw not a uniformed officer, but Mama herself, accompanied by Tandy Bigpond, his long face even longer and sadder than usual.

Vada groaned inwardly. Stepping away from the doorway, she motioned them in. All the children had suddenly become quiet, and the room was so silent she could hear the popping of Mama's knee as she stepped inside. Vada motioned with her head toward the back of the house and gave Nelda a little push. "You all go on back yonder. I got to talk to Mama."

"Hey, Roxanne," Dempsey said, his voice shy. "There's some kittens over at Mr. Gilmartin's. You want me to show you?"

"Not now, Dempsey," Vada told him. "She needs to stay here."

"Can I stay, too?"

"No! You can't stay. Now get out of here, all of you. I don't want to have to tell you again."

"But Mama," Dempsey began.

"Just get out of here!"

Dempsey gave her a mournful look, not yet moving, and Vada turned on Nelda. "You, too. Get on, now. I don't need no help from you."

Nelda rolled her eyes again. "All *right*. You don't have to get hateful. I have to go to work anyway." She, Margaret, and Dempsey moved off down the hallway where Gerald and had already disappeared.

"And no fighting!" Vada screamed.

When they were out of earshot, she turned to see Mama and Tandy standing where they'd entered. Roxanne hovered halfway between Mama and Vada, and Tandy Bigpond watched the girl with undisguised longing.

"I come to get my daughter," Mama said, and folded her arms over her midsection, purse hanging from the crook of her arm. "Tandy's here to see to it," she added.

"Well, now, Esther, I don't want to cause no trouble," he began, but Mama shot him a look that would have withered a concrete block.

"You'll do what I say you'll do," Mama said, and the slight man drew back as if she'd spit at him. Mama reached out and pulled Roxanne to her. "And you. You stay right here by me."

"Now you looky here," Tandy started, but the front door opened and in walked Harmon, cigarette hanging from his mouth.

He removed it and picked a piece of tobacco from his lip. "I think you all need to get back in that fancy vehicle out there and get on down the road," he said. Mama opened her mouth but he held his hand up. "Esther Louise, you got nothing to say that I want to hear. But I bet I know one or two stories on you that'd make mighty interesting gossip if they was to get out."

Mama paled. "You do not," she said, but she sounded unsure.

Harmon shrugged. "Try me." Taking a drag from the cigarette, he blew the smoke upward and bared his little teeth at her.

Mama frowned, and Vada could tell the woman was torn, and might now be at her most vulnerable. "I wouldn't test him, Mama."

Her mother hesitated, giving Harmon a look that Vada was glad was not directed her way. Roxanne must have felt her mother's sudden disadvantage too, for she pulled her arm from the woman's grasp, and sidled toward the hallway.

"Can I go now?" she asked, and as soon as Vada nodded, the girl spun and ran until she slammed the back door.

Sniffing, Mama tossed her head and moved to the divan, where she perched on its edge, gripping the pocketbook in her lap. Vada, engrossed in arranging her thoughts, didn't notice the departure of the two men, but when she next looked up, they were gone. She reached for one of Mama's hands, tried to pry it from the purse.

"Don't you touch me," Mama said, releasing the bag long enough to slap at Vada's.

Vada laced her fingers together in her lap and took a deep breath. "OK, Mama. You know and I know Roxanne's not fit to be nobody's wife—"

"Wife!" Mama said, tittering. "Who's gonna be marrying her?"

Vada managed not to roll her eyes. "You know that's why Tandy Bigpond is hanging around her."

Mama sniffed. "I never told him he could do any such thing."

"Well, then, I guess if you don't have a husband lined up for her, you won't mind her staying here for a while."

For a moment Mama looked like a rat in a trap, but finally she let out a long sigh.

"I guess it wouldn't hurt." She looked at Vada. "But it's sure not because of anything you or that husband of yours might tell people." She removed a folded fan from her purse and flipped it open, fanning rapidly. "Not that anybody would believe anything you might say about me anyway. My life is proof that I take care of my own. And I was a good wife to your daddy, anybody would tell you that."

Vada sat before her mother, a living example of how the woman ran her life, and let the words go in one ear and out the other. *You want something from Mama, you don't rattle her cage while she's beating her chest.* What was important was that her mother had given in.

Later that night, Vada lay in the still house and heard giggling coming from the room occupied by Nelda, Margaret, and Roxanne. She wanted to smile at the sound of girls who were being girls rather than preparing to be wives or to raise someone's children, but she remembered that sloe-eyed, sidelong look Roxanne had directed at her from the tree swing back at Mama's. She hoped that she had not made a mistake in bringing the girl there, but somehow, she felt she had done the right thing. How could it be a mistake if she kept Roxanne safe another few years?

Chapter 28

W hen school started, Roxanne and Dempsey set off together every morning, Margaret, Gerald, and Jacob tagging along. Dempsey and Roxanne seemed to have developed a friendship, or at least an alliance, against everyone else, and Vada was just relieved Dempsey wasn't jealous. The boy was a trial sometime, but at least he wasn't as clinging as he had been, and for that Vada was grateful.

She watched them as they went down the hill the first morning, saw how Roxanne's hip occasionally bumped Dempsey's, how Dempsey's hand went to the small of her back, sometimes lingering there, how even though the other three children danced around them, running forward and coming back, the two seemed alone. As they topped the hill, Vada felt a twinge of something—not alarm, exactly, nothing so strong as that—but maybe concern. *They're good kids, both of them.* But even as that thought occurred to her, an image of Roxanne appeared: the way the girl carried herself—hips swaying, breasts straining whatever she wore, and the way she had of running her fingers through her hair from right front diagonally across her head. Dozens of times a day, she brushed the heavy mane to the left and away from her face, only to have it fall across her face again, giving her a disheveled, just-tumbled-out-of-bed look.

"She's going to be trouble."

Miz Priddy's voice startled Vada—she hadn't even realized the woman was there. "Lordy, you scared the life out of me!" She gave the old woman a playful slap on the shoulder, and then looked back to where the children were disappearing over the crest of the hill.

"But she is," Miz Priddy insisted.

In spite of her own niggling concern, Vada shook her head. "No more than any other young'un," she said. She hoped she didn't have to eat those words.

* * * * *

The next morning, she stood at the sink and looked out at the hazy, almost white sky. It was September and seemed hotter than it had in July, even with the clouds. She thought about going outside, working in the yard a while, but the idea did not appeal to her—nor did any other. It was as if getting Roxanne moved in and all the children settled was the climax to something, and everything after was a long, slow descent into—into nothing, that thing she wished for so fervently after Addy's death. Only now it did not seem like an escape, but something to be escaped. *Has my life always been so empty?* She dropped into a chair at the table and put her face in her hands. *Lordy me! There's got to be more than this. There's got to be.*

But the following two months seemed to prove her wrong; they were nearly as bad as those following Addy's death. Now, as then, Vada moved about with a heaviness that would not lessen. There was nowhere she wanted to go and nothing she wanted to do. Harmon even had people at the church praying for her, something that would have infuriated her a year ago. Now, when he told her they'd had an altar prayer especially for "whatever it is that ails you," she simply stared at him. She didn't even have the energy to get mad, and when he asked her to go with him to a Sunday night fellowship, she actually consented; the event was tedious and people hovered around her until Vada claimed a sick headache and made Harmon take her home. Harmon said nothing, just sighed and drove her to the house as if this were another in a long line of burdens she'd forced him to carry.

And the children hardly seemed to know she was alive. Nelda had just started attending respiratory therapy school, and between school, work, and her boyfriend, Vada saw her mostly coming and going. Cordell was always working or with Jerri Dawn Puckett, and Vada expected they'd marry before long. Margaret had made Roxanne her idol and couldn't be enough like her; Roxanne had become secretive and sly, close-mouthed, talking only to Margaret and sometimes Nelda, mooning around, probably over some boy or other; Dempsey either tagged after Roxanne or hung around the house, bouncing a basketball against the back side of it until Vada thought she'd scream. Even Jacob managed to irritate her, following Gerald and the rest of the children around and tattling on them.

On a day when she had not even bothered to get dressed, she sat at the kitchen table, hands wrapped around a cup of coffee, and glumly considered what it would take to get through the remainder of the dreary day. She looked up when Miz Priddy entered the room with a handful of just-delivered mail.

"We get more trash in the mailbox, I'll swan," the old lady said, and held up a circular. "What in the world they think we're gonna do with horse feed? I'll vow, that Cordell eats like a horse sometimes, and Gerald gets to smelling like one, but we ain't—" She broke off as she tried to catch one flyer, brown and of stiffer paper than the rest, that slipped from the bunch and fell to the floor.

"I'll get it," Vada said, and leaned to pick it up. It was a list of perhaps a dozen offerings from the local extension service, and she started to toss it back to her mother-in-law when something caught her eye. *Greenhouse Gardening at Home.* She felt a stirring of interest. Six dollars was all it cost. *Six dollars!* She'd never had six dollars to spend on herself in her whole life. *Bet Harmon gives that much to them Holy Rollers out there in Kellyville every week.*

"Vada, are you listening to me?"

Vada looked up, startled to see Miz Priddy still there.

The old lady shook her head and tossed the rest of the mail into the trash. "You wasn't. Don't nobody listen to nobody else 'round here, and that's a fact." She held her hand out for the circular in Vada's hand. "Here. I'll throw that away."

Vada stuck it in her housecoat pocket. "No. I want to keep this one a bit."

Miz Priddy shrugged. "Suit yourself," she said, but clearly thought Vada's behavior peculiar.

Vada paid no attention. She went to the sink and fingered the green, segmented leaves of the Christmas cactus that sat above it on the window sill. The plant's claw-like prongs waved, blind and grasping, in the wake of any air movement. But while its lush green seemed healthy, it had never bloomed. Instead, it sat in the window full of a kind of robust potential never fulfilled.

Realizing she had somehow failed with the plant, Vada wondered if she weren't like that cactus: strong and healthy-looking, but never actually doing anything. *Almost thirty years old, and what have I got to show for myself? Not a thing.* She felt immediately guilty. She had her kids. Raising her children had been the only thing in her life that had made her feel productive, and she'd done that mostly under duress. But now they hardly needed her. They all had their own friends, their own activities, and almost the only time they were all together was at meals.

Sighing, she moved back to the table and dropped into a chair, pulling the circular from her pocket and smoothing the wrinkles. Of course, this didn't look like the kind of course where she would learn anything about houseplants, but if this expert knew so much about growing things year round, maybe he'd know something about a plant that was supposed to bloom in the winter. She gazed at the words on the stiff brown paper. She had to do something. Miz Priddy had tried to teach her to crochet, finally giving up when they were mutually frustrated. While yardwork was, in its own way, fulfilling, there was a certain sadness that set in when everything she'd done through the spring and summer faded away in the winter. Besides, she felt herself a run-of-the-mill gardener, having done nothing that anyone with a mower and a hoe couldn't have accomplished. Her yard was striking mainly because of her precise planning, mowing, and edging that contrasted sharply with most of her neighbors' haphazard methods. Even if she were to enter the Garden Club competition as the mailman had urged, she would no more win than she would fly to the moon, and she knew it.

She understood now why so many women had babies born long after the rest of the children had grown, but the thought evoked a shudder. *Having a young'un to feel like I'm worth something! Might as well shoot myself.* To stay sane, she had to find something to occupy her that didn't involve childbirth or needlework. It didn't seem fair. Harmon could go out and work and when he wasn't working he could head for the pool hall if he wanted to, or go fishing, or even hunting, but for a woman it was different. She had to have a reason to leave the house, had to be improving life for her family or her husband. Fingering the edges of the brochure in front of her, she looked at the cactus squatting on the windowsill. *Who says getting me out of the house won't improve the life of this family? It's all in the way you tell the tale.* Standing, she stuffed the circular into her pocket and went to get dressed.

* * * * *

"Vada, what you doing, girl?"

She spun in place, gasped, and almost dropped the clay pot she held. "Harmon Priddy, forevermore! Don't you know better than to sneak up on a person? You nearly scared the life out of me."

He removed his hat, tossed it on top the ice box and went to the sink. Over the sound of running water, he called, "If I got to wait till you get done mooning over that plant, I'll be standing here half the night. What is it this time? Got the mealy-bugs?"

She leaned past him to position the Christmas cactus in the window over the battered cast-iron sink. Fingering the long, segmented leaves, Vada sighed. "I was wondering why it don't bloom."

"You've had it in damn near every window in the house. If it's supposed to

167

put on flowers and it don't, why don't you get rid of it?"

"Because I don't get rid of everything that don't suit me." The words surprised her and she hurried to the back door as if to escape them. That was no way to start. Banging the screen open, she called, "Supper's on. Y'all come and wash up. Your daddy's ready to eat." She paused and looked at her youngest in dismay. "Jacob, get out of that mud right now. And you in your school clothes too. Get in here and get them changed."

"I got to finish making this mountain so I can have a landslide."

"Do what I said!" she screamed. His thin face fell, and she could've kicked herself. Maybe she wasn't even a decent mother. *And maybe I just need to get out of this house.*

Turning back to the kitchen, she nearly ran over Harmon. "Jesus in a treehouse. I can't even walk in here without stepping on somebody."

"Why you always got to be taking the Lord's name in vain?"

"Does somebody being in a treehouse make him a bad person, Harmon?" Vada's heart sank at Harmon's look, a combination of disapproval and disappointment. She sighed. "I'm sorry. I am. I'm—I don't know, nervous." She was, too, and it took all the effort she could muster snap at him again for moving too slowly. The table was already set, and she started buttering bread for the children as soon as she could get around him.

"It ain't good for nothing," he said, sounding like she'd already argued him to the end of his patience.

"What's not good for nothing?" She dropped both the knife and the bread she was buttering and rubbed her forehead. She'd troubled herself to cook the man a special dinner, something besides beans or oxtail stew, and in the middle of the week at that, and he was going to ruin everything.

"That plant."

She turned on him. "What plant?" When he looked at her as if she had two heads, she remembered that they had been discussing the Christmas cactus. "It's good for something. It's good for me, Harmon. I like it, all right? And it will bloom. Sooner or later, that blasted plant will bloom."

He made a wry face. "If it ain't done it yet…" He let the words trail off as if the answer should be obvious.

Oh, *why* wouldn't he let her alone? He was going to keep pushing her until she said something they would both regret, something no number of apologies would remedy. She sucked in a sharp retort. If she fought with Harmon, she could forget about taking the class.

He kept at her, though. "I don't know why you don't make you a vegetable garden like a normal person, 'stead of always trying to grow flowers and such." He shook his head. "Flowers in the house, at that."

"I know I ought to. I never had any luck growing vegetables. Don't you remember the last time I tried? Didn't get hardly nothing out of it. Few measly tomatoes." She poured gravy into a bowl and put it on the table, trying to sound casual. "Fact is, Harmon, I been thinking about that very thing. Growing me a garden. A good one that will save us money." She paused to let that sink in before continuing. "One I could grow all year round."

Harmon dried his hands and tossed the tea towel to the cabinet, rubbing the back of his neck and rotating it as if it were stiff. He patted her on the shoulder. "All year round, huh? Somebody gonna show you how to import sunshine? Pipe it in from California?" Without waiting for an answer, he added, "Where's Ma?"

Vada placed a glass of tea in front of him, a little harder than she meant to. "Sitting with Miz Satterwhite. Been having one of her spells again, and her daughter can't come." Moving back to the kitchen door, she thrust the screen open. "I'm not telling you again," she shouted. "Your daddy's ready to eat." Within seconds, the kids clomped up the back steps. Jacob slid into a chair while Margaret's shrill voice challenged Gerald's froggy one.

"You don't even have big shoulders. You can't play football unless you got great big shoulders like—like—a football player," she said.

"They're not born with 'em." Gerald's overalls hung by one strap, grass-stains marking both patched knees. He rolled his dark eyes at the rest of those in the room. "She's about half stupid," he said, deftly ducking a slap from his sister.

Vada looked at the assembled family. Cordell was eating with Jeri Dawn's family and Nelda was working, but Roxanne and Dempsey ought to be here.

"Jacob, go find Dempsey and Roxanne," Vada said.

Gerald continued his revelation of his sister's ignorance. "She thinks Johnny Unitas and them was born with great big shoulders." He shoved her lightly. "How you think they got out of their mamas if they's that big, stupid? You reckon they—"

"Gerald." Harmon's dead level voice stopped the boy in his tracks. Gerald sneaked a look at his daddy then away, his olive complexion deepening. Margaret's eyes widened in a combination of fear and anticipation, and Vada held her breath. Suddenly the silence was broken by the harsh shriek of swollen wood—instantly identifiable as the door to the girls' room—then a flurry of voices, and Jacob flew back into the room, color high.

"Mama, they was in there kissing. I seen 'em."

Chapter 29

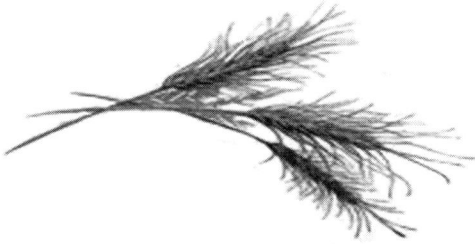

The whole room seemed to hold its breath as Dempsey strode in, his usually placid face mottled. "We was *not* kissing! Can't we even close a door without—"

Roxanne slunk in silently, shooting a glance at Vada, and Vada knew at once that Jacob had told the truth. After one look at Harmon's darkening face she grabbed both Roxanne and Dempsey by an arm. "In the front room. Now!" When Harmon started to rise, Vada put her hand on his chest. "I'll do it. I can take care of it."

"I knew this would happen," he said.

She rolled her eyes, feigned a lack of concern. "I doubt much happened, Harmon. Just stay here, get you some supper. I made chicken-fried steak, special." He looked as if he would protest, but finally relaxed into his chair.

In the front room, Roxanne sat on one end of the divan, her shoulders hunched as she inspected her finger tips, while Dempsey stood at the window, hands jammed into the pockets of his jeans. "What do you two think you're up to?" Vada asked.

Roxanne looked up, all innocence. "We was just doing our homework." That said, she began to nibble a cuticle, watching Vada.

Vada looked at her sister, studying her long enough that it should have made Roxanne nervous, but if it did, the girl hid it well.

"Dempsey?" Vada said.

"What?" He still stared out the window.

"Look at me." He turned around, but his gaze was directed above and to the right of her head. "I said, look at me." Finally, with what appeared to be great effort, he did. His usually clear, light brown eyes were opaque, his lips set in a sullen line. "What were you doing in there?" she asked. His eyes slid away again.

"Nothing." He studied a spot of faded linoleum near her feet.

Something on his neck, visible above the slightly frayed shirt collar, caught Vada's eye, and before he could fend her off, she covered the distance between them and pulled at his collar. "That sure looks like something to me," she said. "Lord almighty, Dempsey!"

He jerked away from her, covering the hickey on his neck. "Leave me alone, Mama."

Vada stood in the middle of the floor, breathing hard, looking from one to the other. "You," she said to Roxanne. "You think I brought you here to see you doing such as this? You want to end up pre—in the family way, and you not even sixteen? That what you want?"

"But Vada—"

"But nothing! Get in there and eat your dinner then get yourself to that bedroom and stay there."

"I'm not hungry," she huffed. With a last look at Dempsey and a great rolling of eyes, Roxanne left the room. Almost immediately, the screeching of swollen wood on wood sounded.

Vada turned to Dempsey. *Jesus in a*—Remembering the look Harmon had directed her, cut the thought short. *But Lord! Shoot! Moses in a rowboat!* Wasn't there a man born who could quit hounding a woman, just for a while, till she got grown at least? She tried to control her rage, to speak calmly, but lost the battle as soon as she opened her mouth. "You keep your hands off her, you hear me?!"

Dempsey flinched with each word Vada spat, but it wasn't until she looked into his stricken eyes that she faltered. "Dempsey...son." She stretched a hand toward him. But he was gone, shut into the boys' room, separated from Roxanne by a wall.

Vada exhaled shakily. She would leave them both alone tonight, and perhaps tomorrow she could speak more rationally, maybe talk to Dempsey about Roxanne in a way he could understand, agree with. She'd always been able to talk him around. Why should this be different?

In the kitchen, Harmon looked at her, one eyebrow raised. She shook her head at him and seated herself. He gave her a long look, but said no more about it. "This some kind of holiday I don't know about?"

"What makes you think that?" she asked, and then remembered: the class, the dinner, softening Harmon up. Only now she couldn't think about the class. The only thing on her mind was Dempsey and Roxanne, and how she could defeat whatever was going on between the two before it really started. "I just decided to cook you something decent. That all right?"

He looked as if it might not be all right, but didn't say more.

* * * * *

The following morning, both Roxanne and Dempsey successfully avoided her, but Miz Priddy, with hearing no doubt developed from years of eavesdropping on her own children's conversations, heard them sneak out the back door, probably to the shed, and alerted Vada. Vada waylaid them as they tried to sneak back into the house, but at the last minute decided to talk to Dempsey first, alone.

She followed him into the boys' bedroom and closed the door.

"Dempsey." He stood, hunched, until she touched his shoulder. When he turned to look at her, the shadows beneath his eyes tore at her and she put her arms around him. "Son, I'm sorry."

He stood rigidly until she released him and backed up, then he went to the bed and sat, face averted.

She sighed. "Dempsey, please. Talk to me."

"I thought you loved me."

"Why, Dempsey—forevermore. You know I do. You're one of my babies, one of my own young'uns, like Jacob or Gerald or any of them." Truly astounded at his idea that she might not love him, she put a hand on his arm only to have him jerk away from her.

"Then why ain't I good enough for Roxanne?"

She stared at him. "Good enough? Who said you're not good enough?"

"You. Yesterday."

"Oh, Dempsey, son. I never meant for you to think that. It's not you. It's anybody. She's too young. Don't you see that?"

He looked at her as if she were simple. "Too young to love?" He didn't wait for her to answer. "I love her, Mama. I want to marry her."

"Oh, phooey. You don't either," she blurted.

Dempsey leapt to his feet. "Don't tell me what I feel. I love her. I'm going to marry her whether you like it or not!" He brushed past her and out the door before she could stop him.

She sank onto the bed. "Jesus, Jesus—Moses in a rowboat," she corrected. "Can I do anything to mess this up worse?"

Chapter 30

Vada had intended to speak to Roxanne again, but the fiasco with Dempsey made her wary. She waited and watched, refraining from talking to either until the situation seemed less explosive. In the meantime, she set into motion once more her plan to get Harmon to agree to her taking the extension class. It began with another supper—not as fancy as chicken-fried steak, but still special.

Even with the situation between Dempsey and Roxanne, the idea of learning something she was actually interested in excited her. For the first time in months, life held promise.

"Vada, are you listening to me?" Harmon's voice, rough with irritation, scraped at her and pulled her back to the kitchen.

"Of course I am," she said. "I always listen to you. I was just so fascinated I could hardly talk myself." Margaret shifted in her chair and Vada looked quickly at her, at the upturned mouth and flushed cheeks, at the stifled laughter in the changeable eyes. Vada looked away before she, too, had to choke back a laugh. She was laying it on a bit thick, but it wouldn't have mattered. Everything was funny to Margaret, who saw through the routine shams of life and inevitably found them amusing, if not downright hilarious. "Fascinated," Vada repeated to Harmon.

Harmon looked from Vada to Margaret, then one by one to each of the other children. "Hmph," he finally muttered into his plate. "I'd like to know where your mind gets to sometimes."

Oh, no you wouldn't. She passed him the platter of fried chicken. "Look here. I think there's a piece of chicken with your name on it right there."

After supper, she did the dishes, staring out the window at the darkness, seeing in her mind the place she would till for the garden in the spring. Or she guessed she would. She could not imagine what kind of garden could grow all year round, but she'd find out soon enough. The day couldn't come soon enough, and not just because she wanted to save Harmon money. She wanted more than that. She wanted something of her own, something she created with her own hands, something beautiful. Her gardening was only so-so, but she knew she could get good at it, real good. She could do what she loved and still make things a little easier on Harmon's pocketbook.

She imagined her vegetable garden-to-be. It would lie along the back fence, a rich, fertile place now gone crazy with hollyhocks. She wasn't worried about losing them—they'd grow anywhere, the poorer the dirt the better. Not like a lot of things. She drew her focus in closer, to the windowsill in front of her. "Like you," she muttered to the cactus. "Pampered and petted and mollycoddled, and you don't do a blessed thing. I've got half a mind to do like Harmon said and pitch you right out that—" An explosion of laughter behind her interrupted her words, and Vada spun in place, back suddenly to the sink, soap suds dripping from her hands onto the faded linoleum.

"Margaret Joyce, you nearly scared the—"

Margaret giggled, dark braids bouncing as she pranced around the kitchen. "I can't help it, Mama. You act like those plants talk back to you." She picked up a small pot of ivy from the center of the table and mimicked Vada. "Oh, little plant, you little darlin', talk to your mama, you sweetie, you—"

Vada flung soapsuds from her hands at Margaret. "If you have to be in here deviling me, you can finish the dishes."

"Nah, I got homework."

Vada wet her hands in the soapy water again and flicked drops at her daughter. "Then go."

Margaret shrieked and set the plant down, running from the room as Vada made a mock charge. When the girl was gone, Vada plunged her hands back into the dishwater, searching for stray silverware. "They do talk to me," she said, "and I guess I understand 'em about as well as I understand anybody." As her hands rested idle in the warm water, she looked through the window into the night, a vague yearning tightening her midsection.

* * * * *

She lay beside Harmon in the dark and waited for his breathing to return to normal, thinking again about the stupidity of people who said the best way to get on a man's good side was to set a fine table. She clapped both hands over her mouth and nose to stifle a snort, and when she had regained her composure, considered the thought once more. Maybe they were right about getting to his heart, but she knew the path to anything else began a little lower.

But oh, to feel *passion* for someone, to really want to make love to a man. Surely there was a grain of truth in Miz Priddy's silly romance stories, and if there was, Vada would like to experience a little of it. She remembered the day so long ago when, Gerald brand new and Margaret not even an idea, Addy's eyes had shone as she told Vada about sex with Alex: that it was fun, and it felt *good*. Vada shut her eyes and tried to imagine the desire Addy had felt, tried to imagine wanting anyone so much she'd bounce and shine, so much she would sacrifice everything else. She tried to conceive of a way that the plots of Miz Priddy's romance books could ever even remotely apply to her. There was always a main female character head over heels after some handsome but possibly evil man she had at first hated. Vada didn't even know any evil men, and she supposed that if she hated someone she'd have a pretty good reason and that she would continue to hate him. But in the books it was never that way. Instead the couple became unable to keep their hands off one another, like magnet and metal, drawn together by so much passion that they could not be separated. Not with a *crowbar!* Vada could think of nothing she cared for that much, except maybe her children, but that was different. She hadn't even wanted them in the first place, but had learned to love them after the fact. *And anyway, it don't do to hang too tight to young'uns. They grow up and leave, and then what have you got?*

The thought of her children's future departures weighed her down, made her feel like crying, and the fact that they were the last thing in her life she had to look forward to depressed her further. Then she thought of growing flowers and vegetables all year round and perked up. *I got to get my hormones looked at. I'm up one minute, down the next, like a roller coaster.* Finally, she turned on her side and looked at the shadow on the wall created by the tree outside her window. *Anyway, it don't do to want. Somebody will find out you want it and see you get the opposite. Mama taught me that if she never taught me nothing else.*

"Harmon?"

"Hm?"

"Did I tell you about them classes they're having out to the fair barn?" She knew she hadn't told him, but he wouldn't remember, and it would at least open the conversation. She lay still, eyes on the ceiling, and listened to the soft creaking of the old house as it settled into the cradle of night. It may have been a tactical error to let him have his way before she got him to agree to the class, but with Harmon, she needed to make sure he was as pliable as possible, even if it meant letting him at her twice in one night.

"Mmm?" His voice was soft with sleep, and he shifted to his side, putting one arm over her midsection. He let out a long gust of air that ruffled her hair, and she patted his arm.

"Don't go to sleep yet. I'm not through telling—"

"I know. Growing things. Ma can tell you all there is to know on that, I reckon."

"No. I want to take a class."

"A class? What for? You smart enough to hook me. What you need to go to school for?"

She suppressed a biting reply. "But there's a—there's a class over at the fair barn. Somebody from OSU is teaching how to grow the best vegetables, and how to fertilize, and all. Plus, they're telling how you can do it year round. It doesn't cost a whole lot, and I'd kind of like to take it, just so I don't waste my time planting things that don't grow."

Harmon lay silent and she thought he'd gone to sleep, but finally he spoke. "Got to teach people how to grow a garden? My mama's been gardening since Hector was a pup, and she ain't never had no schooling for it. And anyhow, till you got to feeling so puny, you had the best looking yard in these parts." He paused. "Not that it was worth a lot but to look at, but couldn't you just take what you done there and move it over to a vegetable garden?"

This wouldn't be as easy as she had wished, but she tried to remain calm as she stroked his arm. "Number one, your mama's getting too old to be out there in the sun helping me. And number two, my yard wasn't nothing. I started out with some good dirt some fool trucked up this hill, and some fine, fine grass must have blowed in from Missouri or somewhere, and I made it all look pretty, at least compared to most yards around here." She let her fingers dance across his chest. "And you know, if I could have took what I done in the yard and done it in that garden, I would have. I don't like to put out all that work and get nothing back."

He sighed. "Well, at least you ain't moping around no more like you lost your best friend. How much is it going to cost me?"

"Six dollars." She squeezed her eyes shut.

"Six dollars!" he yelped. "Why, girl, have you lost what little mind you got? We ain't got six dollars to throw away— "

She opened her eyes, set her jaw, and moved her hand downward, past his stomach to the inside of his thigh. "I got three saved. If you could just give me three more I could do it." She rubbed his leg, then his smooth, barely haired and slightly rounded belly. "I don't have to buy materials or anything, and they even give you some kind of plant book to take home when it's over." A sudden inspiration seized her. "We'd save on groceries if I grew all our vegetables and canned them."

"Save." He sounded more awake now. "On groceries." He rose on his elbow and looked at her a moment, then pushed her gown up and tried to pry her thighs apart.

She clamped them together. "What about that class?" He worked at wedging his big hands between her thighs and she crossed one leg over the other. "I want to take the class, Harmon." She peered at him in the dim light and he eyed her in silence for a long time before he spoke.

"All right," he growled. "All right."

Chapter 31

Outside the barn-like extension building, mere feet from the big doorway, sat a greenhouse, and Vada was drawn to it as ants are drawn to sugar. A plastic building, moist and fertile, it enclosed the fragrance of a multitude of flowers fighting for her attention, and she stared about in wonder. A dozen or so other women, all of whom looked to Vada to be taller and smarter and richer than she, milled around looking at the overwhelming display of vegetation. Only two men were visible, one small and frail, almost lost in the shadow of the other. The burly man had the wildest, reddest hair Vada had ever seen. It was not over-long, but each strand seemed to stand on end, as if his head had caught fire and he'd tried to put it out by shoving it into a box fan. She stood in place, knowing she was staring goggle-eyed, but unable to help herself. *Where would a body get hair like that?* It seemed somehow unnatural, with the curls struggling in all directions as if in a hurry to leave his scalp. They looked soft, though, like they'd curl around her fingers if she ran her hand through them. Heat enveloped her face, and she looked around to see if anyone was watching her. *What a thought! Hussy!* She turned her attention from him to the profusion of flowers, and by the time she looked up again, everyone but she and the red-haired man had left the greenhouse and streamed through the door of the larger building.

Vada scurried after the group, imagining the eyes of the big man following her. *Probably thinks I'm some kind of idjit.* Several long tables were arranged in rows throughout the large room, bucket-shaped plastic chairs hugging one long side of each table. She took a seat close to the door, clutching her pocketbook to her chest as she watched the other women for cues. Finally, the red-haired man appeared before the first row and stood facing them, his back to the black, dusty surface of a portable chalkboard.

"Hey, there, ladies. How you doing?" He looked around the room and grinned as if delighted to at last be in their company. "I'm Levon Jordan, and I'm an extension agent from Oklahoma State University in Stillwater. I'll be teaching you everything I know about gardening." His grin broadened. "It could be a very short class." The skin around his eyes crinkled, and the eyes themselves glinted, but Vada was mesmerized by his white, even teeth, awesome in their perfection. His body seemed to possess a great, untapped energy, and she couldn't believe no visible light encircled him.

"Why don't you introduce yourselves, and tell me a little about why you're here?" He nodded at the black-haired woman seated nearest him. She blushed and cleared her throat.

"Shirley Locke." Giggles tumbled out of her like bubbles from soda pop, and her face reddened even more. "I have a black thumb." The woman waggled it at him, as if in proof. "I thought I should do something while I still have a lawn." Polite laughter followed her remark, and the man's attention moved to the next person. Vada slid lower and lower in her chair, until her tailbone had reached the edge, and she had to sit up again. When her turn came, sweat beaded on her forehead. "Va—Vada," she croaked.

"Vada," Levon Jordan repeated. He stood, one hand in his pocket, using the other to repeatedly toss into the air and catch a stubby piece of chalk. "That it?" She stared at him, dumbly powerless in the face of all that red-haired energy and the eyes of the other women upon her. He laughed. "Just Vada, huh? No last name?"

Heat moved up her body, starting at her feet, bringing with it a pressure that forced out one more word: "Priddy."

Levon burst into laughter, the sound as big as he was and magnified by the huge building. The women tittered, turning almost in unison to look at Vada where she sat miserably erect in her seat.

When he quit laughing, Levon Jordan tossed the chalk into the air a couple of times before he spoke. "A pretty name for…a pretty girl." When he released the last few words, he seemed to lose some momentum, and he looked at her, eyes thoughtful beneath thick red-gold brows. He went on to the only remaining women, a trio who had slipped into the room after everyone else, but his gaze returned to Vada time after time. After all had been named and acknowledged, he gave her one final look, this time in a way that seemed heated, expectant. Finally, he turned to the blackboard and scrawled what he said was a typical root system. As he talked, he seemed to regain a bit of his earlier enthusiasm. Vada scribbled notes on the backs of mimeographed sheets from the folder provided to each woman. She avoided his gaze, but throughout the evening, she was conscious of his eyes on her. Just the feeling of being watched brought warmth to her face.

After a break, he asked for any specific gardening questions, and Vada struggled with her nerve until nearly the last minute. "Christmas cactus," she finally blurted. "I got one in the house that won't bloom." She tried to stare a hole through her hands, white knuckled from clutching each other, but she forced herself to look at him.

He held the chalk still, chewing his bottom lip. "Hm. Where do you keep it?"

"I've had it everywhere," she said. "North window. East window. Front porch. Everywhere. It just don't bloom."

"Is it in a room that's dark a lot?"

She shook her head slowly. "No. I make sure it gets plenty of light."

He nodded as if that explained everything and tossed the chalk into the air, catching it deftly as it fell. "Well, there you are. That kind of thing needs twelve, fourteen hours of darkness a day after about, oh, October. Then it'll bloom right on time for you."

Without even thinking, Vada blurted, "That's the stupidest thing I ever heard!" The other women seemed to turn upon her as one, disbelief clearly written on their faces.

Levon threw his head back and roared, his laughter booming through the place. "You're exactly right, Pretty Girl. It is stupid."

Vada thought her face must be glowing, the heat of her embarrassment was so intense. "I—I didn't mean to dispute your word. I—I never heard of a plant blooming in the dark is all. It don't seem right."

He smiled at her. "Well, it wouldn't be, not for ivy or something, but it's exactly right for a Christmas cactus. They're exotics, got to have special conditions."

His eyes were like wide-open windows, no hidden recesses, just good humor and concern, the kind of eyes that could never keep a secret. This time, when he smiled at her, she smiled back.

When class ended, he had barely mentioned year-round gardening, what she had come to learn about, but had talked only about roots and cells and aeration. What she wanted was the nuts and bolts. "Don't tell me what makes it work. Just tell me how to do it," she muttered under her breath as she gathered her papers and pocketbook and hurried from the tables. Just before she reached the door leading outside, she heard Levon calling her.

"Hey, Pretty Girl—uh, Vada—Miss Priddy, hold it."

Even his voice seemed red and curly, full of laughter. When she turned to face him, he became awkward, starting to speak, then straightening chairs that were already in place. Finally, she could stand it no longer. "I got to go. If you got something to say, say it." Clutching her pocketbook to her like a shield, she fixed her eyes on a place above his top shirt button, where red-gold hair curled out. A warm, weak feeling erupted low in her stomach, a feeling she did not remember ever having before, and it spread through her groin and down her legs. It took every ounce of strength she possessed to stay standing, and she had to put one hand out to steady herself. *Just what I need—a sinking spell right here in front of this fella.* She chastised herself for not having eaten more at supper.

"I—I wanted to apologize for embarrassing you. It's not something I make a habit of doing."

She glanced away, then back. There was that feeling again. She squeezed her legs together. "It's all right. I—I get embarrassed pretty easy." Now it was hard to breathe, and if she didn't get out of this place in the next ten seconds, she'd faint for sure.

He started to speak, emitted a croak and stopped. He cleared his throat. "Listen. Can I buy you a cup of coffee, or a soda, maybe? There's a little café not far from here."

She shook her head. "No. I'm sorry. I—I got to go," she finished and spun around, heading for the door at a trot with her breath caught in her chest.

In the pickup, Harmon waited with an unlit roll-your-own hanging from his thin lips. "Well, how you like being in school, little girl?" he asked, putting the truck into gear.

Gravel crunched under the wheels for a while before Vada managed to answer. "It's not like real school," she said, and stared out the side window at the street so she wouldn't have to talk to him. The pavement, slick and shiny from the humid night, slipped by as the truck gained speed. She heard the sound of Harmon striking a match with his thumbnail, then smelled the pungent aroma of Prince Albert. Lowering the window a bit, she thought again about Levon Jordan and his rowdy red curls. If his hair were longer, she imagined it would spill over his shoulders like clematis over a fence, profuse and startling in all its vivid glory. The funny feeling arose in her middle, and she felt hot, dizzy. *I'll not go back. I ought not to, and I won't.* She pictured the red-gold hairs on the back of the man's square hands. A groan tried to force its way through her compressed lips, but she swallowed it, squeezed her eyes shut, crossed her legs, and leaned her hot forehead against the cool dampness of the window. Why did she feel as if she were in danger? As if she needed someone to catch her when she fell, and sure that she would fall? *I won't go back. I won't.*

* * * * *

The next week, she told herself, "It's the money," all the way to the fairgrounds. *You can't pay good money for something and not use it.* And she really couldn't. Wastefulness was not in her, but she didn't think that was why she had come. She didn't know *why* she had, but here she sat listening to Levon Jordan talking about topsoil and telling them more about aeration than Vada ever wanted to know. She stared at the red-gold hair on the backs of his hands and his forearms, curling from the top of his checked-flannel shirt, and she thought about clematis. Before she knew it, the others were scooting back their chairs and heading for the door, chattering among themselves like so many monkeys. She was nearly out of the barn when she heard Levon call her.

"Vada. Wait. I want to talk to you."

Stopping, she stared at the floor, shoulders hunched, trying her best to be offended at his use of her given name. She felt him come up behind her, actually felt the warmth his body radiated, and any anger she had mustered seeped away. He touched her shoulder, and she expected to hear a sizzle and smell burning flesh. Nervous, she edged out of the larger building toward the greenhouse, and, stepping inside, reached out and fingered a thick, fleshy lamb's ear plant, found the velvety softness strangely familiar, soothing.

"Can't I buy you a cup of coffee? Or even just a bottle of pop from the machine outside?" His voice was like the lamb's ear, surrounding her like a cocoon, and she wanted to nuzzle it, rub her face and body all up and down the softness of it. He stood silent a moment, then leaned around to look directly into her face. "I just want to talk to you for a while."

Vada kept her head down and looked at the crushed rock. She knew she should say, "I'm married," or maybe, "My husband don't allow me to date," or *something*. But she didn't. "I got to go," she said, voice low, stroking the lamb's ear and standing rooted to the floor.

"How about next week?" he persisted. "Just for a while."

She smelled something spicy, fresh, exciting, like he bathed outdoors, and she took shallow breaths to resist the pull of it. Her mind formed the word "No" a split second too late, as her mouth said, "All right." She flew out the door into the night, to the safety of Harmon and the pickup. But the parking lot was empty. She searched through the mist, stupidly turned to look behind her as if she might have accidentally passed the truck. Nothing there, just Levon in the doorway, the light behind him outlining his square form and obliterating his features. She spun and ran through the gravel parking lot to the road, then crossed it and began to walk toward town on the uneven shoulder.

Halfway home, drenched and miserable, she heard the chug-chug-chug of the pickup. He stopped and leaned over to shove the door open. "Couldn't get the gol-danged thing to start," he said.

Vada didn't reply, just hauled herself onto the seat and leaned into the door, face turned slightly away from him, forehead on the window. She felt sad and mad all at the same time, and she wished she would fall out of the truck, anything to end her confusing thoughts.

That night, she lay awake long after Harmon had begun snoring. Every time she closed her eyes, she imagined Levon Jordan's big hands everywhere on her, imagined him kissing her neck, lifting her hair and finding the ticklish spot behind her ear. The last thought as she drifted off to sleep, and the first one the next morning, was *I will not go back. Wild horses won't drag me back.*

* * * * *

Next time, Harmon dropped her off with a grin. "Have you a good time at school, little girl," he told her.

Vada slid from the truck, a sick, excited feeling pursuing her. *He better be doing some heavy duty talking about this year-round gardening he keeps promising.* Her palms felt sweaty, and she turned to walk backward, watching the truck as long as she could see it. She wanted to shout at Harmon to stop, come back and save her from this—from whatever it was she feared. But she didn't. Instead, she cheered herself with the thought that nothing would happen if she didn't want it to. She turned back toward the barn, deep in thought, jerked open the door and collided with the solid red wall of Levon Jordan.

"Hey. Hold up there. Where you going so fast? Didn't you get my message?"

Vada stood breathless before him, peering up at his face, which was partly shadowed by the dimness of the building. All at once she became conscious of the emptiness of the place, empty of everything but the tables and blackboard. And her. And Levon Jordan.

"Where is everybody?" She tried to look at anything but him, and found it necessary to wipe first one palm then the other on her skirt.

"I had to go to Stillwater—didn't think I would be back in time." He swallowed hard, and his voice became husky, as if he were telling her a secret, but he only said, "Regina was supposed to call everyone and tell them we'd cancel tonight and extend class for a week."

Shaking her head, she looked at the ground. "Nobody—well, it'd be the neighbor's telephone—" Her gaze rose as far as his chest, and sweat trickled down the small of her back. A different kind of warmth began in her stomach and groin, and she closed her eyes briefly against it. Desperate to put space between herself and this man, she walked the few steps to the greenhouse and slipped through the door.

He was behind her in a heartbeat, and the heat his body gave off seemed to precede him, to reach her even as he stopped a foot away. He was close enough so that his breath ruffled her hair a bit on top. She shivered, closing her eyes again, and he seemed to take that as permission to come closer. Their bodies almost touched, and he traced a line down her cheek with his finger while she wavered between the heat of desire and the sweat of embarrassment.

"Don't," she whispered, making a move toward the greenhouse door. He closed the space between them. His hand on her breast brought a renewed surge of perspiring, and she backed away, vowing to leave the building in the next thirty seconds and never return. Now his hand was on the first of her print blouse's many buttons, and Vada squeezed her eyes shut against her embarrassment. This was not the stuff of her dreams. She had not imagined her clothing being removed, not by her own hands or anyone else's. Somehow, she had managed to think of his lips on hers, his hands on her body, ecstasy unending without either of them undressing. Now, it all seemed shameful, sordid, but she didn't know how to stop. "I don't want—" she began, but Levon seemed past hearing.

"God, Vada," he moaned, and ran his hand down her sides, behind to her buttocks, picked her up and pulled her legs around his waist, then began to make his way to the rear of the greenhouse.

She tried to drop her legs, push him away from her, but he simply grabbed her thighs, near the buttocks, and resettled her on his hips. Something, perhaps his belt buckle, dug painfully into the tender area between her legs. Biting a lip, she tried to shift her weight, and he groaned again as if she had done something intentionally to arouse him. The air changed perceptibly, became warmer, more moist, and Levon let her down on a stack of burlap bags so compressed they had become solid. Dim light fell through the opaque walls and ceiling, and she could see his face, see herself reflected in his eyes.

His voice trembled when he spoke. "I don't want to do anything you don't want to." Even as he uttered the last words, his lips moved over her eyes, as dry and light and fragile as butterfly wings, then to her ear, her neck, the hollow of her throat, while at the same time working her cotton panties down and off one leg.

Vada shivered, tried to hold onto the panties, but he pulled them from her hand. Why couldn't she just say, "No. Stop this!"? A flurry of thoughts ran rampant, and she whimpered in fright and confusion.

Oh, me. Lordy me. She really didn't want this; what desire she'd felt had fled, and instead of being carried by emotion to a land inhabited by romantic heroines and their darkly handsome men, she was stuck right there with a huge stranger so intent on what he was doing that he seemed to not even know who lay beneath him. *A knothole would probably do him about as much good.* The rough bags irritated her buttocks, and as she tried to squirm away from Levon, he released a long, low moan and grabbed her hips with both huge hands, pushing himself inside her, hurting her far worse than Harmon had, even the first time.

"What do you want?" he whispered, pushing harder. "What do you want me to do?"

"I want—I want you to stop..." she gasped. "Stop, please." As she squirmed more determinedly beneath him, grabbing onto the edge of the stack of burlap for leverage, he let out a hoarse, almost animal-like groan, and collapsed on top of her.

She lay there, barely able to breathe because of his weight upon her, and felt as if she'd lost something precious and irreplaceable.

Chapter 32

She didn't go back to class, and when Mr. Gilmartin traipsed across the lawn to tell her she had a phone call, she pled illness, and asked him to please tell the caller she had the flu.

"Fella said it was mighty important," Mr. Gilmartin wheezed. "Said to tell you it was about that class you's a-taking." His eyes were red-brown and runny, and Vada was sure he knew exactly what she was thinking.

"I can't. I'm—I'm too sick," she said through her nose, and shut the door in Mr. Gilmartin's face. She was sick, too, sick with shame and disgust, and she wished she'd never laid eyes on Levon Jordan. What she had done was horrible, inexcusable, and she had hardly slept since. When she did doze, she woke suddenly, in a sweat, groaning at the memory.

"Oh, Lord, Lord," she moaned as Mr. Gilmartin left. Crawling onto her bed, she pulled the blue and white granny-square afghan over her and looked at the clock. 2:30. The children would be home soon, but she could not drag herself from the bed of misery she had made. She drifted into a heavy, foggy time of nothingness where time wasn't and shame wasn't and despair wasn't, and the next thing she knew, Roxanne was sitting on the edge of the bed, her huge can-can making her full skirt almost cover Vada's swollen, hot face.

"You getting up today?" The girl poked her in the upper arm, but when Vada glared at her, Roxanne slunk from the room, casting looks over her shoulder.

The next time Vada awakened, it was Harmon shaking her. "What you doing in bed, girl? It's near six and there ain't no supper on. Ma's about to have a sinking spell in there, said she's done tried to get you up two or three times."

He peered at her, concern and annoyance moving by turns across his narrow, dark face. When she didn't answer, he gave her another little shake. "What's the matter with you? Are you sick?"

Mute, she shook her head, and turned her back to him, closing her eyes. The room was silent for several minutes before she heard him walk away. Even his footsteps seemed puzzled. She stared at the wallpaper, but the faded vines climbing the trellis at regular intervals reminded her of Levon, and what she had done, and shame washed over her. All the anger and restlessness she'd felt weeks earlier rose again, now directed at herself. Drawing back her fist, she hit the vine-covered wallpaper, once, twice, again and again until her fist was bloody and battered and she knew that even if she broke every bone in her body, she would still be Vada Priddy, a woman who had cheated on her husband and acted like some kind of tramp. She was an adulteress, now and forevermore, and nothing she had experienced with Levon Jordan had been even remotely worth what she felt. She buried her face in the thin pillow and sobbed at how disgusting she was, and how much her hand hurt, until she fell into an exhausted sleep.

* * * * *

Harmon said nothing in the morning, not about her swollen, red eyes or her battered hand, which Miz Priddy had wrapped in a flour-sack tea-towel with much clucking and sighing and pressing of hands to her own ample bosom as if to make sure the stress of other people's lives had not killed her. The children crept around their mother as if they feared she'd gone crazy, and Harmon gave Vada one last bewildered look when he left for work. After that, Vada stared so long and hard at Miz Priddy that the old woman finally removed herself from the kitchen, mumbling something about dusting. Vada remained silent, and when the children left for school she went back to her room, closed the door, and climbed back under the covers. The Christmas cactus sat on the makeshift table next to the bed now, because this was the darkest room in the house. She stared hard at the plant, wondering at the tiny bumps that protruded from the ends of the segmented leaves, and stretched her good hand out to feel them. Her nastiness had probably infected even this plant. It would probably rot and die because of what she and Levon had done.

She squeezed the bumps gingerly, then rose on her elbow and peered at the plant. They were buds! She snatched back her hand as if burned. For no reason she could fathom, the plant's impending bloom seemed a betrayal; words she didn't even know she knew welled in her, filling her throat and chest and threatening to escape in a scream. With a solid, backhanded *thwack*, she sent plant and pot flying from the table to land in a heap of dirt three feet away.

1962

Chapter 33

O ver the next several months, the problems of daily life forced Vada's mind away from her transgression. Dempsey's behavior in general and his relationship with her in particular kept Harmon and his mother in alternating states of worry and prayerfulness. Vada could only seek to appease and to point out that it could be worse, an opinion rejected by both. She stabbed at the dirt with the hand spade. *Least he don't come home drunk.* She hit another clod with the point of the tool. *That'd send them both through the roof.*

She crawled further along the flowerbed. As if she didn't have enough to contend with, Nelda had gotten married, and Cordell, too, both in the space of five weeks, as if wedlock was a virus they'd both been exposed to. Vada had had to help plan their weddings, sewing until her fingers bled, and then there had been Christmas to contend with. Meanwhile, Harmon and his mother moped and moaned over Dempsey. He stayed away from the house, hanging out with older boys who drank, but boys did that. What bother Vada most was Dempsey's belligerence, his obvious disgust with her. *How on God's green earth could this be the same boy who begged me to be his mama?*

And then there was the way Roxanne clung to him. *Like a locust shell to tree bark.* He wouldn't take her with him when he went to meet his friends, or she would probably be drinking as well. Vada sighed and sat back on her heels, staring down at the small spade, the dead roots of last fall's flowers threading through the dirt that caked it.

One positive aspect of Dempsey's behavior occurred to Vada. At least Harmon had something to occupy him so he didn't start trying to fix her. All she wanted was to be left alone to till the ground for flower beds and brood. About what, Harmon always wondered aloud. *About what? I could tell him a thing or two.* But she couldn't. All she knew was something didn't feel right. She didn't feel right. The night in the greenhouse had taken something from her and replaced it with a vague apprehension that followed her everywhere, even waking her in the middle of the night, leaving her lying in her own sweat, heart pounding.

Thankfully, it wasn't just Harmon who left her alone. Only Nelda would have pushed Vada for an answer to her melancholy, and she rarely came to the house since she'd married. Everyone else was preoccupied in one way or another, and seemed to accept this as another of her spells of craziness. She caught Harmon looking at her sometimes, but he never said a word, not even when the certificate of completion for the class she'd taken had arrived in the mail, and she tore it up and dropped it into the wastebasket by the back door. She hadn't completed the class, and she wouldn't take credit; she refused to be both an adulteress and a fraud. Besides, all that money, and she still did not know how to grow a decent garden, much less make a hot house.

But I don't care. And she didn't, too much. At first, right after the night with Levon, she'd felt out of control, like a gasoline-powered lawnmower with the throttle stuck wide open, tearing up one side of a yard and down the other. At least now that was gone, and if this vague fear was what took its place, then so be it.

"We need to talk."

Vada jumped as if somebody had stuck her with a cattle prod and turned to glare at Harmon. "Why are you always sneaking up on me?"

"I wasn't sneaking." Harmon eyed her as he rocked from heel to toe to heel, back to toe, and she knew without looking that his hands were inside the bib of his overalls as they always were when he was preoccupied.

She kept pulling weeds, looking only at the dirt, the weed, and her hand. "About what?" she asked.

"Dempsey and Roxanne."

"Oh, Harmon. I've talked to them till I'm blue. You can see what good it's done." Slowly rising to face him, she grunted against the constricting waistband of her skirt. *I've got to lose me some weight.* "What now?"

He sucked his teeth and stared into the distance, rocking another time or two before answering. "Well, I—I's thinking it might be good if Roxanne stayed out to your Mama's for a while."

"There's no way I'm sending her to Mama's. I can't believe you'd even suggest it."

He cleared his throat, scratched the side of his face, still didn't look at her. "Something's got to be done. I think her and Dempsey's sneaking out to that lean-to after we're in bed."

She eyed him. "What makes you think so?"

He rocked, avoiding her stare. "I guess I seen 'em."

"You saw 'em!" She slapped him with one dirty hand. "Well, did you think to stop 'em?"

"Aw, Vada. It's just been happening since it got warmer."

"Harmon, for the love of God. How long do you think it takes—oh, forget it. I'll have this out with them two once and for all."

"Well, I know they're young, but...if they're that determined—being married's not the worst could happen."

"They'd better not be studying on that."

Clearing his throat, he took another drag from his cigarette and flipped it into the driveway. "They might not be studying on it, but they're sure doing the homework. They keep it up they ain't likely to have a choice."

"You're missing some marbles if you think they're getting by with this." She'd gone to so much trouble to see that Roxanne was kept away from Tandy Bigpond, she was damned if she'd be thwarted by Dempsey Priddy.

Harmon looked at her, shaking his head as he lit another cigarette. "You don't give me no credit." He inhaled and let the smoke out. "It ain't like I'm making it happen. I'm just telling you what is."

Sighing, she dropped the small spade she'd been holding onto the porch, then made her way inside. The house lay dim and quiet, like a great lumbering being napping on a warm afternoon. Voices came from the direction of Margaret and Roxanne's room. Vada couldn't decipher the words, but she didn't care. All she wanted was a minute with her sister. Silent feet carried her down the hallway to the room, and she rapped sharply on the door before pushing against it. At first it refused to open, and she heard the sounds of scrambling and hurried conversation from within. Pushing harder, she heard the scraping sound of wood on wood as the door slowly gave way.

Roxanne sat half erect on the bed, hair in a more-than-usual state of disarray and lips swollen and ripe. Her poodle skirt seemed to hover around her, the crinoline peeking from beneath it, white and frothy with lace. At the foot of the bed, looking equally rumpled, stood Dempsey.

"What are you doing?" Vada's words were directed at both of them, or she meant for them to be, but her glare was solely on Dempsey.

"Nothing," he said, and started to brush past her out the door. "I'm not doing nothing."

She grabbed his arm. "It don't look like nothing to me. What business you got in here?" she whispered, the "s" sound in *business* becoming a hiss. "Haven't we had this talk once?"

The boy looked at Roxanne, and Roxanne moved to his side, taking his arm above the elbow. "Let's just tell her, Dempsey."

His eyes shifted again, this time to the door, and he looked as if he'd give anything to be on the other side of it.

"Tell me what?" Vada's heart began to race. When Dempsey didn't answer immediately, she grabbed his other arm and shook him. "Tell me what? Dempsey Priddy, you better not be fooling with her, I'm warning you. I didn't bring her this far to have you—"

"I'm not fooling with her," he burst out. "We're getting married, whether you like it or not."

Vada released him and backed away as if he'd struck her. "Over my dead body."

He twisted away from Roxanne. "She'll never change, Roxie. She won't ever think I'm good enough for you."

"I didn't mean that," Vada began, but her previous statement hung in the air like some kind of toxic cloud. "I'm not saying you're not good enough, Dempsey." Touching his arm again, she searched her mind for something she could say to undo the damage, but nothing came. It was just like the first time—the wrong words, the wrong tone, everything was wrong. Dempsey shook her off, bolted from the room, and in less time than seemed possible, she heard the front door slam. Roxanne started after him but Vada caught her by the back of her blouse and pulled her back. "I told you this wasn't going to work. You understand me?"

Roxanne jerked away from her sister and pushed her heavy blonde hair away from her face. "Why're you making him choose? Don't you know he worships the ground you walk on?" Her cheeks flushed and her breath came quickly. "When I first come here it was Mama this and Mama that—he couldn't say enough good things about you. And now—his heart's broke and it's your fault, Vada."

"My fault?"

"It's bad enough you don't have two words to say to him anymore, but when you do talk you say the exact wrong thing. Don't you ever get tired of trying to run everybody's life?"

"I don't do any such thing! Don't you even—"

"What? Don't have a thought of my own? Don't disagree with you?"

"That's not what I mean, and you know it. Don't you know what's going to happen, you keep fooling around like this?" A roaring started in Vada's ears, like the rushing of a mighty river, and she could barely hear her own words. "You're going to end up pregnant is what, and I didn't bring you here for that. It won't happen long as I got breath in my body."

"Vada, I love him. Can't you get that through your head?"

Vada flipped her fingers at her and made a "fftttt" sound. "You don't know what love is—you're not old enough to know. You got your whole life ahead of you."

"I don't have a life if I don't have Dempsey. Don't you understand that?" She seemed desperate to make Vada understand. "He's going to quit me because he loves you. Why's he have to choose?"

"He doesn't have to choose. I'm his mama, and your sister—I just want you both to be happy—to stay out of trouble."

"Trouble?" Roxanne cried. "Loving somebody isn't trouble. Trying to live the life you didn't get to, that's trouble." Her chest heaved and her cheeks flamed. "I'm not the one told you to marry Harmon. Why am I the one's got to suffer?"

The roaring in Vada's ears continued, and now she could hear her heart beating above it. "I'm not trying to punish you," she said. "I just don't want you to have to—have to grow up too soon. That's all."

"You don't want me to grow up until I've done everything you didn't get to do." Roxanne went to the bedroom door and turned to look at Vada again. "And you won't be happy if I do anything else." With that, she turned and ran from the room.

Vada folded her arms over her middle, rubbing at the sudden goose-flesh that rose on her arms as she listened to Roxanne's steps through the kitchen and out the back door. *What did I do to cause this? I don't want her to live life for me. And I do love Dempsey. And I do talk to him.* She hugged herself and moved through the darkening house to stare out the back screen at the fast approaching night.

* * * * *

Roxanne ignored Vada as much as possible, coming and going in sullen silence. She and Dempsey studiously avoided each other, at least in Vada's presence, and Dempsey refused to speak to Vada at all.

"You reckon he's going to get over this mess?" Harmon had asked her.

"Sooner or later," she'd mumbled, telling herself that Dempsey would soon see that there was no truth in his accusation of her, but she felt guilty. She didn't want him to marry her sister. She didn't want Roxanne married to a man who would keep her barefoot in the winter and pregnant in the summer, someone who made enough money to keep food on the table and nothing else. Vada loved Dempsey, like a son. But not like a brother-in-law.

* * * * *

She tried to talk to Roxanne again, catching her one day as she sat on the front steps, pocketbook in her lap.

"Where you off to?" Vada asked.

"Beverly is coming after me. We're going out to Annie Barnett's."

Vada searched her memory for a face to go with the familiar name, finally retrieving one from the tunnel of years behind her. "Barnett. Isn't that the name of that old Indian lady lived out by us, out by Kellyville?"

Roxanne nodded. "That's Annie's grandma." The sound of an approaching engine became louder and the girl stood, avoiding Vada's eyes. "I've go to go."

"Wait, Roxanne. I want to talk—"

"No time. See you," the girl called, and reached the street as a red Corvair pulled up in front with music pouring forth.

Roxanne didn't look at her sister again, but Vada stood on the porch and watched the girls drive away, a knot in her stomach. Why had she ever brought Roxanne here? *I'm not up to this.* But she had to finish what she started, and do as her father had asked her to do. She sighed and went back into the house. *I might not be doing a very good job, but at least I'm doing it.*

Chapter 34

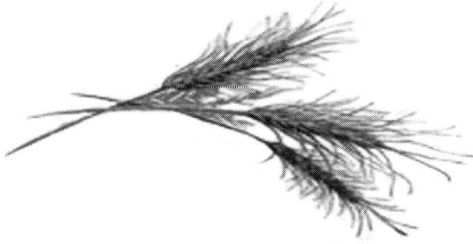

Little time elapsed before something happened that pushed all thought of Roxanne and Dempsey out of Vada's mind, at least momentarily. She'd cleaned up the kitchen and mixed a batch of bread. She could punch it down before bed and let it rise again until morning. *I'll get up extra early to bake it,* she promised herself, and vowed to go to bed as soon as she'd patched Jacob's pants and sewn a ripped seam on one of Harmon's workshirts. When she finally rose from the yellow circle of light over the old treadle sewing machine, the button of her faded skirt popped off from the exertion of her standing.

"Well, forevermore!" She searched for the button, found it and put it on the sewing machine. *Might have to make rags out of this skirt, it's so old and rotten.* She bent her neck as far as possible in order to see the place where the button had come off, and in the middle of that movement a sudden, irrational, and unwelcome thought sprang full-blown into her mind. *I'm going to have another young'un.* So absurd was the idea that she laughed aloud, but even to her own ears the laugh sounded shaky.

In the bathroom, she wet a faded blue washcloth with hot water and soaped it with the sliver of Lux in the soapdish. As she washed her face she looked in the mirror, at the clear eyes, glowing skin, and shiny hair. She remembered how sick she'd been with every pregnancy, and she knew she could not be pregnant now and feel this good. She had gained some weight—needed a shoehorn to get into most of her clothes, and there were some that even a shoehorn couldn't help. And she had missed three or four monthlies, but that had happened last time she'd felt so bad, when Papa had died. Miz Priddy said that sometimes when women ceased eating, their monthlies stopped, too. But the weight gain nagged at her. *What about that? I'm near 30. Everybody gains weight when they get older. And I don't get hardly any exercise. Why, it's a thousand wonders I don't waddle when I walk!*

Thankful for that at least, she made her way down the darkened hallway to the bedroom.

* * * * *

The next morning, she rose an hour before Harmon so she could bake the bread. Poor Miz Priddy had gotten up with a sinus headache and returned to bed to wait it out. By the time Vada took the fragrant bread from the oven, Harmon was at the table, his face buried in a recent *Farmer's Almanac* he'd gotten at the Co-Op, or at least that's what he wanted her to think. She was mortally certain that the rolled up newsprint sticking out his windbreaker was an *American Tattler*, and that he was waiting only for her inattention to whip it out and begin to devour its sensationalistic contents.

"I want you to keep them papers away from the kids," she told him from where she stood at the stove, keeping an eye on a pan of oatmeal beginning to bubble.

"What papers?" He looked up.

Leveling at him the look she usually directed at Jacob when he "accidentally" opened the bathroom door on his sisters or Roxanne, or at Gerald when he sassed her, she turned back to the stove and gave the pot of oats a vicious stir. *Sometimes I'd like to shoot him and tell God he died.* "You know what papers. Them trashy things your mama brings in here." She switched off the fire under the pan and carried it to the table, placing it on a hot pad to cool before the kids staggered out of bed and into the kitchen for breakfast. Steam rose to mingle with the smoke from a roll-your-own Harmon had left burning in the ashtray, and the smell of the burning butt, oatmeal, and fresh bread seemed custom-made for the late spring sunrise creeping through the window.

Harmon lay down the small paperback annual and sopped up his remaining egg yolk with the heel of her homemade bread. When he'd swallowed the last bit and pushed his chair back, he stuck his hands inside his overall bib and shrugged. "They got to learn sometime."

She let a corner of her mouth twist into a grimace as she spread butter and plenty of jam on a thick piece of bread. "Learn what? That every other baby born's got two heads? Or that President Kennedy's been taken away by men from outer space and replaced by a look-alike alien?" She took a bite out of the moist bread. "It's 1962, Harmon. There's a lot more they need to learn than a bunch of old wives' tales and outright lies."

"Well, who's to say that Kennedy ain't some kind of alien?" Harmon asked, beginning to roll another cigarette. "He's Catholic. That could lead to all kinds of things."

She nearly choked. "Sometimes I wonder how you made it this far. There's not a thing in that paper that's true, unless it says somewhere there's a sucker born every minute." She finished the slice of bread, hesitated briefly, and fixed another. *I'm going to have to go on a diet or something. But not today.* She ate the second piece and was contemplating a third when Nelda slipped into the chair beside her.

"Hey, you all."

"Nelda! You like to scared the fire out if me. What are you doing here?"

"What? I can't sleep over? I got to go to a motel?" Her voice radiated peevishness, but there was something else there Vada couldn't identify, something that seemed studied.

"Oh, you know better. I just thought you forgot the way home when you got married."

"Well, I didn't." Nelda tossed her dark hair and let it settle in a cloud around her slim shoulders. "I got clinicals at the hospital here." She cut off a thick slab of bread and buttered it, then layered it with what looked like a half cup of jam. "Nights. All week long." She bit into the bread, then added a little more jam. "You were asleep when I got in."

"You eat like that, that little waist you're so proud of won't make the week." Vada tried to resist the urge for another slice of bread, compromised, and took half a slice.

Nelda and Harmon exchanged a look, and Vada glanced from one to the other. *What the devil's going on here?*

Nelda focused her gaze out the kitchen window and bit into her bread, chewed methodically and swallowed. "It's not me that's getting broad in the beam." The white, pinched face of her childhood had turned flawlessly creamy, but the girl's face was still narrow, fox-like.

"Huh. That's gratitude for you." Vada pursed her lips.

"If you don't quit beating me over the head with that..."

"With what?" Vada asked, but she knew. *And it's too bad.* If not for her, Harmon would never have consented to borrow the money for Nelda's training as a respiratory therapist. "It wasn't for me, you'd be working at Safeway from now on, waiting for some sack boy to carry you off and give you half a dozen porch monkeys." She sniffed. "'Stead of that, here you are married to a professional man, a radiologist. I'd say you owe me."

"Quit changing the subject," Nelda said, but her face showed the difficulty of giving up the argument. "The fact is you're about to bust the seams out of your clothes, and me and Pa—"

"You try having three or four young'uns. See if you don't gain a few pounds." Vada rolled her eyes at the both of them.

Nelda looked at Harmon. "You *said* you were going to talk to her. Do I have to do everything?"

Harmon cleared his throat like he did when he had something on his mind, but he didn't say anything until he lit his cigarette. "Aw, she'd too busy picking at me to listen."

"Talk to me about what?" Vada asked, then glared at Harmon as if she'd just heard him. "And I don't pick at you. I just don't like them papers being around here." She looked at Nelda. "Him and your granny read that Tattler like it was the Holy Bible. It's nothing but lies and more lies."

Harmon looked quickly at Nelda, then to a spot over Vada's head. "There's some of it true. Ma knows one old gal who's been in that very paper." He inhaled deeply and blew a great plume of smoke upward. He still wasn't looking at her, but Vada felt watched just the same. "Fact is, we was talking about it last night whilst you was tending to the bread."

Vada laid a final dollop of jam on the bread. Maybe if she kept quiet he'd say what he was thinking and leave her alone. She looked out the window and chewed her bread and jam, but from the corner of her eye she saw his gaze flicker briefly toward Nelda, and saw Nelda give him a slight but encouraging nod. Vada turned her face full on him, but he refused to meet her eyes.

Studying the floor, he cleared his throat. "This old gal that was in the paper—the one Ma knowed—was plumb out to there." He held his hand a foot away from his stomach. "The doctors thought she had a tumor." He sucked on his cigarette then stubbed it out, releasing smoke through his nose. He cut his eyes at Nelda, and they both looked at Vada like they expected her to say something.

"Speaking of doctors, I thought one of them told you to give up on them cigarettes." Vada finished her bread and used one hand to sweep the crumbs from the oilcloth into her other hand, cupped at table's edge. Harmon's battle with tobacco was old news, but any comment about his smoking usually provoked a flurry of bickering between him and Nelda. It didn't work this time.

"A tumor, they thought," he repeated, ignoring her remark, just as Nelda did.

Vada sighed. "A tumor. All right."

"Only it weren't no tumor, when they got right down to it." She nodded, then rose to take the crumbs to the trash, but Harmon grabbed her arm and leaned forward eagerly. "It was a hairball, Vada! A great, big hairball, with bone, 'n' fingernails in it, they said." His backlit black eyes glittered darkly and he lifted one eyebrow. "She sold it to one of them freak shows, and they went and pickled it. They charge a nickel to see it to this very day."

"That's disgusting." Shuddering, Vada went across the floor to the wastebasket. This was exactly the kind of talk she wanted to keep from the children. She did not want them growing up ignorant. *Like some I could name.* When she'd rid herself of the crumbs, she went back to the table, eluding Harmon's attempt to grab her arm again, and asked Nelda, "That why you're here? You think I got a hairball, too?"

Color rose in Nelda's cheeks, accentuating her large, heavily fringed dark eyes. Avoiding Vada's glare, Nelda pulled at a lock of hair and shifted uncomfortably in her chair. "Can't I even come to see ya'll without you thinking I got something up my sleeve?" Looking at her father, she gave him a weak smile, alarming Vada more than anything had so far.

Vada sat heavily in her chair and folded her small, callused hands in front of her on the green vinyl tablecloth. "What are you two up to?" Her heart pounded so hard in her chest she thought surely it must show through the front of her housecoat, but she didn't know why it beat so. There was no way in the world that Nelda and Harmon—especially Harmon—could know anything about her that she didn't already know. Maybe they knew something she *did* know. Maybe they—one or both of them—had found out about…about Levon. No! They couldn't.

Harmon looked uneasy, but determined. "Me and Ma and Nelda—well, mostly Ma and Nelda—" It was his turn to give Nelda a sickly grin. "—but me too, some—we was thinking, might be you ought to go see Doc Fist. You said it yourself, even when you was a day away from your time, you never weighed more'n a 130 pounds in your life, and this last few months, you been getting plumb fat. Why, I bet you weigh nigh on a 150 pounds now."

Dr. Fist had replaced Dr. Smith six or seven years ago, and generally just the sound of his name made her giggle. Now Vada stopped in the midst of buttering the other half of her slice of bread, knife paused in mid-air. Just one word had penetrated, and it had never been applied to her in her entire life. "Fat? Why, Harmon Priddy, I—" Her mouth snapped shut on the words. She looked at the bread in her hand, laid it and the knife down, folded her hands in her lap and studied them, looked hard at Sarah's wedding ring, buried in the flesh of the third finger of her left hand. When several moments had passed in the silent wake of her shock, Harmon's face appeared before hers, almost in her lap as he tried to peer into her eyes.

"I didn't say nothing wrong, did I?"

She raised her face, and he did the same, the motion so fluid she felt like she was watching her own reflection. Except, of course, Harmon was thin as a clothesline pole, and she was—*fat. Fat and sassy. So fat you couldn't see her eyes. A butterball. Lard ass. A tub of lard. Nine ax-handles across the ass.* A host of other euphemisms flitted through her mind, phrases she'd never applied to another person, much less to herself.

"Vada? I didn't mean—"

Nelda came and squatted next to her chair. "Mama—we wasn't trying to—"

"Not trying to what? Tell me I'm a fat pig?" Her voice did not rise, but she wanted to scream. She pictured herself on her hands and knees, squealing like a big old hog. *A hog!* Shaking Nelda's hands off hers, Vada pulled her cotton housecoat around her—or as far around her as it would go, because yes, maybe she had gained a few pounds, and who had more right? She had had three children—four if you counted the one born dead—and there weren't many women in this world who could do that and not gain a little weight.

She was not about to tell them that, though. "Well, I thank you very much, Harmon. You ever think of looking at my mama? You know what they say— you want to know what a girl's going to look like when she gets up in years, just look at her mama."

"Well, I wouldn't rightly call your mama fat…she's kinda round and…" He looked more closely at her face and blanched, hurrying on. "Your mama ain't fat, not a ounce of fat on her. And you neither. Not all the time I knowed you. No, sir. Just here lately." It only got worse. "And it ain't that you're fat now. No sir, nothing of the kind." He stubbed his cigarette out and she expected him to leave the table immediately, followed by Nelda, but he didn't. Instead, he leaned forward and tried to take one of her hands, one of her fat hands, but she jerked it from his grasp, glowering at both him and his daughter.

Not fat. Ha. Too late for that, mister. "I'll thank you not to touch me," she said. She looked at Nelda. "And you. You—you traitor. I can't believe you'd talk behind my back."

"But Mama," Nelda said.

Vada was surprised to hear the quaver in the girl's voice, but it didn't make her any less mad. "You go on and leave me be. I can take care of my own fat self."

Nelda looked to Harmon, and he sighed, placed a hand on Vada's shoulder. "I didn't say you's fat to be mean, I said it 'cause I been worried about you, and Nelda and Ma has, too. And I didn't really mean fat, not like you might think of it. Something ain't right, and we got to find out what it is." He cleared his throat, and his gaze slid away. "Fact is, Nelda made you an appointment with the doctor."

"The doctor!" It was all she could do not to scream the words. *When I was sick enough to die having babies he didn't lift a finger.* Now she felt better than she'd felt in ages—and he wanted to drag her to the doctor. *A hairball!* Well, this was 1962, and a woman had some rights. She would not be dragged to a doctor just because Harmon and Nelda thought she was fat.

Chapter 35

The doctor's office looked the same as it had—Lord, when was the last time she'd been? She couldn't even remember, but she did remember the odorless room with its orange vinyl chairs and up-to-date *Field and Stream* magazines, and its five-year-old *Ladies' Home Journals*. She flipped through a *Field and Stream*, glaring over it from time to time at Harmon, hidden behind a tattered copy of *Highlights for Children*, very conspicuously not an *American Tattletale*. What would life be like, she wondered for the millionth time, to live with people that didn't have daily fits of ignorance? And when in the world had Nelda crossed over to the other side? *I thought we were doing so good since she got grown.*

"Vada? They're calling you, girl." Harmon stood before her, his hand extended. For the first time, she felt a twinge of fear. He'd never in their whole married life offered to help her up or down, in or out. *He must think I'm on my last legs.* But the sight of the magazine in his other hand, stark symbol of what he was not reading, reminded her of her anger; rising, she swept past him toward Ginger, Dr. Fist's nurse, whose fiery hair was like a friendly lighthouse sent to guide the good ship Vada into harbor. *Hairball Harbor. I'm never forgiving Harmon for this one.*

"Haven't seen you around these parts lately, Vada," Ginger said. They stopped at the scales in the corridor off of which examining rooms lay, and the nurse pushed the weighted metal piece delicately across the tick-marked rod. Vada thought she never would stop, but she finally did—at 148. Ginger's eyebrows crawled nearly to her hairline and she made a clucking sound. "I thought you were looking a little on the plump side," she said as she scribbled numbers on a sheet of paper.

The nurse picked up the conversation as if there'd been no lag. "You got to be dying before you come in?" She led Vada to the examining room and handed her a stiff cotton gown.

Dying? The thought brought a lump to her throat. "Who said anything about dying?" Vada went behind a partition and slipped off her dress, sliding on a faded blue gown with the opening down the back. She emerged to perch on the end of the examining table, arms folded, but Ginger pried one arm free to check her blood pressure.

"What are you here for today?"

Vada winced as the cuff tightened on her upper arm. "Harmon thinks I got a hairball."

Ginger laughed and poked a thermometer into Vada's mouth. "Nah. Seriously. I have to write it on your chart." Vada glared at her, and felt like biting through the thermometer. "Oh," Ginger said. One eyebrow arched and her red beehive seemed to stand up a little higher as she removed the thermometer. "Well, long as you got your panties off anyway, he might as well check you out." When Vada remained silent, Ginger said, "You did take them off, didn't you?" She held the thermometer to the light briefly, then made a note on the same piece of paper she had earlier and clipped it to Vada's chart.

Vada glared at her and slid down from the table, padding across the room and behind the curtain, where she removed her underpants in tightlipped silence.

"So how's Nelda doing?" the nurse called.

Why, oh, why do folks have to talk to a person when she's naked? It's not decent. Vada didn't answer until she had come from behind the curtain and perched once more on the edge of the table. "I'm not going to speak that girl's name after this mess."

"Oh, come on. It can't be that bad."

Vada gave her a look intended to wither, then folded her arms over her chest and tried to glare a hole through the frosted glass window.

"I heard she's taking respiratory therapy training," Ginger said, and when Vada didn't answer, continued, "I sure wish JoAnne'd do something sensible like that. Settle her down some. That child worries me to death sometimes." She shook her head. "We sent her over to Tahlequah, to NSU, and she didn't do a thing but chase boys." She patted Vada's knee. "Doctor'll be with you soon." The door whispered shut behind her, but almost before Vada could take a breath, opened again.

White coattails flapping, Dr. Fist entered, frantically searching for, and finally finding, the glasses that perched atop his iron-gray hair. He slipped them onto his nose. "Oh, me," he said, and fell heavily onto the stool at the foot of the examining table. "If it's not Vada Priddy! Put 'er there, little'un." He held out his hand, but she just looked at it. Finally, he dropped it, pulled her chart to him and flipped through it. "What have we got here today? You feeling bad?" He looked at her chart again, but she knew there was nothing there, just blood pressure and temperature. And weight. He pursed his lips, then puffed out his cheeks. "Gained us a little weight, didn't we?"

We? She wanted to say something smart, but it wouldn't come out.

He patted her knee. "C'mon, young'un, what's the problem?"

"Harmon made me come," she burst out. "He thinks I'm fat, and I can't just be fat, it's got to be a hairball."

Dr. Fist laughed and slapped his own knee, kept laughing until tears stood in his eyes. "Hoo-eee! I tell you girl, you are a case." Raising his glasses, he wiped moisture from beneath his eyes, then let the spectacles fall back onto his nose. "Now c'mon, seriously. What are you here for?"

The injustice of it all brought tears to her eyes, and that made her madder. "I told you. He thinks I got some kind of hairball. I don't doubt he's thinking about selling me to a circus or some such."

He shook his head. "You are something when you get going, I'll tell you that." He consulted her chart again, mumbling. "Hm. You've gained some— 20-25 pounds. But I don't believe I've seen you since—what—" he looked at her chart again, then up at her, alarmed. "Well gawdamighty, Vada, you've not been in here in more'n three years." He shook his head and went to the door. "Ginger! Head 'em up and move 'em out. I need you in here."

Vada groaned and fell back onto the table, forearm over her eyes. He was going to look at her privates. She hated that. *Harmon's going to pay for this.* The snick of a lighter sounded near her head, and she removed her arm from across her eyes. Dr. Fist loomed over her, a Camel hanging from the corner of his mouth.

Blowing a stream of smoke out, he waved his hand at her. "You're looking mighty good. How come Harmon to take a notion to bring you in here? Really."

It wasn't bad enough she had to tell everybody once, they all wanted to hear it twice. "Ask him," she muttered through tight lips.

When Ginger came in, she helped position Vada's hips and placed her feet in the stirrups. Her bottom was hanging over the edge of the table, and her stomach made growling, excited noises. *Probably that cabbage I had last night. Oh, Lordy me, strike that miserable Harmon dead where he stands.* She blinked hard at the ceiling, holding back angry tears. Even as she did, she wondered what Dr. Fist saw down there. One of these days, she was going to get a mirror and see for herself. It could be no worse than she imagined.

At last, after about a hundred years of the doctor poking around in her privates, Vada sat up with Ginger's help, and Dr. Fist patted her on the back. A funny look flitted over his face, then a grin. "You don't have anything that won't be cured." He left the room, leaving behind the smell of Old Spice and Camels.

"Come on into Doctor's office when you get dressed." Ginger squeezed her hand, and, half-smiling, left the room.

For a moment, Vada was frozen in place. She looked into the mirror on the wall above the sink, turned her face to one side, then the other. He'd said she didn't have anything that wouldn't be cured. Why, then, did she have to go into his office? She slid from the table used the gown to wipe the lubricating jelly from between her legs, grimaced, then hurriedly dressed. *Might as well get it over with.*

When she reached Dr. Fist's office, he and Harmon were already there, the air blue with smoke and probably with the lies they habitually told each other about fishing. It had always seemed like the less they fished, the worse the lies got. Harmon reached for her hand, but she batted it away and seated herself in a chair next to him.

"Haven't you done enough?" she whispered loudly, casting a murderous glare in his direction.

Harmon's lower lip protruded a little, like Gerald when Vada gave him a dressing down. Crossing her arms over her chest, she looked across Dr. Fist's big oak desk. She could hardly see him above the piles of charts and journals, copies of *Field and Stream* and stacks of the *Sapulpa Herald*. Behind him on the wall was a picture of Beau, his English Setter, with a pheasant in his mouth.

The doctor leaned back in his chair and lit a cigarette from the stub of another. "Well, Vada. What do you think you'll be doing along about, oh, say, August?"

She frowned. "Same as always, I reckon. Put up a few vegetables. Cook and clean and wash and iron." She glanced at Harmon. "Take care of him. If I let him live." She looked at Dr. Fist. "Unless I'm going to be dead or something."

Dr. Fist started to laugh, but ended up choking, coughing till he was red-faced and panting. When he regained control, he stubbed out his cigarette. "Oh, I reckon you'll be here all right. There'll just be another little Priddy butt to diaper."

Stunned, Vada felt stared at the doctor. Pregnant? She couldn't be. She felt too good. And she'd been careful. She'd been calculating her safe days for years, and rarely even had a close call. "B-but—I had my monthlies. I mean mostly I have. Not lately, but I was feeling poorly." She felt Harmon's eyes on her and she turned to him. "Tell him, Harmon. Tell him—" Looking back to the doctor, she said, "That rhythm thing…I done what you said." But had she? And how long had it been since her period had come along? She couldn't for the life of her remember.

"Well, now, you know what they call women who use the rhythm method, don't you?" Even if she'd known she wouldn't have had time to say before Dr. Fist answered himself. "Mothers!" he said, and slapped his desk, laughing at his own joke.

Harmon laughed too, a grin splitting his dark face in two. "Praise the Lord!" He shook his head. "If you ain't the sly one."

Vada ignored him, swallowing hard. "But this—the first of April? You mean I been—I been—" The words dried up, and she slumped in the chair, sudden visions of Levon and the one night in her life when she had let her guard down whirling in her head, flashing past her closed eyes. *Dear Lord, what have I done?*

Chapter 36

That would have been the time to tell Harmon, if ever there was a time, but she couldn't. She was scared, ashamed, and nauseated by her own capacity for deceit. She could not bear the way he would look at her, the way his eyes would narrow and disgust would be written all over his face. She couldn't bear the way he looked at her now, eyes shiny and soft, doting on her as he never had with any of the other babies, acting as if this one was something special.

That's my punishment. She was sure it was, but even though she probably would have felt a thousand times better if she could have told him, there was no question of doing so for fear of something even worse. Instead, she spent her days and nights wishing with all her might that Harmon's God, the God with a big G that she barely believed in, would strike her dead now so she did not have to bear this child, did not have to live forever with the proof of her infidelity. She wished it so hard that sometimes at night she had to get up out of bed and go to the living room because she was afraid that if God actually did kill her He'd take Harmon, too, just because he was too close to her.

Telling the children was perhaps the hardest thing she'd ever had to do. Cordell, Jacob, and Nelda seemed to be the only ones who took the announcement in stride, Cordell because he was a dumbstruck newlywed, Jacob because it didn't matter to him one way or another, and Nelda because she halfway knew. Margaret had remained silent but worried her lower lip and eyed Vada doubtfully, while Roxanne and Dempsey exchanged disgusted looks with each other before the group drifted out of the living room, leaving only a beaming Harmon, a miserable Vada, and a clucking, grinning Miz Priddy.

Physically, Vada didn't feel any worse than she had when she went to the doctor, so she continued to work in the yard. She could have recruited one or the other child to help her with any heavy work, but she didn't, only half admitting to herself that she wished for a miscarriage. *Anything. Anything to get out of this mess.* It didn't come, though, and she spent as much time outside as possible. When she no longer found work to be done in the yard, she stood out back gazing over the velvety green lawn.

"What's so interesting?"

Vada jumped. "Roxanne. I thought you had to work this afternoon." She reached for the girl, tried to hug her, but Roxanne moved away.

Roxanne tugged on a piece of her blonde hair, now reaching only to her shoulders, and avoided Vada's eyes. "I traded with Beryl Jennings. I'm going to work for her next Friday." She'd only been working at the Do-Ee Drive-In for two weeks, just a summer job, and Vada thought it was a bit soon to be taking off work, but if there was one thing Vada had learned, it was to pick her battles carefully.

"Why'd you trade?" Vada tried to keep her voice neutral and crossed her arms over her bulging belly, fists clenched, but hidden, in the bend of her elbows.

Roxanne stared at the ground for a moment, digging one sneakered toe into the brilliantly green grass, then looked toward the street. "There's a dance at the VFW."

"I don't want you—"

The girl's head snapped up. "Why?" Her eyes bore into Vada's, and she looked as if she could kill her sister.

"I'm tired of arguing with you about this. It's not decent, you going out there by yourself. Half them men's married, and the other half—"

"Not worth having," Roxanne said. "I know. But I like to dance, and that's the best place to do it." Now she crossed her arms over her middle and Vada could see the pulse beat in the creamy hollow of the girl's throat. "Anyway, Dempsey said he'd take me. I wouldn't be by myself," she said, too casually.

That's supposed to make me feel better? "The VFW's not a fit place for a girl your age. As long as you live under my roof, you'll do as me and Harmon say. It's not decent," Vada repeated, massaging her lower back.

Roxanne seemed to be trying to dig to China with the toe of her sneaker, and her reply was almost lost to Vada in the slight rustle of wind through the trees.

"What?"

"I said make up your mind. You don't want me to be with Dempsey and you don't want me to be with anyone else."

Vada's back suddenly ached almost unbearably, and she made her way to the small back porch Harmon had built. She lowered herself onto it, panting slightly from the heat, and looked up at Roxanne, who had followed her. "I don't tell you much, Roxanne, but I'll tell you this—you start going to the VFW, people are going to get ideas about you."

"Then can I go to the movies with Dempsey?" She plopped onto the porch beside Vada and stretched out her long, golden brown legs, studying them as if they belonged to someone else.

"Roxanne." The pain in Vada's back had eased up, but she felt a growing ache behind her eyes. "Why aren't you ever satisfied?"

"Why are you always punishing me because I'm not a boy?"

"I'm not doing any such thing," Vada said. "And if you ask me, you got a pretty good life—enough clothes for half a dozen girls, more hair pretties than I ever saw outside a dime store—I call that a fine life."

Roxanne rested her elbows on her knees and her chin on her fists. "What good is it if you never let me go anywhere?"

"I do let you go places. But the VFW's not one of them." Although Dempsey's name wasn't mentioned again, it hung between them and Vada felt she had to get away from the possibility of talking about him anymore. Raising herself heavily from the porch, she climbed the steps and opened the screen door. As it slammed behind her, she heard Roxanne's petulant voice.

"You'll be sorry someday."

Vada didn't answer as she made her way down the cool, dim hallway to the living room and her chair, and dropped heavily into it. *I'm already sorry. You got no idea.*

Chapter 37

As her delivery date came and went, Vada developed a lethargy that hung onto her like the moist, sweaty clothing that clung to her each afternoon. She sat day after day in front of the radio, swollen ankles propped on a three-legged stool, listening to the Reverend Herman J. Bevenue and his Holy Ghost Revival Hour, a falsely-named three-hour extravaganza divided into almost equal portions of delivering God's word to the unsaved and requesting money so he might continue, to possibly start a television ministry. Harmon appeared each evening midway through the Holy Ghost Revival Hour, kneeling by her chair, patting her stomach, offering to bring her a glass of tea or a butter and sugar sandwich. She wished he'd stop it. Wasn't it enough that she was pregnant in the dead of summer? And that because of her sin and refusal to confess it, the child she carried would probably be born deformed, blind, deaf, ill, even dead? That thought haunted every waking moment to the point that she had no time to worry about where Roxanne was, or Dempsey. She tried to pray, but even in her hour of deepest need she couldn't form the words. Hoping that no god worth having would take His wrath out an innocent child, Vada listened and waited for Reverend Bevenue's assurance of that fact. But he was no help. Instead, the reverend pointed out that the sins of the fathers would most assuredly be visited upon the children. Although Vada was sure they would, it peeved her that women should be included in "fathers" when it came to suffering but ignored when rewards were handed out.

She sighed and wiped sweat from her neck and face. Lord, she was so tired. Resting her head on the back of the rocking chair, she closed her eyes and drifted into sleep.

She woke shortly to sweat trickling down her chest, forming what felt like puddles of moisture beneath her breasts. Lifting her head briefly from the back of the rocker, she let it drop again. The radio droned on, and with a sigh, she shifted her weight to ease the pain in her backside. The rubber doughnut Dr. Fist suggested had done her little good, but who cared? She was dying of hemorrhoids, and nobody cared. Staring at the ceiling, she wondered if screaming would help. Lord knew she felt like she could start now and never quit. Screaming would take too much energy, and even crying was too much work. *Shoot!*

It seemed like everything was wrong. Vada didn't want any child, much less this one. Even if she did, it was far too hot to be pregnant. It was indecent, the way she had to sit, legs splayed, with her dress, the chair, everything, sticking wetly to her. She tried to pull herself a little higher in the rocking chair and groaned. Why couldn't she at least get this over with? Eight days past her due date. If something didn't happen soon she thought she might explode. She pictured herself in another year, sitting in the same spot, 21 months pregnant. Now, that would be one for the *American Tattletale*, all right. At last she gave up trying to raise herself, and moved her hands from the arms of the chair to the swollen stomach, feeling the roiling and bumping and thumping against the walls of her belly. It never stopped. *This young'un has kept me up more nights in the last four months than the others all put together—after they was born.* The kicking and the twisting, rolling over and wedging under her ribs, on her bladder…what was it doing in there, trying to punch its way out? Or punish her.

And didn't she deserve it? She closed her eyes, sighed deep in her chest. One night. Just one night she had lowered her guard, been weak, stupid, and look at her. *Dear Lord.*

"Mama? You awake?" Jacob's voice was soft and she opened her eyes to see him kneeling by the chair, red-brown hair in spiky clumps, his face, beneath the freckles, turning golden from the long afternoons roaming the neighborhood. "Mama?" he repeated.

She placed her hand on his head, rumpled the damp hair even more. "'Course I'm awake. Don't you know mamas never sleep?" She struggled a minute, then groaned. "Help me, son." Obediently, he took her hands and pulled her up from the chair, emitting a grunt as loud hers. "Oh, Lord," she said, hand on her back. Waving at the radio with the other, she added, "Turn that thing off and I'll see what we got in the way of cookies." She waddled toward the kitchen, then stopped and glanced over her shoulder. "Gerald home yet?"

Jacob shook his head, switched off the radio and ambled after her. Not even thirteen for another six months, he was already taller than her five-foot-nothing, and thin as a split rail. There was a lot of her father in him, and even a little of her mother. "I saw him walking with Waydene Phillips over on Lee." He wrinkled his nose. "She ain't even pretty, Mama. Why, she ain't even got a chin."

"Don't say 'ain't.' And anyway, pretty's not everything. Maybe she's smart. Or funny." Even conversation was an effort. She motioned to Jacob and he stretched one long arm into the cabinet over her head to pull down a gallon jar filled with ginger snaps and molasses cookies. Placing a half-dozen cookies on a chipped plate with pale pink roses, she then poured a glass of milk for each of them. Jacob carried the glasses to the table while Vada brought the plate. She glanced out the back door, anxious for the sight of any of the other children coming down the alley.

"Gerald says if her titties were any bigger she'd fall over on her face."

She gaped at him. "Jacob Eugene Priddy! What a thing to say! My lands, who ever heard of a twelve-year-old boy—"

He rounded his eyes at her. "Gerald says it all the time." He drained his glass of milk and started to wipe his mouth on the back of his sleeve, then caught her eye and used the dishtowel lying on the table. "He's always talking about titt—bosoms."

Vada sighed and closed her eyes. "Let's just not have any more of that kind of talk, Jacob." She motioned toward the front of the house. "Go out and see if him and Margaret are coming yet."

"How come you're always worrying about where everybody's at?" Jacob helped himself to another cookie. "You didn't use to."

Vada nibbled on a gingersnap and shifted on the hard kitchen chair, trying to find a position that didn't feel like she was sitting on a stump. She looked toward the alley again. "There's more trouble for y'all to get into nowadays." Pushing lightly on his shoulder, she nodded in the direction of the living room. "Go on, son. See if they're out there."

"Okay." Jacob finished his own milk and took a long drink from her glass, then belched loudly. At the look on her face, he tried to hold back a grin. "Not bad manners, just good beer," he said.

"Jacob." She glared at him.

"Dempsey says it," he protested.

"If Dempsey jumped off a bridge, would you do it, too?" When he didn't answer, she pointed a finger at him. "Don't let me hear such as that come out of your mouth again, you hear me?"

This time, he was subdued. "Yes, Ma'am." He took a ginger snap and went toward the front door. He returned in less than a minute. "Not there yet."

Shaking her head, she fingered his shirtsleeve. "Already outgrown this," she told him.

He glanced down as if surprised he even wore a shirt, then shrugged. "Yeah. Must be a good shirt, though. First Dempsey outgrew it, and then Gerald, and now me."

"Still." They all needed new clothes, the kids, and Harmon, too. And the truck wouldn't last much longer, either, from the look of things. It had to be push-started more often than not, and she sure couldn't help with that anymore. *Can't hardly push myself out of a chair.* The real indicator of vehicle life in the Priddy family was how many times a week Harmon kicked the fender and damned it to hell before stomping into the house for another roll-your-own. Vada bit her lower lip. *Hard to tell what's going to give out first, the pickup or Harmon.* As if on cue, the child within delivered a vicious kick, a reminder of what all else she had to worry her. She tried to draw in enough air to sigh, but couldn't manage it.

"Did Dempsey come home last night?" Jacob asked.

She shook her head. "I guess not. Don't tell your daddy, though."

"I won't." Jacob studied the oilcloth in front of him for a bit, brow furrowed. "Mama?"

"Hm?"

"Where do you reckon he goes? When he doesn't come home, I mean."

Vada released a gust of air in a combination sigh and groan and shook her head. "I wish I knew, son." She experienced a sudden spasm of fear as she did frequently these days. Life used to be so much more simple, a known quantity that she could cope with, even if she didn't like it. Now though…it seemed as if one thing after another went bad.

And now here I am bringing another young'un into it. Makes a body feel plumb guilty, like I got this way all on my own. A sickness began down deep and she wanted a hole to open up and swallow her. How many times a week now did she completely forget that this wasn't Harmon's baby, that she was an adulteress? What was wrong with her? Just because Harmon did not know about her night with Levon Jordan didn't mean she was allowed to forget about it. She could pretend to, but she couldn't *really*. She was a juggler keeping the balls of worry, guilt, and fear up in the air, and to drop one would bring disaster. Lord.

She was so confused. Jacob poked her, demanding her attention again.

"What, Hon? I didn't hear you."

"Dempsey told Roxanne you're not his Mama. How come him to say that?"

Vada shrugged, tried not to let his words hurt her. "Well, if you get technical about it, I'm not. You know that." She swallowed hard over a lump that had suddenly formed in her throat. The rift with Dempsey killed her soul every time she thought about it. In her eyes he'd forever be the sweet child who had demanded her love. *But I got to take care of Roxanne.* She sighed and chewed the inside of her cheek. When had everything become so complicated?

Sometimes, as she lay half on her side and half on her stomach and rocked herself to sleep, toe against the foot-rail of the iron bed she shared with Harmon, pushing, pushing, she imagined this new child as a combination of her and him, maybe her eyes and his hair this time, maybe with Harmon's long fingers and toes and her good teeth. Then, in the gray time between dreams and waking, when feelings were blunted with approaching sleep, anything was possible. But in the stark light of day in Sapulpa, Oklahoma in 1962, the reality of her mistake haunted Vada, and she knew she would pay for it.

In the days that followed Vada thought less about her children and more about sin and forgiveness. Would God really take one of her children? Or let her die? And if he did, wouldn't that be punishing a dozen other people too? Harmon would be one of them, and he hadn't done anything; he never questioned that the coming child was his. Only Vada knew it wasn't, and really, even she did not know for a scientific fact. She just knew. Levon's name and her sin beat with the rhythm of her heart, rode on the wave of fluid surrounding the baby growing in her.

Maybe Dempsey's distance from her was punishment. Vada couldn't decide if that made her feel better or worse. After all, it had already happened. If this was as bad as it got…but, oh, Dempsey! She'd never thought she could so deeply miss his love, his regard. If she could only pray…would that ease her heart? Maybe not—even Harmon had left off his "Praise the Lord" and "Thank you, Jesus!" of late. He seemed a bit disillusioned. Maybe that was just it—there was no comfort.

* * * * *

"What? You all right?" Harmon's voice in the dark was mighty like the voice of God, except for the wheeze. Even barely awake, Vada knew God did not wheeze like a worn-out accordion.

"Of course I'm all right. Why wouldn't I be?" Couldn't he let her be? She struggled to fall back into the eiderdown of sleep.

"You commenced to moaning there for a minute. Sounded like you's hurting."

"Have you lost your mind, Harmon? I never moaned in my life." She felt his hand on her belly, and she moaned again. "Shut that noise up," she said, not sure to whom she spoke. When she looked at Harmon she saw two, and the moaning turned to panting, back to moaning, getting louder and louder. *My head, Lord. My head. And my belly, my back.* Which hurt worse? She tried to bat a prodding hand away, and it was her own, coated with something wet, warm. Suddenly the light was on, blindingly on, and all she could think was that she must look like a mole in pain, with this blinking. "Can't you turn that thing off?"

"Not if I'm going to get dressed and get you to the hospital, I can't." Harmon stood there in his longhandled underwear, the scratchy ones he wore every day of the world, even now, in the heat of August. Only now there was a dark patch on the crotch and down one leg. She giggled, or maybe not, and tried to rise on her elbows.

"You wet all over yourself, Har," she said and pointed at the red long johns. But they weren't red. Not all over. Only on the crotch and the leg, and she suddenly saw her hands, all half dozen of them where they'd lain on her own thigh, and they were red, too. "Well, forevermore." Puzzled, she looked up and there stood Dempsey, but not the grown up, twenty-year-old Dempsey. This was the little boy who had followed her up and down the rows in the cotton field.

"You be my mama?" he asked now, but he backed away when she held out one or two or five of those red hands of hers.

"I'll be your mama, Dempsey, I will. I just got to get through this—"

Then Dempsey, not little Dempsey but long tall Dempsey, broke in. "Pa? Is she—what's wrong?" The words were right, but the fact that there were two not-quite-separate Dempseys was not. The combination of longing and fear written on his dark face seemed as mysterious to Vada as the wet stuff slipping from her, and the moans that would not be silenced.

"Har, can't you shut her *up?* I can't hear myself think with that racket." She tried to sit up, to move at all, but her body would not obey her. "Har," she whimpered, eyes following him.

By now he was out of the red-stained long johns, paying no attention to his lanky nakedness as he dragged out a pair of khakis and pulled them over his bony legs. "Dempsey, get the truck started. We got to take your mama to the hospital."

Vada felt frozen, her many bloodstained hands stretched in front of her. Then, like wind sweeping across a field of wildflowers, sweet relief overtook her. Now the worst had happened and she could finally relax. She didn't know what the worst was, but she knew it hurt, knew she was woozy from the pain and sick to her stomach, but when she thought she couldn't hurt anymore, she couldn't take anymore, that blissful breeze had found her, and she drifted away, buoyed upon the knowledge that she could let it go…let it all go now.

The last thing she heard was a cacophony of voices—Gerald's—teary and scared, hollering at his daddy—"We choked and choked, Pa, but that dang truck won't start, and Dempsey—he took off—" Harmon, more frightened than angry—"I'm going to kill that boy when I get hold of him"—and finally, Dempsey, panting, terrified—"I got Mr. Gilmartin, Pa. He's bringing the car around."

Chapter 38

Vada awakened slowly, fighting her way upward from the quicksand of sleep that tried to suck her back down. She'd been having the best dream she'd ever had. She was somehow not herself, but an odd combination of Nelda and Addy, and she was at a wedding in a big fancy house. She was watching the ceremony, and suddenly noticed high up, near the ceiling, cracks running along the board trim where ceiling and wall meet. Dozens and dozens of mice, noses twitching and wiggling, scampered back and forth, but the wedding party, all of them, were blind to the mice. All but Nelda-Addy, who tried to point to the mice, to raise her arm and her voice when the preacher asked if any man knew why this couple should not be joined in holy matrimony, but she couldn't. She couldn't, but in an instant the mice disappeared, leaving behind only quivering black noses and an occasional whisker. She threw back her head and laughed aloud, and when she opened her eyes, she was in a hospital bed, and everybody she'd ever known seemed to be in the room with her, but they didn't look completely familiar. It was as if their faces had been broken and re-assembled crookedly. A tall, skinny man with a hawk nose, thinning dark hair, and eyes flat black and glittering, approached her.

Vada tried to reach out to him, but her right arm felt numb. "Har? I can't move my arm." She tried to shift her body, and found her whole right side was weak, heavy feeling. "Har?"

"Well, you finally decided to wake up, did you, girl?" He took her hand. "You going to be fine," he said, his voice loud, as if the numbness extended to her ears. "Doc Fist says there ain't nothing ain't going to be put right in a few months." He paused. "Well, old Gilmartin's seatcover ain't never going to be right. You nearly scared the life out of that old man." He chuckled. "I think he seen Jesus, sure enough."

She didn't reply, but little by little, she began to recognize the faces around the bed: There was Nelda-Addy—no, not Addy. Addy was long gone, long dead. It was Margaret, but she looked so grown up. And Harmon, Miz Priddy, Gerald, and a woman Vada didn't know. Harmon moved closer to her.

"Got us a young'un, a red-headed baby girl," he whispered. A vague sense of dread washed over Vada, and she lay still, alert to his every move, word, look. He nodded and spoke to the room at large. "A whopper, ain't she?" Pride had straightened his back and puffed out his chest, and she wouldn't have been surprised if he had begun to strut around the room. Relief now replaced dread, and she wanted to hug him—would have, if she could have moved. But what would move, hurt, and what didn't hurt, wouldn't move.

The unfamiliar woman edged in next to Harmon. "I'm Marjorie Parmentier." She patted Vada on the shoulder, then squeezed it. "You don't know me, but I have heard so much about you, Vada—spent many an hour on my knees praying for you."

Vada squinted. She looked the woman up once, down once—tall, thin, a bun on top her head that looked like a pan of bread left rising too long.

"Thank you kindly," she said, and was startled at the weak, pathetic sound of her voice. She rolled her head on the pillow and looked around the room, finally resting her gaze on Harmon. "The baby? She's all right?"

Marjorie Parmentier let loose a squawk that bounced from the walls of the room and made Vada jump, then wince in pain. "All right? That rascal weighed ten full pounds, Vada. I'll swan, I don't know when I seen a bigger baby come out of a littler gal. And oh! That awful head of hair! Why, I was telling Harmon here that if I didn't know better, I'd say there's a nigger in the woodpile somewhere, what with that hair and the size on her! Harmon here's a stick in overalls, you, you can't be no more than ninety pounds with your britches full of bricks."

"All right, all of you yahoos, out, out, out." Dr. Fist roared through the door, white coat tails flapping, glasses perched atop rumpled hair. "What y'all think you're doing in here, worrying this little gal to death?" he asked. He slapped Harmon on the back. "What's wrong with you, Harmon? Vada's not but half-way back from death's door, and here you are having a house party! God almighty, man, get these people out of here."

Reduced to shuffling and cutting his eyes at Vada, Harmon prodded everyone out of the room while Dr. Fist flipped through her chart, then hung it back on the end of the bed before dragging a vinyl chair up beside her. He plopped into it and grinned at the huge expulsion of air that came from the cushion. "Cafeteria cooking," he said. "Does it to me every time." He looked at her in the high bed, and his face sobered. "So how you doing, darlin'?"

He suddenly reminded her of her father, and she felt like a little girl. "I hurt," she said in a tiny voice.

He nodded. "I'll bet you do. But I can't give you anything now if you expect to be nursing that little girl." He laughed. "They tell me she doesn't like that bottle worth a damn." He scooted forward, to the edge of the chair, and patted her hand. "Now, listen, hon. You're going to be weak on your right side for awhile. You've got a little nerve damage from that big baby, but you'll be right as rain before long."

Vada searched his face. "She's all right?"

"All right? Why, sh—spit fire and save matches, Vada! She's almost twice as big as any of your other babies. Ten pounds, four ounces, twenty-two inches long." He shook his head. "I believe one of us miscalculated. That child is plumb overgrown—had to cut her cotton-picking fingernails right off the bat, and that head of hair—of course Harmon tells me some of you-all's babies have had hair pert near to their little fannies when they were born." He patted Vada. "But me and old Mother Nature have seen to it this is the last of your babies, little'un."

A huge tide of relief rolled over Vada and she closed her eyes. *Finally. Thank you, thank you, thank you, God.*

"Now, don't take on." Dr. Fist patted her hand. "You got kids aplenty—"

She opened her eyes. "If I could get out of this bed, I'd dance you a jig. You got no idea what you done for me here."

He looked at her steadily for a moment, his blue eyes bright, intelligent. "Maybe I do, now." As if something important had been settled, he slapped his leg and rose, grinning at her. "You better thank your lucky stars that old man was home when that boy hollered for him, because I'll tell you the truth, we like to lost you, what with her being a little lumberjack, and you trying to give us the afterbirth before the baby—it's called afterbirth for a reason, you know." He broke off as the door opened and a nurse entered carrying a bundle topped with a froth of red hair. "Well, look here," Dr. Fist said. He slapped Harmon on the back, watched him as he trailed after the nurse and cranked up the head of the bed. "You all enjoy this one. She might not be least, but she's sure-god last!" His laughter died away to a smile, and he crossed his arms over his chest, clearly enjoying the scene before him.

Harmon's gaze followed the nurse as she placed the baby in Vada's good left arm, then pulled the other up to cradle the child's backside. Surprisingly, it stayed, and Vada found there was a little strength in it, after all.

She looked into the smooth, pink face with its fine webbing of blue veins, ran her finger along the satiny cheek, over the button nose and pursed lips, across the tiny eyelids that twitched in the wake of her fingertips, inspecting the baby at first because she felt it was expected of her, and then because she fell under the spell of this late child, her last. Still, she was looking all the while for a sign, something that announced this baby's difference, that told the world the child was a punishment from God for her mother's sin. There was nothing outside the baby's size and the red hair. And if Harmon didn't wonder at it, she would not prompt him.

He made some kind of noise, and Vada looked up, noticed for the first time the doctor was gone. Harmon put a huge hand out then retracted it, holding it with his other hand as if he didn't trust it to behave itself, and the look on his face became one of yearning and…something else…shame?

Well, forevermore. "You want to hold her?" Vada asked. Something made her desperate for his bonding with this tiny creature, and when he at first shook his head her heart froze. But from his shamefaced, longing look she quickly realized how big a lie that headshake was. She jiggled the baby a bit. "Take her, now. I'm worn out from doing inventory here."

He hesitated but a moment before taking her into his large, veined hands. The baby, big as she was, looked tiny, helpless. Harmon made his careful way around the bed, walking lightly as a man on new-tilled soil, hooked a foot around the chair leg there, and pulled it close to the bed. As he settled himself, baby on the bony knees that were nearly under his chin in the low seat, the child stirred. Eyelids fluttered, lips pursed, sucked air, relaxed, and she punched at the swaddling blanket until the upper half of her long body lay free. Yawning hugely, she stretched her hands and arms over her head, stiffened her legs, kicking them out of the blanket, too, and spread her toes, each long, creased digit going its own way. Finally, she drew in on herself, muscles relaxing, and opened her eyes. Deep and dark, they were almost not a color, but an absence of it, and under scowling red-gold brows, they studied Harmon's face as if memorizing it inch by inch by rugged inch.

Vada watched the two consider each other; then the child's eyelids fluttered once, twice, and closed, and her lips curved slightly as if she found humor in the world she had so recently entered. One arm drawn to her chest, she seemed to retract her limbs until she made a rounded compact bundle again, like a flower closing at sunset. Vada's breasts ached and she longed to take the child back to relieve them, but she remained silent. Finally, Harmon looked up at her, his face as new and smooth and free of worry as that of the child on his lap.

"Ain't she a whopper?" he whispered. "A Priddy and a half is what she is." He smiled at Vada. "You done good, girl."

Chapter 39

W hat's her name?" Gerald asked. He, Jacob, Roxanne, and Margaret ringed the wheelchair where Vada sat with the new baby in her arms.

"Did you name her after Granny Ross like she wanted?" Margaret asked.

Vada made a snorting sound. "We did not." Gazing down at the sleeping baby, she said, "Adelaide Maureen's her name—we're going to call her Maureen." She looked up. "One of you all go see where your daddy is. I don't want to be here another week."

"I will," Gerald said, and had barely disappeared when Harmon and a young man in white approached from the other direction.

Anticipating his father, Jacob said, "I'll go find Gerald."

"Find him and get to the car. It's out front." Harmon looked down at Maureen and rubbed his hands together as if he couldn't wait to hold her again.

"Where's Dempsey? I thought he was coming."

Harmon shook his head and took the baby. "I don't know. I ain't seen him since last night." He glanced pointedly at Roxanne, who stared back blandly. "I ain't studying on hunting him down, though, I can tell you that. He can stay gone, he wants to act this way."

"He did get Mr. Gilmartin when the truck wouldn't start."

Harmon cradled the baby against his chest, stroking her cheek. "We're all overcome with common sense sometime. That don't mean it sticks."

Vada wanted to disagree, wanted to send Harmon to find the boy, not draw any more lines in the sand. But she was tired and just wanted to go home, away from the antiseptic smell and the poking and prodding of the nurses.

"Well, get me out of here, then."

Harmon looked at the young man in white and nodded. To Vada's relief, the orderly began to push her out of the room. *Finally.*

The 1949 Buick that had replaced the pickup just that week sat in front of the hospital's double doors, and Harmon motioned toward it proudly. "Got me a good deal on this one," he told her.

Vada eyed the car that had once been rust colored, now mostly just rust. "Well," was all she said. The girls piled in back while Harmon helped Vada in and handed the baby to her.

After ten minutes of sitting—the car idling with barely a sound, she had to admit—Gerald and Jacob finally appeared.

"Where in blazes you boys been?" Harmon asked. "Don't you think we got better things to do than sit here and wait on you?"

"It's not my fault," the boys said in unison. Harmon growled and put the car in gear.

Vada's stitches were uncomfortable, and she could not help shifting her position several times. "Maybe when we get home you could go look for Dempsey."

"I'm not looking for him. If I found him, I'd have to wring his dad-burned neck," Harmon groused. "If he don't watch out he ain't going to have a home to come to."

Sniffling sounds came from the back seat. Vada sighed. "Your daddy didn't mean that, Margaret."

"What if he don't come back?"

"He'll be back."

"I don't know about that," Roxanne said. "He's probably taken off for good." Margaret's sniffling increased.

"He's probably clear to the state line," Roxanne added. Barely suppressed sobs came from the back seat. "He's probably—"

Roxanne's words abruptly stopped when Harmon made a sharp turn and pulled up next to the curb. He put the car in neutral, set the brake, and turned in his seat. "Number one, you're just agitating. You don't no more believe that than the man in the moon, or you'd be bawling and squalling and carrying on like nobody's business." He was breathing hard now. "Number two, he ain't took off, and you know it. And if you don't shut your yap, I'll put you out right here."

"That's three," Roxanne mumbled but Harmon's look silenced her this time.

Harmon drove, staring straight ahead, lips so tight a white line circled them. Relief flooded Vada when they reached the house and pulled smoothly into the driveway. Miz Priddy waited on the front porch, face creased in delight. As soon as the car stopped, she was at the passenger door. "Let me see that little angel," she cooed, and took the child from Vada. "Mercy sakes alive! Looks like she could take off walking on her own any day. And that hair!"

Every comment on the baby's hair was like a fist in Vada's stomach, and she wondered if it would always be so. Not that she wanted to let the feeling go. She deserved it, and without this punishment, she feared an even greater one might befall her. She made her way into the house slowly, Harmon at her elbow.

Inside the front door, she sniffed the air then paused and looked at Miz Priddy, a mock frown tightening her forehead. "Is that pot roast?"

Miz Priddy bobbed her head, delighted to be found out. "It sure is—we ate beans around here this whole week so's we could have this special, for when you and the young'un here come home." She looked down at the baby in her arms. "You know, I think she favors Jeanette. Don't you think so Harmon?"

He didn't even bother to look, but continued down the hall with Vada's bag. He called over his shoulder, "Well, I hope she don't grow up to marry every Tom, Dick, and Harry who asks her." No one could bring up Harmon's sister without his mentioning her many marriages.

Miz Priddy shook her head, and led Vada to the couch. "Maybe if she was living in sin he'd have something nice to say," she whispered.

Vada smiled as she lowered herself to the divan. "Is Dempsey here?"

Miz Priddy shook her head, intent on the baby. "Haven't seen him." The old woman turned her attention immediately back to the baby. "My lands, Vada, this young'un is full-growed, ain't she?"

"Sure felt like it to me," Vada said, and managed a faint laugh.

* * * * *

Well after midnight, Vada sat in a rocker in the kitchen nursing the baby, eyes so heavy she worried she would doze off and drop the little girl. She jerked herself awake several times, and had just switched the baby to the other breast when a shadow fell across the kitchen floor. Dempsey stood in the doorway. Or perhaps "stood" was not the right word. He swayed from one side of the doorframe to the other, and she could smell the liquor on his breath even from where she sat.

She hastily covered the nursing child and her own breast with a clean diaper she'd been using as a burp cloth. "Lord have mercy, Dempsey! You scared the life out of me."

He stared at her, one unruly lock of hair falling over his forehead. "You don't fool me."

Her heart seemed to stop in mid-beat, then resumed in a pounding rhythm that deafened her to all other sound. "What—what do you mean?"

He swayed across the cracked linoleum to stand in front of her, fixing his gaze on the child for a long moment, then lifting his eyes to Vada's face. She expected to see in those eyes bitterness but instead saw sorrow. His lips moved, but she heard nothing, saw nothing but the moonlight spilling through the windows, highlighting the glistening wetness on his cheeks. She wanted to pull him to her, hold him the way she had in his childhood.

"Dempsey, son," she whispered, reaching for him.

"Don't 'son' me," he said, voice like acid. "All I ever wanted out of you—" The words dwindled to a whisper. "I just wanted you to love me."

"Oh, Dempsey. I do."

He laughed, a harsh, grating sound. "No, you don't. You did till push come to shove, then you left me blowing in the wind. You—"

"Boy, what do you think you're doing?" Harmon's voice came from the same doorway in which Dempsey had stood moments earlier, and the younger man whirled to face his father. Harmon crossed the floor in two strides and caught Dempsey by the shirtfront. "What do you mean coming in here in the middle of the night, drunk as a badger?"

Dempsey batted his father's hand away. "I'm not drunk."

"You stink of it, and I ain't having it. You coming in all hours of the night, upsetting your ma—"

"She ain't my ma!" Dempsey cried, and the anguish in his young voice tore at Vada. "I've never been good enough. Just ask her!"

Before she could make a sound, Harmon had stretched one long arm out and smacked his son's cheek. "Don't you talk about your ma that—"

Dempsey put a hand to his face and backed away from his father. "She's not my ma. I don't have a ma, and it looks like I don't have a daddy neither." He spun away, his anguished sobs bouncing from the walls of the room. Jerking open the back door, he turned to Vada. "I don't need you," he said, voice rasping. With that, he banged out of the house, Harmon on his heels.

Vada sat speechless, unable to even comfort the child who had begun to protest at the top of her lungs this interruption in her feeding. Miz Priddy appeared and pulled the string on the kitchen light, producing a glare like a streak of lightning. The old lady stood blinking at the stunned mother and squalling infant.

"What is it? What's wrong?" she asked.

Vada shook her head and handed the baby to her, then went to the back door. Harmon stood in his underwear, overalls pulled on over them but the bib not fastened, and stared toward the street.

"Har?" She put a hand on his arm.

His shoulders slumped and he turned toward her, his face haggard. "Your sister has changed that boy into a raving idiot. He was always the best of the bunch." He trudged toward the house.

Vada had certainly never heard *that* before, but ignored it. Her heart felt pummeled. In the house, Miz Priddy handed Maureen back to Vada and tsk-tsked her way back to her room. When Vada had finally soothed and fed the child, Harmon carried the baby down the hallway and placed her in the cradle at their bedside.

It was a long time before Vada slept. She ached for Dempsey, imagined his heartbreak at the thought that he was unloved and unwanted. *How did I manage to foul this up? What didn't I do?* It wasn't until Vada resolved to talk to Roxanne in the morning, to do whatever it took to make everything right, that she was able to rest.

* * * * *

That conversation was one that would have to wait, for not only was Dempsey not in evidence, but Roxanne, too, was gone. Vada wanted to ask her mother if she'd seen Roxanne, but could not. Mama had been waiting for Vada to come crawling to her for years, even before Roxanne had come to live with the Priddy's, and Vada could not give the woman the satisfaction. Besides, she and Harmon both knew where the girl was—she was with Dempsey, wherever he was.

Finally, a few weeks after the two of them had disappeared, Vada and Harmon were sitting in the splintery porch swing, talking about nothing much, when Roxanne appeared at the edge of the front yard.

"Roxanne, my lord," Vada said, and went the girl, who sagged into her sister and let herself be led to the splintery swing. "Where you been? We've been worried sick."

"Where's Dempsey?" Harmon asked her. "You tell me and I'll fetch him home. This ain't no way—"

Roxanne looked at him, eyes dull. "He's gone." Twisting her hands in her lap, she repeated, "Gone."

"What do you mean, 'gone,' sugar?" Vada spoke gently, feeling instinctively the girl's fragile state.

Roxanne stared at her hands where they now lay motionless in her lap. "We went to Oklahoma City. We was staying at a—at a motel. I thought it was going to be different—but Dempsey—all we done was fight and carry on—it was like living with Johnsie, or something." She sighed. "I got a job waitressing, and I wanted to go out dancing, do things. But he—" Her voice quavered. "He just sat and drank. I woke up one day and he was gone. There was no note, nothing—just a little bit of change from my last night's tips and a bus ticket back here."

Vada placed her hand over her sister's and felt a tear splash on it, then another and another, and she pulled the girl close. "Shh, it's all right. And he's all right, I know he is."

"I catch that boy, I'm going to warm his britches, I don't care how old he is," Harmon said, his voice a growl. "And you, girl. What the—"

"Harmon," Vada said, and shot him a warning look over Roxanne's blonde head.

"Well, hell's bells, Vada. What if—"

"Harmon, please!" she said, and this time he shut up. A few moments later, looking as if he still had words in him that needed out, he expelled an irritated breath and stalked into the house.

Vada smoothed Roxanne's hair back and kissed the girl's forehead. "It'll work out, sugar. Don't you worry." Even to her own ears, the words sounded unsure.

Chapter 40

Two weeks after Roxanne came home, Vada received a letter postmarked Fort Knox, Kentucky. There was no salutation, just a couple of paragraphs in Dempsey's scrawling hand:

> *I reckon you can see by the postmark where I'm at. I didn't want to worry you no more so thought I'd tell you I'm in the army. Tell Roxanne I'm sorry about everything, but I reckon Mama was right—not the good enough part, but the too young part. Isn't it funny how you can love somebody so much it makes you crazy, and then all of a sudden you see you can live without them? At least it wasn't just me—seems like Roxanne got the same way. I'm still sorry about what happened. I know what you always say—sorry didn't do it, but I really am. I don't know what got into me there for a while.*
>
> *Anyway, tell everybody I said hey, and maybe some of you all could write sometime.*
>
> *Love, Dempsey*

Even before she felt the relief of knowing Dempsey was safe—if anyone could be safe in the Army—Vada closed her eyes and clung to one thing—he *had* written. Maybe he didn't really believe what he'd written, or the things Vada had tried to tell him, but he'd written. Maybe they'd finally turned the corner. She would write—oh, yes, she would write, every day if she had to. Whatever it took, she would do.

* * * * *

Roxanne seldom caused any trouble now, but more than once Vada thought the girl had been crying. She didn't know what to say to her, so she let it go, counting on time to make it right. As long as Roxanne behaved well enough at least to keep peace in the family, Vada was happy. And really, she had nothing to complain about. Roxanne went to school, went to work, and came home, keeping mostly to herself. Sometimes she played with Maureen, but her heart never seemed to be in it. The last person Vada expected to notice what went on around him finally made her aware that Roxanne suffered from more than emotional turmoil.

"What's wrong with Roxanne?" Jacob asked.

Vada shrugged. "Just growing up, I guess." She smacked his hand away from the fried potatoes she'd just dumped into a bowl. "Quit. Nobody wants to eat after you got your hands all over everything."

Jacob grinned. "I ain't hurting them. That hot grease'll kill my germs."

"Hot grease'll burn your fingers is what it'll do. And don't say 'ain't.'"

After a pause during which Jacob inspected his fingers, he looked up. "Does growing up make you sick? Is it like her-mones or something?"

She paused in the middle of turning the second batch of potatoes. "What?"

Jacob seated himself at the table and propped his chin on the heel of his hand. "You said Roxanne was growing up. I just asked how come growing up makes you sick. She's all the time puking in the alley."

Vada felt blood draining from her face and head. For a moment she thought she would faint, but she managed to turn the fire out under the potatoes and fall into a chair across from Jacob.

"Is it her-mones?" he asked again.

"It's hormones, and no, that's got nothing to do with it." She cleared her throat. "When—when exactly did you see her puk—throwing up?"

He shrugged. "I don't know. Just about every day, I reckon. Out there where those stick flowers are."

Vada sighed. "Hollyhocks," she said. "They're called hollyhocks." For some reason, she found herself thinking, *I always said there wasn't nothing could kill a hollyhock.* Pushing the idea aside, Vada motioned toward the back door. "Go out and play while it's light. Supper will be ready in a little bit."

The boy stood reluctantly and moved toward the door. When he got there he stopped. "I'm not going to get sick, am I, Mama?" The sprinkling of freckles across his nose stood out against his skin, growing pale now that autumn was nearly over.

She smiled and rose from the table. "No, son. You're not going to get sick." Giving him a little push toward the door, she added, "You know Roxanne. She doesn't eat enough to keep a fly alive. That's why she's sick. Now don't worry."

He looked at her doubtfully, but finally his brow relaxed and he went out the door.

Vada turn the fire back on, though down low, and walked through the house to the girls' room. Even though Dempsey was far away, getting ready to be shipped out to Vietnam, Vada had learned her lesson, and she rapped on the door, then waited for the answering murmur before entering.

Gloom held the bedroom like a captive. A bare minimum of light seeped through the curtains, illuminating where Roxanne lay on the bed. Vada bent over her sister and placed the back of her hand on the girl's face. Clammy, damp with either sweat or tears, and warm. Too warm. Vada reached up and pulled the string on the single bulb fixture hanging from the ceiling. Roxanne stared up at her, eyes glittering, face shiny with sweat. Backing away to the door, hand to her chest, Vada shouted for Miz Priddy.

"Go over to Gilmartin's and call Harmon. Tell him to get home now!"

* * * * *

The ride to the hospital, although short, seemed excruciatingly slow, Harmon cursing under his breath and Roxanne bolt upright in the back seat with Vada, blonde hair plastered to her forehead, breathing in strange, shallow little gasps.

"Sugar, how long you been like this?" Vada finally asked, remembering Jacob's earlier words. Wordless, Roxanne shook her head, never pausing in the shallow breaths, and Vada wanted to shake her. This was Addy all over again. She was going to lose her last sister, and she was powerless to stop it. She hugged Roxanne close to her while the girl clutched her abdomen with both hands.

When they finally reached the hospital, Vada had to pull Roxanne from the car. Both nearly fell as she did, and an orderly rushed out with a wheelchair, flying from the double glass doors. Behind him waddled a round doughy figure. Vada nearly sobbed with relief.

"Oliver!" she cried. "You remember me?"

He frowned for a moment before his chubby face broke into a smile. "You bet I do." He quickly and efficiently flipped down the foot rests on the wheelchair and helped Roxanne into it before looking Vada up and down. "Look at you! You sure have grown up." The man nodded at Roxanne as he pushed the girl into the emergency room. "This can't be one of yours, though."

"My baby sister," Vada said, chest tightening almost to the point that she could not speak. She tried to force the words out. "I don't know—I'm not sure—maybe it's her gallbladder or something."

Oliver patted her on the back. "Don't you worry. We'll take care of her. Whatever it is, she's better off here than a lot of places." As if on cue, Roxanne moaned, bringing Vada to her side.

She knelt by the wheel chair where it had stopped at the front desk. "What is it, sugar?"

"Don't tell nobody. Don't," she whispered. Her pale, moist skin took on a new sheen and she clutched Vada's hand. From the corner of her eye, Vada saw Harmon hovering to the right and behind the wheelchair. For the first time she realized how much strength she drew from his presence. Keeping her attention fastened on Roxanne, she smoothed the hair back from the girl's forehead, squeezed her hand.

"You can't help being sick. It's nothing to be ashamed of."

Grabbing Vada by the front of the dress with surprising strength, Roxanne pulled her close. "Don't!" The word burst from between cracked lips. "Don't tell nobody. Promise me!" The last word turned into a moan and Vada hastened to appease her sister.

"I promise. I won't tell. And you're not about to—" She had to swallow over a sudden lump in her throat. "You're not going to die." She tried to straighten but Roxanne refused to let loose of her.

"Don't tell Dempsey." The voice refused containment now, becoming a rasping demand.

In that instant, Vada knew. She knew what had been wrong with Roxanne, knew not what the girl had done to remedy it, but knew it was something desperate and dangerous, maybe even fatal.

And it's my fault. If my sister dies, it's my fault.

* * * * *

Dr. Fist was out of town, and the doctor who tended Roxanne was a stranger to both Vada and Harmon. He wore a toupee of an unnatural shade of black that contrasted sharply with his dull, dark brown hair. Worried though she was, Vada could not help wondering if the man had ever looked in the mirror. Not that it mattered *as long as he's a good doctor.*

"Dr. Farrell," he said, and stuck his hand out first to Vada, then to Harmon. "That your sister? That right?"

Vada nodded, her stomach tied in knots. "Is she going to be all right?"

"I don't know." Farrell removed his wire-rimmed glasses and pinched the bridge of his nose, eyes closed. When he opened them, he looked at Vada. "But I know one old Indian woman who better pray this girl don't die."

"Old Indian woman?" Vada closed her eyes, remembering Roxanne on the front porch, waiting for Beverly somebody to take her to Annie Barnett's. She suddenly found her tongue stuck to the roof of her mouth, and wished desperately for a glass of water.

"Barnett. Lives outside of Kelleyville in a shack. Grows all kinds of plants and herbs. Sells them to fools like your sister." He jerked his head toward the room where Roxanne lay. "Tells them they can take this or that and not get pregnant, or if they already are, that she's got something that'll get rid of a child." He puffed his cheeks out and shook his head as if disgusted with the world at large.

Vada's heart thudded slowly in her chest as she recalled the plant—what had it been? Foxglove?—that she had gotten from that same old woman all those years ago. "So she's pregnant."

"No. Hard to tell if she ever was, at this point."

"And you—you think Roxanne took something the old woman gave her?"

He nodded. "Said she did." He shrugged. "Thinks she got pregnant anyway, and still she goes back." He shook his head and put his glasses back on. "I get a woman in here once in a while, drinks some kind of tea made out of mandrake. It doesn't get rid of babies, but it sure will give whoever drinks it a hernia from vomiting. Had one once stuck a piece of slippery elm up in her, into her cervix. Lost her." He looked at Vada's face and hurried on. "I don't think your sister's that bad off. Nothing we can do but wait. She's dehydrated from vomiting." His face softened a bit. "She's young and strong. And the body's got a way of taking care of itself."

Nodding at the two of them, he plunged his hands into the large pockets of his white lab coat and walked away from him, the unlikely toupee bouncing slightly.

"Doctor?" Vada called.

He turned, one eyebrow lifted.

"Can I stay with her?"

"Don't see why not. I'll have somebody bring a cot down for you."

Vada folded her arms over her chest, rubbed the goosebumps on the upper area. "Why don't you go on home? Try to get Maureen to take a bottle, all right? You can come back in the morning before you go to the plant."

He looked relieved. "You want me to get hold of your mama?"

Vada shuddered. "Good Lord, no, Harmon. This'll be our little secret.

Nobody else needs to know." *Especially not Dempsey.*

Harmon nodded at her as if she'd been making his decisions for him all his life, then squeezed her shoulder and followed the doctor's path.

* * * * *

Vada woke in the small hours of the morning to the slight sound of Roxanne moving about on the stiff sheets. She crossed the few steps to from cot to bed, cutting in half the light that spilled from the hallway.

"Roxie?" The childhood name fell from her with complete ease as if no time had passed since she'd been Roxanne's favorite person in the world. "How you feeling?"

Roxanne's eyes glittered in the dimness. "Thirsty," she whispered.

Vada poured a glass of cold water from the metal pitcher and held a plastic straw to Roxanne's lips. "Don't drink too fast. You'll make yourself sick again."

The girl sipped a bit of water and dropped her head back onto the pillow. "I've never been so sick."

"You'll be all right, now. You've got a good doctor up here."

"Am I—is the baby…" The words trailed off and Vada hesitated only briefly before answering the girl.

"There's no baby. Not this time."

A look of relief crossed Roxanne's face before she nodded and closed her eyes. Vada sat and watched the girl sleep for a bit, then sighed and went back to her cot.

1965

Chapter 41

Vada smoothed the slipcover on the divan, perched on the edge of it for less than a minute, then leaped up to straighten it again. Margaret wandered into the room, accompanied by the smell of nail polish, and her mother as she compulsively straightened and sat, straightened and sat.

"What's wrong with you, Mama? You act like you got a bunch of fire ants in your pants."

"Nothing's wrong," Vada lied, cross that Margaret had called her on it. Dempsey was coming home today was what was wrong. Any minute Harmon would pull into the driveway, and there would be Dempsey. *Or what's left of him. My fault, my fault, my fault* was all she could think. The letters that passed between Sapulpa and Vietnam had seemed normal, with no hint of rancor on Dempsey's part. Still, Vada couldn't help blaming herself for what had happened to him.

"When are they going to be here, Mama?"

Vada jerked her attention back to Margaret, and went to the open front door to peer through the screen. "I don't know. His plane was due about nine. It's near eleven now, but it's a good ways to the airport." She sighed. "You know your daddy—drives like an old man." *He is an old man*, she thought with a pang. At least he seemed to be, more and more, with his hacking cough and slow movements.

Once he'd gotten over his anger at Dempsey, Harmon's heart had slowly broken open with grief at his son's absence. Vada wanted so much to comfort him, and she had forgiven Dempsey long ago for anything he had said in anger, but Harmon resisted comfort. He preferred expecting the worst, then being pleasantly surprised when it didn't come to pass. Sighing, Vada wandered back to the divan, sat, then immediately rose to straighten the slipcover.

"You make me nervous, hopping up and down like that," Margaret said, blowing on her nails and glaring at Vada.

"Go in the other room, then." Heading back to the door, Vada stared at the lush grass and thought about Harmon's words when Dempsey had been sent to Viet Nam—the conflict, not the war, she reminded herself. She had repeated them over and over, like a prayer: "Well, at least he's not in any real danger. Clerks don't get shot at." But then who would have thought Dempsey Priddy, at least the boy he was when he left home, considerate enough to lie to his family? As they had found out, he was no clerk. He was about the furthest thing from a clerk a soldier could be—at least according to Cordell. He was something called a LURP—somebody who traveled about with four or five or six other men looking for…well, that she'd never gotten clear. All she knew was that the enemy had apparently found them first, and Dempsey was the only one left breathing when the medics arrived. *Clerk! My foot!*

On the one hand, she was angry that he'd lied to them. Maybe if she'd worried more, he wouldn't have been wounded. She felt guilty that they had all been living their lives as if everything were normal while Dempsey had been chased from one end of that little country to the other, seeing horrors she could not even imagine. After hearing that he'd been hurt, Vada had wanted to laugh and cry and throw things at the wall, or maybe at Harmon. She should never have listened to all that "not a war" garbage that Harmon and newspapers insisted on. If you went to a foreign country in a uniform and everybody was trying—and often succeeding—in blowing everybody else to kingdom come, it was a war, and she could slap herself stupid for not having been prepared for Dempsey's being shot.

Yes, Dempsey's I'm-a-clerk routine, and the world's insistence that what was happening in Vietnam wasn't a war, had fooled her, but now he was coming home. That was what mattered.

Margaret moved up beside Vada to look out the door, and, slipping her arm around her mother's waist, squeezed her. "I'm sorry, Mama. I guess I'm just nervous already."

Vada patted her arm, then looked up and smoothed the glossy dark hair. "I know. We all are."

"What's Dempsey going to do now? I mean, like he is and all."

Although she was seventeen, there was enough of the child left in Margaret that she looked to Vada for the answers to questions like that, and it broke Vada's heart to know that not only did she not have them, but neither did anyone else. "I don't know. I reckon he's wondering the same thing."

"Nelda says some men that come back from the war have got something wrong with their heads, you know, like it made them crazy or something." Her voice dropped almost to a whisper. "Nelda says some of them take dope."

Because Nelda was a respiratory therapist and her husband Joe a radiologist, Nelda considered herself an expert on illness of all kinds. Her know-it-all attitude irritated Vada, but what could she do?

"Is Dempsey crazy?" Margaret prodded.

Vada shook her head. "No. 'Course he isn't. He's just bound to be a little—upset."

"Upset," Margaret mused. "Mmm. I guess so." She blew on her nails once more and touched one pink tip lightly with a forefinger. "Is Roxanne coming over after work?"

"No, but she'll come for Sunday dinner." Roxanne had gone to beauty school in Tulsa, and in spite of all Vada's fears, had found a job in a fine salon, dated from time to time, and seemed content with her life. She'd sometimes stuck notes in with Vada's letters, but they were mostly of the "Hi, how are you" variety, as were Dempsey's when he wrote back. Vada knew because Roxanne made sure to share the letters, whether coming or going, as if reassuring Vada that that chapter of her life was closed.

The sudden crunch of gravel propelled Vada, followed by Margaret, onto the front porch and into the yard as Harmon pulled the new old pickup—the one that had replaced the old car that had replaced the old old pickup, which had replaced the old old car—into the drive. To her surprise, Dempsey sat behind the wheel. She and Margaret exchanged glances, and for just a moment her heart leapt—maybe it had all been a terrible mistake, and Dempsey still had everything he'd left with. Otherwise, how could he be driving the pickup? How?

She lifted her eyebrows at Harmon, but he shook his head slightly, so she let it go. Moving around the front of the truck, she reached the driver's side door just as Dempsey slid out of it and balanced himself on his crutches. Vada felt the dull weight of reality settling around her shoulders as she struggled unsuccessfully to keep her eyes off the little bit of a stump that was once his left leg, now covered by creased khaki neatly pinned up. She was surprised at how glad she was to see him, and even more surprised at how happy he looked. Not healthy, maybe, but happy. Mostly happy, but something behind the eyes…Vada tried to shake off the thought.

"Dempsey! Dempsey's here!" shouted Jacob. He barreled around from behind the house, colliding with Dempsey, nearly sending him over backward. Maureen, who had followed at a distance, abruptly stopped, suddenly shy. And why not? Until this moment, Dempsey could have been nothing more to her than a name and a picture on a wall.

Dempsey reached out to tweak Maureen's nose, but she backed away from this one-legged stranger. Dempsey laughed and put his hands behind him. "OK, I won't touch." He shook his head. "But will you look at you? You're nearly grown!"

Jacob had moved a step or two back, but when Dempsey turned his brilliant smile on him, he threw himself at his older brother. Dempsey laughed and hugged the boy. "You got to slow down—I haven't got but the one leg to stand on now. You can't be knocking me off of it."

For one long moment the sound went out of the world, and the Priddy driveway was silent as a church on Saturday night. Dempsey finally broke the quiet.

"Come on. Lighten up, why don't you?" Then everyone was talking at once as they moved toward the house, only Harmon and Vada lagging behind.

"Why was he driving?" she asked. "And how could he? I mean, with one—with one—" She was relieved when Harmon cut her off.

"Said he wanted to." He ignored the "how could he" part and looked at her, hope in his eyes. "He looks better than I thought he would. Don't he look good to you?"

She nodded, but she was not so sure. Something behind the happiness in Dempsey's face frightened her. He looked—desperate, maybe, like somebody was chasing him and he was barely keeping his lead.

"He looks good," Harmon repeated as if reading her mind. "Real good." He spoke with great force, as if by saying it he could make it true.

Vada remained silent, but her mind raced. *He doesn't look good at all. Got no color, got no meat on his bones—looks like he's been starved near to death.* And the look in his darkly circled eyes—Lord God, it scared her just to see it. How much more frightened must Dempsey be trapped inside it?

When they reached the kitchen, Miz Priddy was crying and wiping her eyes with her apron as she ushered Dempsey to the table. She sat him down and placed an enormous mayonnaise cake before him, with knuckle-deep fluffy chocolate frosting. "Just like I said," she told him. The rich cake stood before Dempsey, the tangible manifestation of at least one promise kept.

He looked puzzled for a minute, then grinned. "But it's not my birthday. You said for my birthday."

She patted his shoulder. "Well, you done missed three of 'em. You eat this one, I'm going to make you another'n." A tear ran down her cheek and she wiped it away with the back of her hand. "Granny's just glad you're home safe and sound."

He grinned crookedly. "Well, most of me is, anyway."

There was that silence again, and Miz Priddy broke it by hugging Dempsey once more and saying, "You all get on out of here now. Me and Vada's got us a dinner to cook." She shooed Harmon and the children out, then went to Dempsey and put a hand under his arm to help him up.

He jerked away from her, his face twisted into an unrecognizable grimace. "Don't," he said, voice harsh. "I don't need no help." As Miz Priddy's face whitened, his own returned to pleasant blandness as if a curtain had dropped over it, and he put a hand on her arm. "I'm sorry. I'm sorry, Granny. I'm just tired." Standing on his own, he pulled her to him with one arm. "I'm so tired," he said again, as if just discovering it.

Vada cut in. "Come on. Your bed's all made up, and you can lay down awhile before dinner."

"I don't need to lay down," he said, but followed her down the hallway to the room that had been his, Gerald's and Jacob's. "Got it all to myself, huh?" He grinned and moved past where she stood in the doorway.

"Jacob has the other bedroom since Cordell got married, and you know Gerald—he'd rather sleep with a bunch of cows than get up one minute earlier than he's got to," Vada said, and Dempsey laughed. Gerald had worked at a dairy several miles distant for over a year. In the beginning, he'd slept in his clothes on top of the blankets so he would not have to waste time dressing and making the bed in the mornings. When even that seemed to cut into his sleep time, he began staying in a tackroom at the dairy barn. After completing his morning chores there, he caught a ride in to school on one of the milk trucks.

"Those boys are something, ain't they?" he asked, but Vada knew he wanted no answer. He looked around him, at the faded wallpaper, the worn-out, rose-patterned linoleum, the lone window with the curtains Vada had made—bright pink daisies on a green background. "Hasn't changed. Nothing's changed," he said, and it seemed as if he were talking to himself, convincing himself. His light eyes, almost the same color as the khakis he wore, moved from the dresser, adorned with a starched, embroidered scarf and a jar of wildflowers, to the bed, its iron head and foot showing a little rust. He poked the bed with his crutch, the rubber tip contrasting starkly with the worn green chenille of the bedspread. "Still plenty of spring left in it." He cut his eyes at Vada, gave her one of those endearing, lop-sided grins that had saved him from many a well-deserved punishment. "Cordell coming by with that wife of his?"

She laughed, hugged him. "He'll be here, but he won't let Jerrie Dawn out of his sight as long as you're around."

Dempsey didn't reply, just suddenly looked far older than his age. Sinking onto the bed, he lay back, placing his crutches on the floor beside him.

"How's Roxanne? She said she got a good job."

"She did. Doing fine. She'll be over here for Sunday dinner."

He nodded. "Hope I'm awake by then. Feel like I could sleep for a week," he said, and yawned as if to prove it.

"Can I get you anything?"

He smiled, shook his head. "Naw. Thanks, though."

She turned to leave the room and he said something unintelligible, his voice almost a whisper. She looked back at him. "I didn't hear you."

"I said—I said it wasn't so bad over there." He swallowed hard, and she saw his Adam's apple bob a couple of times. He patted what remained of his leg. "This isn't the worst that could happen." Like his daddy, he seemed to be looking for confirmation. "I saw worse."

She nodded. "I know. I know." She tried to smile, but could feel the sag when it collapsed on her face. Standing there, she suddenly knew she had to hear that he was her Dempsey again, the boy she'd raised and loved and almost lost, both physically and emotionally. Closing the door behind her, she went to the bed and sat beside him.

"Son, are we okay? The two of us, I mean?" She searched his face. "You know I wouldn't hurt you for the world."

He raised himself on an elbow and touched her shoulder, tentatively at first, then when she put her arms around him, hugging her with a frightening ferocity. "We're okay, Mama. We are."

When they had released each other, she looked hard into his face, searching for a sign that would tell her he meant it, that they were all right, were who they'd always been to one another. Though he smiled up at her with shining eyes, if the reassurance she sought was there, it was hidden in his exhaustion and excitement at being home. "You rest now." She patted him, briefly put her cheek next to his, and went to the door. She turned to look at him one last time. His eyes were closed now. His face wore a hollowed out look that scared her, and she felt her heart skip a beat. One deep breath, then another and she left the room.

In the kitchen the whole family had returned to huddle around the table. They looked up, almost as one, when she entered the room.

"What's he doing?" asked Jacob.

"Is he all right?" Margaret wanted to know.

"Why, 'course he's all right," Harmon said, but he too looked at Vada.

She lifted her shoulders in a slight shrug. "You know as much as I do." Unable to bear the sight of the hopeful faces in front of her, she turned to stare out the window over the sink. Folding her arms over her midsection, she rubbed them, trying to smooth the goose bumps that refused to leave.

Chapter 42

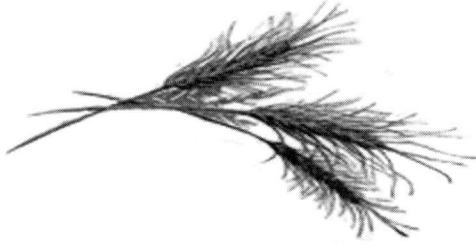

Vada shut off the alarm and lay quietly, trying to orient herself to wakefulness. She heard movement in the kitchen—probably Miz Priddy. Swinging her legs over the edge of the bed, she slipped her housecoat on and went down the hall. As she entered the kitchen, she stared in surprise at Dempsey, crisply dressed, his back erect, pouring a cup of coffee from the blackened, battered coffeepot.

"You're up mighty early," she said. "I thought you'd probably want to sleep in."

He shook his head, grinning. "Nope. Not me. I'm ready to get out there and hunt me a job."

Despite his grin, she felt as if she were in the presence of a man wound so tight he might fly into pieces any minute. "You have to do it today? It can't wait a little till you're rested?"

He shook his head. "Early bird gets the worm," he said. "I'm going to drop Pa off at the plant and take the truck."

As if summoned by mention of him, Harmon appeared in the kitchen, wheezing, carrying his work boots. He lifted his eyebrows at the sight of Dempsey. "Still bound and determined to get out there and find some work, are you?"

Dempsey nodded. "Yessir. Can't be too soon for me."

Harmon dropped his boots to the floor and sat with a grunt. Clearing his throat, he began rolling a cigarette, paying far more attention than usual to the process. "You know you ain't got to do that—you got money coming to you if you want it. Let 'em give you that disability check. Then you could take your time finding a job."

Dempsey didn't look at Harmon, but through the back door. "I don't want charity. Don't need it." He swallowed, and it was loud in the quiet of the kitchen. Still not looking at either of them, he said, "I can take care of myself."

Harmon and Vada exchanged glances, and Vada shook her head slightly. Harmon lit his cigarette, nodding to Vada or Dempsey or the room at large—it was hard to tell because his eyes were everywhere. "All right, son. You'd know best about it." This uncustomary giving in told Vada that nothing was all right, that Harmon was more worried than he'd ever been, but Dempsey just seemed to take the agreement as his due.

She turned to the stove and cracked eggs into the sputtering bacon grease, her scalp prickling.

* * * * *

Dempsey returned to the house at the end of Harmon's shift, driving him home like he was the father and Harmon the child. They both looked exhausted. When Dempsey went to his room and closed the door, Vada didn't expect to see him again for a couple of hours at least, maybe not even all night, but he soon emerged in denim pants and a tee shirt, one pant leg neatly pinned up.

"Have any luck?" she asked from where she stood peeling potatoes.

His handsome face, broader and more open than Harmon's, creased in a smile that stopped short of the light brown eyes. "Lotta leads," he said. "Lotta leads."

They made small talk for a bit, and relief was almost palpable in the room when Maureen, Jacob, and Gerald traipsed in.

"Gerald!" Dempsey said. "Where you been, boy? I thought you never would come home. What's the matter, you made one of them cows your girlfriend?"

Gerald flushed bright scarlet and grinned, offering a mumbled explanation of why he slept at the dairy, but Dempsey laughed and ruffled the spikey dark hair.

"Dempsey, you coming to our game tonight?" Jacob asked, snatching a piece of raw potato from the pile his mama was slicing. "Ow! Mama!" He moved away from her, holding the hand she had rapped with the dull side of her paring knife. "You coming?" he asked Dempsey again.

Harmon snorted, then fell into a fit of coughing. When he had regained his breath, he pulled a handkerchief from his back pocket, wiped his mouth, and said, "He's too tired for that kind of thing. Whyn't you let him get set?"

"I was just asking," Jacob said. "Are you, Dempsey?"

"Why, sure I am," Dempsey said before anyone could answer for him. "Wouldn't miss it. What position you boys playing?" As they launched into a discussion of the upcoming game and their places in it, Vada looked at Harmon and shrugged. Dempsey always had done what Dempsey saw fit.

"You boys get outside and let me get dinner on," she said, and when Jacob started to protest—as he did at every opportunity—she grabbed him by the upper arms and firmly turned him around, toward the door, and gave him a little push. "Go."

Once they were in the backyard, Vada watched them through the window over the sink as they perched on the picnic table. Miz Priddy wandered in from the front room, crocheting even as she walked, but without looking at her hands.

Moving up to stand beside Vada, she continued to force the small hook rapidly in and out of the soft pink thread. "Poor Dempsey," she said. "He just ain't the same."

Vada didn't reply, but stood with folded arms. Much as she cared about what he was going through, more than anything she wanted him to be normal so she could make certain the two of them really were all right—that their relationship was back on solid ground—but she couldn't imagine a more selfish thing to do than to worry him when he had so much to contend with. And hadn't he said they were fine? Why couldn't she just take him at his word?

She heard a wail and saw Maureen run through the backyard to the picnic table, Margaret sprinting after her. The three-year-old gave Dempsey a wide berth and went to Gerald, crying and gesturing at her older sister. Vada watched as Dempsey sat silently by for a moment, then reached over and tugged on one red curl. Maureen stopped crying abruptly and looked at him, and when he motioned her to him, she hesitated only briefly. Once on his lap, she glared at Margaret, jabbing her forefinger in the older girl's direction and no doubt confiding to Dempsey all the evil done to her by the wicked sister.

Dempsey nodded, as serene as if soothing small children was all in a day's work, and Vada felt a very small lifting of the weight of worry. She turned back to her cooking, looking out only occasionally as she listened to Miz Priddy's prattle and Harmon's terse replies. If she did not look too closely at Dempsey's face, or at the empty place his leg used to be, she could almost forget that things were not as normal as they seemed. As she busied herself with supper chores, she tried to forget the panic in his eyes, tried to banish the doom-laden thoughts that pursued her.

* * * * *

The first Sunday after Dempsey returned home, he accompanied his father, grandmother, and siblings to church while Vada prepared dinner. She had just put a red velvet cake in the oven and begun peeling potatoes when she heard Roxanne call from the front of the house.

"Vada?"

"In here, Roxie." Vada rinsed the potato starch from her hands, dried them on her apron and met her sister in the hallway.

Roxanne held up a big jar of honey. "Look what I brought for Dempsey."

Vada laughed. "He'll appreciate that."

"Remember when he used to just eat it out of the jar?" Roxanne asked, placing it on the table.

Vada nodded. "I don't reckon he's changed any in that respect."

Roxanne found an apron and put it over her sleeveless, bright pink shift. Her curly blonde hair was piled loosely on her head and tendrils fell around her face and on her neck. Her skin, with the late summer's tan, was like cream with a little coffee. The promise of her girlhood had been realized, and Vada often thought her sister was as beautiful as any movie star, but even better than her outward beauty was her inner goodness. In the last few years, Roxanne's teenage self-absorption had gradually disappeared, replaced by a reflective, sometimes even wistful, attention to those around her.

"How's he doing?" Roxanne asked, slicing tomatoes onto an oblong platter.

Vada sighed. "He says he's fine." She peeled most of another potato before she spoke again. "All I know to do is treat him like the same old Dempsey."

"Do you think he hates me?" Roxanne kept her eyes on the tomatoes she was slicing, but Vada heard the tremor in her voice.

"Forevermore, Roxie," Vada said, and stopped her paring knife in mid-peel. "Of course he doesn't hate you. Why would he? And if he did, don't you think he would have said so by now?"

Roxanne shrugged and looked at Vada. Tears stood in her deep blue eyes, but none fell. "I feel so guilty," she whispered.

Vada put down the paring knife and embraced her sister. When she released her, she searched the gorgeous face. "Why would you feel guilty? Dempsey didn't have to join the army."

"I know, but..."

"Roxie," Vada said. "You came home. He could've done the same." She turned and picked up the paring knife again. "Now, if we don't get to cooking we're going to be in a fix."

* * * * *

Vada leaned against the door frame, her arms folded over her midsection, watching Dempsey and Roxanne. Roxanne perched on the picnic table with her feet tucked under her, while Dempsey straddled the bench, the pinned-up pant leg hidden beneath the table. Vada couldn't see Dempsey's face, but Roxanne's was unmarred by tension, softened further by an occasional smile. Vada sighed. *I wish everything could be as normal as that picture right there.* But it wasn't, and she feared—no, knew—none of their lives would ever be normal again.

Chapter 43

Every day for more than a month, Dempsey left the house in search of work. Every day when he came home, his spirits were lower. If she asked him, he always gave her the same anwer: *Everything's great. Couldn't be better, got a lotta leads, lotta leads.* Finally came a day when he didn't get up, not even after Harmon had gone to work and Margaret and Jacob to school. Vada sat in the kitchen, hands wrapped around the cup of coffee grown tepid, a well of dread inside. Maureen played on the floor with a basket of clothespins, making "pin peoples," while Miz Priddy hovered around Vada, hands making nervous patterns in the air like birds afraid to light.

"You going to see about him, Vada? You don't reckon he's took sick?" Her rheumy eyes betrayed her fear for her grandson.

Vada looked into her coffee cup as if there might be an answer there. *God, where are you now? I know Harmon's been praying double time. Where are you when we're losing Dempsey?* And there was no doubt in her mind that they were losing him, that whatever horror had been gaining was finally about to overtake him. She closed her eyes, took one long, quavering breath, and pushed herself up from the table. Pulling the frayed blue flannel shirt she wore as a sweater more tightly around her, she forced her feet out of the kitchen and into the darkened hallway. At Dempsey's door, she tapped.

"Son?" It was on the tip of her tongue to ask, "Are you all right?" but suddenly, seeing it for herself was the most important thing in the world. She tapped again. "Son? Can I come in?"

When he still did not answer, she turned the knob and pushed open the door. Expecting darkness, at least dimness, she was surprised to see the room ablaze in light, not just what little light spilled through the north-facing window. Light shone from the ceiling fixture, from an old drop-light of Harmon's clipped to a hook on the wall, and from from several shadeless lamps she had never laid eyes on before. The room was absolutely spotless but for the random light fixtures and a towel rolled into a long cylinder lying by the door, as if it had been pressed against the gap at the bottom.

Dempsey lay on his side in an undershirt and a pair of khaki pants, both hands under one cheek as he had slept when a child. Believing him to be asleep, Vada moved toward him. His eyes opened, and she jumped as if he had suddenly leapt at her. She knew by the desolation on his face that whatever he had so determinedly avoided had finally overtaken him. His dull eyes set like two rocks in a face that had aged years in the last month.

As much as she wanted to kneel in front of him, she remained standing, afraid that to go to her knees would be an admission that he could not return from that awful place into which he had retreated. If she remained standing, she, like one of Harmon's preachers, could demand that Dempsey rise and be whole.

"You getting up today?" She forced cheer into her voice, but he didn't move, only looked at her as if to say, "Who are you kidding?" She tried again. "Come on, boy. Up and at 'em. I got mulch to spread. Sure could use the help."

"Mama," he said. Just that. "Mama."

She hesitated, steeled herself against the tenderness for him that threatened to overwhelm her. Her arms ached to cradle him as she had when he was three, but she could not succumb now. *It's for his own good. His own good.* "You got to get up, Dempsey. You can't lay here and give into this."

He looked at the ceiling, one arm over his forehead. "Give in to what? Being half human? Half a man?"

"Who told you that?" She moved his chin so he faced her. "Who?"

He jerked away. "Nobody had to tell me. I can see it when they look at me." He drew the back of one hand over his eyes as he squeezed them shut, as if by closing them he could forget. "I see it," he whispered.

For a moment Vada studied him, this boy who had made her love him in spite of herself. "Dempsey, you can't stop people from being curious. Or from showing it." He turned his face to the wall. She tried again. "If you see somebody with a head wrapped up in bandages, aren't you going to look at him, wonder what happened?" He didn't make a sound, so she knelt on the bed and grabbed his chin, turning his face toward her. "Look at me." When he did, she tried once more. "You're not the first one this has happened to. There've been other wars. Other men who've been...war heroes."

He pushed her away, and his laughter was a bark. "War hero! That's a laugh. Can't be a war hero if there's no war going on, can I?" He swung his leg over the bed and sat up, the movement so sudden that the blood drained from his face. "Just because thousands of people get killed over there in a week doesn't make it a war in this great land of ours." He ran the fingers of one hand through the light brown hair that had grown in the last six weeks from a brush cut to a shaggy cap. "Conflict. Ha." His voice echoed bitterly from the faded wallpaper, reminding Vada of Harmon's words.

"Not a war—a conflict. Can't you get nothing through that thick skull of yours, Vada?" But Harmon was human, like all those who had denied the reality of it. "Dempsey, they're just scared of it." She struggled with the words, barely understanding the rationalization herself. "Calling it a war would make it real," she finished, voice cracking, and knew immediately this had been the wrong thing to say.

"No!" Face twisted in anguish, he pounded on his thigh. "This makes it real. This makes it real, and I have to live every day for the rest of my life with this, and with faces of dead people in my head, and with knowing there's no good reason for me to be alive and somebody else dead!" He fell back on the bed, pulled his stump onto it and turned over. "I'm tired. I want to go to sleep."

"Dempsey, listen to me. Arms and legs—that's not what makes you a man, a person." Vada motioned toward the closed door. "You tell the VA you want a leg, somebody'll make you one. And you ought to do that, but whether you do or you don't, what makes you a man is inside."

He did not respond, and she stared at his back in mute helplessness. Were there words enough in the world to give him back what he'd lost, not just physically, but within? Finally, when he did not turn toward her or make any sound, she left the room, closing the door softly behind her.

* * * * *

And so it went, with Dempsey alternating between shouting at all of them to leave him alone, glaring at anyone who crossed his path, and engaging in hours-long staring contests with the ceiling of his room. At first, he at least talked to Roxanne when she dropped by, but eventually even she could not penetrate the malaise in which he had become mired. Harmon, for once, did not order Dempsey to do this or that, but seemed almost as depressed as the boy himself. When Vada broached the subject of "what to do" about Dempsey, Harmon looked blankly at her, a cigarette hanging from his thin lips, as if he couldn't quite make out her words. At night, when they were in bed, she heard the "bzz-bzz-bzz" of his whispered prayers. She hoped on the one hand that they did some good, and on the other that they wouldn't, if only so she would be proven right about God, and Harmon wrong. But then she felt guilty, and squeezed her own eyes shut and tried to pray, but nothing came out. *Spiritual constipation,* she always thought, but laughing about it made it no easier to bear.

Miz Priddy was no better than Harmon. She moped all over the house, and it was "Poor Dempsey" this and "The poor boy" that until Vada could scream. Finally, one evening almost three months after Dempsey returned home, Vada and Harmon were in the kitchen, Vada peeling potatoes, Harmon smoking, both looking from time to time out the back window at Dempsey, sitting atop the picnic table, unshaven, hair spiked from lack of care, watching Jacob and Gerald alternate between tossing the football back and forth and chasing one another around the sun-dappled green and gold of the back yard.

"I wish he'd go see somebody," she said, eyes on the potatoes she was cutting into cubes and dropping them into the big pot on the stove—*thunk. Thunk. Thunk.*

"See who?" Harmon asked.

"I don't know. A doctor. One of those psychiatrists."

"I been through that with him—told him them people down at the VA hospital probably see this all the time. But..."

Vada heard the shrug in his voice and wished she could encourage him. She was all out, though—out of encouraging words, positive thoughts, hope. Even if those doctors had seen boys—men—like Dempsey before, and of course they had, that didn't mean they'd know what to do for him. She lay awake many nights worrying about him, but lately she had started to become angry. *He's not the first person to expect one thing and get another, to lose a part of himself through no fault of his own.* It was tragic, certainly, but as Dempsey had said the first night he was home, "This isn't the worst that could happen."

She watched him and searched her own imperfect memory for some comparison to draw that might make sense to Dempsey, that might make him look at her with something besides pity that she could not understand the depths of his pain, or surliness because he hated the whole lot of them.

Just before Christmas, the answer came, not from her own mind but from the mailbox. It was a class schedule for spring classes at the Vo-Tech in Drumright. Trying to block out the memory of another time, another class, she ran her eyes down the list of offerings—Bookkeeping, Welding, Nurse

Aide, Cosmetology, Auto Repair—not a lot of things suited to Dempsey, but surely this was not all they had to offer. She sat down at the kitchen table to study on it a minute. Miz Priddy came in with the dustmop and placed it in the corner nearest the stove.

"What you got there?" She looked over Vada's shoulder. "Vo-Tech. You thinking about going back to school?" The old lady clucked. "You didn't even finish that last class you took." Vada ignored her, pushed back from the table, and went to Dempsey's room.

She tapped on the door. "Dempsey?" Pushing it open, she found him lying on the unmade bed, right leg bent at the knee, listening to the old Motorola radio that once sat in the living room. The twang of a guitar and Johnny Cash's inharmonious voice sounded faintly.

Dempsey's hollow eyes seemed to have some trouble focusing on her, but she plunged ahead. "Look here. This just came in the mail, and I bet there's two dozen things over yonder at the Vo-Tech that—that you—that a man with one leg could do."

He laughed, no longer piss and vinegar, but only vinegar. "A man. Right. When you find one, give that to him."

She took a deep, calming breath. "Dempsey, you've got to give up this self-pity. You act like you're the only person ever been hurt." He started to speak, but she dropped to the edge of the bed and put her fingers over his lips, feeling the bristles around them, above the lip and on the chin.

"Hush. I just want you to hear me out." Stubbornness dropped down over his eyes like a venetian blind, and the color of the iris went noticeably darker. He stared out the window, lips a thin line, while she talked to him. "Your daddy might let you sit in here till the end of time, and I might too, if I thought it would make you feel better. It won't. You keep laying in here wallowing in self pity, the rot that took your leg is nothing compared to the rot that'll go on in there." She thumped his chest, gone soft now from months of inactivity.

He tried to bat her hand away, but she grabbed his, shoving the circular in front of his face. "Look. Find you something to do that doesn't take two legs, or—"

He jerked the circular from her and wadded it, threw it as hard as he could, its weightlessness stopping it at the foot of the bed to drop onto the wrinkled sheet. This failure seemed to feed Dempsey's fury and he threw himself on his side, dragging a pillow over his head.

"Just go on," he said, voice muffled. "Go on and leave me be."

She put her hand on his shoulder, bare around his none-too-clean undershirt, and with slow, steady pressure, turned him to face her. "You can't stay in here and feel sorry for yourself for the rest of your life."

Jerking away, he rolled to the other side of the bed, where he lay glaring at her. "You don't know," he said. "You don't have any idea what it's like to be—to be not even twenty-two years old and trapped—laying in here like a turtle on its back." He was breathing hard sat up and leaned against the wall, leg and stump stuck out before him. "You don't know," he said again.

She looked at him for a few long seconds, then down at her hands, twisting the ring that had been his mama's. All right. She'd try it another way. "Look, Dempsey. You got hurt, you got hurt bad, and it's going to take a long while to get used to doing without your leg, but some didn't make it back at all—"

"Yeah. They're the lucky ones." Sweat beaded his forehead and upper lip.

Vada sighed. "What happened to you was horrible. But at least you were doing some good. Can you look at it that way?"

"You don't know!" Dempsey shouted, then his voice dropped until she could barely hear him. "Did good, did I? I'll tell you what I did. I'll tell you." His breathing became raspy. "I set fire to a whole goddamned village, burned it to the ground. Wasn't that good? Must be, because why else would we be told to do it, huh?"

"Well, I—"

Dempsey's eyes reddened. "How about this one? I went after a buddy to drag him to where they couldn't shoot him no more, and his arm came off in my hands." He banged his head against the wall behind him. "If I'd known the good I was doing, I don't reckon I would have puked all over him." Exhaustion crept into his voice. "Another time. There was a girl, five-six years old. Cutest little thing you ever saw, shoebutton eyes, mouth like a rosebud. Well, a G.I. offered her some candy out of a little sack. That girl pulled the pin on a grenade and dropped it right into that sack, took off running." His face was a mask, so old and pale that he looked like he could be his own grandfather. "When it blew the shit out of him I stood there with his brains all over me and body parts falling from the sky. And you know what I did, Mama? You want to know?" He didn't wait for an answer. "I shot that child in the back. How good is that?"

"Dempsey, son. Please."

"I have shit myself because I was so goddamned scared, and then walked around with my drawers full because I didn't dare stop long enough to change them."

She stood motionless, appalled, but still not willing to let him lie back down and give up. "All right, Dempsey. I'll grant you I *don't* know about that. It must have been horrible." Looking briefly down at the floor, she steeled herself. "I'll tell you what I do know," she said, looking up at Dempsey. "I know what it's like to be sixteen-years-old and to pick cotton in hundred-degree heat with a baby in a buggy and a baby in the dirt under it and another one in my belly. I know what it's like to pick that cotton all day long then drag myself back to a two-room cabin that's 130 degrees inside and fry fatback and turnip greens and gag on my own vomit while I got all of you fed." As she looked at him, the forced rage meant to snap him out of his self-pity became real and spilled over, a palpable thing on the bed between them, lumpy and misshapen. "I know what it's like to keep having young'uns after I was worn out, and to be worn out by the time I was eighteen." She tried to shut up but the words kept coming, spewing out of her like water from a faucet. "You don't know what trapped is, Dempsey, but you keep laying here feeling sorry for yourself and you will. You sure will, and you won't have a living soul to blame but yourself." She went to the door, backbone rigid. As she grasped the knob, she turned to him.

"I wouldn't take a million dollars for a single one of you—not you or Cordell or Nelda or the ones that was born to me, either. But this isn't what I would've picked, if I'd had a choice. And if you're smart, you're going to make a choice now, one that'll make this just a short, ugly little bit of your real life."

His expression didn't change, but seemed frozen into lines of belligerent outrage. He looked so much like he had when he'd displeased her as a child that Vada's anger began to dissolve.

"At least you could walk away," he said, voice quiet.

"I couldn't have walked far enough to get away from what I knew I had to do," she said, voice just as quiet. "You can buy you a leg, but I couldn't buy me a different life." They stared at one another for a long moment before she went out, closing the door behind her.

* * * * *

Later that day, Vada was in the back, turning over ground for a new flowerbed in anticipation of a predicted early and hard freeze, when Miz Priddy came around the side of the house.

"Where's Dempsey?" the old woman asked. "I went to see did he want some dinner, and he was gone." Her face creased in worry, and she scanned the backyard like he might be there. "You sure been at him."

Vada straightened and stared at her mother-in-law. At him? Is that how they all see it? She sighed. "Gone out? Or gone?"

"That bag he brung home with him is gone. So's most of his clothes."

Her voice dropped low. "And he took every light bulb in every socket in that room."

Vada leaned the shovel against the house and went to the back door, not even taking off the old boots she wore to garden in. When she reached his room, she stared at the unmade bed, the radio, the open closet door, and her heart dropped to her knees. She didn't mean this. Didn't mean for him to leave. She'd just been trying to pull him out of the sinkhole of self-pity he was mired in, to force him to stand up to life. Oh, Lord. What would she tell Harmon? She sighed, closed her eyes against the thought, then squared her shoulders and turned, almost running into Miz Priddy.

"He's not there," she told the old woman.

"I told you that." Miz Priddy set her jaw, turned and shuffled toward the front room, a sure sign that she had no desire to discuss this dreadful thing her daughter-in-law had done.

Vada went through the kitchen and stood at the screen door. "He probably just got tired of feeling sorry for himself. He'll be back," she said aloud, but the words sounded as empty as his room had been. Sighing, she left the house through the back door. Returning to her flowerbed, she dug with single-minded intensity, pushing thoughts of Dempsey as far away as possible. They kept coming back, though, and the harder she rammed the shovel into the ground, the more frightened she became.

Chapter 44

V ada waited up for Harmon, who was working a double shift at the
glass plant. She heard the squeal of the pickup brakes and then his
tired steps on the porch, in the front room, and down the hallway toward
where she waited in the kitchen. Pulling his plate from the oven, she placed
it on the table and stood behind his chair as she waited for him to wash. He
glanced at her as he seated himself, but remained silent, dropping his face into
his hands and rubbing it hard. Running his fingers through his thinning hair,
he picked up his fork.

"You going to stand there, or you going to sit down and talk to me while I
eat?" He took a long swallow of the buttermilk she had poured for him, and
she slid into the next chair. He forked a piece of meatloaf into his mouth and
looked at her, at first blankly, then with dawning realization. "What's wrong?
Something wrong with Ma? One of the young'uns?"

She shook her head and looked at a spot directly in front of her on the vinyl
table cover. "No. I mean, yes. Dempsey." Just his name, coated with guilt as it
was, seemed to catch in her throat.

Harmon laid his fork down. "What about him?"

"He's—he—we had some words, and he's gone off. I don't know where. Or
how. I was outside, in the back. Your mama told me he was gone." Her face felt
swollen, hot with shame. "I'm sorry, Harmon. I don't know what ails him—I
just tried to talk sense to him is all, and he—he…" Her voice trailed off at the
look on Harmon's face.

"What did you say to my boy?" His breathing came in gasps, and she was afraid he'd have another one of his spells.

"My boy, too. He's my boy. And it wasn't nothing, Har. It wasn't. I was only trying to help—"

He looked at her as if she'd just said she'd hit the boy in the head with a crow bar. "Help? How is it you was trying to help and Dempsey ends up gone?"

Her mouth moved, but nothing came out, and she finally rose and left the room, clutching her robe closed at the throat. Stumbling down the darkened hallway, she found her way to their bed and fell onto it. *Jesus, Jesus, Jesus.* She couldn't even remember why it was so important that Dempsey see things her way, but within her, a circle of words spun round and round: *He had his leg blown off. Wasn't his mind. Just his leg.* This little voice, her defender, was met with the sound of Dempsey as a child, running up the dirt road from the school bus, hollering "Mama? Mama? Where you at?" Only now it was she who cried out for him— "Oh, Dempsey, where you at, boy?"

* * * * *

At first, Harmon took off every Saturday and Sunday afternoon in the old truck, looking for Dempsey. Tulsa. Kellyville. Mounds and Kiefer. Okmulgee. She knew he went to those places because she heard him tell his mama so, but he never told Vada. He hardly spoke to her. None of them said much of anything anymore. Even Margaret. Always the child closest to Vada, she was now the one most reproachful. Each time she passed her mother, the girl seemed to shrink to a smaller size so as to avoid their touching, and she never came to Vada anymore for hair curling, or button sewing. And although Vada felt certain neither Harmon nor Miz Priddy would actually say out loud that she had caused Dempsey to leave, the whole family seemed to have caught the idea like a virus.

The one exception was Nelda. Her husband now worked in Oklahoma City and came home only on weekends, so she often came to the house, bringing her two-year-old twins and the baby. "It's not your fault, Mama," she would say, her lovely face set in the same firm lines Harmon's were when he told her if she had left Dempsey alone he'd still be there. Vada didn't know who to believe, but no matter who was right, she couldn't honor the idea that there was ever a good time to wallow in self-pity. The people who made it through life were like good gardeners: they tilled and planted and weeded, hoping for just enough rain and sun to make a decent crop; if that failed, they plowed it under and started over.

Christmas came and went. Gerald was there, with Jacob, Margaret, and

Maureen, and Nelda brought Bill and the children, shyly announcing the expected birth of another child seven months away. Cordell and his eight-month-pregnant Jerrie Dawn waddled in—Cordell appeared to be the one eating for two, but Vada didn't say so. Roxanne came, bringing Allen, a young man she'd been seeing with some regularity, and Vada's spirits were buoyed a bit to see that her sister looked so happy. Allen and Bill assembled the tricycle Roxanne had given Maureen for Christmas, and Maureen pedaled it through the house, screeching and ringing the bell mounted on the handlebars.

The sun seemed to shine twice as brightly that day, the sky to blaze more blue than ever, but the wind held a chill that portended the winter to come. Every time anyone entered through the front or back of the house, Vada's attention jerked toward the silhouetted figure in the doorway just long enough to make sure it was not Dempsey. It never was.

The whole family gathered around the big table in the kitchen for ham, candied yams, mashed potatoes, giblet gravy, pumpkin pie, and whatever else Vada and Miz Priddy were able to think up. Dempsey's name was not mentioned once. Although there was no empty chair at the table, there nevertheless seemed to be an empty space, one that only Dempsey could fill.

Nelda and her family left last that night, and she hugged Vada tightly. "Don't worry, Mama. It's going to be all right. I know it."

The comfort Vada often found in Nelda, usually such a hard-headed realist, was absent. She simply hugged her back, afraid to speak for fear she would cry.

* * * * *

By the middle of April, temperatures climbed to near eighty, and humidity bleached the sky almost white. Vada rose early, leaving Harmon asleep propped up on a stack of pillows so that he might breathe more easily. He was in his third day of absence from work because of a stubborn cold, one of many he caught each year, and he had been up half the night choking for air. After she had seen Jacob and Margaret off to school, she went to the backyard, found herself perspiring just walking to the shed. Slapping one of Harmon's old caps on her head to shade her face from the sun, she pulled the mower from beneath the small overhang Riley and Gerald had built to cover it, and began pushing it over the lush green grass. The scent of cut grass filled her nostrils and she inhaled even more deeply, as if she could store it up for a time when it would not be available to her.

She knew she'd have the day to herself. Miz Priddy was at a local church that provided a hot midday meal, quilting, dominoes, and other pastimes for older people. After Dempsey left, she had begun going every weekday for dinner and then an afternoon of quilting. Margaret and Jacob no longer came home to eat at noon, but took sandwiches or leftovers to school wrapped in newspaper or the occasional paper bag. Only Maureen kept Vada company most days, and she, a most self-sufficient child, needed her mother very little. Each day seemed endless to Vada, although she remembered the days when she had craved time by herself. And it was not the being alone that distressed her now, but the isolation, and the isolation was made worse by the fact that she could not bring herself to admit that she had made a mistake. She was sorry Dempsey was gone, Lord yes, as sorry as she'd ever been for anything, but she hung on to one thought: *I couldn't let him just lay down and give up.*

Behind that idea was one that battered at her defenses without ceasing, but to which she refused to give place—she could have approached Dempsey some other way, talked more nicely. There were times when she would have given anything to be held, coaxed, coddled—talked into getting up and going on instead of stonewalled, forced into continuing in the face of what she saw as impossible barriers. Like when Addy died. Harmon had not babied her, no; he had been sympathetic, but she'd still had to carry her share of the load. He'd practically forced her to go care for her mother. And even if he had not made it clear that she had to continue to work, to pick cotton, cook, and tend babies, she would have forced herself. *I'm always going to get up and do what I have to, eventually. Some won't. They don't have the heart. Or the spine.* This made her think of her mama. *Nobody ever made her do anything she didn't want to. That's what's wrong with her to this day, why I see her two, three times a year. So maybe I didn't make a mistake with Dempsey, but oh, Lord, I miss him. I do.*

These thoughts haunted her, and sometimes she felt as if she were in a fight with herself. That's how it was when Dempsey walked up and planted himself in front of her, and so surprised was she to see him that her first words were a continuance of her internal argument.

"My mama'd be a different person today. I'm hanged if she wouldn't."

Dempsey's look was only a little quizzical, like he already knew what she was thinking, but her second question brought an outright laugh.

"Where'd you get that leg, son?"

He looked at his denim-covered thigh, rapped it with his knuckles, and brought his gaze back up to meet hers. "Stole it off a stinking Indian when he wasn't looking. You want it back?" He grinned and she did, too, her heart so full it felt like happiness was going to choke her. For a minute it was as if he had never left, never gone to Viet Nam, never lost his leg, never come home and got mad and left again. He enveloped her in his arms, and when she swayed a little from the heat and the surprise and the intense pleasure of his presence, he held her firmly upright, as steady on those two legs as he had ever been on his own.

Mindful of Mr. Gilmartin's ever-present eyes staring from his back door to hers, Vada dragged Dempsey into the house and made him sit at the table. Her hands shook as she poured him a glass of iced tea, muttering under her breath, "Dempsey's home, he's home, he's home," as much a verbal pinch to verify the reality of it as for the sheer joy of saying the words. Three or four months ago she might have been torn between kissing him and slapping him, but not now. Right and wrong had gone the way of the winter snow, and all she felt was glad to see him.

"Where have you been all this time? Don't you know we was all worried to death?"

He held up a hand, wagging his head back and forth. "I know, I know. Don't give me any grief about that, now." He took a long swallow of tea. "I had to get myself together, finish feeling sorry for myself."

"Oh, Dempsey…don't. I didn't mean…" While only minutes before she'd assured herself she'd done the right thing in rousting Dempsey from his sorrowful state, her voice now trailed off and heat rose up her neck at her embarrassment over having to hear her own words parroted back at her. "Just stop," she finished weakly.

He swiftly stood, grabbed her and swung her around the room. "You stop it." He twirled her around as if in a complicated dance and pulled her back to him, smacked her big and loud on the cheek, then held her at arm's length. "You've got no reason to be sorry." He grinned. "I took your advice, Mama. At least I did after I got over being mad at you and the whole world." He punched her lightly on the arm. "I got myself into school, going to learn how to do something that means something."

She clapped her hands together. "You're going to the Vo-Tech. I knew—"

He cut her off, pulled a piece of paper out of his pocket. "Nope. Not Vo-Tech. You're looking at a genuine Oklahoma A and M aggie."

She took the paper, looked up at him, down at it. Back up at him. "When? When are you going to do this?"

He laughed. "Don't you see those grades? I did it," he said. "One semester anyway." He sat down at the table again, took a drink of tea, popped back up to where she still stood holding the paper. "I tell you, Mama, you'd be surprised how little you think about your body when your mind gets busy." He rapped on his thigh again, a hollow sound that made her wince in spite of herself. "Wouldn't have gone this far but the VA paid for it, and I needed to get where I'm going a little faster than I could on those crutches."

"You went clear to Stillwater?"

"Mama, I've been to Viet Nam." He grinned. "Getting to Stillwater's nothing." As if that settled *that*, he looked around the kitchen. "Everything looks the same. Isn't that something? I thought everything would be so different when I come back."

They were the same words he'd said all those months ago, but were no longer filled with pain and desperation. Now he was Dempsey again, more Dempsey than he'd ever been before, if that was possible.

Vada finally went to the table and dropped into a chair. It didn't look the same to her. The worn linoleum was somehow brighter, the air a little lighter, the window more sparkling, just to have Dempsey back. "Gerald is sleeping in your room. Decided he could get up a little earlier after all."

Dempsey made a dismissive motion with one hand. "It doesn't matter. I've got a job in Stillwater, for the summer anyway. I just couldn't wait to see you all."

"Why didn't you call, Dempsey? Your daddy's been near about frantic." Which was only partially true. After the first few weeks, Harmon had lost the desperate fear he'd had for his boy's safety, and lapsed into resigned sadness. If anything bad was to happen to Dempsey, they'd hear about it. It was Vada whose frantic fear revealed itself only by her constant cleaning and yard work. Now that Dempsey sat here in front of her, she suddenly felt very, very tired, as if it had all caught up with her.

He ducked his head, then gazed out the back door. "Aw, Mama. I was…I was mad, at first. Then I was…embarrassed, I guess." He looked back to Vada, his face set in earnest lines. "The first few weeks of school, I was just looking for a fight." He grimaced. "I hated all those people, walking around like there wasn't a war going on, acting like their world was the only one there was. But then once I got interested, got to talking to them, you know, in my classes, and once I got to studying, I found myself going hours, even days, without even thinking about my leg, about…Viet Nam, and all that." He stood, his back to her. "Then I woke up one morning, and I thought, 'Boy, you must be crazy. What was it you were so het up over?'" He turned to face her, spread his arms wide. "And here I am."

She searched his face, looking for hidden anger, fear, but saw none. "You're sure?" she couldn't help asking. "Sure there's nothing wrong, that we're all right, me and you?" Her chest and throat tightened, and she had to force the next words out. "You know I love you, Dempsey, love you just like I gave birth to you myself."

He caught her small hand in both his. "I know that! I always knew it, but something—I don't know. When you were fixing to have Maureen, I got it in my head that somehow this young'un would be the one that would use you up, suck you dry and there wouldn't be anything left of you for—for me." His eyes glittered in the bright light that shone through the window, and she could only look at him, wait for him to continue. "I used to be afraid every time you'd get ready to have another baby, afraid you'd die, like my mama. And you're the only mama I really remember. I couldn't have stood that." He swallowed hard. "And the way you didn't ever get on me when I was growing up, not like you did the rest of them—sometimes I thought you were going to kill Cordell, honest to God."

She stared at him, dumbfounded and incredibly relieved all at the same time. "I—I didn't *have* to get after you like I did them. You were…" Her voice trailed off as she searched for words. When she couldn't think of a better one, she said simply, "You were good." She hugged him, held him as tight as she could, and when she released him, looked into his light brown eyes, searching for the demons he'd brought home from Viet Nam. "I could never love Maureen or Gerald or Margaret—none of them, any more than I do you." She looked down at her hands. "And Roxanne…you just have to understand about her. And about Addy, and my mama and all."

He ducked his head, blushing, then looked back up. "I know. I do." He examined his hands then swallowed hard and met her eyes. "She all right?"

Vada shrugged, then nodded. "She'll be by this weekend, I reckon." She hesitated before she spoke again. "What about the—the nightmares, and the lights and all?"

He shrugged. "I talk to a guy at the VA every so often, when I can get to Muskogee. But just knowing you and Pa are here—knowing that you love me and you're going to be here for me—that'll go a long way toward learning to sleep with the lights off."

She clapped her hands to her mouth. "Oh, Good Lord! Your daddy!" She smiled through brimming eyes and hugged him again. "You stay here. I don't want him to go another minute without knowing you're back, and safe." As she hurried down the hallway to the bedroom, she felt lighter than she had in months. They'd all sleep that night.

1975

Chapter 45

Vada watched Harmon and Dempsey through the back door, torn between running out and throwing her arms around Harmon and picking him off with the .22 he kept behind the kitchen door.

"I ain't seen a woman yet could drive proper," he was saying. "And that was them been doing it all their lives." He clutched the back of the lawn chair and wheezed the words out. Although he was visibly trembling, he held out a hand, palm up. "Just pass them keys over to me, now, hear?" He waggled his fingers, but Dempsey stood pat, his light brown crew cut tipped with blond from the summer's sun, and topping his dark face like a brush.

"You can't drive anymore, and somebody's got to," Dempsey said. He looked toward the back door where Vada hovered. "Mama, we'd better get going if you don't want to be down there all day."

Harmon's gaze was full of reproach. "Can't believe you'd talk to your daddy that way, and you a war hero."

Dempsey laughed. "Number one, what's being a war hero got to do with how I talk to my daddy? And number two, if you gave me a quarter to go with that war hero business, I could come pretty near having enough to get a cup of coffee."

Just then, Maureen tore around the side of the house and skidded to a stop in front of Dempsey. She pulled at the cut-off denim shorts that seemed always to work themselves into the crevice of her buttocks. "Where you going,

Dempsey?" Without waiting for an answer, she said, "I want to go, too."

As Vada came down the back steps, purse in hand, Dempsey pulled the lanky thirteen-year-old redhead to him, placing his chin atop her head. "You can't go, darlin'. I'm taking Mama to her driving test." He tousled her already wild hair. "They've got Highway Patrolmen over there giving the tests. They see this mess of red stuff on top of your head, they're liable to put you in jail for impersonating a match."

"I'm not skinny, and that stuff on my head is called 'hair.'" She scowled at him and struggled out of his grip, running to Vada. "Mama, I can go, can't I?" The short run had apparently forced the shorts back into their accustomed space, and she jiggled from foot to foot, finally using her fingers again to pull them out.

Vada slapped the girl lightly on the arm. "Quit digging, Maureen. It's not ladylike. Now go wash your hands."

"But you said if I didn't tell Daddy you were driving you'd—"

Harmon collapsed into the wooden-framed, hammock-like chair. "God almighty, does the whole world know my wife's took up driving and running around?"

Maureen kissed the top of his head. "The whole world doesn't know," she told him. "You didn't know, and there's people in China that don't know."

Vada could see him relax, trying not to grin. She patted Harmon's shoulder. "I'll be back before you know it."

"No, Mama," Maureen cried. "I want to go with you. You never take me anywhere. Ever since Granny died I just have to sit here like I'm dead, too." Her face reddened and Vada knew this was not a conversation she wanted to have, especially in front of Harmon. He would know she was afraid to leave him alone, and he would become apoplectic at the idea that Maureen had to be left at home to care for him. But Miz Priddy's stroke and subsequent death earlier in the year had created a void that someone had to fill.

She looked up at the girl and was astonished all over again at the six inches Maureen had on her. If she was 5'8" now, going on thirteen years old, Lord knew what she'd be when she was fully-grown. Although it was hard to exert any authority from this angle, Vada grasped Maureen's arms at the biceps. "I'll bring you something if you behave, all right?"

"Something good? Not just a candy bar?" Maureen's gold-flecked eyes regarded her mother with suspicion.

Vada thought, not for the first time, how different this child was from the ones who had come before. Any one of them would have been thrilled with the prospect of a simple piece of gum. "Something good," she promised.

"A magazine," Maureen said. "I want a *Mad Magazine*. Or *National Lampoon*."

"All right, all right." She leaned over to kiss Harmon's cheek. He'd never have stood for such public shows of affection five years ago, but he couldn't get away from her now, and Vada took a double-edged pleasure from the acts.

"Wish you'd just let me be," he groused. "Guess you feel guilty, though, seeing how you ain't never around no more."

"Harmon, for pity sake, I'm the one ought to be saying leave me be! I haven't been anywhere but to learn to drive and to the grocery store for months. I'm taking this driving test, I'm getting a license, and we'll talk about what I'll be doing when I get home."

Clutching her purse with the few dollars in it that she would need for the license, she took off at a trot, eager to be away from his whining. He became more childlike every year. "Lord!" she said, and heard a laugh behind her. She glanced over her shoulder, and there was Dempsey, hurrying toward her in his stiff legged gait, grinning from ear to ear.

"Quit laughing at me," she said. "And Maureen's right. You do walk like Chester." Since Dempsey had bought Vada and Harmon a TV, reruns of *Gunsmoke* had become an indispensable part of the week for Maureen, and she saw likenesses to Chester, Matt Dillon, Miss Kitty, and the other characters in nearly everyone.

"Go ahead. Insult me. It doesn't bother me a bit," he said, sliding behind the wheel of his yellow '73 Chevrolet.

Vada sniffed. "Your daddy gets worse every passing day. Makes me wish he'd take up drinking."

"I don't know about that," Dempsey said, "but I sure as hell wish he'd give up cigarettes. He'd sure feel better."

"Not to hear him tell it."

Dempsey laughed. "Yeah." He began to hack and cough, spitting imaginary phlegm on the floorboard of his immaculate car, wiping his mouth on the back of his hand. "My pa coughed worse than this every day of his life," he said in perfect imitation of Harmon. His voice rose several octaves. "'And didn't have a lung left when he died.'"

"I never said that," Vada said.

"Well, you ought to. You baby him too much."

"I guess. Sometimes. But wait till you've got a wife and she's dying. Then see how you treat her."

"Aw, if I ever get married it'll be to somebody that'll outlive me by a long shot. For that matter, Pa's going to outlive me and you both. He's tough as a boot. He ain't going to die."

Vada glanced at him, saw the stubborn chin and set jaw. Regardless of his statement, Dempsey knew as well as she did that Harmon wouldn't live many more years.

"Unless he busts a blood vessel in that hard head of his when you tell him you got a job."

Vada shuddered. "I don't have it yet," she said. She knew she would, though, but had deliberately avoided telling Harmon until she had a driver's license and didn't have to depend on people to get her to work. He'd burst more than one vessel if he thought she—and by extension, he—was going to ask a favor from someone.

* * * * *

Dempsey let her out at the curb when they returned. As she shut the car door behind her, he called to her. "You still fixing dinner for Maureen's birthday Friday? Even if you start to work before then?"

Vada put a forefinger to her lips. "Shhh! Don't tell the whole world." She walked back to the car. "I'm perfectly capable of cooking, job or not. Just make sure you remember that record player you promised her, or I'll never hear the end of it." She waved a hand at him. "Now go on before you get me in all kinds of trouble." Turning, she walked slowly toward the house, holding the small document in her hand. She was glad they didn't have her picture on it, like Gerald's did when he returned from California. *5'1", 112 pounds, black hair, hazel eyes.* The least they could have done was get it right. Inaccuracy irritated her, more now than ever. She was five feet, one and three-quarter inches tall. As good as five foot two, as far as she was concerned. She distinctly remembered telling them so.

Rounding the corner of the house, she saw Harmon where she'd left him two hours ago, head slumped onto his chest. Her heart raced and she ran across the grass. *Oh, Lord, not yet, please,* she prayed.

She touched the side of his face, then his neck. He was still warm. "Har, you sleeping? It's me, Vada," she said.

"Well, who else would it be?" He raised his head and looked around. "And I wasn't asleep," he lied.

"How you feeling?" She put a hand on the back of his neck again, frowned. "You sure are warm. Maybe you ought to come in the—"

He waved her back with his own hand. "'Course I'm warm. The sun's out ain't it? And don't you come nosing around me, girl." Wheezes punctuated every word, and he fell into a fit of coughing. Vada dropped her purse and hovered about him, searching for anything she could do to stop the phlegm-filled, choking cough. Someday this cough would take him away before her very eyes.

He tried to say something, and she knew the strangled noises, understandable only in context and accompanied by his violent motioning, meant "Get back, get away and leave me *be*," but she couldn't. When the fit finally subsided, he lacked even the strength to keep Vada from wiping his sweaty face, touching the ragged muslin that passed for a handkerchief to his lips, and inspecting what she found there.

Breathing hard, he glared at her, and she understood. *How dare she hover around him and yammer about helping him and then draw breath like it was nothing?* Twenty-eight years of marriage had taught her something, even if it wasn't exactly what she needed to know.

"Where you been so long?" he asked when he could speak. "It don't take no three hours to get a driver's license."

This would have been the time to tell him about the hospital and the job she'd been interviewed for, been hired to do. But she couldn't. Not yet. She stared at him, feeling resentful and deceitful at the same time, until a tremendous clattering noise jerked her attention to the house, and Margaret crashed through the back door in hot pursuit of Maureen, who ran behind her father.

"You stay out of my stuff, you miserable little brat." Margaret made as if to step forward and Maureen backed up a step. Margaret stopped, shaking with indignation. "*When* are you people going to teach that child some *manners?*" Her long black hair made a valiant effort to curl about her narrow face in spite of what Vada knew to be hours spent trying to straighten it.

Harmon pulled Maureen closer. "Nothing wrong with her that wasn't wrong with you at her age." He poked Maureen in the ribs, and she giggled.

"Plus, you're stoooopid," Maureen told her sister.

"Mama!" Margaret's flawless skin reddened and she became more visibly rigid, quivering again, a bow pulled a little too tight for Vada's comfort. Margaret had moved to Oklahoma City with a boy she'd gone with for several years and finally married, only to have the marriage fall apart before the first anniversary. Now she was home, working at Safeway and carping at Maureen, who, to be sure, usually deserved it.

"It ain't your mama's fault," Harmon said. "She tries."

Margaret snorted. "Nobody around here tries." She glared at Maureen and pointed a finger at her. "*She—*" a pause for dramatic effect—"has got the devil in her, and I'm not just saying that." When Vada and Harmon both simply stared at Margaret, she dropped her hand to her side. "Well, she does."

Maureen put her hands on hips that had not yet gained shape. "Huh-uh. The devil'd be afraid to get in me."

"You got that right," Margaret muttered.

Vada rubbed her temples, two fingers on each side, and then looked at Margaret. "Why do you have to fight with her like you were her age?" Margaret did not answer, and Vada glanced toward Harmon, who, with shaking hands, had begun to roll a smoke.

He hadn't even creased the paper before Maureen was by his side. "Let me do it, Daddy." Without waiting for permission, she took the paper from him, creased it, and, after her father had added Prince Albert, rolled a perfect cylinder with expert fingers. Looking slyly at Margaret, she twisted both ends and held it up. "Here's how Lonnie rolls 'em," she said. She put one end in her mouth and inhaled deeply, holding the imaginary smoke in, cheeks puffed.

Puzzled, Vada looked from Maureen to Margaret, whose face seemed ready to explode into a million brilliant red shards. "You little sneak," Margaret hissed between her teeth, and quick as a flash seized the child by the neck of her striped T-shirt while Maureen's eyes widened in gleeful terror. Maureen was the taller of the two by a good three inches and the sight of Margaret holding her by the shirt was almost comical.

"Daddy!" Maureen shrieked. Margaret grabbed the girl's long, unruly hair and pulled her head back so their faces were close together. "You better quit your spying—"

"Here, now," Harmon said, and grabbed at Maureen. The exertion caused a bout of coughing and by the time it had subsided, Margaret was gone and Maureen stood behind him, slapping him on the back with great vigor. "You got to stop that hacking, Daddy," she said, voice stern.

"Don't I know it," he wheezed. He wiped his mouth and settled back.

Vada folded her arms over her chest and looked at Maureen. "Why do you torment your sister that way?"

Maureen shrugged, giggling. "'Cause it doesn't take anything to get her goat." She came around in front of Harmon and dropped to the ground, leaning against his legs and grinning up at him.

The corners of his mouth twitched, but he didn't laugh. "It ain't just your sister you want to torment, is it?"

Maureen giggled, and Vada had to smile. Although she had long ago forgiven herself for the act that had brought her youngest daughter into being, she couldn't help observing the irony that it was this child with whom Harmon shared the strongest bond.

"I don't want to torment you, Daddy," the girl said, pulling a dandelion up and blowing the fuzzy head away. "I'm going to live with you forever and ever, till I'm dead, so I can take care of you."

Harmon pulled her to him, and Vada was as suddenly and sharply filled with pain as a funny bone hit with a hammer. She almost groaned aloud at the thought of ever losing either of these two people. She wanted to hold onto this moment, measured in heartbeats and wheezes.

"Mama! My magazine!" Maureen looked at her mother's face bounded to her feet like an oversized puppy. "You forgot!" she accused.

"Oh, sugar, I did forget. I'm sorry."

"You *always* forget." Maureen plopped back down at her father's feet. "Guess I'll just grow up ignorant."

"I'll get you one when I go grocery shopping. Maybe you could go with me." Maureen seemed satisfied with that, and Vada turned toward the house. "I better get supper on before I forget that, too," she said.

* * * * *

Later that night, Vada readied herself for bed as Harmon watched. Her movements were precise, at times overly so, because she dreaded telling him about her job.

"How does it feel to be you?"

Vada turned toward him, her dress unbuttoned but not yet removed. "Do what?" She frowned. "To be me? How does it feel?"

Harmon wheezed with the effort of raising himself a bit higher on the pillows, and he looked embarrassed, as if he wished he'd not asked the question. "Quit repeating everything I say. You're worse than Maureen and her mocking people."

"I can't help it, Har. It's a strange question. I don't hardly know what it means." She stepped out of her dress and slip, deftly sliding a nightgown over her head almost in the same motion, a clothing sleight of hand.

"It ain't so strange. I just wondered what it's like to be little and pretty and young and waiting on your husband to die."

Vada felt her jaw drop, half-surprised it did not thud to the floor. "Harmon Priddy! I never in all my born days—what foolishness is this?"

His face, usually a uniform gray, reddened, and his brows knit over black eyes. "Well. What am I supposed to think? Here I am all stove up, and you going off with Dempsey every time I turn around." He swallowed hard and looked at a place somewhere to the left of her. "I can't—I can't—cut the mustard no more."

She stared at him, stupefied. "Harmon, I was with *Dempsey*. Your son. Remember him?"

"Ain't that what I just said?" Stubbornness radiated from him.

She put her hands on her hips. "Now you're just being silly."

He said nothing, just lay against the pillows miserably, waiting for her to tell him what he didn't want to hear.

Instead, she climbed onto the bed and put a hand on one side of his face. What was she to tell him? *The best day of my life was the day that part of my life was over? I haven't missed sex no more than I'd miss having gas?* No. She couldn't. She sighed. "Listen to me. Whether or not you can 'cut the mustard' doesn't matter. You understand me? That's not what I married you for, and whether you can or can't—it doesn't mean a thing."

He closed his eyes and leaned more deeply into the pillow, his breathing so unusually slow and quiet it worried her.

She squeezed his hand. "You all right?"

His eyes snapped open like window shades wound too tight. "You can't seem to wait till I'm in my grave. Go on, admit it. I ain't nobody's fool, by damn."

Removing her hand from his, she switched off the light and placed herself carefully on the edge of the bed, away from him. He was going to drive her crazy before it was all over.

He raised slightly on his elbows. "What? What's this? Now you can't stand to lay beside me? Maybe if you're lucky you'll wake up next to a corpse!"

Vada looked toward the ceiling for a moment, then wriggled closer, jaw set. She lay next to him, her body touching his from shoulder to ankle. He lay back too, but within a minute or two, sighed and nudged her. "Get over. I can't get comfortable with you right on top of me."

Clenching her teeth to keep from shouting at him, she scooted to the other side of the bed. Both lay in silence for a few minutes before Harmon spoke, seemingly to the air. "None of this is my fault," he said. "Raise a woman up and take care of her, and what does she do but stick a knife in your back." When she didn't answer, he elbowed her. "Vada?"

"Har-*mon*," she moaned. "Stop it. You are driving me crazy."

"I just want to talk to you." He hitched up the pillows and sat a little higher in the bed.

"No you don't. You just want to fight. You want to find somebody to blame for you being sick."

"No I don't," he scoffed. "I want you to turn over here and tell me why you went and lied to me, the husband that's took care of you all of these years, never asking for nothing in return, just giving and giving and—" The words broke off suddenly as she snapped the light back on and glared at him. "All right, all right." He stared straight ahead and she turned off the light once again and turned onto her side, trying to relax and get ready for sleep. Not thirty seconds later his voice came once more. "But why you got to go behind my back and learn to drive? You might just as well stick a knife in it as to go behind it like you done."

She had planned to tell him about the hospital, and her job, but now she didn't want to. Why couldn't she simply leave the house on the appointed day and return that evening, no questions asked?

"Har," she began, but he spoke at the same time, cutting her short.

"Where was you and Dempsey so long? It don't take three hours to take a driver's test, no matter how bad you are."

She lay silent for several minutes, but for some reason he didn't prod her. Finally, she sighed. "After I took my driving test I went to see a man about a job."

"You did what?" He sat up, leaned over her and switched on the lamp.

She sat up too, sliding back against the headboard as if to brace herself. "Saw a man about a job. I applied last week, and I had an interview today." She yearned to slide under the bed and curl in on herself like Maureen had when she was little and knew she was in trouble.

"That dog won't hunt. Nossir. Ain't no wife of mine going to work. You can just put that right out of your head."

"Somebody's got to do it, and it can't be you, Harmon. The doctor has told you, they've told you at the plant, and if you'd just look in the mirror, you'd see it yourself. You're not getting over this. You have to get used to it." Her voice started out firm, but the last words quavered.

"You ain't working," he repeated. "Even if you could get a job, you ain't working. It shames a man." His face grew increasingly red.

"Har, I have *got* a job, and—"

"Shut up. I ain't got to listen to this."

His words were strangled, and she simultaneously wanted to comfort him and retaliate. She remained silent, hoping he would get it out of his system, but he sat glaring at her, his breath coming in watery gasps. Finally, he spoke.

"If you go out that front door to a job," he said, "you ain't got to bother coming back in it."

She gaped at him, and then closed her mouth with an almost audible snap. Swinging her legs to the floor, she grabbed her housecoat. When she had belted it around her with vicious movements, she stomped to the door, tossing words over her shoulder like firecrackers. "You've got no right to tell me to get on down the road the first time I do something on my own, something that doesn't suit you." Her breath came fast and furious, and when she reached the door, she turned to face him.

"You listen to me, Harmon Priddy! I picked cotton just like you did, and I lived on fatback and cornbread just like you did. Besides that I had your babies, took care of your young'uns, and cleaned your house, and washed your clothes. If that ain't work, I don't know what you'd call it."

"That's what a woman does, Vada. That's what you ain't never got in your head." He wheezed between the words. "What you did wasn't nothing special, and you owed it to me. You *owed* it to—" He broke off, gulped air, and was immediately held prisoner by the deep, wracking, breath stealing cough. With visible effort, he brought it under control, but his next words were barely a whisper. "Hadn't been for me, your mama'd been beating on you another five, ten years." His head dropped back onto the pillow and she could see the barrel chest move up and down in strained movements.

She struggled to keep to herself the words that had festered within her for years, even before she could articulate them, but it was a futile effort. That they had very little to do with the argument at hand meant nothing. "That's right, I would've been. I would've been left with my mama and daddy till I was grown, till I was a woman. You took a little girl, Harmon, a fourteen-year-old girl who didn't even have titties yet, and *you forced* her into that bed and you raped her."

For a moment his chest didn't move, then it began to rise and fall again, and he closed his eyes. "You was my wife." Horrified, she watched a tear slide down his face, heard him draw a ragged breath. She pressed her back against the closed bedroom door, one hand to her mouth, the other out toward him, palm up, as if to capture the words she had spoken and bring them back, unspeak them. "You was my wife," he whispered, eyes still shut. "I loved you the first time I seen you, blinking them long eyelashes at me, rubbing your toe in the dirt."

Vada pressed the heel of her hand to her front teeth. *I won't cry. I won't and he can't make me.* Stumbling from the room, she ran down the long hall to the kitchen and out the back door, kept running until she reached the shed. Panting, she worked the rusty hasp until she got the door open, then flung herself through it and closed it behind her. Falling onto two bags of lawn fertilizer, she beat on them with her fists, screaming into the plastic, mouth barely open. *I'm stupid. So stupid! Oh, Jesus, what have I done?* How could she have said such a thing to Harmon?

Oh, God, oh, God, please don't let him hate me. I didn't mean it. I didn't. She rocked back and forth, face hot and sweaty, eyes burning with unshed tears.

* * * * *

Harmon barely spoke to her in the following days, and Vada didn't try to force the issue. *He doesn't have to talk. But I've got to work.* On the day she was to start, she rose early and dressed in the bathroom. Running a brush through her hair one more time and straightening the skirt of her white uniform, she admired her reflection, allowing herself the slightest bit of vanity. "Not bad for an old married woman," she said aloud. Gathering her car keys and a paper bag with a biscuit and sausage sandwich in it for her lunch, she went to the front door, stopping along the way to peek in the children's rooms. It was still early, not yet 6:30, and Margaret slept in one room while Maureen sprawled in another, legs brown against the white sheets.

Passing her own bedroom, she saw the empty bed, and as she entered the kitchen, she glimpsed Harmon through the back door, already in his lawn chair underneath the willow tree, his back to her. Sighing, she went out and squatted before him.

"Har, I'm going now." His eyes flicked to her face, then away, but she saw the pain in them, the knowledge that this day marked the end of something for them. She couldn't put a name to it, and he probably couldn't either, but it was an ending just the same. *Or a beginning.* The thought came unbidden and she felt herself flush as the words were a betrayal of Harmon. She put her cheek next to his, and when she moved back he grabbed her fingers, put them to his chest as if he'd captured a small bird and didn't want it to get away.

"I'm sorry," he said.

Her breath caught in her throat. "No. No, I'm the one should be sorry. I didn't mean what I said."

"Not that," he wheezed. "I know you didn't mean it. I'm sorry I took on like I did. You're right." The last words were cut off by a violent bout of coughing, and several minutes passed before he caught his breath again. "You're right. Somebody's got to earn some money, and I can't." His hand shook as he brought hers to his lips, kissed it lightly and let it go. "It's just a hard thing for a man, knowing he can't do what a man ought to."

"Oh, Harmon." Heedless of her white stockings, she knelt and put her arms around him, noticing once more his frailness, the heaving of his barrel chest. "It isn't the end of anything." Harmon had just voiced the thoughts she'd had for days, but suddenly, in the face of what really was and not just the picture her fear had painted, she knew it was not the end. It was just another step in the journey that she had begun long before in Papa's dusty front yard.

Returning her hug, he pushed her back gently. "You best go. Don't want to be late your first day."

She nodded, rising to her feet and trying in vain to brush the grass stains from her knees.

"Vada?"

She looked up. "What?"

"They're lucky to get you. Them hospital people."

"Why, thank you, Har. I hope they think so." Smiling, she patted his shoulder and walked quickly across the thick carpet of grass to the car.

1979

Chapter 46

It was a dismal spring day, damp, rainy, unpleasantly warm for the black dress Vada wore. The children had tried to get her to purchase a new one for the funeral, but she'd been too frugal for too long. She'd worn this dress to her mother's funeral, and to Miz Priddy's, and she would wear it for Harmon's.

"You okay, Mama?" Maureen, seated beside her under the canopy provided by Owen Funeral Home, put an arm around her mother and squeezed.

Vada stared at the rectangular hole into which Harmon would shortly be lowered and bit her lip. "I'm all right," she whispered. And she supposed she was as all right as she would be for quite a while, because she was numb from exhaustion and felt little. The last few weeks had been a nightmare of doctors and the hospital and tubes and Harmon's gasping attempts to breathe. Now, she was glad to feel nothing.

"Pa had a lot of friends," Dempsey said from her other side.

With great effort Vada looked around her. Fifteen minutes before the graveside service was to begin, most of the seats were filled—many, but not all with Priddy offspring and their offspring—and people flowed in. "I guess he did," she replied.

She stared at the dark wood of the casket, tried to imagine Harmon in there, wearing the suit the children had bought him. She had argued against it, but in the end she let them have their way. What did it matter? Harmon was gone. He was as gone as a man could get, and she missed him already. Vada let her gaze drop back to her lap. How many times had she wished him away from her? How many times had she wished to be left alone, to have a few minutes peace without the demands of a husband and children? And now she would be alone. For the first time in her life she would be alone, except for Maureen darting in and out between school and basketball practice, and all she wanted was Harmon there to squint at her through cigarette smoke, to snort at her ideas about nearly everything, to lie with her at night and worry about the grandbabies or the roof or how long the car would last.

A stirring of something in her chest, a burning in her eyes, threatened to overwhelm her and she tried to summon the blackboard of her girlhood, the one with NOTHING scrawled across it, the one that had kept her steady when Addy had died, but it eluded her.

"Mama, the preacher's here." Maureen again. "You want to talk to him before we start?" When Vada didn't reply, too intent on finding NOTHING, the clean, shampoo smell of Maureen was replaced by the scent of Wind Song, and Roxanne squatted in front of her.

"Vada, honey, they're getting ready to start. Do you want to tell the preacher anything else about Harmon, anything we didn't think of last night?" She placed a piece of notebook paper, crinkled and covered with Gerald's scrawl, on Vada's lap.

Vada smoothed it. These were the facts of Harmon's life. Born 1913. Died 1979. Retired from Liberty Glass. Father of seven, grandfather of nine. His church membership. In the end, was this what he was reduced to, words on a piece of paper, a box lowered into a hole? Was this all there was for any of them?

"No," she murmured. Roxanne seemed to take that as an answer to her question, but Vada hadn't meant it as such. She lifted her head to look around at the assembled crowd—their children, strong and tall and good, every one—and their children's children, the few old enough to be there—with the same potential for goodness and strength. The friends, so many friends, church folks, too, though Harmon hadn't attended services the last year of his life. Co-workers, neighbors, people to whom he somehow meant something, to whom he still meant something, gone though he was.

As the crowd quieted and the preacher's wife began to sing "This World Is Not My Home," Vada's thoughts drifted to the occasional Sundays when she'd sat beside Harmon in church and listened to that song. From there, she followed those thoughts: to the feed store, the feed store to Papa, and at last to the fields she'd run through as a child. In her mind she saw the thistle and goldenrod, the sunflowers, Queen Anne's lace, jimmy weed and holy clover, all the wild flowers she'd loved as a child, and she heard Papa's voice: "Them's everlastings, Sister. They'll be here long after me and you are gone." But he had been wrong.

"It's not just the flowers, Papa. It's us, too," she whispered. No matter what it was called, whether it was the soul or spirit, the work of God or some other mysterious power, a part of them lived on, from everlasting to everlasting. A part of Harmon and Miz Priddy, and yes, even of Mama. *Some part of us that's deeper and truer and richer than any life we could have lived, that's what's left.* She gazed out at the cemetery now, seeing not the leavings of winter but the advent of spring, the beauty and sorrow of it all somehow mixed up with the grief of losing Harmon. Her eyes burned, her chest felt filled with too much of something, sadness or loss or shock at how much she would miss Harmon, and this time she did not look for a way out of the pain. Instead, she let the tears slide down her cheeks and turned her face up to the single ray of sunshine that struggled through the clouds.

Reader's Guide

1. A number of people have a vested interest in Vada's marriage to Harmon. Who are they and what are their motives?

2. Is Harmon a good husband, given the time and place?

3. How might Addy's life have differed from Vada's, had she survived?

4. Why does Vada's father allow her to marry Harmon?

5. What qualities do Kenneth Ross and Harmon Priddy share?

6. Is Vada's decision to bring Roxanne to live with the Priddy's a good one?

7. Is Vada a good mother?

8. Vada comes to care deeply for Harmon. What characteristics does he possess that draw her to him?

9. This book is set in a particular place—rural Creek Country, Oklahoma. Could it have happened anywhere else?

10. What role does religion play in Everlasting?

11. What characteristics does Vada share with her mother?

12. What are the major themes of the book? How are they dramatized?

13. What about Levon attracts Vada to him?

14. Does Harmon realize Maureen may not be his child?

15. In what areas is Vada's growth apparent through the years?

16. Before he goes into the army, Dempsey is angry with Vada. What causes his anger?

17. What do you think is the true relationship between Dempsey and Roxanne?

18. After Dempsey returns from Viet Nam, is Vada's treatment of him too harsh?

19. Could the characters have moved in different directions than they do, or do their lives seem predetermined by place and time?

20. If you could ask the author one question, what would it be? What would you expect the answer to be?